THE FOURTH
LABYRINTH

THE FOURTH
LABYRINTH

CHRISTOPHER GOLDEN

BALLANTINE BOOKS NEW YORK

Book design by Diane Hobbing

For my amigo, Jim Moore

Acknowledgments

Thanks are due to my excellent editor, Tricia Pasternak, for her hard work and for her patience, and to Naughty Dog's fantastic creative director, Amy Hennig, for her support and enthusiasm. Much thanks also to my awesome agent, Howard Morhaim, for his wit, his understanding, and his sage advice. Last but not least, thanks to Rio Youers for the music and for loving Nate Drake as much as I do.

UNCHARTED

THE FOURTH
LABYRINTH

1

Tropical birds scattered as Drake veered the Jeep onto an old rutted track, snapping branches and tearing away vines, plowing through the rain forest with killers in pursuit, bullets flying, a gorgeous but pouty girl in the passenger's seat, and a bitch of a headache. With only one of his arms on the wheel, the Jeep slewed to the left, and the pouty girl screamed as he forced the vehicle back onto the trail just before they would have crashed into a felled tree.

Nathan Drake was beginning to hate the jungle.

He glanced in the rearview mirror an instant before a bullet shattered it, forcing him to risk glancing back over his shoulder. There were three vehicles in pursuit, a lumbering truck that had fallen to the rear and two Jeeps just like the one he was driving; which made sense considering that this one had been parked next to them when he'd stolen it.

The jungle had closed in around them, a wild tangle of rain forest the people of Ecuador called El Oriente, which seemed to him a pretty ordinary-sounding name for a place full of things that could kill you—like brutal sons of bitches employed by pissed-off South American drug lords.

The rutted track he'd taken forced the three vehicles into single file; which was good since it meant only one carload of them could be shooting at him at any given time. Bullets tore at leaves and cracked branches, the Jeep juddered up and down, rattling his teeth, and Drake kept his head down.

"This is your idea of a rescue?" the girl shouted.

He glanced at her wide eyes and her pretty mouth and her soft skin the color of cinnamon and decided he didn't like cinnamon. It ruined a good piece of toast as far as he was concerned.

"What the hell makes you think this is a rescue?" he snapped.

She blanched a little at that, and then her eyes narrowed. "Maybe the fact that here you are, rescuing me."

Drake laughed, but then his smile vanished as he heard bullets plink into the metal rear of the Jeep. The spare tire bolted to the back blew, but that was a damn sight better than losing one of the tires he was actually using.

"Does this *look* like a rescue?" he asked. "You're along for the ride by accident, sweetheart."

In truth, it hadn't been entirely by accident. He'd infiltrated the rain forest compound where Ramón Valdez tended to hide out from the rest of the world, running his drug cartel from a place so remote that nobody wanted to go hunting for him there. *No one with half a brain*, Drake thought. That hadn't stopped him from tracking Valdez down twice in three years.

He didn't like jobs that involved outright theft, for reasons that were best explained by the situation unfolding around him that very moment. But in the case of Ramón Valdez, he'd made an exception because he had a prior claim on the item he'd been hired to steal. He'd stolen it once before.

The girl had been a wrinkle in his plan. He'd found her trussed up in Valdez's bedroom and had intended to leave her there until her efforts to free herself gave him the idea that maybe she wasn't a willing participant in her bondage. That had complicated matters significantly, because timing was vital to his plan. For a few seconds he had tried to persuade himself that he wouldn't regret leaving her there—that her struggle was some kind of playacting she'd rehearsed for Valdez's benefit—but as he had started to walk away, he'd known he was lying to himself. Drake knew a prisoner when he saw one.

"What were you doing there, anyway?" he asked, jerking the wheel to the right.

"Vacation," she said bitterly in that aren't-you-a-dumbass tone young women seemed to perfect so early. "What do you think?"

"Not really the question," Drake said.

A burst of gunfire tore up the trees to his left; the last few bullets stitched the side of the Jeep and then blew out a taillight. A macaw exploded in midflight in a bullet-riddled burst of blood and feathers.

"Maybe you should focus on driving?" the girl asked, panic in her eyes as she ducked lower in her seat. "How can you be so calm?"

"Oh, this isn't calm," Drake said, twisting the wheel to veer around a felled tree. The Jeep rumbled over brush and roots and sideswiped a giant kapok tree. "This is me terrified. I can tell by the white knuckles and the way my jaw hurts from clenching."

The girl glanced at his hands on the wheel. She must have noted the whiteness of his knuckles, because she went a shade paler than before.

"You going to tell me who you are?" Drake demanded.

"My father really didn't send you?" she asked.

Her disappointment softened him as much as a guy driving through the jungle pursued by people trying to kill him could be softened. He saw the split-trunk tree he'd been watching for, the only kind of landmark that could be expected out here, and cut the wheel to the left, crashing the Jeep through a curtain of hanging vines and onto a trail that had been trodden by hooves but rarely by tires. The Jeep bucked like crazy; it felt like it would shake apart in his hands, leaving him sitting on the driver's seat and holding the steering wheel with no car around him.

"Sorry, kid. I don't have a clue what you're talking about."

She lifted her chin, trying too late to hide her withered hope. "My name is Alex Munoz. My father is mayor of Guayaquil. He's been fighting a war against drugs in the city, and he can't be bought."

She said this proudly, and Drake didn't blame her. For the mayor of a major South American city to take on the drug cartels, he had to be either courageous as hell or absolutely nuts. Alex didn't have to tell him the rest of the story, either. Beautiful girl, no more than nineteen, bound and gagged in a drug lord's bedroom? She had been a hostage, a negotiating tactic, and probably about to become the victim of something worse.

How do I get into these things? Drake thought.

But then, it wasn't Alex Munoz's fault that he was being shot at. Sure, untying her and getting her out of the compound had given him away and slowed him down, but it had been a risky plan to begin with, and in his experience risky plans almost always ended up in him being shot at—and sometimes actually shot.

"So if Papa didn't send you, who are you?" Alex asked, her pouty look returning. "What are you going to do with me?"

Drake ignored the second question. If there was anything he'd learned over the years, it was that while running for his life with a woman at his side, it was best never to tell her you didn't have a plan. "My name's Drake. Nate Drake."

If she got the James Bond reference in his delivery, she didn't let on. "What is this?" Alex asked. "What did you do to make Valdez so angry?"

Drake gestured to the backseat. "See that?"

When Alex glanced into the back, Drake knew what she would see. The staff was wrapped in burlap kept tight by strips of duct tape. The burlap had come from the poppy farm on the other side of the compound from Valdez's house. Drake had brought the duct tape himself. He'd managed to get the display case in Valdez's study open without setting off any alarms, had bagged and tagged the staff, and had been making his exit when he glanced into the bedroom and saw the girl with the cinnamon skin. The rest was dumbass history.

"I see it," Alex said.

"Have you heard of the Dawn Tavern?"

"Are you talking about a bar or Pacariqtambo? The place of origin? Or are you talking about the lost colony?"

"You know the story?" Drake said, glad he didn't have to explain. Just the fact that they were having this conversation was absurd enough, but he figured it was better than her screaming at him not to let her die or him cursing himself out for coming down here in the first place.

"Of course," Alex sniffed. "I go to university."

Great, Drake thought. *The only brat in the jungle, and she's in my Jeep.*

In Incan myth, Pacariqtambo was a cave from which the first people had emerged into the world. One of those brothers and sisters was a guy named Ayar Manco who carried a golden staff that was supposed to indicate where his people should build the first Incan city. Legend said that he'd changed his name and founded the city of Cuzco, that he and his sisters had built the first Incan homes with their bare hands. To many people in the region, the story was more history than legend, which meant that the discovery three years ago of the ruins of a lost colony—supposedly an offshoot of those original Incans, going all the way back to Ayar Manco—had stirred up a serious controversy. A local tribe whose people claimed to have known about the lost colony all along insisted that the ruins were the real and actual Pacariqtambo, that after being betrayed by his siblings, Ayar Manco had returned to the cave of his birth with his wife and children and founded this hidden village. The public argument about what was real and what was myth had been raging ever since.

"Three years ago, Valdez hired me to lead a team into Pacariqtambo and bring back whatever artifacts we could find. But what he really wanted was the golden staff of Ayar Manco. After I brought it to him, he decided he'd rather kill me than pay me. I barely got out of Ecuador with my life."

Alex looked at him like he was crazy. "So you decided to steal it back?"

Drake laughed. "Are you nuts? Valdez eats guys like me for breakfast. No, I figured I was lucky to still be breathing. But the Cuiqawa—the tribe that made those claims about Ayar Manco? They figure they're probably his closest descendants, so the staff should be theirs. They hired me to get it back."

"And you took the job? After Valdez almost killed you?"

"A guy's gotta work," Drake said. "And hey, Valdez went back on a deal. That just doesn't sit right, y' know? I figured the least I could do was annoy him a little."

They held on as the Jeep dropped into a streambed, splashed through, and roared up the other side. The guns had gone quiet, and Drake took a moment to hope Valdez's goons had given up the chase. Then one of the pursuing Jeeps burst through the vines behind them, and he realized he should have known better. It was never that easy.

"Hey," Drake said, glancing at Alex as he drove, a fresh burst of gunfire blasting the trees off to his left. "Do you think your father's offering a reward for your safe return?"

She stared at him. "You said this wasn't a rescue."

"No," Drake replied, "I don't think I did. And anyway, it's a moot point, isn't it? I mean, once a guy's actually done the rescuing—"

"You haven't rescued me!" she shouted as a bullet shattered the rearview mirror on her side, showering her hair in shards of glass and metal.

"Well," Drake said. "Not yet."

He aimed the Jeep at a gap in the trees that looked too narrow, but they roared through with inches to spare on either side. Alex swore at him and covered her head, then looked up in blinking astonishment that they had not crashed even as Drake floored the gas pedal and the tires spun clods of damp earth into their wake. For a few seconds the clatter of gunfire ceased again, and as they passed through a strangely uniform alley of trees and vines, the hush of the rain forest embraced them, muffling their engine noise.

The Jeep hit a rise, then topped it, and the tires spun without traction for a heartbeat before touching down in a small clearing. Stiff-armed, Drake kept the wheel steady over the rough terrain, but they had run out of room. Thick brush bordered the clearing, and trees grew close and leaned together, conspiratorially close. The only way out was the way Drake had driven in, and Valdez's gunmen were right behind them.

"Oh, my God, we're dead!" Alex cried.

Drake drove full tilt toward the far side of the clearing, the trees rushing toward them. At the last second, he cut the wheel to the right and hit the brake, causing the Jeep to fishtail and then shudder to a stop. The engine kicked and died, ticking with the heat of its exertion.

"Put your hands up," he said.

Alex glanced at him in confusion. "What?"

Drake threw his gun on the floor of the Jeep and climbed out, raising his arms in surrender. "If you don't want to get shot, put your damn hands up!"

The first of the pursuing vehicles roared into the clearing. Several shots rang out, but Drake started shouting out his surrender in both English and Spanish, lifting his hands higher to show he meant it. He stepped away from the Jeep as Alex finally put up her hands and slipped out, imitating him as best she could. She had started to cry.

Drake thought it was a bad idea to smile, but he had to struggle to keep a straight face. Fear did that to him. He figured Valdez had ordered his thugs to retrieve the girl and the staff of Ayar Manco, and it seemed pretty damn likely that he'd ordered them to kill the thief who had stolen both—which would be him—but he thought surrender would confuse them. Hoped it would, anyway.

The second carload of killers arrived in the clearing as the first came to a shuddering stop twenty feet away from him, their weapons trained on him and Alex. The big truck would be lumbering along somewhere behind. In one of those vehicles would be the guy in charge, some bastard smarter than the other bastards, and in their moment of confusion the killers would wait for him to make the call. If Drake was surrendering, did that mean they should take him back to Valdez alive, or were they still supposed to shoot him?

While they were waiting, they climbed out of the two Jeeps, all of them shouting, spreading out in a circle around Drake and the crying girl, who didn't seem to understand that they would take her alive to preserve her value as a hostage. Or maybe that was why she was crying, Drake thought. Maybe being taken alive scared her more than dying.

Or maybe you're just being melodramatic, he thought. The killers gestured with the barrels of their guns, shouting in Spanish for Drake to get down on his knees. He complied, and Alex did, too, even though nobody had asked her. A short, slender, deadly-looking guy with a mustache that looked like it had been drawn on with a marker jumped down from the back of the second Jeep and walked toward Drake with his gun held down at his side like he was trying to sneak up on them, even though they were all watching him expectantly. This would be the guy, then. Drake waited for him to give the order to fire.

Stencil-mustache man didn't say a word, though. If his buddies were waiting for orders, they were going to have to keep waiting, because he was a hands-on kind of guy. He pulled a pistol from an armpit holster and strode over, lifted the gun, and pointed it at Drake's forehead.

"Any time now!" Drake called out, his voice shaking.

The little commandant frowned in surprise, apparently assuming that Drake was trying to rush him into pulling the trigger.

"What are you—" Alex began.

A single shot rang out, sending a flurry of colorful birds shooting skyward from the trees around the clearing. The little man with the ridiculous mustache staggered backward, glanced down in confusion and maybe a little regret at the hole in his chest, and then collapsed into the grass.

Only the fact that Drake and Alex had their hands thrust into the air and so obviously empty kept them alive in that moment. The baffled killers spun around, aiming into the trees, trying to figure out who they were supposed to shoot. One of them even fired a few rounds at nothing.

Then the shadows moved, branches swaying as dozens of guns and faces appeared in the trees. Some were above and some below, some were dressed in the style of local tribesmen and others in the plain garb of migrant workers, but they were all armed. There were guns as well as bows with arrows strung and even some knives ready to be thrown. Other than the cocking of the weapons and the rustle of the trees, they made no sound.

One of Valdez's men started shouting at the others to fire, as if he needed to have someone else pull the trigger so he didn't have to go first. An arrow thunked into the ground inches away from his mud-crusted left boot. He stared at the arrow for a second or two and then threw his gun into the grass.

A moment later, the rest of the killers started discarding their weapons and the Cuiqawa tribe swiftly emerged from the trees and surrounded them. Several of the tribesmen hurried to Drake's stolen Jeep, and one of them lifted the burlap-wrapped staff from the backseat, shook it in triumph, and nodded his thanks. Drake hoped the guy realized he hadn't gone in after the staff just to win the tribe's gratitude.

He stood and went over to Alex. The girl still looked terrified, staring at the Cuiqawa as though they might be a new threat. Drake helped her to her feet.

"How 'bout now?" he asked. "Does this count as a rescue?"

2

Drake spent most of the flight from Guayaquil to Chicago catching up on his sleep. After the adrenaline rush of days spent trying not to die, he felt completely spent, yet at the same time he was filled with a rare contentment. He'd set right a wrong Valdez had done him, restored a cultural artifact to its rightful owner—granted, he'd been the one to steal it in the first place—and now was going home with more real money in his pocket than he'd had in a long while.

The tribe had paid his fee for retrieving the golden staff, but the mayor of Guayaquil had paid even more for the pleasure of getting his daughter back alive. The fact that the latter deed had been purely, if somewhat irritatingly, accidental only made the reward that much sweeter. It was the kind of luck that didn't come his way often, and he couldn't wait to share the story of his good fortune with Victor Sullivan, his best friend and sometime partner in ventures like this one.

There were several squalling children on the flight, and the sumo-size passenger in the seat behind him didn't seem very happy about Drake reclining his seat, but he felt impervious to the world's attempts to disrupt his contentment. With in-flight music quietly piped into his brain through the free headphones, he managed to sleep through the movie, waking up just long enough for the gooey chicken and broccoli dish that might have been dinner or maybe some kind of breakfast omelet if the congealed stuff around the chicken and veggies turned out to be egg.

The flight landed almost fifteen minutes early—just before ten o'clock in the morning—and when Drake unbuckled his seat belt and stood up, obviously content and well rested, he thought he caught several envious glances from other passengers. Most of them looked pale and weary, but he felt good as he retrieved his backpack from under the seat and his duffel from the overhead compartment. The sumo who'd been unhappy about his reclined seat was still trying to unwedge himself from 17D when Drake filed off the plane.

As he traveled from one terminal to another, he smelled cinnamon rolls, and his stomach rumbled. He had managed to keep down the hideous concoction the airline had fed its passengers, but he was definitely hungry again, and cinnamon rolls were one of his lifelong weaknesses. Like kryptonite—if kryptonite was soft and warm and covered in sugar and Superman liked to eat it. *Or something*, he thought.

While waiting in line for his cinnamon roll and looking forward to American coffee, he reached into his pocket and took out his cell phone, which had been off for the duration of the flight. He turned it on and saw that he'd missed some calls during the flight and had some messages. The first one consisted of a woman's drunken rambling, and he decided it must be a wrong number. The second message was from Vivian, the woman who operated as his travel agent whenever he needed to make a journey that kept his movements off the grid. Drake did a little too much improvising for Vivian's taste and she often chided him for not using her services more often, but this call was to admonish him for flying from Ecuador to the USA using his own passport. He didn't like to do it, afraid to draw any scrutiny from Homeland Security, but he was just a guy visiting South America, not some jihadist taking flying lessons and then spending a few weeks training to blow himself up in some secret mountain stronghold in Afghanistan.

The third message was from Sully.

"Nate, it's me. Call me as soon as you get this. Something's up, and I could use a second set of eyes. Another brain wouldn't hurt ei—"

The phone beeped, and he glanced at it, surprised to see that it was Sully calling again. He thumbed the button to switch over to the incoming call.

"Sully," he said, frowning. "What's so important?"

Motion out of the corner of his eye drew his attention, and he flinched, on edge after the last few days, but it was just the girl behind the counter handing him a bag that exuded the delightful aroma of cinnamon.

"You on U.S. soil, Nate?" Sully asked.

"I've got a layover in Chicago," Drake said as he made his way to a small table where he could sit with his back to the corner.

He could hear Sully pausing and thought he heard the man exhale. Smoking a cigar, Drake thought. Sully quit about once a month and spent a lot of time chewing the end of an unlit Cuban, as if daring himself to light it. This morning, he had obviously needed a smoke.

"Chicago," Sully said, his gruff voice even raspier than usual. "How fast can you get to New York?"

Nate paused with the sticky cinnamon bun halfway to his mouth.

"What's in New York?"

He could hear Sully blow out another lungful of cigar smoke before answering.

"Murder."

Just after three-thirty in the afternoon, Drake sat in the back of a New York City taxicab, breathing in smoke from the incense the cabbie had been burning and watching the green street signs go by on the way to Grand Central Station. He could have taken a shuttle bus directly from JFK International Airport in Queens to Grand Central in the heart of Manhattan, but Sully's urgency had been clear, and for once Drake was flush with cash.

He wished only that Sully had been more forthcoming over the phone. Drake had spent his whole life learning how to roll with the punches, and a big part of that had been Sully's tendency to spring things on him at the last minute. But he didn't think Sully's reluctance to go into detail had anything to do with the aging treasure hunter's usual games. Just before Sully had rushed off the phone, Drake had heard a woman crying in the background. If his old friend and mentor didn't want to talk about murder, he figured it was because someone else in the room was grieving. Sully would never be accused of being the sensitive type, but neither was he heartless.

A grieving friend also would explain why Sully hadn't come to the airport to meet him when his plane landed. If he needed Drake for backup for some reason, normally Sully would have wanted to brief him as soon as possible. Instead, he had just asked Drake to meet him under the clock on the main concourse of Grand Central Station.

The cab dropped him off in front of a restaurant called Pershing Square that was practically hidden beneath the elevated Park Avenue Viaduct. Drake paid the cabbie but barely looked at the man, his thoughts running ahead of him. He'd been lucky enough to catch a flight from Chicago within half an hour of talking to Sully on the phone, and throughout the nearly two and a half hours in the air and the duration of the cab ride, he had mostly been able to let his mind drift or focus on other things. But now that he had arrived, he couldn't help being worried.

Victor Sullivan had practically raised him from his early teens and taught him everything—or nearly everything—he knew about staying alive in the "hard-to-find-acquisitions" business. They'd been all over the world hunting for treasure and antiquities for pretty much anyone who could afford to pay the tab. And in all that time he had never heard Sully sound as grim and weary as he had on the phone.

A taxi driver laid on the horn as Drake hustled across the street. A chilly October wind blasted him, and he shivered, wishing he had a coat. He had left his bags in a locker at JFK, figuring he would be headed back to the airport on his way out of the city, but nothing in there would have helped. Ecuador had been warm and humid. Drake had spent too much time in hot and sticky locales in his life, so he didn't mind the chilly autumn wind, but it was a rapid shift, like stepping through a door to the other end of the world.

Wouldn't that make my life easy? he thought. But of course that kind of stuff happened only in science fiction and fantasy stories, where the heroes were all noble and dead wasn't always forever. Real life had less convenient rules.

Drake hauled open the heavy glass-and-brass door and walked up the pebbled incline between the outer and inner doors. A man with a long, filthy, matted beard and sunken eyes stood to one side wearing a sign announcing the arrival of the End Times, but there was no way to tell if he was celebrating or regretting the moment.

When he stepped into the main concourse—the enormous, ornate chamber that came immediately to mind when he thought of Grand Central Terminal—he made a beeline for the huge clock. He spotted Sully standing beneath it, but the older man was turned away, watching the stairs across the terminal, probably thinking about the baby carriage scene in De Palma's *Untouchables*, a homage to the Russian flick *Battleship Potemkin*. They'd passed through Grand Central together a few times, and every time Sully had to tell him about those stairs. Sully saw him coming and perked up, shaking off whatever he'd been thinking about. From the haunted look in his eyes, Drake decided maybe it wasn't old gangster movies, after all.

"Nate," Sully said. "Thanks for coming."

"I was already traveling. Just had to take a detour," Drake replied. Their rapport mostly consisted of banter, but for once he thought maybe the lighthearted approach wasn't appropriate. "What's going on, Sully? You said 'murder.' One look at you and I'm guessing this isn't some cozy mystery."

Sully frowned, smoothing his gray mustache. "I'm not my usual jovial self, huh? I guess not. But you look more than a little like crap yourself, so maybe you shouldn't judge."

Drake raised his eyebrows. "Great to see you, too."

A tired smile touched Sully's face and a bit of the usual mischievous twinkle lit his eyes, but then the smile faded and his gaze turned dark. He nodded his head toward the row of arched doorways that led through into the train tunnels and platforms.

"Come on. This way," he said.

Drake followed without asking any more questions. If Sully

had a particular way he wanted the answer to unfold, Drake would indulge him. He'd earned that, and far more, in the years they'd been friends. He studied Sully as they reached a staircase and started down to a lower level. A drinker and an inveterate ladies' man, he looked, as always, as if he would have been more at home gambling in 1950s Havana than dealing with twenty-first-century America. His graying hair looked a bit unruly, and dark circles under his eyes implied he hadn't gotten a lot of sleep the night before. He wore a brown leather bomber jacket over one of his guayaberas—linen shirts that were most popular in Latin America and the Caribbean. Both the shirt and the khaki pants he was wearing were rumpled, indicating that whatever sleep he had gotten, he'd been wearing the same clothes since the day before.

It had been almost two months since Drake had seen Sully, but they'd spoken on the phone less than a week ago, and at the time there'd been no indication that anything was amiss. But murder gave no warning.

Sully led him through the lower-level concourse and past the arched entrances to a warren of underground railway tunnels until at last he turned through one of those archways and walked down a dozen steps to a train platform. Lights flickered unreliably in the darkness of the ceiling above them. The rumble of trains both near and distant made it feel like at any moment the world might shake itself apart. The noise reminded Drake of counting the seconds between thunder strikes as a child, trying to figure out how far away the storm might be and if the lightning might be coming his way.

No train awaited them at the platform. Drake had half expected that they were about to embark on a journey, but if they were, it apparently wouldn't be by train. The tracks were empty, and other than themselves, the platform looked abandoned—except for the yellow line of police tape that had been used to cordon off the end of the platform from the public. Drake didn't have to ask; he knew where they were headed now.

Two platforms over, a train clanked and hissed, waiting as a few stragglers hurried alongside it. A conductor stood outside the door, ushering them along. The man glanced at Drake and Sully. Once upon a time he would have minded his own business—New York had been that kind of town—but after 9/11 all that had changed. Sully knew it, too, because he stopped at the crime scene tape, making no move to go beyond it. They were suspicious enough just being down here without any obvious reason. Drake thought maybe the conductor would think they were plainclothes detectives, but then he realized they were probably underdressed for that. And if he had caught a glimpse of the guayabera under Sully's bomber jacket, the man would know right off the bat they weren't cops. Most police kept their quirks on the inside.

Standing by the police tape, Sully withdrew a cigar from inside his jacket pocket. He wasn't much for rules, but he didn't light it, just stuck it between his lips and rolled it around in his teeth for a minute, thinking. Drake had never known him to be a man prone to rumination.

"You're starting to freak me out a little, Sully. How about you start by telling me who died?"

Sully stared at a spot beyond the police tape for a moment longer, then took the cigar from his mouth and turned to Drake.

"This platform's been closed since last night. A train came in from Connecticut—plenty of stops along the way—and when it left, there was an old steamer trunk on the platform. Mostly people were getting on, leaving the city, but there were some arriving, too. One of the conductors remembered the trunk and that two men were sitting near it. He assumed they had carried it on but didn't look too closely at them. Dark coats; that's all he remembers."

Sully shook his head, eyes narrowed in frustration. "Think about that, Nate. Anything in the world could have been in that trunk. The whole thing could have been full of Semtex or something. Can you imagine explosives in that kind of volume detonating under the city? We're so obsessed with planes, but nobody's paying attention to . . ."

He trailed off, taking a breath. He looked more angry than

grieving, but Drake knew Sully well enough to see that he was both.

"So, this trunk *wasn't* filled with explosives?" Drake ventured.

Sully shot him a hard look. "I was making a point. But no, it wasn't. Place reacted like it could've been, though. Hundreds of trains were prevented from coming in, thousands of people evacuated. Transportation Authority brought in counterterrorism agents, and NYPD had a bomb squad down here. Bomb-sniffing dogs didn't get a read on it, but they were still treating it like it was going to explode. A couple of the guys who wrangle those dogs—one of them used to train them to sniff for corpses, and he knows the smell pretty well. He said he thought there was a body in the trunk. Turned out he was right."

Drake put a hand on his shoulder, hating to see his friend in pain. "Sully—"

"It was Luka," Sully said, his jaw working, eyes flashing with anger. "But not all of him, Nate. No arms and no legs. Just his torso. They'd cut his head off, too, but at least that was in the trunk. Whoever killed him, they didn't amputate his limbs to make it harder to ID him or they wouldn't have put his—"

Sully faltered. Sneering, he jammed the cigar back into his mouth and stared again at the area beyond the yellow tape. The train two platforms away pulled out, clanking loudly, and Drake wondered if the conductor was still watching them. He wondered why the cops or the FBI weren't on top of them already, wondering what they were doing there. If the trunk had been filled with explosives instead of Sully's dead friend, they would never have been able to come down here without being stopped. But murder didn't get the same attention.

In his life, Luka Hzujak had been an archaeologist, a college professor, and a collector of antiquities. He had also been one of Victor Sullivan's oldest and dearest friends, a man who saw the modern understanding of history as just as much a mystery as the unfolding of tomorrow. Luka was known for pissing off his colleagues and employers because he refused to settle for the currently accepted versions of historical episodes, particularly from ancient times. In recent years he had established himself as a successful author of controversial histories written in language accessible to the general public. Drake had met Luka perhaps a dozen times and had liked him a great deal. He could picture the man's mischievous face and the way he'd always stroked his goatee like some cartoon devil. Luka had never condemned Sully for the work he and Drake did, mostly because he thought the most significant evidence available to challenge historians' version of the past came from tomb raiders and treasure hunters.

"I'm sorry, Sully," Drake said. "Something like that—it shouldn't happen to anyone, never mind someone like Luka. Have the cops turned up anything?"

Drake didn't bother asking where Sully had gotten his information about the discovery of the body. It seemed clear he had a source in the NYPD, which really came as no surprise. Sully seemed to have a drinking buddy or a gambling compadre just about everywhere. Six years past, they had spent a few rainy weeks in Bhutan searching for ancient demon and animal masks. The first day, they had gone to the marketplace to find something to keep the rain off them, and a man selling goat cheese and wine had clapped Sully on the back and hugged him like a long-lost brother. When the guy had stepped back, Drake had seen the wary suspicion in the merchant's eyes. He and Sully were friends, but they didn't trust each other. That seemed to be a common dynamic, and it extended from Bhutan to the United States to Easter Island. Drake trusted Sully, at least most days, but one of the first things the man had taught him was that a certain amount of mistrust was healthy and would keep him alive.

But Sully's NYPD contact hadn't been much help.

"They've got squat," Sully said.

Drake frowned, turning to look up at the flickering lights. "Seriously? It's Grand Central. They've got to have cameras everywhere."

"'Course they do. Doesn't mean they all work. When the budget's tight, choices have to be made. Some things fall by the wayside," Sully said, turning to look at him again. "But we've got something the cops don't."

"What's that?"

The look in Sully's eyes was a mixture of pain and pride. "We have Jada."

3

Drake and Sully took the subway train that shuttled passengers between Grand Central and Times Square, then boarded another subway car, this one headed north. They sat quietly together, Sully warily watching other passengers. The lights flickered on and off, making strange scars out of the scratches some vandals had put on the windows. The seat beneath Drake had been sliced open, but that didn't bother him as much as the smell that permeated the air, trace aromas of sweat and urine, like the ghost of someone else's stink. The car rattled on the tracks, rocking back and forth in a lulling motion that might have put Drake to sleep on a day without murder in it.

Sully glanced around, more paranoid than Drake had ever seen him.

"What's going on, Sully?" Drake said, voice low. He glanced around to see if anyone was paying attention to them, his friend's paranoia contagious. But it was the New York subway; as a rule, people tended to pretend they were the only ones on the train. "How come you've got Jada hidden away?"

"It wasn't my idea," Sully muttered, glancing sharply at Drake. "She won't talk to the cops 'cause she's afraid of ending up just as dead as her father."

"She knows who did it?" Drake asked, intrigued.

"No. But she might know why. Now shut your trap. We'll be there soon enough."

Drake didn't argue. He could see Luka's murder had Sully spooked. If he wanted to be overcautious because he feared Jada might also be in danger, Drake wouldn't blame him. Sully was the girl's godfather, and he took the role seriously. With Luka dead, he would do whatever he had to in order to make sure the girl was taken care of.

Though she wasn't really a girl anymore, was she? The last time Drake had seen Jadranka Hzujak, she had been eleven or twelve years old. In the intervening years, he had been vaguely aware that the girl had been growing up, but it had been happening so far off his radar that it was difficult to imagine Jada as an adult. Five or six years ago, he and Sully had gotten together with Luka and had dinner in a little dive in Soho that looked like it hadn't changed in decades. Over dinner, Luka had mentioned that Jada had been enjoying college, which meant she had to be in her mid-twenties now. But he couldn't shake the image of the little girl she'd been out of his mind.

As the train pulled into the 79th Street station, Sully tapped Drake on the knee and got up, slipping through the standing passengers. Drake followed, smiling as he made his way around a prodigiously pregnant young woman.

On the platform, Sully leaned up against the side of a newsstand and waited for the train to close its doors and pull away. Drake thought he was being overly cautious, but he had altered his travel plans and come to New York and been in motion since he had gotten off the plane at JFK. A couple of minutes just standing still was welcome. Besides, he knew this game. Sully wanted to wait for the platform to clear to make it more difficult for anyone who might be trying to follow them to remain inconspicuous.

When the disgorged passengers had scattered and the train was gone, Sully fell into step beside Drake and the two of them went up the stairs in silence. Outside, the chilly autumn breeze swept along the sidewalk and the afternoon shadows had grown longer. Sully turned uptown, and Drake waited patiently until they were half a block from the subway station entrance before speaking again.

"Come on, Sully," Drake said. "Patience is a virtue, but it's never been one of mine. You dragged me halfway across the country—"

"You were in Chicago. That's not even close to halfway."

Drake frowned. "I was never good at fractions. And that's not the point. Luka is dead, and from the way you're acting, it's obvious you think whoever killed him isn't going to stop there. If you're gonna drag me into a situation where I might end up in a trunk with some of my pieces missing, I'd at least like to know what I'm getting myself into."

Sully shot him a hard look. "So would I."

He let out a long breath, relenting, and glanced around to make sure no one was paying them any extra attention, then shoved his hands in his pockets and kept his gaze forward, talking quietly.

"Here's the lowdown," Sully began. "Maybe you remember that Jada's mother died when she was a kid."

"Breast cancer, wasn't it?" Drake asked.

"Lungs," Sully corrected. "Luka remarried a couple of years back, a woman named Olivia. Jada called her the 'wicked stepmother.' Olivia Hzujak works for a company called Phoenix Innovations. CEO is a guy called Tyr Henriksen—Norwegian, I think. Phoenix is mainly a weapons manufacturer, with business partners around the world, but they have a research division that keeps things pretty hush-hush."

"Why does the name ring a bell?" Drake asked, wary as a car slowed in his peripheral vision. It turned out to be a taxi letting off a passenger, but Sully had him jumping at shadows. "Tyr Henriksen, not the corporation."

"Thought you'd catch that," Sully replied. "Henriksen's an antiquities collector, and he doesn't mind acquiring things in a shady fashion if the aboveboard approach doesn't work."

"He'll hire smugglers and thieves if he has to," Drake clarified.

Sully arched an eyebrow. "I know. Can you imagine? Rogues and villains."

Drake said nothing. Sully was joking, but Drake didn't think it was funny. He bent the rules and sometimes he broke them, and his line of work put him into contact with some pretty unsavory characters, but he didn't consider himself one of them.

"Three months ago, Henriksen reached out to Luka through Olivia, trying to get him involved in a private project," Sully went on. "Luka had a bad feeling about Henriksen's proposal, I guess. He did some poking, started doing the research Henriksen wanted, and stumbled across something that worried him enough that he quit. Only he didn't *really* quit. He kept working on the project, but for himself instead of for Tyr Henriksen."

"This is all pretty vague."

They'd walked a couple of blocks and now came to a stop at the corner of 81st Street and Broadway, waiting for the light to change. There was a Starbucks at the southeast corner of the intersection and Drake found himself craving coffee, but he kept his focus on Sully and the people around them. A young professional woman, he guessed Indian or Pakistani, walked a tiny mincing dog. Two men crossed at the light, carrying Starbucks cups and laughing together. Drake didn't see any threat, but he felt it, though he figured that was mostly the picture the day had painted thus far.

"At first, all Luka would tell Jada was that Henriksen had wanted him to solve a mystery for him and that there was treasure at the heart of it. Something priceless," Sully said. "Something—"

"Worth killing for," Drake finished.

"Looks that way, doesn't it?" Sully asked.

The light changed, and they continued north along Broadway.

"So Luka wanted the treasure for himself," Drake said.

"It doesn't feel right to me. Luka wouldn't have put himself on the line like that. He loved his work and he loved his daughter, and I always had the impression he was content with that."

"No offense, Sully, but you saw Luka once every couple of years. People change. And even if Luka didn't change, you can't climb inside someone's head and see the world the way they see it."

But Sully was shaking his head. "No way. I knew him as well as I know you. And Jada's with me. She says her dad wasn't excited the way someone who thought they were going to get their hands on something special would be. She says her old man just seemed afraid. When she pressed him about it, he told her Henriksen's project was dangerous and the only way to stop him was to find the treasure before he did."

They turned on 82nd Street. An old man passed them, his long wool coat too large for his age-shrunken frame, and Sully waited until they were a dozen paces beyond him before he paused and faced Drake.

"Look, Nate, here's what it comes down to. Luka—he was one of the good guys. I want to make sure whoever killed him pays the price. Beyond that, Jada wants to finish this project. It cost her father his life, and she intends to see it through for him. I plan to be a part of that. I'm not as young as I used to be, and she's not used to people trying to kill her, so we could use your help. If you end up in a shallow grave somewhere, at least you'll know you went out doing something good."

Drake arched an eyebrow, unable to hide his wry smile. "Well, when you put it that way, how could I resist?"

Sully clapped him on the shoulder. "Thanks. It means a lot."

"Don't get all mushy, Sully. You'll make me blush."

Sully rolled his eyes and turned away, cutting diagonally across the street toward a five-story building that took up half the block, which consisted of a row of apartment houses. Drake waited for a messenger on an old moped to buzz past and then followed. The Upper West Side of Manhattan seemed like a nice place to live, with trees planted along the sidewalk and waist-high wrought-iron gates in front of short pathways that led to front doors. The apartment building had red doors, dormers on either end and a little chalet-style peak in the center. Sully went all the way to the last door at the end of the block, where 82nd Street met West End Avenue.

Drake followed him into the foyer. Sully hit a button labeled Gorinsky, and they were buzzed in immediately.

Their destination turned out to be an apartment on the fourth floor at the rear of the building. According to Sully, it belonged to an old college friend of Jada's who was studying overseas and had left her a key and an invitation to use the place any time she was in the city. If there was an elevator, Drake didn't see it, and he was impressed by how little difficulty Sully had with the stairs. Not that he expected his old friend to collapse halfway up, but Sully wasn't getting any younger, and smoking cigars wasn't exactly the athlete's number one hobby.

The apartment door opened before they reached it. The woman who stood just across the threshold could have passed for a teenager at first glance. She wore a long-sleeved cream-colored top, tight black pants, and plain black boots, useful instead of trendy. Her hair was black, but the long bangs that framed her face had been dyed a vivid magenta. But with a second look, Drake saw the power in her five-foot-three frame and the intelligence glinting in her hazel eyes.

Jada Hzujak was definitely not a kid anymore.

"What the hell are you doing?" Sully asked quietly, hustling her back into the apartment. "You didn't even ask who it was before you buzzed us in."

Jada lifted her chin, ready for a fight. "I'm not stupid, Uncle Vic. There's a camera in the foyer, remember? I watched for you."

She jerked a thumb at the intercom panel by the door. Drake couldn't see it from out in the hall, but he figured Sully was getting a look at a screen where someone in the apartment could see who was buzzing from down below and feeling pretty sheepish. That made Drake smile. He didn't get to see Sully put in his place very often.

Then Jada looked at him. "Are you just gonna stand in the hallway, smiling like an idiot, or are you coming in?"

"I wasn't sure myself for a minute," Drake replied, "but I guess I'm coming in."

Jada stood back to let him enter, then shut and locked the door behind him. Drake glanced at Sully.

"Cat got your tongue, 'Uncle Vic'?"

"Shut up," Sully snarled.

The apartment was neat to the point of being spartan, decorated in bland colors by someone without a lot of imagination. The few pieces of art on the walls all seemed to have been chosen to match the decor instead of the other way around. The only signs of habitation were the throw pillows in disarray on the sofa and the mess of papers and books on the floor and coffee table nearby.

"Jada, you may not remember Nate—" Sully began.

"I remember him just fine," Jada said, tucking a magenta lock behind her ear as she regarded Drake coolly. "Though in my memory you're taller."

Drake smiled. "Well, to be fair, you were shorter back then."

"You were cuter, too."

His smile vanished. "So were you. In a bossy ten-year-old girl kinda way."

"I was twelve."

"I know."

Jada laughed, then immediately sobered, as if she felt guilty for feeling any levity at all in a world where her father had been brutally murdered. She managed a small, melancholy smile, just the slightest acknowledgment that she'd enjoyed the sparring, and then turned back to Sully.

"I kept working while you were out," she said. "I wanted to have something to show you when you got back."

Sully followed her over to the sofa and sat on the edge as she started to arrange the papers on the coffee table, then lifted a few of them off the floor. From where he stood, Drake saw that many of the papers were drawings of what looked like mazes, but they were fully rendered illustrations, not a crude puzzle maker's doodling.

"How much did you tell him?" Jada asked Sully.

"Just about Henriksen, and Luka being afraid. I didn't get into any of the historical stuff," Sully replied.

" 'He' is standing right here," Drake said, then looked from Jada to Sully. "And I thought she didn't know what this mysterious project was."

" 'She' knew a little and is trying to figure out the rest," Jada said, cocking her head and studying him. "What do you know about alchemy?"

Drake shrugged. "What's to know? Crazy people thought

they could turn random other metals into gold. And how cool would that be? Although treasure hunters would be out of work."

Jada picked up an old book, its dust jacket yellowed and torn at the edges. He could barely make out the title, *Science, Magic & Society*.

"You don't look like the homework type," she said. "But if you want to read up, it might not be a bad idea. There were a lot of men through the ages—almost always men—who presented themselves as alchemists and claimed to be able to make gold. They claimed all kinds of other things, too. St. Germain told all of Europe he was immortal. Fulcanelli had a reputation as a sorcerer. Nicholas Flamel supposedly unlocked the secrets of the philosopher's stone."

Drake picked up the book and flipped a few pages. "Actually, my favorite was always Ostanes the Persian. You know, the guy who was with Xerxes during the invasion of Greece? Apparently introduced the black arts into the Hellenic world? Quite a rascal, that one."

Jada gave him an appreciative nod.

"The crack about homework?" she said. "I take it back."

Drake sat on the sofa, attentive as a schoolboy.

"Don't be impressed," Sully sniffed. "You can't be in the business of acquiring antiquities without knowing the major alchemists."

"I collect all the trading cards," Drake put in.

Sully shot him a withering glance. Drake wondered if it was meant to stop him from making jokes or from flirting. Not that he meant anything by the flirting. It was a nervous habit he'd developed when he was around women who intrigued him, and Jada definitely intrigued him. Stunning, smart, and fierce, she still managed to have a sense of mischief that he admired. However, Sully was obviously protective of her, and Drake had no intention of testing that.

"I've been taking notes, trying to make sense of the things I remember my father saying in the past few weeks," Jada explained, gesturing to the papers. "Uncle Vic and I went to the library this morning after he called you, and I tried to find the books I remembered my dad was so fascinated by late in the summer. A couple of them I couldn't find, but I tried to get things that seemed the most similar."

"What interests me the most is what I *didn't* find," she went on, turning to Drake. "One of the last things I remember my father saying about all of this was that he'd found some connection between all of what he called 'the great alchemists' and King Midas."

"Not much of a stretch," Sully said. "Midas was supposed to be able to turn things to gold just by touching them."

Drake leaned forward, reaching for one of the maze drawings. "Maybe I missed something, but last I checked, Midas was just a myth."

Jada nodded. "Maybe. But my father always said that every legend has at least a little history at its core."

"What are all these?" Drake asked, holding up the maze drawing.

She took it from his hand. "My dad had been doing tons of research, but his inquiries were split pretty evenly on two subjects. The first was alchemy. The other one was labyrinths."

"What's the connection?" Drake asked.

"We don't know yet," Sully said, sifting through the illustrations. "Jada dug up references this morning on some of the more famous labyrinths."

"Sketching helps me think," Jada said. "Most of the ancient labyrinths only exist as ruins and foundations, but archaeologists think they've got some of them figured out. There are diagrams. I tried drawing them, trying to find design connections, that kind of thing."

"Any luck?" Drake asked.

Jada's expression turned contemplative. "A little," she said, reaching for a larger book from the coffee table. "But the biggest piece of luck was right in front of me from the second we found this book in the library, and it took me until about twenty minutes ago to realize it."

She tapped the cover, drawing their attention to the author's name: Maynard P. Cheney.

"You know him?" Sully asked.

"No," Jada said. "But my father had been talking to the guy constantly in the last few weeks. Cheney is working on a new exhibit for the Museum of Natural History. Want to guess the subject?"

Drake held up the labyrinth illustration in his hand and raised his eyebrows.

"Exactly," Jada said, nodding.

"The museum's only a few blocks from here," Sully said as he stood.

"Let's go have a talk with Mr. Cheney," Drake replied, setting the illustration aside.

Jada rose, and they both turned to look at her. She seemed confused for a moment, and then her eyes flashed with anger.

"Oh, hell no," she said, glancing back and forth between them. "My father is dead, and this guy might help us figure out why. If you want some girl who's going to lock the door and hide behind the sofa, then you've got the wrong damsel in distress."

Sully looked like he might argue, the thought of Jada in danger making him go pale, but one look from her and he didn't put up an argument. Drake liked her more and more.

As Jada opened the door and led the way into the hall, he glanced at Sully. "I guess she's coming along."

Sully gave a wan smile. "You want to try to stop her?"

Drake followed Jada out the door. "Not in the least."

As they walked down 81st Street, Drake hung back a ways, keeping an eye on Sully and Jada but also keenly aware of their surroundings. He checked every pedestrian and every vehicle but saw no sign that they were being followed. On the way uptown, he had considered Sully's paranoia excessive, but now he wasn't so sure. They had only the edges of the puzzle surrounding

Luka's murder, but if he had made some huge discovery involving alchemy, that likely meant gold. Maybe a lot of gold. And there were a great many people who would do just about anything for such treasure. He scanned the windows and rooftops but realized that it had become his turn to be overly paranoid. Even if Luka's killers—and logic suggested there was more than one, considering how much effort it required to sneak a steamer trunk with a corpse inside it onto a train platform without anyone noticing—had found out where Jada had been hiding, they could not have predicted which route Drake and Sully and Jada would take when leaving the apartment.

Still, he was worried. As they walked, he turned the whole thing over in his mind. Luka's wife had made the introductions between her husband and her employer. Drake wasn't sure what her position was at Phoenix Innovations, but it stood to reason that she knew at least some of the details of the secret project Henriksen wanted Luka to work on. When Luka turned him down and started working on it himself, that would have put Olivia in a difficult position. Would she have told Henriksen what her husband was up to?

Jada referred to Olivia as her "wicked stepmother." It might be a family joke, but Drake doubted it. The question was whether Olivia Hzujak valued her job more than she did her marriage. And if she had told Henriksen what Luka had been up to, would this billionaire CEO have gone so far as to have the man murdered?

Drake didn't know. But someone had killed Luka, and to do it in such an odd and gruesome fashion—well, the killers hadn't tried to hide their work. On the contrary, they had virtually assured that the whole world would know of it. By now, details of the discovery of Luka's body would be on every news channel and all over the Internet.

Something didn't click there. If Henriksen had wanted Luka dead, would he have made such a spectacle of the crime? It seemed far too great a risk for a man with so much to lose.

Ruminating on it, he picked up his pace as Sully and Jada passed the museum on the right and reached the corner of Central Park West. They looked comfortable together, like father and daughter. Sully spent most of his time focusing on his own fortunes, so it was fascinating to watch him become so wrapped up in someone else's. He had no children of his own, but Jada was his goddaughter, and it was pretty clear he would do anything to protect her. Even if Drake hadn't wanted to help Jada—which he did both for her own sake and because the puzzle intrigued him—he would have been on board just because Sully had asked.

It was the one thing that Drake and Jada had in common. As of this morning, Sully was the closest thing either one of them had to family. Drake hustled up the museum steps and through the door, finding Sully and Jada waiting for him just inside.

"Anything?" Sully asked.

"Not that I saw," Drake replied, "but I'm no detective, so what do I know?"

Sully frowned. "Nah. If they knew where Jada was, they'd have tailed us from the apartment."

Jada looked relieved as Sully headed off toward the information desk. For a person who had learned of her father's murder only half a day before, she was holding together well.

By the time they caught up to Sully, he already had spoken to the neatly attired man behind the desk, who had picked up a phone and was having a conversation while half turned away from them. A moment later he hung up the phone and informed them that someone from Dr. Cheney's team would be down to fetch them momentarily. Drake fought the temptation to make a crack about anyone "fetching" them and joined Sully and Jada in standing around an enormous plant, trying not to look awkward.

An attractive young woman arrived to fetch them, introducing herself as a graduate student working with Dr. Cheney. She wore her hair up in a loose bun, artfully disarrayed, and though her dark red sweater and gray skirt were fashionable and neat, Drake thought she looked more like a movie superspy masquerading as a museum employee than an actual graduate student. She made him want to enroll in classes or become a museum curator, and though Jada and Sully asked her questions while she let them up to the second floor, Drake missed the initial bits of conversation.

"—honestly surprised that the board went along with it," the woman said as she marched up the stairs ahead of them. "Whitney Memorial Hall has been used for special exhibits numerous times, but in this case, they actually relocated the oceanic birds exhibit to the Akeley Gallery. Most of the birds, I should say. The Akeley is a smaller space, so some had to be put into storage. In any case, it underscores how enthusiastic they are about Dr. Cheney's work that they're willing to go to that extent. He's been working night and day for weeks in preparation."

They reached the top of the stairs in a wide rotunda. Through a huge entryway behind him, Drake saw elephants, and the sight saddened him. He had seen the real thing, up close and personal and on their own territory, and encountering them here felt almost grotesque.

"I'm sorry," he said, tearing his attention away from the elephant. "I zoned out for a second. What's this exhibit Mr. Cheney's working on?"

The question earned him a look of scorn from their guide. "Dr. Cheney's exhibit is called 'Labyrinths of the Ancient World.' His research into historical records and the physical evidence has been groundbreaking."

"And he's the curator of the exhibit?" Jada asked.

"Of course," the graduate student sniffed, growing impatient and visibly irritated at their ignorance.

Without another word, all courtesy forgotten, she strode from the rotunda and down a short corridor past restrooms and a coatroom. A velvet rope blocked the huge rollaway doors at the end of the corridor. A small brass stand bore a sign that asked patrons to pardon the museum for its appearance while a new exhibit was being installed.

"They should switch her to public relations," Drake muttered to Sully and Jada. "Doesn't she just exude a welcoming warmth?"

Sully shot him a remonstrative glance, but Jada said nothing. She wore a hopeful expression as they followed their guide past the velvet rope. The graduate student used a key to unlock the large doors and slid one side open just wide enough for them to pass through.

"Dr. Cheney's locked in here?" Jada asked.

"There's an employee entrance as well. This was just the most convenient way to bring you in. And Maynard has a key, of course."

Drake tried to hide his smile. *Oh, it's Maynard now.* Someone had a little crush on her boss. It would have been adorable if she hadn't been such a condescending witch.

They entered the exhibit after she and Drake nearly collided with Sully and Jada, who had stopped to admire Dr. Cheney's work. Drake's eyes widened as he took in their surroundings. Just ahead of them were two massive stones engraved with ancient languages: Greek on one side and Egyptian hieroglyphics on the other. A banner hung on the wall to the right, trumpeting the name of the exhibit—"Labyrinths of the Ancient World"—along with the tagline "Can You Find Your Way Out?"

"No way," Jada whispered.

"Actually, I kinda think 'way,'" Drake replied.

The graduate student slid the door shut behind them but didn't bother with the lock. Apparently she didn't think they would be there very long.

"If you'll follow me," she said, "I'll take you through the labyrinth. Please don't touch anything, and no photographs, of course."

"Of course," Sully said drily.

The labyrinth exhibit had been constructed as a maze, with information imparted along the way through diagrams and scale models. Monitors had been installed in the walls to show animated re-creations of the construction of the labyrinths, and at regular intervals there were cutouts in the walls where ancient artifacts had been placed behind thick glass. Some of the plaques identifying those objects were not yet in place and some of the cutouts were still empty, but Drake had the idea that the time was not far off when the exhibit would make its debut. And what a debut it would be. He felt certain that crowds would flock to the museum to lose themselves in the labyrinth Dr. Cheney had built.

What the irritated graduate student led them through was not a full-size labyrinth but only a tiny fragment created to give visitors the illusion that they were lost in a vast, sprawling maze. As they turned sharply angled corners and then doubled back again, Drake decided that Dr. Cheney had done an excellent job. In fact, being lost was no illusion at all. He imagined that when the exhibit was completed, there would be arrows or some other indicator to let people know if they were headed in the right direction, but he would have been lost without their guide, and he thought the same must be true of Sully and Jada.

"Is there a Minotaur?" Jada asked.

The graduate student glanced back at them over her shoulder and smirked. "No. But there will be a false turn that will be very dark, and you'll hear a roar coming from it. Then the lights go out, and there's a whole display about the legend of the Minotaur. We're supposed to focus on history, not myth, but people who come to an exhibit on labyrinths are going to expect *something* on the legend."

Jada started to reply but never got the words out. Whatever she might have said was interrupted by a horrible scream that echoed through the labyrinth, seeming to come from everywhere and nowhere at once. A man's voice, in panic and pain.

"What the hell—" Sully growled.

The graduate student froze. "Maynard?" she called, panic in her eyes.

Drake and Jada exchanged a glance, and he could tell by the way she stood that they were doing the same thing: listening, trying to figure out the source of the scream. In the labyrinth, it might be impossible to pinpoint.

"This way," Drake said, taking a left turn.

"No," their guide said, grabbing his arm. "That's a dead end."

She walked straight ahead, and for a heartbeat Drake thought she would collide with the wall. Only when she passed through it did he see the opening; an optical illusion had made it seem like an unbroken surface. Dr. Cheney had outdone himself in creating his labyrinth exhibit, but the time to appreciate it had passed.

Drake, Sully, and Jada followed her through the opening and around a sharp turn that brought them to a fork.

"Which way?" Jada asked.

The graduate student seemed about to go right, but then there came a crash of glass and the thump of a heavy impact against the walls. Drake darted past the woman, down the corridor to the left. The sound had been close, and with the thud on the wall, there was no question about direction now.

Drake darted around a floor display, brushed the fake stone wall, and took a jag to the right. It felt like he'd reversed direction; for a second he thought the maze had misled him, but then it split into two narrow passages, one in either direction, and he turned left again, rushing in the direction of the crash. He heard Sully, Jada, and their guide pursuing him but didn't slow. That scream had been one not of fear but of pain. And more than pain. He had heard men scream like that only in the worst of circumstances, when blood had been shed and life was fleeting.

"Nate, watch your ass!" Sully shouted.

Drake slowed, taking heed of the warning. They'd heard no gunshots, but he had no way of knowing what waited for them ahead. He dashed past a yawning darkness to his right and wondered if that was where the Minotaur's roar eventually would be heard. Then he reached a turn where the ceiling sloped downward to an arched entryway. He ducked through and nearly tripped over a man sprawled on the floor.

"Damn it," he muttered, regaining his footing.

A quick glance at the man's dull, vacant eyes—and the stab wounds in his chest and the blood staining his clothes and pooling under him—was enough to tell Drake he wasn't going to make it.

4

Blood bubbled from Dr. Cheney's lips as he tried to breathe, and his whole body shook.

Drake surveyed the scene in an instant. A display case had been shattered in the man's struggle with the murderer. Blood smeared on the wall showed where the dying man had crashed into it, trying to keep himself from falling.

Sully, Jada, and their guide ducked through the low passage, and when the graduate student saw the dying man, she screamed his name.

"Maynard!" she cried, and rushed to kneel at his side, murmuring denials and prayers in a torrent of heartbreak.

"Don't touch him," Sully warned as she went to try to lift his head.

The woman glanced up in confusion, but Drake saw in her eyes that she understood Sully's caution. The police would not want the crime scene disturbed. She wanted to help the curator, but anyone could see there was nothing she could do.

Drake turned away from her anguish. He ran to the next bend in the corridor and peered around the corner, listening for retreating footfalls. They were no more than thirty seconds behind the killer, but that could be an eternity if the bastard knew where he was going. He was about to give chase anyway but hesitated.

"Hey," he said, rushing back to the others, realizing he didn't know the graduate student's name. "Which way is the staff entrance you were talking about?"

She blinked, lifted her gaze from the dying Dr. Cheney, and looked at him. "Back there," she said, glancing the way they'd come. "Through the Minotaur's alcove. It's the dark area on the left as you—"

But Drake had stopped listening. He remembered. They had just passed it, probably only a second or two before the killer had gone into that darkness. He might even have been hiding there in the shadows, waiting as they went by so as not to make any noise.

"Stay with her," he told Sully.

Sully nodded, though he didn't look happy about it.

Drake ran through the passage in a crouch, standing as he emerged in the corridor. He heard Jada following, wished she would wait with Sully, but didn't take the time to argue with her. A couple of hours with the adult Jada Hzujak and he knew she wasn't the sort of woman who was going to sit idly by when it came time for action.

They raced through two turns of the labyrinth, retracing their steps, and came to the Minotaur's alcove. Drake didn't slow, plunging into the darkness, hands in front of him. He stumbled over loose cables on the floor but caught himself on the wall at the rear of the alcove.

"Watch your step, Jada," he said, his eyes adjusting as he found a doorknob and twisted it, bursting through into a narrow, dimly lit corridor that looked nothing like the interior of the labyrinth.

Sound equipment and a workbench blocked the way to the right, so they went left, hurtling down the narrow hall created by the hollow backs of the labyrinth's walls. Plywood and two-by-fours and bare bulbs made him think of being backstage in a theater.

What the hell am I doing? Drake thought. Luka had been murdered, and now Dr. Cheney, who apparently had helped him in his labyrinth research, was dying. Whatever Luka had discovered, someone didn't want anybody talking about it. If the killers thought that Jada's father might have shared his secrets with her, she would be a target as well, just as she had feared, and yet here they were chasing after one of the very people who would want her dead.

The corridor cut diagonally to the right, and he followed it. It zigzagged in between turns in the labyrinth, a hidden space, a

maze within the maze. He could hear Jada's footfalls right behind him, her breathing so close that he practically could feel it,
and he knew they were being foolish taking this risk. But he also
knew that she wanted answers and would never stop just to save
herself.

The maze ended abruptly. The walls on either side cut away,
the halls of the labyrinth turning, but their narrow corridor arrived at a pair of double metal doors with an exit sign glowing
above them and a warning placard stating the door was for the
use of staff only.

Drake slammed through the door and found himself on a
stairwell landing. Jada skidded to a halt beside him, looking first
up and then down.

"Which way?" she asked, her hazel eyes alight with fierce
determination, her magenta bangs framing her face.

"No way to tell," Drake said. "And we'd be fools to try
guessing. We've gotta get back to Sully and get out of here."

"What?" Jada snapped, turning on him. "Dr. Cheney's our
one lead, and he's back there dying. If we catch this guy, we
could make him tell us—"

Drake shook his head. "We're not gonna catch him. He's got
a head start, and we don't know where he is or what he looks
like. Whether he went up or down, by now he's mixed in with
employees or with visitors and is on his way out of this place.
Best thing to do right now is get you the hell out of here."

Jada's eyes narrowed. "You think I'm in danger?"

"You were hiding out in a friend's apartment because *you*
thought you were in danger," Drake reminded her. "It's just that
now I believe you."

"Nice," Jada said. "Didn't you used to be charming?"

"Yeah. Strangely, I'm not in the mood today."

Jada's flinty exterior gave way, and for a moment he saw the
pain and vulnerability beneath.

"Come on," she said. "Let's move."

She ran back down the sawdust-smelling corridor. Drake followed, wondering where it would all lead. He and Sully weren't
bodyguards or private detectives, and they sure as hell weren't

cops. This wasn't a job for them, but Sully would never see it that way, and Drake had the feeling that he himself was already in too deep to walk away.

Jada had left the door to the Minotaur's alcove partway open, but when they went back through it, Drake closed it tightly and wiped the knobs on both sides, his mind racing ahead. The police would be there any minute, and then all their options would be taken away from them. Whatever happened after that would be decided by the detectives running the case.

They ducked and went through the low-ceilinged passage, emerging just a few feet from where two security guards stood by Dr. Maynard Cheney's body, one of them on his cell phone, reporting the crime, and the other just scratching his head in dismay.

When Drake and Jada came in, the guards turned and one of them reached for the Taser at his side.

"Whoa!" Drake said, putting his hands up. "We're with them, pal."

The guards looked over to Sully and the graduate student, who sat against the wall a short way down the corridor.

"It's okay," the woman said. "They were with me when I found him."

The guards ignored Drake and Jada after that. They looked quite shaken, and Drake thought they would be very relieved when the police arrived.

He glanced over at the body. Dr. Cheney lay in the same position, still bleeding, flesh turning paler as the blood drained from him. The man's chest had ceased to rise and fall. One glance at the graduate student's red-rimmed eyes and her tears and the way Sully held her—self-conscious and awkward at the intimacy of her grief and the comfort he offered—and it was clear no ambulance would be needed. Not that Drake had needed confirmation. The moment he had seen the extent of Cheney's wounds, he had known the man's fate was sealed.

"Uncle Vic," Jada said softly, her eyes beginning to well up at the sight of the dead man. "We need to go."

Sully gave a shake of his head, cautioning them to be wary of what they said around the guards. He leaned in and spoke to the graduate student in gentle tones Drake rarely had heard from him.

"Gretchen," he said quietly, "tell them what you told me. And quickly, please. We don't have a lot of time."

Apparently the graduate student had a name, and Drake thought it fit her well. Drake and Jada drew nearer, and he glanced over his shoulder to make sure the guards weren't making any effort to overhear them.

Gretchen looked at Jada. "You're Luka Hzujak's daughter?"

Jada nodded.

"And he's really dead?"

Jada took a deep breath, wiping away a tear, visibly fighting her grief. "Yeah. Murdered. And whoever killed him probably killed Dr. Cheney, too."

"What's the connection, Gretchen?" Drake asked quietly, glancing again at the guards, wondering how long before the police pulled up in front of the museum. "Jada's father was studying labyrinths. He made some kind of discovery, figured out some kind of mystery that had him excited."

"I don't know everything," Gretchen said. "It's just—my God, it's just *history*. But I know that Maynard told Professor Hzujak about a connection he'd found between the labyrinthine tomb from Egypt's Twelfth Dynasty and the labyrinth of Knossos—the one with the Minotaur—"

"I thought that was just a legend," Drake interrupted.

"So did I," Gretchen said, nodding. "But the historical record says there was something being shown there in the first century A.D. It's accepted that the labyrinth of Knossos existed, but the question is how much of the story is real and how much is myth.

"Maynard thought he had found part of the answer. The museum is running an archaeological dig near the City of Crocodiles in Egypt right now—my brother Ian is one of the managers on the project—and they've found some amazing things."

"My father was in Egypt just a few weeks ago," Jada said in a hushed voice.

Gretchen nodded. "Yes. He visited the dig. You didn't know why he traveled there?"

Jada hugged herself. "Research was all he told me."

"Maynard had been translating the writing on the artifacts that have been coming back from the dig," Gretchen went on. "He found references to three different labyrinths, all in use at the same time and all designed by Daedalus."

"Another myth," Drake said.

"Based on a real person," Gretchen said.

"Come on, Nate," Sully put in. "How many times have we proven that most legends have at least a kernel of truth?"

Drake nodded. There was no arguing with their own experiences.

"What about Midas?" Drake asked, thinking of Luka's research into alchemy.

Gretchen shook her head. "No. As far as Maynard knew, all of that 'Midas touch' stuff, turning things to gold, was just a story. It meant something, but he hadn't figured out what just yet."

"Dr. Cheney thought he had proven the rest, though?" Jada asked.

"He was sure of it," Gretchen said, a bit breathless now, wiping at her tears as she glanced at the guards. She had no reason to believe their story except that she saw Jada's grief reflecting her own and must have felt how vital this information was to them.

"There were even references to the Minotaur," she went on. "Not just the one in Crete, but in Egypt, too. Both labyrinths had monsters in them, according to the writing at the Egyptian dig. There's more than a kernel of truth to this stuff, and he had the evidence. As soon as he started accumulating all of that, he got the go-ahead from the museum to proceed with this exhibit."

Sully began to rise. Gretchen reached for him, as if fearing to be left alone, though the security guards were there. Sully took her hand and helped her stand as well.

"Jada," Sully said, "Dr. Cheney told Gretchen that he thought whatever your father was searching for must be at the center of the third labyrinth."

"Where was that one?" Drake asked.

"That's the thing," Gretchen said, glancing back and forth between Drake and Jada. "It's a mystery. But your father called Maynard a couple of days ago, and when they got off the phone, Maynard was so excited. Your father thought he'd worked out the location of the third labyrinth. He wouldn't say where it was until he'd confirmed it, but Maynard believed in him. He said if anyone could find it, Luka Hzujak could."

The two young women exchanged a look of shared sorrow, and Drake lowered his eyes, feeling like he and Sully were intruders. But then Jada touched his arm, and he looked up at her.

"This has to be it," she said, but she was staring at Sully. "This is why they killed him, Uncle Vic."

"To keep the secret?" Gretchen asked, doubtful.

"Or to keep Luka from getting there first," Sully said, turning to Drake.

"Henriksen?" Drake said. "He was already our best guess."

The security guards' radios crackled with voices and static. The police were on their way up. They would be upstairs in moments.

"We need to go," Sully said, looking at Jada.

"Gretchen, listen," Drake said, staring at her intently. "You said your brother's working on that dig in Egypt. If we can get there, can you put in a word for us? We need access to that site."

"What?" Jada asked. "Egypt?"

But Sully was nodding, looking at Gretchen expectantly. "It's the only way we're going to find out who's really behind this."

Gretchen glanced at the corpse of Dr. Cheney. Then she nodded. "I'll call him."

"Good," Sully said. "I'm sorry, but we've got to go. When this is all over, you'll hear from me. We'll make sure you get the truth."

"Thank you," she said, her expression crumbling as they walked away and she was forced to contend once more with the murder of a man she so obviously had admired and loved.

"Where do you think you're going?" one of the security guards asked.

"The police are coming up, aren't they?" Drake said in the most reasonable tone he could muster. "They'll never find their way through all of this. We're gonna meet them and guide them through."

"Right," the guard said. "Should've thought of that."

"Hey, don't sweat it," Sully replied. "None of us is thinking straight right now. What a horrible day."

"Exactly," the guard said.

As soon as Drake, Jada, and Sully were through the crouching passage, they bolted along the twisting corridor to the Minotaur's alcove. They could hear voices and the crackling of police radios coming their way as they slipped silently through the door at the back of the alcove and then hurried along the narrow "backstage" hallway to the staff exit.

"How the hell are we going to get to Egypt?" Sully asked Drake.

"We'll figure it out."

"We can't go yet," Jada said as they raced down the employee stairwell. "Not until after my father's funeral."

Sully stopped and turned to her, taking her by the hands. "Jada, listen. The way he died—it's going to be days before the coroner releases his body for burial. If Henriksen is behind this, he's been working on it for a while. Whatever secrets Luka discovered, Henriksen either knows them or he's trying to crack them right now. If we're gonna get to the bottom of it, we can't let him beat us to them."

Jada looked frustrated and confused. "What if they're ready to release him and I'm not back?"

"We'll leave word," Drake promised. "We'll make sure either someone is there to claim him or the coroner's office holds on to his remains until you can do it yourself. But the other problem is that if your father's killers really are looking for you, a funeral would put you out in public, make you vulnerable."

Jada narrowed her eyes. "Once they find out you're helping me, you guys will be targets, too."

"Nah," Drake said, smiling. "Who'd want to hurt a guy as charming as me?"

"Sometimes *I* do," Sully said. "Come on."

They hurried down to the first floor, took a moment to compose themselves, and opened the door. No one tried to stop them. Drake had considered security cameras, but he figured that if these staff doors were under video surveillance, either the killer had disabled them to avoid being seen—in which case they had nothing to worry about—or the cops would scan the video as far as the killer and stop there. He hoped.

They had to answer a few questions and be patted down by police officers as they were leaving the museum and provide their names. Then they were on the street again and walking back toward the apartment where Jada had been staying.

"We need to go to Luka's place," Drake said.

Sully shot him a look. "Not a good idea."

"The cops will already have searched it," Drake argued. "And they won't be looking for the same things we'll be looking for. If there are any notes or computer files about this stuff, we want them. We need all the information we can get on this. Until we find out what Henriksen is really after and get our hands on it—"

"And expose him," Jada put in.

"—Jada will never be safe."

"I don't know," Sully said. "Maybe we should talk to Olivia."

Jada flipped her hair back and stared at him. "No way. That bitch is involved in this somehow. I know it. It's the only thing that makes sense."

"You can't really know that," Sully replied.

"But I do," Jada insisted, reaching into her pocket and pulling out her slim red cell phone. She flipped it open and turned it on, waiting a moment while it powered up. "Huh, look at that. No messages. The cops had to have told her hours ago that they found her husband murdered and—" Her voice broke. "—and stuffed into an old *trunk*. But she hasn't tried to get in touch with me? His daughter? Her stepdaughter?"

"You're right," Sully said, throwing up his hands. "I'll buy it.

We'll go to Luka's place. But we've gotta watch our asses. If it *is* Henriksen, he's likely to have people watching the place."

"We have to risk it," Drake said. "And if they come after us, maybe we can grab one of them and confirm what we're all thinking about Phoenix Innovations."

In agreement, they walked in silence for more than a block before Sully flagged down a taxi, preparing themselves for whatever trouble awaited them at Luka Hzujak's apartment.

By the time they got there, the whole building was in flames.

Before someone had decapitated and mutilated him and put most of his pieces in an old steamer trunk that smelled of low tide and mothballs, Professor Luka Hzujak had lived in a four-story brick building on 12th Street, just west of Abingdon Square Park, in the West Village. Slender trees grew from slots in the narrow sidewalk. With the stone lintels above the windows, the dormers on top, and the small smokestacks on the roof, the building might have looked like something out of *Oliver Twist* if not for the fact that it was on fire.

Drake spotted the smoke out the window of the taxi from several blocks away. A few seconds later, Sully frowned, sniffing the air. The smell of a fire that large never presaged anything positive.

"Pull over here," Drake said.

The cabbie obliged, and Sully and Jada climbed out while Drake paid the man, including a generous tip mostly because he didn't have time to wait for his change. He slammed the door and shoved his hands in his pockets as he hurried along the sidewalk after Sully and Jada. None of them had said anything as yet, but he felt sure they all knew which building was on fire.

When they reached the corner of West 12th Street, there were no surprises awaiting them, but Jada looked like she had been punched in the gut. She hugged herself tightly and took a step back from the sight of her father's burning apartment building.

Sirens wailed, and a police car pulled up at the other end of the street. The firemen were already at work, hoses twisting along the pavement and over the curb. An old woman sat on a gurney behind an ambulance, staring at the building in shock as an EMT put an oxygen mask over her face. Several other people—apparently residents—stood across from the building in various stages of undress, most of them at the very least shoe-less, while a pair of police officers questioned them.

Drake wondered how long Luka had lived there and if there were remnants of his life stored anywhere else. Otherwise, Jada had lost not only her father but all of his papers and photo-graphs, all of the mementos of his life. He watched her cover her mouth with shaking hands, and his heart broke for her. She looked like she wanted to scream or run or hit someone, but she didn't know what to do next.

"This is all happening damn fast," Drake whispered to Sully.

Sully narrowed his eyes and nodded in agreement, then went to Jada and slipped an arm around her.

"Listen, kid," Sully rasped, "we're not going to get anything useful here. We stick around and we're just asking for trouble, especially if whoever did this is on the lookout for you."

Jada spun on him, curtains of magenta hair flying across her face. "We *know* who did this!" she shouted. "And I'm not going to hide anymore."

Thanks to streetlights and New York traffic, the taxi that had just left them off hadn't gotten very far. As the cabbie acceler-ated across the intersection, bending to glance at the burning building and all the emergency vehicles, Jada rushed into the street and flagged him down.

"You don't think—" Sully began.

"Phoenix Innovations," Drake said.

Sully swore. "This is a really bad idea," he said as he ran after Jada.

"Yeah," Drake agreed. "But are you gonna stop her?"

Sully ignored the question, but they both knew the answer. With the kind of pain Jada was in, they didn't blame her for wanting to confront the man she suspected was responsible for killing her father or the stepmother she thought had betrayed him. But that didn't make it a good idea. Drake doubted they would have been able to talk her out of going to Tyr Henriksen's office, which meant the best thing they could do was protect her.

"Fifty-ninth Street and Broadway," Jada said, practically hurling herself into the backseat of the taxi.

"I just dropped you off," the cabbie said, mystified.

"Yeah," Sully growled. "Change of plans."

Sully paused before getting into the cab and looked back at Drake.

"Whatever goes on, it's gotta be as public as possible," he said. "Make sure security cameras pick us up, that people see us going to Henriksen's office. It goes against every rule we've ever had—"

"No, you're right," Drake said. "If we're going in there, we have to make sure Jada gets noticed. No matter how much they want to silence her, they're not going to kill her in the office if a hundred people saw her go in."

Glass shattered behind them, and they turned to see black smoke and bright fire billowing out of the exploding upper-story windows. The building was going to be a total loss, and you didn't get that hungry a fire without some kind of accelerant. The investigators would know right off it had been arson, but that didn't matter if they couldn't figure out the identity of the arsonist.

Sully climbed in beside Jada. Drake glanced at the baffled-looking cabbie, but the man seemed focused on the spectacle of the firefighters at work. Then an ambulance rolled up behind them and gave a blast of its siren, urging them out of the way, and the cabbie looked irritated and motioned for Drake to get in.

As Drake ducked his head to get into the backseat, the window of the open door exploded in a shower of glass shards.

"What the—" Sully began.

A bullet punched through the roof and lodged in the seat behind Jada's head.

"Down!" Drake shouted as another shot plinked the outside of the cab.

With a loud roar, a black SUV sped past the ambulance and

slid to a shuddering halt beside the taxi. Its glass was tinted, but the passenger window started to glide down, and Drake knew that one way or another they were dead. If the sniper on the roof across the street didn't kill them—only that would explain the angle of the first shots—these bastards in the SUV would make their deaths look like a gangster drive-by.

"Drive!" he screamed to the cabbie.

The guy behind the wheel of the ambulance smartened up, putting the vehicle in reverse, and it sped backward in retreat. Down West 12th Street people had started to tear their attention from the fire, hearing the gunshots.

"Damn it, drive the car!" Drake shouted, banging the partition to get the terrified cabbie's attention.

The man had ducked down, hiding behind the dashboard. Something—Drake's command or his own sense of self-preservation—made him realize that if they just sat there, they were dead, and he sat up and threw the cab into gear.

A sniper's bullet punched through the windshield and took him in the chest. He jerked against the seat and then started to slide sideways, his hands twitching on the wheel.

"Son of a bitch!" Sully snapped. "I need a gun, Nate!"

But they didn't have any guns. Not yet. They were damn well going to get them, but for now, running was the only choice. Drake popped the rear passenger door, staying low as he yanked open the one in front. The cab had started to roll but hadn't picked up any speed.

He spotted a gun jutting from the open window of the SUV as he threw himself into the front seat. With both hands, he grabbed the cabbie and hauled the man toward him, then started climbing over him.

Bullets punched the side of the cab, shattering front and back windows and plinking through the metal doors. One caught the driver in the thigh. Drake had time enough to think that what he was doing was insane, that it was suicide to put himself in the way of the bullets. But he knew that doing nothing would also be suicide.

He got his hands on the wheel, kept his head to the side, and was about to hit the gas when a loud, crunching impact filled the air. He risked looking up and saw that the ambulance driver had purposely rammed the back of the SUV.

"Crazy bastard!" Sully whooped appreciatively.

"Bought us a couple of seconds," Drake said.

Jada cried out as another bullet punched a hole in the roof, a new attack from the sniper, letting daylight in.

Drake gritted his teeth. They had to get away from both attacks, the sniper and the SUV, and there was only one direction open to them that he knew would accomplish that. He slammed it into reverse, backed the taxi up thirty feet, then put it back in drive, cranked the steering wheel to the right, and skidded into a turn down West 12th Street.

"Are you *nuts*?" Sully shouted.

"You're going to hit the fire truck!" Jada warned.

Knuckles white on the wheel, Drake drove straight for the closest fire truck. Firefighters shouted and tried to wave him off. Survivors of the burning building scurried out of the way. The two cops on the sidewalk pulled their guns, but not fast enough, as Drake shot the taxi through the gap between fire truck and ambulance and careened down the street toward the police cars waiting there.

Gunfire punched the air, echoing off the buildings, but he didn't slow down.

"Jada, are they following?" Drake asked.

She spun in the backseat and looked out the rear window. "Yes!"

"Are you kidding?" Sully said. "Who the hell are these guys?"

"We'll be out of range of the sniper as soon as we turn the corner," Drake told them.

"What about these nutjobs in the SUV?" Sully barked.

Drake smiled. He gunned the taxi past the two police cars parked diagonally at the curb, grazing a parked Mercedes, tearing off the taxi's sideview mirror, and then accelerated even more. At the intersection, he hit the brake, turned into the skid, and slung the taxi into a right turn, driving the wrong way up Washington Street. Car horns blared, and a white box truck swerved to avoid a head-on collision.

He glanced over his shoulder and saw one of the two police cars pulling out to block the road. Two officers on the street had their guns drawn and were rushing up to the SUV as it skidded to a halt.

"We're clear!" Sully said.

"For how long?" Jada asked, leaning forward, looking at Drake in the mirror. "They'll have cops crawling all over us in a minute."

Drake hung a quick left on Jane Street, no longer heading into oncoming traffic. He glanced over his shoulder at Sully.

"What do you think? Chelsea Piers?" he asked.

"No choice," Sully agreed.

"What's at Chelsea Piers?" Jada said.

Drake smiled, glancing at her in the rearview mirror. "Same thing you generally find at piers. Boats."

5

The High Line elevated park had started its life as a freight train track built above the city to keep the trains away from public streets. The elevated platform that ran through the Meatpacking District all the way to 34th Street had been converted to a long green oasis. Drake had never walked the park, but he had read an article about it in some in-flight magazine or other, describing it as a hidden gem of New York City. Someday he hoped to get a closer look at the High Line, but today he needed it only for cover.

He pulled the taxi to the curb on Little West 12th Street and let it roll into the shadows under the High Line. In the backseat, Jada was still shaking.

"Oh, my God," she said. "What the hell are we going to do?"

Sully took her hand, forcing her to meet his eyes. "We're gonna improvise, sweetheart. Don't worry. If there's one thing Nate and I know how to do, it's improvise."

Drake watched the rearview mirror for cars. The street was one way, so at least they had that going for them. He waited for a red Accord to buzz past them, hoping their shattered windows would earn no more than a quick glance. The Accord slowed and the driver gave him an odd look, but Drake glared at him and the guy accelerated, minding his own business. He might be on his cell phone to the cops in a second, but they had at least a couple of minutes.

He popped his door.

"Get out," he said. "Let's go."

Sully opened the back door and climbed out, with Jada hurrying after him. As Drake stepped from the taxi, she looked at him and then bent to peer through the open driver's door at the dead cabbie. His blood had started to pool on the seat.

"We can't just leave him here," Jada said.

"We sure as hell can't take him with us," Sully grumbled.

Drake glanced back at the dead man. "The police will take better care of him than we could. And if we stick around, they might end up burying us right next to him."

He shut the cab door, then noticed Sully staring at him.

"What?" Drake asked.

Sully pointed at his chest. "There's blood on your jacket."

Drake stripped off the coat, but he couldn't leave it in the cab. There was enough evidence of their presence already. If they were lucky, no one had gotten a good look at their faces and they would never be connected to the gunfire or the dead taxi driver, and so the police would never have a reason to test their DNA against any hair fibers found in the cab. He thought that probably would work out in their favor. His larger concern had to do with the museum. If Gretchen talked about them and helped the police make the connection between Dr. Cheney's murder and the burning of Luka Hzujak's apartment building, eventually he and Sully and Jada would get caught in the net.

They had to rely on Gretchen's discretion, and Drake didn't like that. Not that he didn't trust strangers easily. He tended to go with his instincts; it was just that there had been times when his instincts had been dangerously wrong.

Drake turned the jacket inside out and used it to brush broken glass off Sully and Jada's coats.

"Let's move," he said, carrying the coat bunched under his arm in a bundle.

They crossed the street and headed west, and by the time a battered gray Mercedes came growling along the road, they were far enough from the abandoned cab that no one would have made an instant connection between this trio of pedestrians and the damaged taxi. But Drake kept them moving at a swift pace, knowing that the police would not make any presumption of innocence.

They turned north, six short blocks from where the Chelsea

Piers complex was situated. It was mostly sports and recreation now, though it still had a private marina. Despite the autumn chill and the lengthening shadows of the fading day, he felt a circle of heat in the center of his back, as if a target had been painted there.

"Jada, where's the wicked stepmother right now?" Drake asked.

Sully shot him a glance. "You planning to pay her a visit? I'm not sure I like that plan. Or did you forget the guys with the guns and how eager they were to kill us?"

"It's not a plan," Drake said. "I have no plan. Well, not much of one, and the one I do have doesn't involve Jada's stepmother. I'd just like to know what we're dealing with here."

As they turned into a small oval park, cutting diagonally across from Tenth Avenue to Eleventh, Jada pulled out her cell phone.

"What are you doing?" Sully asked.

"Getting an answer to Nate's question," she said, punching a couple of buttons before she put the phone to her ear. She listened a moment, and then her eyes narrowed. "Hi, Brenda, it's Jada Hzujak. Is Olivia there?"

Drake saw a momentary confusion furrow her brow.

"Sorry, Miranda," Jada said, glancing down at her feet as she walked. "I expected Brenda to pick up, and I'm—well, I've got a lot on my mind. Listen, I know you're just covering the desk, but I didn't realize this was the week Olivia was going to be out of town, and I was hoping to take her out to lunch. Do you have any idea when she'll be back?"

Jada smiled thinly, but there was no amusement in it. She thanked Miranda and ended the call, then immediately began placing another.

"What's going on?" Drake asked.

"If Olivia's regular assistant hadn't been at lunch, we probably wouldn't even know this, but my stepmother's away on business. Yeah, in her grief, instead of planning her husband's funeral, she's skipped town. I gathered from the way Miranda was talking that she doesn't even know my father's dead. Olivia hasn't told her coworkers that her husband's been murdered."

Sully grunted. "Yeah, that's not weird or suspicious."

"So where did she go?" Drake asked.

Jada held up a finger to forestall him, turning her attention to her current phone call. She gave her name and cell phone number and then answered a couple of other questions, and it quickly became plain that she was calling her cellular service provider.

"Yes, I hope you can help me," she said once she had proved her identity to the satisfaction of the AT&T rep on the line. "I'm not at home, but I'm desperately seeking a phone number. Last month, my father was in Egypt and I called him several times at a hotel there. I know it's a strange request, but I'm hoping you can just glance at my bill from late September and give me that number. I need to get in touch with him and it'll be awhile before I'm home and I don't remember the name of the— Yes, that'd be great. Thanks so much."

She paused, waiting for the information.

As they emerged from the park, where they could see the river across several lanes of traffic, she covered the phone with her hand for a second and looked at Sully and Drake.

"I'll give you two guesses where Olivia is right now."

"She's in Egypt?" Sully asked.

"Look at that," Drake said. "You didn't even need your second guess."

Sully shoved his hands into his jacket pockets. "Guess that answers our question about whether or not Olivia's in on it with Henriksen."

"For me it was never a question," Jada said.

Drake cocked an eyebrow. "You know we're jumping to a lot of conclusions, right? Henriksen is chasing the same mystery Luka was working on, and it sure looks like Olivia's been working behind her husband's back, but none of this is proof that they killed him or sent those nice men with the guns after us."

Jada waved him to silence, focused on her phone call again.

"Yes, I'm still here. That's perfect, thanks." She looked around and realized she had nothing to write with or on. "Actually, if you could do me one other small favor? Could you e-mail me that number? I know it's probably not what you're supposed to do, but—"

She paused again, listening, and then smiled. "Even better. Thanks again."

Jada ended the call and slipped the phone into her pocket. "He's just going to e-mail me the whole bill. Should've asked for that in the first place." She glanced at Sully. "So now we know where to start when we get to Egypt—at the hotel where my father stayed. But how the hell are we going to get there?"

"One step at a time," Sully said as they turned north again, the vast Chelsea Piers complex in view up ahead. "First we get a boat."

"You're just going to walk into the marina and take one?" she asked.

Drake gave a small shrug. "Maybe not walk so much as skulk. Or slink. Possibly just a good old-fashioned sneak. What we lack in stealth we make up for in brazen stupidity and desperation."

"Come on," Jada said, turning to Sully. "Is this really going to work?"

Sully grinned his most rakish grin. "Seriously, kid. You don't think we've never stolen a boat before?"

Jada seemed to ponder that for a moment, then let out a breath. "Actually, after the past few hours, that doesn't surprise me at all."

Drake glanced at Sully. "You know, I'm not sure if I should be flattered or insulted."

They stole the boat on a Tuesday just as the sun was going down. As they walked onto the dock, a guard eyed them warily, trying to figure out if they were trespassers. Drake took Jada's hand and then turned and gave her a radiant smile, and she went right along with the charade, snuggling up against him. They were pretending, but it was a nice sort of make-believe, and Drake had to remind himself that the girl was Sully's goddaughter.

"Hey, there," Sully said, sauntering up to the guard as if he belonged there.

The guard frowned at Sully, taking in the bomber jacket over the guayabera and the neatly trimmed mustache, clearly wondering if this was somebody he was supposed to know. Sully drew him aside, lowering his voice so that only the guard could hear, but Drake knew the gist of what he was saying. They had discussed it moments before, and it was a ruse they'd used more than once.

"Listen, amigo, here's the deal. I'm working for Theresa Fonseca. I'm brokering the sale of some of the assets she's received in her divorce settlement. I've got this couple on the hook, but they're a little skittish because the divorce is turning ugly, and they're looking for an excuse not to buy. They keep making noises about security down here, so what I need from you is to act like you're busting my chops. Be a hardass—"

The guard looked confused, glanced at Drake and Jada, and then shook his head. "I don't know any Theresa—what was the name?"

"Fonseca. She—"

"Nah," the guard said. "No Fonseca down here."

Sully turned to Drake and Jada and put his hands up in a see-what-I-mean gesture, as if trying to show them just how tight security was at the marina.

"That's good, man. Perfect," Sully said.

The guard narrowed his eyes. "I'm not playacting here, pal. There's no one named Fonseca."

Sully bopped his palm against the side of his head. "Right, right. Divorce, remember? Crap, what's the husband's name? Starts with a K, I think. Keller? Kramer?"

"Kurland?" the guard suggested.

Sully pointed a finger at him, pistol-style. "That's it. Yeah. Look, I just need to walk them down and show them the boat and I'll be out of your hair. If I do my job right, Miss Fonseca—Mrs. Kurland, I guess—gets a decent price for the thing, and it'll serve the son of a bitch right for making babies with his girlfriend on the side."

The guard's face twisted in deep disapproval. "Babies?"

"I know. Awful stuff. Imagine finding out your husband was having an affair for, what, six years? Bad enough, right? But the guy fathered two children with the other woman. How does a lady pick herself up after getting kicked like that?"

By then the guard was nodding in agreement.

"What an ass," the guard said.

"Fortunately, the judge agreed," Sully said, smiling conspiratorially. "Now, look, do me a favor? Tell me we've got thirty minutes, no more. I have another appointment before I can go home tonight, so I don't want to be hemming and hawing with these folks for hours."

The guard did better than that. He walked Sully over to Drake and Jada, looking as though he were doing them a mighty favor.

"I'm sorry, but the marina has strict policies about visitors," he said. "Without the owner present, I can only give you half an hour. You'll have to sign in and show your ID. Please respect the privacy of the other owners and see me on your way out."

Jada squeezed Drake's arm, apparently concerned about having to show her ID.

"Not a problem," he said. "We wouldn't have it any other way, especially if we might be owners ourselves."

"I—um—left my purse in the car," Jada said.

The guard furrowed his brow.

Drake only smiled wider. "I've got it, sweetie. I'll sign us in."

The guard glanced at Sully, clearly trying to decide whether to push the ID issue, but then he let it go. Apparently, he didn't want to make trouble for Mrs. Kurland, because he led the three of them to a small guard booth not far from the marina entrance and barely glanced at the false identification Drake and Sully showed him as they signed the guest book.

Drake still had his bloodstained coat folded under his arm, and the guard shot a quizzical glance at it as Drake signed in, as if he thought he might be hiding something inside.

"What've you got there?" the guard asked.

Drake sighed in regret. "Not a damn thing. I spilled juice all over myself like an idiot. Ruined my coat."

Careful to show only the inside of the coat, he unfurled it to show that there was nothing wrapped inside it and then draped it carefully over his arm.

"Thanks, amigo," Sully said, giving a private little nod to the guard that Jada and Drake weren't supposed to see. "Say, what's the slip number again?"

He patted at his pants pockets as if looking for the piece of paper where he'd written the number down.

"One forty-seven," the guard replied.

Drake felt sorry for him. It wasn't the guard's fault he was dumb enough to fall for their hustle. He probably was going to get into serious trouble over this, maybe even lose his job. But if Drake had to choose between getting shot or thrown in jail and causing problems for this guy, well, it was really no choice at all.

Sully thanked the guard, pressing a twenty into his palm as they shook hands—a tiny fraction of the reward money Drake had brought back from South America. Then they were walking along the dock, the boats swaying on either side of them, rocked by the river.

Compared to some of the luxury crafts that were docked at the marina, the boat in the Kurlands' slip wasn't much to speak of—a thirty-five-foot Chris Craft with a fiberglass deep V-hull, maybe twelve feet at the beam—but that was all right. They didn't want anything huge or ostentatious. Even better, the Chris Craft was moored in a slip at the outside edge of the marina.

They boarded as if they belonged there, Sully behaving as if he were giving them a tour. Then Sully ducked out of sight, working the key switch off the ignition and pulling at the wires, figuring out which ones were for the starter. Drake kept watch out of the corner of his eye until the guard got a phone call at the booth. He was one of those people who paced while they were on the phone, and as he talked, he strolled back and forth between his security booth and the walkway that led from the dock to the marina club.

The third time he strolled up the walk, Drake gave a nod and Sully twisted the wires together. The motor growled to life, and Sully grinned up at Drake.

"You guys are a little too good at this," Jada said.

"Our line of work requires a lot of improvising," Drake said. Jada gave him a dubious smile. "Right."

Sully backed the boat out of the slip. Just as he throttled forward, pulling away from the dock, the guard came running toward them, shouting and waving at them to pull back into the slip. Drake knew that even then the man wouldn't know exactly what to make of it all. If he had believed Sully's story—and it was clear he had—Mrs. Kurland might have just given her broker the key so he could take the prospective buyers for a spin. The guard would suspect, certainly. But he wouldn't be sure, and he wouldn't do anything drastic until he was.

As they sped upriver, the boat whipping over the water, Drake watched the guard growing smaller in the distance.

"That guy is having a bad day," he said.

"Could be worse for him," Jada said. "He could be with us."

Drake and Sully both glanced at her, saw the sarcastic glint in her eyes, and laughed. She was right. Her father had been murdered, and they had encountered two other dead men today. Someone had sent men with guns to fire lots of bullets at them in hopes of making them very dead. Another someone—or maybe the same someone—had burned down Jada's father's apartment building.

They were having a day far worse than the guard's.

"Still," Drake said. "When we get back into the country, I'll send him something. Wine of the month, maybe."

"Cigars," Sully said, as if wine had been the stupidest suggestion Drake could have made. "Maybe steaks."

"Steaks?" Drake asked.

"Man's gotta eat. And did you get a look at him? You don't get that big eating Brussels sprouts."

"You guys are unbelievable," Jada said, raising her voice to be heard over the wind whipping past them as Sully throttled up and the boat went even faster.

Drake nodded. "That is actually not the first time we've heard that."

Jada whacked his arm. "It wasn't a compliment."

But she couldn't quite erase her smile, and Drake was glad. After all she had been through since the discovery of her father's remains, she needed all the distraction she could get. Now that they had a moment's respite, though, he watched her amusement quickly fade until she gazed at the city passing on their right— lights coming on as evening arrived—her expression solemn and somehow lost.

He hoped her stepmother wasn't involved in her father's death, but he had a terrible feeling that Olivia Hzujak was exactly as wicked a stepmother as Jada suspected.

Troubled, Drake reached into the inside pocket of his ruined coat and pulled out the slim leather case that held a good portion of the reward money he'd earned in Ecuador. There was more in his bags, which were safe in a locker at JFK, and some in his wallet. The rest had been put into an account he sometimes used in the Cayman Islands. For now, what he had on him would be all they had at their disposal, so it would have to be enough.

He dropped the coat overboard and watched it floating, soaking in the water as they swiftly left it far behind.

So far, so good. They would ditch the stolen Chris Craft just north of the 79th Street Boat Basin—Jada's suggestion—and stop by the apartment where she'd been hiding out just long enough for her to pack a small bag. Drake and Sully would have to improvise. They would pick up a couple of go phones—cell phones that could be loaded with as many minutes as they wanted, used, and then thrown away, all without creating an account that could be traced. Sully had suggested they call the marina and let them know where the boat would be, and both Drake and Jada had given the idea a thumbs-up. If they were ever caught, they would still be arrested, but a joyride would go over a hell of a lot better with a judge than outright theft.

From the apartment, they would head north. They needed to get out of the city fast but as under the radar as they could manage. Grand Central was no good just in case there had been cameras that had picked up their faces at the marina. So they would take a cab to 125th Street station in Harlem and board a

Metro North train to New Haven, Connecticut, where they could rent a car. The ID they had used at the marina would be no good now, but Drake was counting on Sully traveling with more than one set of false identification.

Once they were in a car, he thought they would be all right. Drake knew a guy in Boston who could whip up passports and other ID for all three of them. They would take the ferry to Nova Scotia and then a boat over to mainland New Brunswick rather than face the greater scrutiny of crossing the Canadian border in a car. From there, another rental car would bring them into Quebec. Montreal-Mirabel International Airport was used almost exclusively for cargo flights, and he and Sully had friends there. They had needed to sneak themselves—and various acquisitions—in and out of North America on numerous occasions. He expected that it would all go off without a hitch.

Even so, he knew he would be on edge until they were in the air and on their way to Egypt and the archaeological dig at the City of Crocodiles. In Drake's experience, the closer he got to the source of a secret—or a treasure—the easier it became to sense an imminent threat or perceive an enemy. People tended to reveal their true colors when things as valuable as treasure and secrets were at stake. He didn't like snipers taking shots at him from rooftops or thugs hiding behind dark windows.

If someone wanted to kill him, he liked to know who it was.

It made it a hell of a lot easier to fight back.

On Tuesday night none of them got more than a few hours' sleep in the back of the rental car before they arrived in Boston, where the forger had Drake and Sully's new identities waiting for them. The forger was a third-generation professional they called Charlie, though they all assumed it wasn't really his name. He'd had Drake and Sully's photos on file, which allowed him to prep their passports in advance, but he had to create Jada's on the spot, along with various other items—everything from an American Express platinum card to a library ID.

On Wednesday morning they stopped in Portland, Maine,

where Drake and Sully bought small duffel bags and several changes of clothes. By midnight they found themselves in a shabby motel near the cargo airport in Montreal, with one double bed for the three of them. Drake took an extra pillow and blanket from the closet and made a nest on the floor while Jada and her godfather took the bed.

They watched television, waiting to see if there might be some report of the violence in New York, but Montreal was a world away from Manhattan. That night Drake barely dozed, kept awake by the anticipation of the morning's departure, after which he would finally feel like they had gotten away safely. Jada lay awake as well. Several times he noticed her curled up on her side, watching him with eyes that gleamed in the darkened room, but neither of them spoke.

Only Sully managed to sleep. He always seemed able to doze, no matter how terrible the circumstances. He snored deeply, sometimes exhaling loudly, his mustached upper lip trembling with the noise.

On Thursday morning, the flight they thought they had arranged left without them. Desperate hours passed before they were promised another. At last, late that afternoon, they were airborne, comfortably ensconced in a small compartment behind the cockpit.

Finally, Drake slept.

When he woke, with the muffled thump of Irish punk rock coming from the cockpit, he found Sully gone and knew his old friend must be up front with the crew. He lay quietly, watching Jada sleep. With the magenta streaks that framed her face, she usually had an air of confidence even in the middle of her grief. But now in the peace of sleep, she seemed vulnerable, and he had to wonder about the wisdom of their journey. Drake had known plenty of capable women—had had his ass kicked by more than one of them. They had been skilled fighters, survivors, totally able to take care of themselves.

Jada, in contrast, was a question mark. He hoped that she would prove just as tough and capable for her own sake and for Sully's—and for his, as well. He didn't want to see her hurt any more than she already had been. At the same time, he knew he would have to keep an eye out for Sully. The old man clearly thought it was his job to protect Jada instead of letting her protect herself. That kind of thinking could distract him enough to be fatal.

"What are you thinking?" she said, her voice a hush, barely audible over the loud airplane engines.

"Have you ever been in a fight?" he asked. "A real one, I mean."

Jada frowned. "Not a real one, if you mean blood and bruises. Like a beatdown. But I hold my own in the dojo pretty well."

He arched an eyebrow. "Dojo? What do you study?"

"Aikido, mostly. Why?"

Drake smiled softly. Another woman who could kick his ass.

"You know, if we find it—this treasure, whatever it is—I already told Sully we can share it. Even split, three ways," she said.

Drake would have been offended if the idea hadn't appealed to him so much. Even so, he didn't want her to think the potential for personal gain had been his motivation for helping her.

"Treasure's always nice," he said. "But that's not why I'm along for this ride."

"No?" She studied him as if trying to see behind his eyes. "Why, then?"

For the first time, it occurred to Drake how close they were. Reclined in their chairs, facing each other, only a couple of feet separated them. He could have reached out and touched her face. If he had been any closer, he could have felt her breath on his cheek.

"Your father was a good guy," he said quickly. "I liked him. And Sully's my best friend, so it's not as if I could really say no."

"You have before," Jada reminded him. "Uncle Vic told me there was no guarantee."

"Someone tried to shoot me. I take that personally. Historically, I'm not a fan of people who point guns at me, never mind pulling the trigger."

"And that's it?" she asked. "Those are the reasons you're on this trip?"

Drake nodded, frowning. She was fishing for a different reply. What else did she want him to say?

"Pretty much," he said.

Only when he saw the disappointment in her eyes did he realize where he'd gone wrong. Jada had been hoping he had also come along because of her—because he didn't want to say goodbye to her just yet. The look in her eyes lasted for only a second before she hid her reaction from him, but he had seen it, and she knew he had seen it.

"Uncle Vic said you like the mystery, too," she said.

"What do you mean, 'the mystery'?"

"History. Digging up bits of the past that have been hidden for ages."

Drake smiled. "Yeah. That, too. Archaeologists think they've got it all figured out. They write books and papers explaining the ancient world as if there's nothing more to learn. It's arrogant and foolish, and every time we find something that proves them wrong—proves there are things about the past they don't understand or never imagined—that makes me happy."

Jada curled up a bit tighter in her chair. "It is kind of exciting. I've been hearing this sort of thing from my father all my life. And it was his—well, his last mystery, really. I want to know what it was he discovered, and I like that you want to know almost as much as I do."

This time Drake said nothing. The urge to touch her cheek, to push back her hair, was almost too much to resist, but he did. It wasn't meant to be. He wasn't here for that, and his life was way too complicated and unsettled to get involved with Jada Hzujak.

But damn, she was beautiful.

"Plus, there's the treasure," he said.

She narrowed her gaze, looking both amused and irritated all at once. He often had that effect on women.

"Yeah. The treasure. Whatever it is."

6

Drake stepped off the cargo plane onto the tarmac of Cairo International Airport, stiff and parched from the long flight. He had slept at least seven hours, more than half the journey, but he still felt tired. Though he had been there multiple times, Egypt had not lost its magic for him. Its cities were modern, full of car exhaust, loud music, and stressed-out people just like everywhere else, but you could feel the ancientness in the air. There were places just miles outside of any city—Cairo included—where it felt as if he'd stepped back in time.

He dropped his duffel on the tarmac and stretched, glad to be off the plane and able to breathe fresh air. The reasons for the journey were grim, but it felt good to be in motion and trying to do something to solve the puzzle of Luka's death. He figured it would be nice if they could accomplish that before someone started shooting at them again.

"I need something to drink," Jada said, hefting her duffel as she followed him off the plane.

Sully had been the first one off. He had walked around, doing a visual reconnaissance of the little corner of the airport where the cargo plane had taxied to a stop.

Now Sully turned at the sound of Jada's voice and arched an eyebrow.

"I like a drink as much as the next guy, but don't you think it's a little early? It may be past noon here, but it's barely sunrise back in New York."

"Water, Uncle Vic," Jada said, smirking. "Just a bottle of water. I'm dried out from the flight."

Drake grinned at Sully's chagrined expression.

"Yeah," Sully said, pulling a cigar from his jacket and pinching it between his teeth. "I could use some water, too. Flying always makes the inside of my mouth feel like steel wool."

When Jada went to thank the pilot for the ride and for delivering them safely to Egypt, Drake sidled over to Sully.

"Maybe you want to dial down the protective parent vibe a little."

Sully gnawed on his cigar. "You'd love that, wouldn't you, Romeo?"

"What are you talking about?"

"You know what I'm talking about."

Drake waved him away with both hands. "Look, Sully, I don't have any interest in romancing this girl. But I'd like to keep us all alive, and if you keep thinking of her like she's some kid you have to protect, you're liable to get us all killed. She seems capable of taking care of herself. Let's focus, okay?"

Sully's expression turned to stone. "I'm reading you loud and clear. I'm not her father. You think I don't know that? But Luka is dead, and I couldn't live with myself if anything happened to Jada."

"The best way for you to make sure that doesn't happen is to stay alive yourself," Drake countered, lowering his voice as Jada strode back toward them. "Just try to stop worrying about her long enough to not get shot, okay?"

A thin, humorless smile touched Sully's face. Whatever retort he might have come up with—and Drake had no doubt he had been formulating one—he let it pass and turned to face Jada.

"You done playing Little Miss Sunshine with the flight crew?" Sully muttered.

Jada smiled. "Don't be such a cantankerous old man. I know you didn't sleep well, but when you're trying to travel without anyone knowing you've left the country or thinking you're a terrorist, you take whatever accommodations are available. Maybe if you speak up, they'll give you a nice soft pillow next time."

Sully seemed about to bark at her, but then he just muttered something under his breath and marched off toward a small hut outside the cargo terminal. Beads of sweat already had popped out on his skin, and Drake watched him wipe a hand across his forehead.

"He hates Egypt this time of year," Drake said, hefting his duffel.

"Yeah?" Jada said as they fell into step side by side, leaving the plane behind. "What time of year is better?"

"He doesn't mind the second week of January. Usually the Wednesday, around three in the afternoon, you can actually breathe for a minute," Drake said.

Jada laughed. "Actually, I don't mind the heat. Better this than winter back home."

"Don't let Sully hear you say that," Drake replied.

"What about you?" she asked. "What's your take on Egypt?"

"Sultry and mysterious. I need a little of that in my life."

She shook her head. "Listen to you. If I didn't know better, I'd think you were a romantic instead of a sarcastic."

"I could be a sarcastic romantic."

Jada arched an eyebrow. "I like that. I think I'm going to steal it."

"I give it freely and of my own will."

"Aw, it's no fun if it's not stealing."

They both faltered then. Drake figured they had taken their flirting to its natural conclusion and any more would be strained and awkward, so he let silence fall between them. Jada didn't object. Their shared quiet was comfortable, as if their brief encounters years ago had built a foundation for a friendship now. Getting shot at had contributed to their budding friendship, too. Drake knew all too well how quickly a bond could form between people who were in danger.

"So, what is it with you and Uncle Vic?" Jada said, switching gears. "You guys have friends everywhere."

A pair of cargo trucks rumbled past, their engines almost as loud as the planes coming in and out of the airport.

"Not friends," Drake said. "Connections. We know who to call when we need something: information, equipment, transport—"

"A new identity," Jada added.

Drake nodded. "And weapons when we need them. But knowing who will take your money to do something that might not be strictly legal isn't the same as having friends. A connection who'll sell information about a treasure hunter to me is just as likely to sell info about me to the competition."

"I thought you were an 'antiquities acquisition consultant,'" Jada said.

"That, too," Drake replied.

"So you trust your friends not to sell you out?" she asked. "I mean, everybody has a price, right?"

"Almost everyone. As for friends—I choose carefully."

Jada nodded, but a cloud seemed to pass over her face, and he knew she must be thinking about her father.

"What is it?" Drake asked.

"My dad always gave advice like that," she said. Switching the weight of her duffel from one hand to the other, she gazed off into some middle distance, as if she could peer into her own memory. "He always had these great quotes about choosing your friends wisely and all that, but I guess he was a pretty crappy judge of character, considering he married Olivia."

"I don't know about that," Drake said. "Sully may smoke the smelliest cigars in creation—sometimes I think he buys tobacco scented with manure or something just to aggravate me—but I've never known anyone more loyal. Luka picked him as a friend, so he had to have at least some idea who to trust."

"Then why did my father marry the wicked witch?"

"To some men, women are a mystery. We don't understand how their minds work. Which makes it a lot harder to avoid a knife in the back."

Jada smiled. "Oscar Wilde said a friend is someone who stabs you in the front. And by the way, women have the same problem with men. We can see the treachery in other women easily enough, but guys might as well be from another planet for all we understand them."

Drake glanced sidelong at her. "'Treachery'?"

"It's a good word," she protested.

"Yeah. I like saying it. 'Treachery.' You don't get to say that word enough in life." He frowned. "Actually, that's probably a good thing."

Up ahead, Sully had reached the little hut on the tarmac. Drake wasn't sure if it was a security booth or a spot for incoming crews to check in with their cargo manifests, maybe some kind of traffic office. A skinny man in khaki pants and a loose shirt of blue cotton stood leaning against the side of the hut, smoking a cigarette. He wore sunglasses too large for his face, but he smiled as Sully approached him, and the two men shook hands.

"Not a friend?" Jada said, keeping her voice low as they neared the hut.

"A connection," Drake confirmed.

By the time they reached Sully and the thin Egyptian man, Sully was in the middle of lighting his cigar, which Drake took to mean things were going well. Sully's cigars were a form of communication all their own, and sometimes lighting up could be a sign of frustration, but not this time. Sully looked pleased.

"This is Chigaru," he said, and the Egyptian gave a little bow of his head. "Chigaru, meet Jada Hzujak and Nathan Drake, the closest thing I've got to a family in this world. I take their health and well-being very personally."

"Not to mention your own," Chigaru said in British-accented English.

Sully laughed, and it turned into a short cough. He frowned and looked at his cigar. "Gotta give these damn things up." Then he leveled his gaze at Chigaru. "Yeah, I take my well-being pretty personally, too."

"Not to worry, Sully. You have friends in Egypt."

At "friends," Drake glanced at Jada and saw her raise her eyebrows at the word.

"The best friends money can buy," Sully said.

Chigaru grinned and nodded sagely. "Absolutely." He regarded the three of them, obviously taking note of their meager complement of luggage. "Shall we go?"

"It was a long flight," Drake said. "And it's a long ride to Fayoum. We were hoping for something to drink."

Chigaru's expression blossomed into a brilliant smile. "My friends, do you think me so poor a host? I have Coca-Cola, beer, and sparkling water on ice in the car. If you like, I will stop at a market and pick up some takeaway food before we leave Cairo."

"That would be fantastic," Jada said happily.

Drake couldn't disagree. Chigaru might only be a connection, but at the moment Drake felt pretty friendly toward him. A meal and a cold Coke sounded like heaven.

Chigaru started to lead the way toward a Volvo station wagon with tinted windows parked between the hut and the cargo terminal. Just before they reached the car, Sully spoke in a low voice so that no one else would hear.

"What about the weapons we talked about?" Sully asked.

"Didn't I tell you not to worry?" Chigaru said. "Our first stop is for guns."

He opened the driver's door and slid behind the wheel. Sully smiled at Drake and Jada like it was Christmas morning.

"That's more like it. We run into any more trouble, I wanna be able to give some back," he said before climbing into the passenger seat.

Drake opened the rear door and held it for Jada.

"Looks like we've got everything covered," she said, strained amusement in her voice. The idea of guns and more shooting obviously did not appeal to her any more than it did to Drake.

"For the moment," Drake agreed.

But even as he climbed into the back of the Volvo with her and heard the clink of ice as she drew a bottle of sparkling water from a cooler, he couldn't suppress a shiver and the temptation to look back over his shoulder.

He'd just had the strangest feeling they were being watched. It was a sensation he'd had before, and far too often he'd been right.

The Auberge du Lac had been built as a hunting lodge for King Farouk, the last monarch of Egypt. Drake thought it looked more like the kind of place where Sinatra might have appeared in the early days of Las Vegas, with its whitewashed walls and palm trees. The hotel stood on the shore of a lake that was part of the Fayoum Oasis, not far from Fayoum City, which was modern and industrial by local standards.

An hour in any direction and the whole world changed. The Valley of the Whales was within that radius—quiet endless desert where the sand hid fossils of ancient sea life—but so were off-the-tourist-path pyramids, as well as the waterfalls that were a part of the Fayoum Oasis. Some of them had been part of an irrigation plan that went back as far as Ptolemy, diverting water from the Nile for agriculture, but others—the Wadi el Rayan—were part of a modern hydro project. The area had little tourism, but from what he'd learned, it had been growing.

And all of it, the whole damn area, was a part of what had once been called Crocodilopolis. The City of Crocodiles had taken its name from the reptiles that had been plentiful around the lakes in ancient times. Like Kom Ombo, which had come later, Crocodilopolis had been a center of worship for the Egyptian crocodile god, Sobek. The cult of Sobek had built an enormous temple where a single crocodile would be chosen to represent their god and encrusted with gold and gems.

Archaeologists had found the ruins of the Temple of Sobek decades ago. Though legends of a labyrinth in Crocodilopolis persisted, that part of the temple had never been unearthed—until more than a year into the Wadi el Rayan hydro project, when spill-off water from the Fayoum Oasis was being diverted into man-made lakes. Two of the lakes were still in use, but the third had dried up without explanation. Upon investigation, the engineers had discovered that the water had not evaporated; it had drained into the remains of the labyrinth of Sobek.

The final mystery of the cult of Sobek had been located purely by accident. But to learn the secrets of the labyrinth, the archaeological expedition's first task would be to draw the water back out of the ground. More than a year had passed before the team had been able to begin mapping and doing further excavations, and Luka Hzujak had been consulting with the dig's director—Hilary Russo—since day one.

All this, Drake and Sully had learned from Jada during the final hours of the flight from Montreal to Cairo. They knew all there was to know, at least until they could make contact with Ian Welch, whose sister Gretchen was the grad student who'd been working with Maynard Cheney on the labyrinth project at the Museum of Natural History in New York. Gretchen had promised to enlist her brother's help. If she couldn't deliver on that promise, they had come a very long way for nothing.

For the moment, their most vital task was trying not to melt.

Plumes of dust rose from the tires as Chigaru drove the Volvo up the driveway in front of the Auberge du Lac and pulled the car into a parking space in the small lot beside the hotel.

"You are not as close to downtown Fayoum City as you might wish," Chigaru said in his mannered accent. "But this is a beautiful hotel. Certainly you would not find a hotel like this in the city."

Drake thought he detected some slight resentment, as though Chigaru felt put out that they hadn't arranged their accommodations with him. He wondered if the skinny Egyptian would have gotten a cut of their room fees. He might be able to acquire guns and vehicles and information, which were higher-ticket items, but Drake suspected Chigaru would not have minded taking a commission on just about anything. Like the tour guides who received kickbacks from souvenir shops if they directed tourists there, Chigaru wanted his percentage—a chance, as Sully often put it, to "dip his beak."

"It looks nice," Jada agreed, popping open the door. "I'll be happy just to lie down."

Drake slid from the backseat and dragged his duffel with him. They had stopped in the middle of nowhere—and nowhere might have been exaggerating its significance—to divvy up the guns Chigaru had acquired for them. Sully and Drake each had tucked Belgian FN Five-sevens in clip holsters at the small of their backs. An armpit holster would have been too conspicuous, and so would a jacket worn in the Egyptian heat. With their shirttails out, the guns would be hidden but easily accessible.

Jada had taken the SIG P250, a smaller, more compact

weapon that carried a few rounds less. Her father had taught her to shoot at a range in upstate New York, but she had never even pointed a gun at another human being, so though she reluctantly accepted the weapon, she kept it in her duffel.

With a cold Coke in hand, the glass bottle dripping, Sully climbed out and leaned on the roof, looking over the top as Chigaru got out of the car.

"You know how to romance a guy, Chigaru," Sully said. "You always take me to the nicest places."

Chigaru smiled and patted his pockets, digging out his cigarettes and a lighter.

"You are on your own from here, my friends," he said, glancing around at the three of them. "The car is yours. Leave it at the airport in Cairo when you're done or text me and let me know where you've abandoned it and I'll send someone to get it. You have my number should you require anything else."

Sully grabbed his duffel and walked around to shake Chigaru's hand. "I think we've got it as under control as we're ever going to. I'll see to it that the second half of your money is wired into your account before my head hits the pillow tonight."

Drake fished another bottle of water out of the cooler in the car. The ice had melted almost completely by now, but the drinks were still cold enough to be sweet relief.

Chigaru gave a small bow, then dropped the car keys into Sully's hand. "Good hunting, my friend."

Jada and Drake thanked him as well and then fell into step with Sully, headed for the hotel. Chigaru remained by the car, leaning against the trunk of the car with his sunglasses glinting in the late afternoon sunlight.

"What, he's just going to hang around out here?" Jada asked, her voice low.

"A guy that suave? I'm sure someone'll be along to pick him up," Drake said.

"You're just jealous that you're not that suave."

"Suave is overrated and very last century. I'm rugged and sometimes adorably awkward," Drake replied.

Before Jada could fill the obvious opening with good-natured mockery, Sully pushed between them, shouldering them apart like a teacher worried that his young charges were dancing a little too close at a junior high school mixer.

"Can you two cut it out with the cute banter?" Sully said. "You're making me nauseous."

Drake smiled innocently. He would have liked to tell Sully that he was just trying to keep Jada's mind off her father's death and the reason they were in Egypt to begin with, but he didn't want to talk about it with Jada right beside them.

"I'm sure Chigaru's arranged for transport," Sully told Jada. "I figure he'll be gone within the hour."

Drake glanced over his shoulder at Chigaru, who leaned against their car, smoking, as if he hadn't a care in the world. Even at a distance, the man looked in control of the world around him. He might have been little more than a minion for hire, but it was clear he didn't see it that way.

"As soon as it gets dark, I'll sweep the car," Drake muttered to Sully.

"Sweep for what?" Jada asked.

"Bugs," Sully said. "Maybe explosives."

She paled. "We just drove more than two hours in that car."

"He wouldn't blow it up with himself inside. He's an entrepreneur, not a suicide bomber."

Jada narrowed her eyes and glanced back at the parking lot. They were almost to the hotel door, but they could still see Chigaru leaning against the car. She pressed her lips together in irritation.

"It just seems wrong. You paid him."

Sully laughed softly. "There's always somebody willing to pay more, darlin'. Remember that. Money can't buy more than a minute's worth of loyalty."

Drake glanced over the lake—visible to him now only through the fronds of a young palm—and despite the glare off the water, he saw a silver go-fast boat jet into view. It must have cut its engines a moment later, for it seemed to stop short in the water, rising and falling on its own wake as it settled and drifted, the nose turning to point toward the hotel like an arrow. Or a bullet.

Narrowing his gaze, he saw a second, apparently identical boat about a hundred yards farther out, also drifting with its nose pointing toward the Auberge du Lac. The sudden arrival of the second boat couldn't have anything to do with them—he knew that would be too much of a coincidence—but both of the crafts seemed to have an air of purpose around them, as if they were there on business rather than pleasure.

Then Sully called his name, breaking his train of thought, and he saw that Jada was holding the interior door open for them. Drake followed them in, basking in the cool, air-conditioned interior of the hotel, and the go-fast boats were forgotten.

As late as the 1940s, political figures from around the world had met and stayed at the Auberge du Lac for minisummits that helped determine the fate of global relations. The hotel still had the flavor of that bygone era, with its lazy ceiling fans and huge round arched windows and the woodwork in the lobby that seemed to hint at the architect's love of Swiss ski chalets. It seemed to Drake like the sort of place that Rick and Ilsa would have escaped to for a romantic tryst if only *Casablanca* had ended differently.

Sully glanced right, then split off to the left, taking up a position with his back to a pillar. From there he could watch them at the check-in counter and still watch the door and most of the lobby. Drake fought the temptation to wisecrack. The time for digressions had passed. Once they had stepped into the lobby, they had entered the territory of mystery. Somewhere here there were clues as to why Luka Hzujak had been cut up and dumped on a train platform in an old steamer trunk, and Drake's usually mischievous nature was tempered by the weight of the man's death.

Drake and Jada approached the front desk. The man who greeted them gave only the hint of a smile. His red jacket was neatly pressed, and his gray hair and seamless features seemed to have undergone the same process.

"Good afternoon, sir," the man said, nodding first to Drake and then to Jada. "Madam. How may I help you?"

"We have reservations. This is Mr. Merrill," Jada said,

indicating Drake as she gave the name on his fake passport. "You'll have mine under Hzujak."

She spelled her last name for him. Drake was glad she had remembered to grab her real passport when they had stopped at the apartment she'd been hiding out in back in New York. She had traveled under her new, false identification—just as Drake and Sully had—but here it was important that she be Jada Hzujak.

The clerk tapped keys on a computer keyboard and studied his monitor, frowning. He'd seen something in the reservation he didn't like. He took their passports—Jada's real one and Drake's fake—and set them beside his computer. A few more taps, some sleight of hand, and then he was handing Drake a small envelope containing a pair of plastic key cards.

"There are two booked into your room, Mr. Merrill. You are traveling with a Mr. David Farzan?"

"Right here," Sully said, his gruff voice carrying though he had spoken in a sort of stage whisper. He waved a hand as he strode up to the desk to join them and slipped his fake passport onto the counter.

The clerk smiled and nodded. "Excellent," he said, taking Sully's fake passport, keying in the passport number, and then handing it back. "You gentlemen are in Room 137. I trust you'll find everything to your liking, but if you need anything at all, just ring the front desk."

He frowned as he realized they didn't have any luggage other than the duffels but did not comment. Instead, he handed another envelope to Jada with her single key card inside and returned her passport.

"Miss Hzujak, you'll be in Room 151."

Jada stiffened, then shook her head. "No, that's wrong."

Drake and Sully exchanged a look, realizing what was happening.

"I spoke to someone on the phone," Jada said emphatically. "I'm supposed to have Room 213."

The red-jacketed man narrowed his eyes. "Yes, I see there is a note in the computer system to that effect. But that room is un-available."

"You mean it's taken by someone else?" Drake asked. He didn't like the vibe he was getting off the clerk. The whole situation felt strangely tense and awkward, and not just because the hotel employee didn't want to upset his customers.

"Not precisely."

"What does 'not precisely' mean?" Sully asked. "If the room isn't occupied, you have no reason not to give it to her."

The clerk seemed at a loss for words, itchy and nervous, and he glanced around as if he were hoping a supervisor would come to his rescue.

"Why don't we talk to your manager?" Drake suggested. "If you can't explain this, get us someone who can."

Offended, the clerk sniffed in irritation. He glanced around, but this time he spoke in a surreptitious fashion, not wishing to be overheard.

"The room is not available because it is being refurbished. There has been a little bit of damage since it was last occupied."

Now Drake got it, and he didn't like it. A trickle of ice ran down his back.

"So one of your guests trashed the room?" he asked.

"Certainly not," the clerk said, even more insulted, but this time on behalf of the hotel. "Room 213 was vandalized. Repairs are being made but if you please, it is not something the hotel wishes its other guests to learn. It isn't good for our reputation, you understand?"

"We do," Sully said. "But she still needs that room. And if you want us to keep quiet about your troubles, you'll give it to her."

For the first time, the clerk's expression turned from irritation to anger. Then his smile returned, forced and insincere.

"Sir, I have explained that this is quite impossible."

Drake moved up against the counter and leaned in close so that he could speak as quietly as possible.

"Listen. We don't want to make some kind of spectacle, here.

Maybe the person who arranged this for Miss Hzujak didn't explain the circumstances to you, but here they are. Several weeks ago, her father stayed in Room 213. Soon after his return to New York, he passed away."

A flicker of sympathy in the clerk's eyes. That was good. Drake forged ahead.

"This is her goodbye to him, understand? And she's going to have it. I'm sure most of the damage in the room has been cleaned up. Are the windows broken?"

"No, but I—"

"Everything else is cosmetic. Send a maid up there to put fresh sheets on the bed and give her the damn key to 213. You can charge us twice the normal rate. Call it a surcharge, whatever you want. But she's going to have that room before the next hour expires or things are going to get *really* messy."

7

It was closer to twenty minutes when they escorted Jada to Room 213. The maid had come and gone. There were clean sheets on the bed and fresh toiletries in the bathroom, but the entertainment center had a gaping hole where the television ought to have been and the lid was missing from the toilet tank. The in-room safe had been forced open and not yet replaced. A single piece of art—a piece of papyrus covered with a primitive painting of a hunting scene—hung from the wall. Two other hooks were conspicuously bare, with squares of paint around them that didn't match the rest of the walls, which had faded in the sunlight. Other art obviously had hung there, keeping the paint from being bleached by the sun.

"I've stayed in worse," Jada said, tossing her duffel onto the bed and then flopping beside it. She seemed to have forgotten the gun she carried, but Drake thought it was a bad time to remind her.

Sully made a circuit of the room while Drake went straight to the windows. The room had a water view, and he could still see the go-fast boats out there, drifting. He opened the French doors and stepped onto the small balcony, searching the railings and beneath the chairs and the little round table for anything Luka might have left behind.

When he reentered the room, Jada was by the door, fiddling with the knob that controlled the old ceiling fan. It began to rotate slowly, making him realize just how hot it was in the room. He went to the small air-conditioning unit in the corner and found that it was broken. More accurately, someone had taken it apart and it hadn't been properly put back together again.

"Whoever ransacked the place, they did a job on the AC. It's screwed. You're going to be sweating tonight," he told Jada.

"The fan will help," she said. "I'll open the windows. With a breeze off the water, it'll be fine once the sun goes down."

Sully stood back with his hands on his hips, staring at the bureau. He had pulled the drawers out and set them on the floor, working much more neatly than whoever had broken in and searched the room before they arrived.

"Get the bed, will you?" Sully asked.

Drake dropped to his knees, searching underneath, then stood and stripped the fresh bedclothes, checking under the mattress. They both knew there was no point to the search. If there had been anything here, whoever had ransacked the place would have found it already. But he looked just the same, checking the seams of the mattress to see that nothing had been cut and re-sewn. If they were going to look, they might as well be thorough.

While Drake went over the bed, Sully moved the bureau and then the entertainment center, then went into the bathroom. Jada watched the proceedings with fascination at first and then with growing amusement.

"I hope you're going to remake the bed," she said, pushing her magenta hair behind her ears.

Drake frowned at her. "We're looking for—"

"Anything my father might have left behind," Jada finished for him. She kneeled on the mattress, hands defiantly on her hips. "Do you think I'm stupid, Nate? If someone tossed this room, they were looking for something. Stands to reason that there's something to look for. Whoever Henriksen has working for him, they must know a lot of things we don't. My father came here, he figured something out."

"We knew that part already," Sully said.

They both looked up to see him standing in the bathroom door with his arms crossed.

"Yeah, but if they're searching, it doesn't just mean he was on to something," Jada continued. "It means they knew it, and he knew—or at least suspected—that someone was going to try to take those secrets from him. They think he was worried enough to hide something."

Drake looked around the room. "The question is, Did they find it? Whatever 'it' is."

Jada threw the sheets back on the bed, not bothering to make it up, and flopped onto the mattress again, staring at the ceiling. She crossed her ankles, making herself right at home.

"My father was a pretty smart guy," she said. "If he had something important, something he was afraid other people might try to take away, he'd find a way to get it home safely."

Sully chuckled and rapped his knuckles on the door frame as if for luck. "You can say that again. He did it more than once. But if Henriksen, or whoever killed Luka, thinks it's here . . ."

He trailed off, thinking, then nodded to himself. "Maybe they burned his apartment to destroy records or notes he made since he got home, but if they're still looking, they must be damn sure Luka didn't bring whatever it is home with him. So let's assume he did leave something here. Why would he do that? And where would he hide it?"

Drake had kept walking while they spoke, feeling the door and window frames, checking the curtains, testing the floor with his shoes. Now he paused and looked at Sully.

"He made it home alive," Drake said, trying to infuse himself with the kind of fear and paranoia they believed Luka must have been feeling. "But if he thought he might not make it home—if he thought he might not make it out of Egypt alive . . ."

Sully nodded, pointing at him. "Yeah. That makes sense. Okay, so let's say he did hide something, but like Jada says, he's smarter than they give him credit for. Would he really hide it in this room? I'm going to say no."

"Which puts us exactly nowhere," Drake said. He ran a hand over his stubbled chin, confused and frustrated. Luka's killers were way ahead of them, had so many more pieces of the puzzle. He and Sully and Jada were essentially starting from scratch, and they'd already nearly been murdered once.

Jada laughed softly.

Drake frowned and stared at her.

"What's funny?" Sully asked.

She propped herself up in the bed, staring at the ceiling. She barely seemed to notice they were still in the room.

"Jada?" Drake said.

"This place is old. Faded glory, right?" she said. "But the ceiling fan—that's pretty new. Quiet. You can barely hear it except for the swish of the air. No rattling or anything."

Drake shot Sully a worried glance, then turned back to her. "And?"

Jada crawled onto her knees and then rose unsteadily to her feet on top of the bed. She bounced a little, smiling at them.

"Uncle Vic, turn off the fan."

Sully made a beeline to the knob by the door, not stopping to ask why. It was clear Jada thought she was on to something.

"I talked to my dad the night before he came home from Egypt. I heard the—the fear in his voice, I guess. But at the time I just thought he was tired, y' know? Wiped out. He was getting too old to be running all over the world at a moment's notice. I told him I was worried about him, and he told me I had nothing to be afraid of, that he'd be okay as long as he didn't dry up and blow away in a sandstorm. He didn't like the heat."

"Do you think he was trying to tell you something?" Drake asked.

"I didn't notice it then, but yes, I think he was. In his way, without saying it, I think he was trying to warn me that he—that he might not make it back."

She'd stopped bouncing, lost in the memory, her sadness painful to see. Sully moved to the edge of the bed and reached out, taking her hand. Drake said nothing, not wanting to interfere with a moment so intimate. This grief was between family members.

Jada looked down at Sully. "He kept complaining about the fan, Uncle Vic. I'd forgotten all about it, but now that we're here—I've been trying to imagine I'm my dad, and I'm afraid and alone and talking to my daughter on the phone. I was watching the fan and thinking how quiet it is, and then I remembered."

Drake looked up at the fan, its rotations slowing now that Sully had shut it off. He wanted to check it out, but this was Jada's to do.

Tears had started to slip down her cheeks. She wiped at them, smiling sheepishly.

"He said—"

"What, Jada?" Sully prodded.

"He said he hated having the AC on, but the fan rattled so much, it was like having someone in the room that wouldn't shut up. He said, 'This damn thing's got a lot to say.'"

Jada turned to Drake, excitement building in her now. "Those weren't the exact words, but something like that. I know it's not much, but it's weird, right?"

Drake nodded to her. "Go ahead. Look."

She took a deep breath, reached up, and began to run her hands over the tops of the fan blades, one at a time. On the third one, she froze, her breath catching in her throat. Drake heard the sound as she peeled off a scrap of paper that had been taped to the top of the fan blade.

"What does it say?" Sully asked.

Jada stared down at it, and a smile blossomed on her face. She handed the paper to Sully, who glanced at it and then passed it on to Drake.

On the tiny scrap of paper, inside a hastily scrawled heart, Luka Hzujak had written the number 271.

Drake glanced up at Sully. "*Room* 271?"

Jada laughed, drying her eyes. "They were searching the wrong room."

They raced one another to the door.

Intimidation didn't work on the front desk clerk a second time. Drake and Sully explained that the accommodations they had been given simply wouldn't do and that Room 271 would be significantly preferable, but the clerk did not seem interested in cooperating. It had been one thing for Jada to claim she wanted to stay in the same room her father had been in, but the little man in the red jacket clearly thought that now the Americans were just being difficult or they were up to something. Not to mention that they hadn't exactly endeared themselves to him by bullying him when they'd first arrived.

Money solved it all. Once again, Drake had reason to be grateful for his trip to Ecuador, though the money he had made on that job seemed to be vanishing faster than a magician's assistant. The clerk kept a stern, suspicious look on his face all through their transaction but eventually produced a pair of key cards for 271 and handed them to Drake.

The little man patted the pocket of his red jacket, in which Drake's money made a little crinkling noise.

"A pleasure doing business with you, sir," the clerk said. He smiled, his yellow teeth like dark kernels of corn under his mustache.

"You're a walking cliché, buddy," Drake told him.

Jada grabbed him by the arm, tugging him away, in a hurry to get back upstairs. The clerk was taking a reservation as they departed, but he spared a glance at Drake and smiled, patting his pocket again. He gave Drake a thumbs-up.

"Bastard has my money," Drake muttered as they hurried up the stairs. "I liked that money."

"You'll have a lot more than that when we track down this treasure," Jada said quietly. "You can take your expenses off the top."

Her tone held nothing bitter, but just hearing her say the words made him remember why they were there. This gig was costing him a lot of money and he did want to recoup whatever he could, but he felt like a jerk focusing on the money.

"Sorry," he said as they reached the top of the stairs.

Jada touched his arm. "Don't be," she said, glancing first at Drake and then at Sully. "Thank you. Both of you. Whatever comes of this, I wouldn't even have gotten this far without you."

They passed a man wheeling a room service cart in the second floor corridor. At a bend in the hall there were floor-to-ceiling windows with a beautiful view of the lake. The late afternoon sun had turned golden, and a single sailboat moved slowly across the surface. The sight of it reminded Drake of the two cigarette boats he'd noticed earlier, but if the pair of silver bullets was still on the water, they must have moved to another part of the lake.

At Room 271, Sully held out a hand and Drake slipped him a key card. They glanced up and down the corridor. Luka's killers had not known about whatever secrets he'd hidden in this room—they couldn't have without finding the note on top of the ceiling fan—but Drake was feeling cautious, anyway.

"Pretty lucky this room wasn't booked for tonight, right?" Sully asked, as if their good fortune had some other significance.

"Sometimes luck is just luck," Jada said.

Drake nodded. "True. But we don't usually have the good kind."

Sully ran a hand over his face, smoothing his mustache, and then slipped the key card through the lock. Drake felt the weight of his gun against the small of his back but wouldn't draw it without an immediate threat. The door clicked, and Sully opened it, nodding to Drake even as he held out a hand to indicate that Jada should remain in the hall. She looked as if she might burst with anticipation, but she crossed her arms and waited while they entered and did a quick check to be sure nobody was lying in wait.

"Okay, you can come in," Sully said.

Jada strode into the room, letting the door swing shut behind her. As Sully started to speak again, she stiff-armed him, shoving him back onto the bed, and Drake burst out laughing.

"That's the last time you treat me like the damsel in frickin' distress," she said, looking fierce despite her diminutive stature.

"That ain't what it's about, kid," Sully said. "Nate and I— we've been in situations like this before."

He started to rise, an apologetic look on his face, and she shoved him down again. Drake laughed, but he shut up when Jada shot him a bristling look. Then she drew her gun, and none of it was funny anymore.

"I know how to fight, Uncle Vic. And I know how to shoot. He might have been your friend, but he was my father. As far as I'm concerned, this little trip is my mission, not yours. I don't work for you. I don't take orders from you. Yes, I'll defer to your experience, especially if whoever wants us dead takes another crack at us. But for the last time, don't protect me. I'm not a goddamn liability, I'm an asset."

Drake leaned against the bureau, trying not to smirk as he studied Sully. "I tried to tell you, but noooo—"

Sully glared at him. Drake shrugged.

Jada glanced back and forth between them. "We're a team on this, or the two of you should just wish me luck and move on to your next bit of thievery for hire."

Sully stared at the gun in her hand. Drake couldn't blame him. She hadn't pointed it at Sully—the barrel was aimed at the headboard—but any time an unholstered gun was in the room, you wanted to know what it would hit if someone pulled the trigger.

"Admit it," Drake said. "We're just so damn charming that you can't bear the idea of being parted from us."

Jada started to grin, then looked even more irritated that he had succeeded in defusing her righteous fury.

"You're a couple of scoundrels," she said.

"But charming scoundrels," Drake replied.

When it was clear that Jada didn't plan to shoot him, Drake started searching the room, whistling the Seven Dwarves' work song from *Snow White*. Jada laughed and returned the small gun to the holster she wore under her flowing beige blouse.

"Is it safe to get up now?" Sully asked, hands raised as if he were under arrest.

"Shut up and get to work," Jada said, wearing half a grin.

Sully stood, but as she moved away, he reached out and grabbed her, pulled her in close, and kissed the top of her head.

"It's not that I don't think you're capable," he said, his voice a rough whisper Drake could barely make out.

"I know," Jada replied.

Drake thought of half a dozen wisecracks but said nothing. The mirror above the bureau was bolted to the wall, but he had run his fingers around it. Now he was searching the drawers, down on his knees so he could see if Luka had taped anything to the bottoms. It didn't seem likely. If he really had expected Jada to be suspicious enough to come looking or send someone to investigate, he wouldn't have hidden anything someplace that could easily be discovered by accident.

Sully checked the closet and then went into the bathroom. Drake heard him moving around, heard the scrape of the toilet tank lid being removed and replaced. Jada busily stripped the bed and then started to shove the mattress aside. Drake couldn't check under the bureau—there was no room even to slide his fingers beneath it—but he dragged it out to look behind it.

As Sully emerged from the bathroom and he and Jada started going over the nightstands, Drake worked on the entertainment center. He had his hands behind the television when he realized the others had stopped working. He glanced over to see Jada and Sully staring up at the ceiling fan, but when Jada climbed onto the bed to search, she found nothing.

"He'd have been in a hurry," Drake said, glancing around. "Nothing too elaborate. Somehow he snuck into this room. He'd have put whatever it is somewhere it wouldn't be found easily or quickly, but he'd have known that nobody would be searching *this* room, so it might be he'd put it somewhere he could be sure it would be found eventually."

"Not the safe," Jada said. "I'm sure it's left open before a new guest checks in."

Sully narrowed his eyes, then turned to look at the air-conditioning unit beside the window. He hurried over to it and knelt down, prying the face panel off the machine. When he removed it, a small bundle fell to the floor.

"Bingo," Sully said.

He picked it up and tugged off the thick rubber bands around it, and the bundle separated out into a small sheaf of folded pages and a shabby journal of the sort sold in any office supply store in the world. A piece of hotel stationery fluttered to the ground, and Sully snatched it up, gave it a quick, grim scan, and then handed it to Jada, who climbed down from the bed.

Her hand trembled a bit as she took it, but when she read, her voice was steady.

" 'To whom it may concern. Upon your discovery of these documents, please contact my daughter, Jadranka Hzujak, and arrange to see them delivered to her.' " Jada glanced up at Drake. "He's got my address here. Nothing more."

Sully had unfolded one of the papers and now laid it on the bed. The three of them stared down at the map of Crocodilopolis on which Luka had drawn the location of the labyrinth of Sobek and what he suspected were its dimensions and basic design. There were scribblings on the map as well, most of them apparently references to the lengths of corridors but some evidently comparisons to the labyrinth at Knossos on the island of Crete.

"Here. You should be the one," Sully said, handing Jada the journal.

She opened it and began to read, but immediately her expression turned to disappointment.

"What is it?" Drake asked.

Jada frowned, turning and scanning pages. "Notes, mostly. I was kind of hoping it was a real journal, y' know? Something that would lay it all out for us. But it's his notes to himself."

She moved between them, turning so that Drake and Sully could peruse the pages with her. Drake saw what she meant. There were drawings of labyrinths, some larger and some with more intricate details.

"Is that a trap?" Sully asked, indicating one sketch. "Like something from the pyramids?"

"Looks like," Drake agreed.

There were scribbles about Daedalus. "Knossos first," Luka had written. "Then Croc City—and then, where's number three?"

"So he's confirming that Daedalus designed three labyrinths?" Drake asked.

"Yeah," Jada said, flipping two pages back. "It's right here. 'Fundamental design of Cretan labyrinth used three times. Honey a constant.'"

"Honey?" Sully grumbled. "What the hell does he mean?"

None of them replied. Jada flipped a few more pages, pausing only momentarily to study the small maps Luka had drawn in the journal. They depicted the progress of the dig on the labyrinth of Sobek. One of the maps had another reference to honey: a design that seemed to indicate four separate routes that led into a single location in the labyrinth. Beside it, with an arrow, Luka had scrawled the words "Honey Chamber location differs from Knossos, but command is the same—Mistress of the Labyrinth must be given an amount equivalent to all other gods put together."

Luka had drawn an arrow to indicate that his thoughts were continued on the next page, one of his habits, if this journal was any indication. With a dry rustle of paper the only sound in the room, Jada flipped the page.

"Amazing," Luka had written. "In Temple of Sobek—labyrinth of Sobek—but Sobek's worshippers give Mistress of the Laby. greater tribute than they give to their god? Why?"

"Damn good question," Sully growled.

"Even better question if we knew what honey he's referring to," Drake replied.

"You don't think he just means regular honey?" Jada asked.

Drake glanced at her. "Do you? I mean, all jokes about anything called a 'honey chamber' aside—okay, it sounds like a special room Elvis would take his babes in Graceland—but if the other gods are being offered this honey, too, it's probably not the Winnie-the-Pooh variety."

Sully gave him a sidelong glance but ignored the babble. "Jada, didn't you say the worshippers of Sobek actually decorated living alligators with gold and gems?"

Jada nodded.

"So they've got gold and gems," Sully said. "Enough gold that they can make new—what, armor?—for generations of alligators to represent their god. The gems they can maybe pry off, use again, but if they're making gold plating for the gators, they might be making a new one each generation."

"How did they get that much gold?" Drake said. "This place isn't exactly El Dorado."

Jada sighed. "We're not getting any answers from this thing," she said, flipping another page.

"Maybe not," Drake said. "But at least we're getting a better idea of what the questions should be."

Jada turned another page and hesitated. A note had been scrawled hastily there, and when she quickly flipped ahead, she found that the rest were empty. She went back to the final scribble in the journal. It had been written weeks ago, but in a way it was her father's last message to her.

"Talk to Welch," Luka had written. "Golden touch? Maybe Daedalus. Where'd he go? That's the question. Henriksen doesn't care about the Three Labyrinths, he's after the treasure of the Fourth."

"Fourth?" Drake read aloud. "Didn't he say, right at the beginning, that Daedalus designed three labyrinths?"

"Welch," Jada said. "That's got to be Ian Welch, Gretchen's brother."

"Call him, Sully," Drake said. "We need to see this guy tonight. Henriksen's trying to kill everyone who might know whatever it is Luka found out."

"There's no big secret in here," Jada protested, waving the journal. "They trashed his room looking for it, but whatever he found, it's not here."

"Henriksen must think it is," Sully said, going to sit at the edge of the bed and picking up the phone.

"Jada," Drake said softly, "we might not have it figured out, but your father wouldn't have hidden this stuff if he didn't think there was something important in what he's written."

"You're right," she said, crouching down to smooth out the map Sully had opened on the bed. Jada shook her head. "But whatever it is, we'd better figure it out before Henriksen does."

"If he hasn't already," Drake said. "It could be that he already has all the secrets and wants to make sure nobody else does."

Sully dialed the phone, referring to a scrap of paper he'd pulled from his wallet.

Jada flipped open the journal, turning again to that last page. Drake didn't like the furrow of her brow.

"What's wrong?" he asked.

"Just reading it again. 'Talk to Welch.' Is that a message to me? An instruction? Or is it a note to himself, like his one-task to-do list? If so, then whatever mystery he unraveled, he might've told Ian Welch. It would've been right before he left Egypt to head back to New York to continue his research."

Sully had a quick conversation on the phone, and Jada kept her voice low.

Drake frowned. "You're saying maybe we can't trust Welch?"

"I'm saying my father seems to have trusted him, and now he's dead. I'm saying we should be careful."

Sully hung up the phone. They turned to look at him.

"Guess we'll find out soon enough whose side Welch is on," Sully rasped. "We're meeting him for a drink in Fayoum City in two hours."

8

The sun went down as Drake drove them into Fayoum City, the sky becoming a vast indigo field of stars. They passed the ancient waterwheels that kept the narrow canals moving in the city, then crossed a bridge into the city proper.

Drake tapped the brake when he spotted a police car parked beside a building that resembled an upside-down pyramid. In some parts of Egypt it was customary for Westerners to be accompanied by police in the larger cities. Chigaru had assured them that the insignias he had pasted on the bumper and the dashboard would keep most cops away. Either he had been as good as his word or this particular cop didn't feel like rousting Westerners. The police car remained where it was, and Drake kept driving.

The desk clerk at Auberge du Lac had given them directions, which meant Drake wasn't sure if they would end up in the right place until he actually had pulled into the parking lot. He had half expected the little man in the red jacket to send them the wrong way on purpose, but the directions turned out to be impeccable. The only distraction was the small black van that had picked them up as they passed the waterwheels and stuck with them as they drove through the city.

"You see it?" Drake asked.

Sully, in the passenger seat, glanced back. "Got it."

"Keep an eye on it."

Jada stole a quick glance as well. Though she said nothing, her body language spoke volumes, and when they turned onto Halma Street and the van kept going, she visibly exhaled. Drake felt the same relief but couldn't shake the feeling that they had been observed almost from the moment of their arrival in Egypt.

It was impossible, of course. They had driven across wide expanses of nothing where a pursuing vehicle would have been impossible to miss. Even so, he felt the pressure of malign eyes on them as he drove.

The restaurant was tucked into the corner of the lobby of the Queen's Hotel, whose general shabbiness was a persuasive argument for why Luka had chosen to stay outside the city. Despite the dingy interior of the hotel, the restaurant seemed almost cheerful. The rich aroma of spices and cooking meat filled the place, and Drake found his stomach rumbling as he realized how long it had been since he had had a proper meal.

"I could eat a horse," Sully murmured as they entered, scanning the place for Ian Welch.

"From the looks of the place, change that to camel and you might get your wish," Jada muttered.

Drake spotted a thin, edgy-looking man—one of the few Westerners they'd seen thus far in the city—sitting by himself at a corner table, his clothing and overall mien giving him away as American. Welch had chosen a table set apart from most of the dining room, the better to discuss things they would all rather not have overheard.

"I don't know," Drake whispered to the others. "Add enough spices and camel might be pretty tasty."

A uniformed waiter walked toward them, but Sully waved him off, making a beeline for Welch. Drake and Jada followed, and Drake noticed her glancing about the restaurant uneasily.

"Feel like I'm in the Twilight Zone," she said into his ear, her hot breath on his neck. "Lilting Middle Eastern music and an entire restaurant of people staring at me."

"This isn't Cairo," Drake said. "And it's no tourist destination. They don't see a lot of Westerners here and even fewer pretty young women with streaks of magenta in their hair."

Even with the dim lighting of the restaurant, he could see Jada blush.

"It's not very manly to even know the word 'magenta,' never mind being able to recognize the color," she said.

"I'm a new breed," Drake assured her.

They arrived at the table smiling, but Ian Welch's grim expression sobered them both. He looked nothing like his younger sister with an unruly mop of dark hair, round spectacles, and a deep tan acquired from months in the desert. Wiry and intense, Welch shook hands with all three of them as introductions were made, but his focus was on Jada.

"I'm so sorry to hear about your father," the archaeologist said. "When Gretchen told me about his murder—and then Dr. Cheney . . ."

Welch trailed off, then shook his head, at a loss for words. He gestured to the chairs. "Please, sit. I've ordered some tahini and pita to start. The waiter will bring water as well. But, tell me, please—what can I do for you?"

Sully slid his chair back to give himself the best view of the restaurant. Welch had taken the corner seat, but Drake knew Sully would be on guard and let them know if trouble might be coming. The shooting in Manhattan had left them on edge, and the constant feeling of being observed gnawed at Drake, but he would let Sully worry about that for the moment. His focus had to be on Welch.

"There are two things, Mr. Welch," Jada said, tucking a lock of hair behind her ear. "First, we have some questions and we're hoping you can enlighten us. There's so much we don't know."

"I'll do my best," Welch said, nodding.

"Second," Jada began, "well, we'd like to get in and have a look at the dig, but with as few people knowing we're there as possible."

Welch started to reply, brow furrowed, ready to shake his head. Then he stopped himself, perhaps thinking of the murders of Luka Hzujak and Maynard Cheney. He glanced at Drake, then back at Jada.

"You really think this all has to do with something your father figured out after he came here?"

Jada nodded. "We do."

Welch took a deep breath. "Okay," he said, exhaling. "I'll see if I can make it happen. In the meantime, what can I tell you about the work we're doing?"

The waiter arrived with glasses of water for all of them, and then a second appeared and set the tahini and pita on the table. Drake would have rather had nachos, but as hungry as he was, the sesame paste and soft bread would do just fine.

"All right," Drake said before taking a bite. "Tell us about Daedalus and the three labyrinths."

Welch sipped his water. "That's the biggest thing to come out of the dig so far. How much do you already know?"

Drake chewed, trying to swallow so he could reply. Jada jumped in.

"My father talked about his work a lot," she said. "The way I understand it, he believed that Daedalus was an actual person, not a mythological character, and that he designed not only the labyrinth at Knossos—as most stories tell it—but also two others, including the one you're excavating right now."

Welch nodded all through her statement. "Oh, there's no doubt about it now. Look, most scholars will agree that the most enduring myths eventually prove to have had some real-life antecedent. The ancient Greeks, for instance, believed that the Trojan War had taken place and that Troy was an actual place. In modern times, historians had basically decided the whole thing had been made up, that it was just a story, right up until a German archaeologist named Heinrich Schliemann actually *discovered* the ruins of Troy in 1870. So much for the people who dismiss myth as just stories.

"The thing about ancient Greece is that the people who tried to write the histories tended to pull from a variety of sources. A Mycenaean ruler might be confused with a figure in some older Phoenician story, and two pieces of truth might get jammed together, through oral tradition and exaggeration and superstition, into something else. My job as an archaeologist is to try to unravel the threads that time has wound together."

Drake glanced at Sully, whose attention was on the other guests and the waitstaff. To someone who didn't know him, he would look bored and disinterested, just a guy hungrily anticipating his dinner instead of a guy ready for a fight. Sully had Luka's journal and maps stuffed into the rear waistband of his pants, right next to his gun. They had agreed it would be unwise to leave it back at the hotel, but Drake felt constantly aware of its presence among them. More than anything, it explained why Sully was so on guard. But Welch didn't seem put off by Sully's ignoring him at all.

"All right, so—Daedalus?" Drake asked.

"He *was* real?" Jada said.

Welch took a breath, reached up and removed his glasses, and began to clean them with the hem of the tablecloth.

"In the late Bronze Age, there was an inventor and builder considered to be one of the cleverest men in the world. Stories were told about him in many languages and cultures under many different names, but the one that seems to have stuck is Daedalus. He was a craftsman, an artisan, and the labyrinth of Knossos was long considered his greatest achievement.

"There is a great deal of disagreement in academic circles about whether or not the palace discovered at Knossos in the 1870s is actually the labyrinth Daedalus designed," Welch went on, replacing his glasses and reaching for his water glass. He looked intent now, lost in the history inside his mind. "The structure contains thousands of interlocking rooms, but many, myself included, have maintained that it was not the labyrinth itself, that the actual maze was located somewhere nearby."

The waiter arrived, interrupting him, and they all gave their orders. Welch waited only moments after the waiter's departure, eager now that his story had begun.

"What you have to understand is that our current excavation— the labyrinth of Sobek—essentially proves that theory. The main palace of Crocodilopolis, the Temple of Sobek, has been a given for decades. But the labyrinth is a separate structure, not far from the temple. The Cretan labyrinth at Knossos must have been the same."

Drake shook his head. "Wait," he said, holding up a hand. "You're saying they've never found the labyrinth at Knossos? The one with the Minotaur? King Minos, the whole thing?"

Welch smiled, scraping a bit of tahini onto a piece of pita.

"Amazing, isn't it? This stuff is legend, but it gets mixed up in the public consciousness. People don't know what's real and what isn't. So here's what *is* real."

He took a bite, chewed a few times, and swallowed, barely conscious of the action.

"The palace at Knossos is there. But an English gentleman, Sir Arthur Evans—an amateur, because there weren't a lot of professionals in those days—oversaw the excavation of the palace. During the process, he hired people to 'restore' the place." Welch made little air quotes with his fingers. "Some of that restoration included taking entire rooms and having artists paint frescoes on the walls in what he claimed was the style of the Minoan civilization—Minoan for King Minos, right?—only it was all bullshit. Instead of restoring what was there, Evans's restoration team covered it all up, ruining a huge opportunity. A lot of what might have been learned was lost, which is part of the reason no consensus has been able to be formed about whether or not the palace at Knossos and the labyrinth of King Minos are one and the same.

"But our dig—well, it makes a pretty persuasive argument that there's a separate building somewhere at Knossos. Not only that, but every day we're finding more and more evidence connecting the labyrinth of Sobek to the labyrinth at Knossos and to a third, as yet unidentified labyrinth. We've found tablets with writing and markings in sacred chambers, most of them written in Linear B, that establish pretty firmly that Daedalus designed three of them and Knossos and Crocodilopolis were two of the three."

"Not four?" Sully asked, startling them all by speaking.

Welch frowned, turning to him. "I'm sorry?"

"My father left some notes," Jada said. "We got the impression he thought there was a fourth labyrinth."

"That's the first I've heard of it," Welch said. "No, all of the writings we've found talk about 'Three Labyrinths of the Master Builder.' Notations elsewhere make it pretty clear Daedalus is the Master Builder, and we've been going on that theory."

Movement caught Drake's attention out of the corner of his eye, but it was only the waiter bringing a plate of oven-fried cheese that Sully had ordered and a glass of Coke for Jada.

"Luka's notes talked about 'honey,'" Drake said when the waiter departed. "Something about 'the Mistress of the Labyrinth' getting the most."

For the first time, Welch lit up with real excitement. All of his sympathy about Luka's murder and his concern were thrust aside by enthusiasm.

"That's both one of the greatest finds of our dig and one of the biggest mysteries as well," Welch said, eyes bright behind his spectacles. He looked almost like a little boy in that moment, his grin beatific. "A tablet found during the original excavation at Knossos referred to the Mistress of the Labyrinth. Yes, there's the legend of the Minotaur, but set that aside for a second. The tablet told of honey being brought as an offering to the gods in the temple at Knossos but also said that worshippers brought some to the labyrinth as an offering to its mistress. She received enough to equal that given to all of the other gods combined.

"We've found the same thing here in the labyrinth of Sobek. The people feared crocodiles, and Sobek was the crocodile god, so offerings to him were plentiful. But the rule about the honey and the Mistress of the Labyrinth existed here as well. And in the third labyrinth, wherever that was. Each labyrinth had a mistress who had to be propitiated."

Drake stole a bite of Sully's fried cheese. The lights had been dimmed a little and the lilting music turned up as the evening wore on.

"But we're not talking about ordinary honey," Drake said.

"I agree," Welch replied. "Though my whole team's been arguing for weeks about what it might have been. Of course it might have been honey, but it might have been some concoction, even a drinkable opiate or some similar drug. On the other hand, I lean toward the other extreme, which is that it was something far more tangible."

The archaeologist had a strange weight to his words, as if he had just reached the point in the story that he had been building up to all along, some turning point that he presented as a riddle, as if he expected them to be able to fill in the rest on their own. But Drake was too tired for riddles, and he knew his companions were as well.

"Such as?" Drake said.

Welch swirled the ice in his water glass, glanced around to be sure no one was listening, and leaned over the table, forcing a new intimacy into the conversation. Even Sully pulled in nearer.

"Gold," Welch whispered. His eyes were still bright, but he was no longer smiling. There could be no doubting his sincerity.

Jada stiffened, glancing at Sully and then Drake. She said nothing, but she did not have to. Luka Hzujak had written that Henriksen was after the treasure of the fourth labyrinth. Welch might not know anything about a fourth labyrinth, but here was at least a theory about treasure.

"Have you found gold in the dig?" Sully asked quietly.

"Not as much as I'd expected," Welch said. "The cult of Sobek used it in their worship, even in decoration of their sacred chambers and the crocodiles. But there's little of it in the labyrinth."

"So where's the connection?" Jada asked.

Welch sipped his water. "Back up a second. You need to understand that many scholars believe that Minos might not have been the name of the king but a title, the way that Caesar became a title for the emperors of Rome. So the king for whom Daedalus built the labyrinth at Knossos, the king who was the father of Ariadne, whom Daedalus loved, might not have been named Minos at all."

Drake shrugged. "Okay. So?"

"We've found evidence that he had another, more familiar name. That his sons and grandsons scattered to Anatolia and Phrygia and Thracia and Macedonia, all taking his name, causing historians a massive amount of confusion. But there's a tablet in my boss's office at the excavation site that tells a familiar story with a different setting and gives a name to the king of Crete, the founder of Minoan civilization."

Sully snapped. "For God's sake, man, just spit it out!"

Glasses clinked. Conversations stopped. People paused in their dinner to stare at the rude Americans. Drake smiled awkwardly and gave a friendly wave to the people at the nearest occupied table, a pair of silver-haired Arab businessmen, maybe Saudi or Bahrainian.

Welch looked hurt.

Jada reached across the table to put her hand over his. "Mr. Welch, I appreciate your excitement. My father shared it, I have no doubt—"

"He did," Welch agreed, nodding.

"—but we're trying to find out who killed him, and your sister's boyfriend, Dr. Cheney, as well. Before we left New York, someone tried to kill us, too. So I hope you'll forgive us if we're not in the mood for any additional suspense."

Drake stared at her, wondering if he'd had half her poise at the age of twenty-four. He seriously doubted it.

"Of course," Welch said. "Sorry. I was just trying to lay a foundation for what at first blush you might find a bit astonishing."

Drake leaned in and lowered his voice, just as Welch had done. "Astonish us."

Welch smiled, and the four of them became conspiratorial again. "We have evidence to suggest that King Minos of Crete and King Midas were one and the same."

Drake stared at him. The music seemed to grow louder, and the susurrus of conversation in the restaurant ebbed and flowed. He tore his gaze from Welch's face only to glance at Sully and Jada and saw surprise and disbelief that mirrored his own.

"That's—" Sully began.

"Remember, Mr. Sullivan," Welch said, "most legends have a core of historical fact, some precedent. I'm not suggesting a man existed who could turn base metals to gold with the touch of a finger, but there was a King Midas, well known for his hoarding of gold. Stories in different cultures refer to him, though we now believe most of them are references to his sons and grandsons of the same name, and that the patriarch of the family, Midas the First, if you will, was the father of Ariadne, the monarch of Cretan civilization—Minoan civilization—at the time the labyrinth was constructed by Daedalus."

Jada had gone pale, her gaze lost and distant. Welch seemed about to go on but then noticed the look on her face.

"Look, I know it's hard to accept the idea that something so widely viewed as a myth could be real—" he began.

"It's not that," Drake interrupted, a frisson of excitement making the hairs rise on his arms. He glanced at Jada. "Tell him."

Sully had lost several seconds just gaping at Welch, but now Drake saw his mind working behind his eyes as if puzzle pieces were falling together inside his skull. Drake thought that was exactly what it felt like. They didn't have all the pieces, not by a long shot, but suddenly the puzzle had a little more shape than it had had even a few moments before.

"Mr. Welch," Jada started.

"Ian, please."

"Ian, then," she said. "My father's research style was pretty immersive. You could even say obsessive. At the time of his murder, he had buried himself in research on two subjects that were obviously related, but when I went through his notes and things, I could never figure out how. One of those was obviously labyrinths. He had been here, and he had been talking frequently to Dr. Cheney in New York.

"The other subject was alchemy."

Welch nodded. "That's perfect, yes. That makes sense."

"Luka thought there was some connection between Midas and the great alchemists of history," Sully put in.

"There may be," Welch said. This time he looked almost nervous as he glanced around. Drake figured he was worried that the wrong people, overhearing him, might think there was treasure up for grabs at the dig and that could lead to theft and violence.

"Alchemy is impossible," Jada said, her frustration showing. "Gold is what it is. It doesn't start as something else."

"You know that, and I know that," Welch said. "But there have obviously been times in history when people believed in alchemy and some pretty charismatic individuals who claimed to be alchemists."

"The trick was in having the gold to back it up," Drake said.

"Exactly," Sully agreed, scanning the restaurant, talking to them while at the same time acting as their sentry. "All of those guys—St. Germain, Fulcanelli, young Nathan's friend Ostanes—their claims would never have been believed if they hadn't had gold to show for their efforts. Enough to be amazing."

Welch raised his eyebrows appreciatively. "It seems I won't need to educate you all on the history of alchemy."

"Back to Midas," Sully prodded.

"And to the labyrinths," Welch agreed. "On the tablets we've translated so far, there's a story that establishes that the designer of the labyrinth of Sobek—obviously Daedalus, though he's not named—paid the workers in gold and was said to have been able to transform *stone* into gold with a touch."

Drake frowned. "Wait, it says Daedalus had the touch, not Midas—not the king?"

"Exactly," Welch replied, smiling thinly. "It's written that the designer had a great stockpile of gold at the center of the labyrinth, that the workers built from the inside out, and that they would have to go and see him to get paid. He never left the labyrinth, but he paid them their wages in gold."

The archaeologist looked at Jada. "Your father helped me translate that tablet. He and I both believed this story referred to Daedalus. It went on to say that thieves attempted to steal from him constantly, even after the labyrinth had been completed. There are references to the Mistress of the Labyrinth and her honey and to a monster as well."

"A monster?" Jada asked. "This is here in Egypt, not on Crete?"

"Yes," Welch replied, clearly enjoying his revelations. "There are references to all three labyrinths having guardians. Monstrous men. Maybe scarred and certainly huge, but obviously not man-bulls like in the myth. It seems that Daedalus lived in the labyrinth here, and the mistress and the monster were also living inside it. But at some point, a group of builders banded together and attacked the cult of Sobek, killing many people and invading the labyrinth. The would-be thieves found no trace of gold or of Daedalus. Both had apparently vanished. Maybe when we figure out the location of the third labyrinth, we'll solve that mystery, too."

Jada started to ask him more, but then the waiter arrived with their dinner and the conversation halted while he served them. When he'd gone, Drake turned again to Welch.

"I can see why this would be like Christmas for you, Ian," Drake said. "This dig has turned up more information about the ancient world than anything found in a century. You and your boss will have your careers made by this. You'll write books and go on talk shows. You'll be set. But as cool as a lot of this is— and believe me, to someone like me, it is extremely cool— I haven't heard anything yet worth killing over."

Welch shot Jada an apologetic look. "Whatever your father discovered, whatever connection he made that put him in danger, I have no idea what it is. And maybe it makes me a coward, but I confess I'm glad I don't know."

Sully slid his chair nearer to Welch. "Be careful, Dr. Welch. Cheney didn't know, either—or at least your sister didn't think Cheney knew whatever secret Luka had discovered. But Cheney's still dead. You've gotta be on guard until we figure it all out."

For the first time, Welch looked frightened. "But I don't know the secret, either. If there is some kind of treasure and we don't find it during this dig, I have no idea where it could be."

"Just be careful," Sully said, taking a bite of his koshari.

"Maybe we'll find some answers at the dig tomorrow," Jada suggested. "If we can put this puzzle together and prove who killed my father and why, then you'll be safe."

Welch nodded. "Let's hope so," he said, but he had gone rather pale and seemed to have lost much of his appetite.

As soon as he could get away without seeming rude, Welch excused himself and left his dinner half eaten at the table. He didn't even wait to have coffee with them after the meal. For several minutes after he departed, the three of them said nothing, finishing up their dinner, lost in their own ruminations.

Drake's first hint that something was wrong came when Sully started choking.

"Uncle Vic?" Jada asked, worried.

Sully coughed, taking a sip of water to wash down whatever it was he had swallowed wrong. But Drake knew him too well to think the food had been the only problem. He saw the worry in Sully's eyes and the way Sully had sat up, making sure the journal was hidden under the tail of his shirt but that he could reach his gun if he needed it.

Drake glanced at the entrance to the restaurant and saw a woman walking toward them. A beautiful creature, she had blond hair to her shoulders, stylishly cut, and Drake put her in her early forties, though she could have passed for younger with less makeup. Her dress was long enough not to offend the Egyptians, but there was no mistaking the allure of the body beneath it.

"Jada," Sully whispered behind his water glass. "Your stepmother just walked in."

Chair legs shrieking, Jada slid back from the table and stood, barely controlled fury on her face. Drake snatched her wrist and held on tight, forcing her to look at him.

"You're in public, in Egypt, and we're all carrying guns," he whispered through his teeth.

She took a deep breath, wet her lips, and gave a single sharp nod. Sully stood slowly and took up a position beside her, providing her with moral support. Drake stole Jada's Coke and took a long gulp, but he didn't rise. Anyone in the restaurant would think they were greeting the new arrival to their party despite the distress on the faces of both Jada and her stepmother.

"Oh, I'm so glad I found you," Olivia Hzujak said as she threw her arms around her stepdaughter.

Jada stood frozen, her gaze cold, as she endured her stepmother's embrace. Olivia took a step back and looked at her at arm's length.

"When I found out you were here, I just thought—my God, it's like fate," Olivia said. Her lower lip trembled, and she brought a hand up to halfway cover her face as tears began to spill down her cheeks. "Jada, I can't believe he's gone. I don't know what I'm going to do without him."

Her voice shook with grief. Drake stared at the woman. Whatever he had expected from Olivia Hzujak, this was not it. A glance at Sully told him that his old friend had had the same reaction. Yes, the woman fit the mold of classic older femme fatale, but life didn't follow the rules of old Humphrey Bogart movies. If this woman's pain wasn't real, she was a damn fine actress.

Jada, though, did not seem convinced.

"What are you doing here, Olivia?" she asked.

Olivia flinched at the steel and ice in her stepdaughter's voice. She let go of Jada's arm and retreated a step, pushing her bleached hair away from her face. The older woman searched the eyes of the younger for understanding.

"I know what you must think," Olivia said.

"Really? I'm not sure you do," Jada replied.

Olivia glanced at Sully. "Victor. Thank you for taking care of her."

Sully arched an eyebrow. "Somebody had to."

Again Olivia flinched. She nodded slowly, wiping at her tears, but Drake saw the effort it took for her to get herself under control and still thought her grief had to be genuine.

"I couldn't stay in New York, Jada," she said. "Your father—when he first turned up missing, I suspected the worst. But when the police called to say they'd found him and—*how* they'd found him—I feared for my own life."

"Come again?" Sully said. "Why would you think you were in danger?"

Olivia shot him a hard look. "Don't be obtuse, Victor. I know why you're here. You and Jada and Mr. Drake." She glanced at Drake. "I assume this *is* your friend Nathan."

Drake raised Jada's Coke glass in a toast. "Hey."

The woman turned back to Jada and Sully and lowered her voice. "Please, let's work together on this. Tyr is here in Egypt as well. His men have been following me. I'm afraid they'll kill me like they did Luka. I came here in the first place because I thought the only way I would be safe is if I could figure out what he was trying to keep secret and make it public. If it's out there, if it's not a secret anymore, there'd be no point in killing to keep it quiet."

Sully tilted his head, studying her, stroking his mustache. "You're not working with Henriksen on this?"

Olivia paled, looking stunned. "Luka was my husband."

"Oh, please," Jada snorted. "You treated him like a dog who messed on your rug."

"That's awful," Olivia said, her lip trembling again. She shook her head. "I know you never liked me, Jada, but you weren't in our home. You didn't see our relationship the way it was, only the way it inconvenienced you."

"Really?" Jada said, her voice low. One of the waiters had started to approach but thought better of it and retreated. "That's the story you're sticking to? The loving and misunderstood wife?"

"Jada," Sully said warily.

"No, Uncle Vic," Jada snapped, raising her voice just a little, trying to control herself. "Don't tell me you're buying any of this crap. How did she find us, huh? That's what I want to know. We're in a restaurant in a random hotel in Fayoum City. How the hell did she know where to even start looking for us?"

Olivia stared at her. "I'm staying in the same hotel. It's where Luka stayed. I was out most of the day, but when I got back, the desk clerk mentioned there was another guest named Hzujak, and what a strange coincidence. You asked for directions to get here, which is how he knew where you were going."

"You couldn't have waited for us to get back to the hotel?" Sully asked.

"I couldn't know when you'd be back," Olivia argued. "And I told you, I think I'm being followed. Now, are you going to invite me to sit so we can talk about this, or should we all just stand here looking more and more conspicuous."

Drake watched Jada's face, then glanced at Sully. He saw the hesitation there, and he understood it, but Olivia's explanations

seemed at least halfway believable, and he didn't like the attention they were drawing.

"She should sit down," Drake said, looking at Sully. "We've
got too many eyes on us right now."

Jada swung around to stare at him. "You can't be serious."

Drake returned her gaze. "We can't do this here, Jada. Or do
the words 'international incident' mean nothing to you? We
don't have an exit strategy. So please, sit down."

Jada turned and stared at her stepmother. Olivia's expression
was almost pitiful, even more so in a woman who seemed so
practiced at projecting an air of aloof sophistication.

"Not a chance in hell," Jada said. She glared at Drake and
then turned to Sully. "You want to make nice with her, have a
blast. But don't be surprised if you're the next one who turns up
dead."

She turned on her heel and made a beeline for the exit. Sully
and Olivia called after her, but Jada didn't look back. When
Sully started to follow, Drake stood up quickly and grabbed his
shoulder.

"No. You stay with *her*," he said, indicating Olivia. "I'll get
Jada back. Whether she likes it or not, there's a conversation
that needs to happen here."

Drake took off after Jada, all too aware of the eyes on him.
Most of the people were watching his quarry, however. An attractive young American woman with magenta streaks in her
hair would have gotten a lot of attention even if she hadn't been
storming off like a spoiled teenager.

That's not fair, Drake thought, catching himself. If their posi-
tions were reversed and he truly believed Olivia had had a hand
in killing Sully, he wouldn't stand there and listen to her spin
lies, either. But Jada had hated Olivia even while her father was
alive, so Drake had to make her see that she might not be view-
ing things objectively. He had to make her see that if there was a
chance she was wrong, they'd be leaving an innocent woman
alone in the path of a killer.

As he emerged from the restaurant into the lobby, he caught

sight of Jada leaving the hotel. There were lights outside the doors, but their glow did not reach very far into the darkness, and he quickened his pursuit.

Pushing out into the night, he paused outside the door, squinting at the night.

"Jada!" he called, wondering in which direction she'd gone.

Back to the car, he thought. She was stubborn, but she wasn't stupid. That meant to the left, where the parking lot was three-quarters full. He picked up his pace, scanning the cars, and caught sight of the people struggling beside a dark sedan.

His eyes adjusted to the starlight, and he saw magenta.

Jada screamed and struck one of the dark-suited men, trying to break free, and then Drake saw the glint of a gun barrel. Reaching for his gun, he started to run.

9

Drake crouched behind a dented Sahin sedan and took aim.

"Leave the girl or I drop you right here!" he shouted.

One of the thugs spun and took a shot at him, blowing out the Sahin's rear window. Drake pulled the trigger twice, and the grim-eyed man danced backward, one bullet taking him in the shoulder and the other in the chest. His gun flew, clattering to the ground.

Jada punched the goon who was holding her in the throat, and he let go, gasping for air. She launched herself full-out after the gun and skidded on the pavement on her belly, hands reaching. One of the remaining men went after her, the other two drawing their guns.

Drake fired again and missed, the shot echoing off parked cars and the side of the hotel. The two armed men opened fire, bullets punching the flimsy body of the sedan and bursting the rest of the windows. Drake threw himself to the right, counting on the night to veil his movements. He scuttled behind a red Tata minitruck and stood up, looking through the driver's window. The parking lot was on the side of the hotel and poorly lit, but the men were out in the open and the glow of the city was enough for him to make out some details. The two still standing were in dark suits like the one he'd shot, and though one had the olive complexion of the Middle East and northern Africa, the other was Caucasian.

Their car was a dark gray BMW, and it was still running, a low growl coming from the engine. Three of the doors were open. They'd been trying to force Jada into the car when he had come out, which meant that they had been lying in wait for her and that they were quick and well organized. This wasn't some random tourist abduction; that much was clear.

He heard Jada scuffling with the third one, and he wanted to intervene, but rushing in now would only get him killed and it seemed clear they wanted her alive. However, the men who'd come after them in New York hadn't seemed all that concerned about whether she lived or died, and if these bastards were working for the same employer, they wouldn't hesitate to kill her if it came to that.

One of the standing thugs gestured for the other to circle around to their left—Drake's right. They were a few cars away, but if they split up now, they would flank him in moments. He'd have to try to take them down from cover, which would mean revealing his precise location.

He took a breath, finger resting on the trigger. He'd shoot the one who seemed to be giving the orders first.

A single gunshot split the air, and Drake flinched, thinking they'd found him. But then he realized that the shot had come from the gun Jada and the third thug were fighting over, and ice twisted in his gut.

"Son of a bitch," he muttered.

Throwing caution to the wind, he ran between the truck and the bullet-riddled sedan, taking aim at the broad-shouldered white guy. The thug had been waiting and started to take aim, when a shot came from off to the left. It sang through the air and shattered glass but missed its target.

Sully stood at the edge of the parking lot, pistol clutched in both hands. Olivia was behind him, pressed against the hotel, looking frantic, like she wanted to bolt. The black-suited line-backer dropped behind a car; he was smarter than he looked. If he'd taken the time to aim at one of them, the other would have shot him, though it looked like Sully needed target practice.

"Nate, watch your three o'clock!" Sully shouted.

Drake spun, saw the olive-skinned goon appear between two rows of cars, and squeezed off a shot. A bullet screamed past his ear, close enough that he felt the displacement of air against his cheek. He swore and took cover, glanced over at Sully, and saw that his old friend had done the same thing, hidden behind the corner of the hotel with his gun barrel pointed heavenward like a cop about to break down a perp's door.

Or James Bond without the suave, Drake thought. Sully would love that. Or maybe shoot him.

Olivia stood ten feet behind him, well out of range of the shooters. She was trapped there unless she wanted to go back into the hotel and deal with the chaos that would bring. The guests and restaurant patrons would be freaking out now, some under tables and others at the windows, trying to figure out what was going on. They weren't alone in that.

"Jada, you alive?" Drake shouted.

In answer, she struggled to her feet. For a second he thought all would be well, but then he saw that she wasn't alone. The third guy held her tightly from behind. White, early thirties, ex-military by the way he carried himself. But he didn't look well, and the bullet hole in his shoulder probably had something to do with it. He'd been the only guy not in a suit. His shirt had been gray or blue, but a stain had spread out from the wound Jada had given him, the blood looking black in the dark.

Drake twisted and took aim, but there would be no way for him to take the guy down without shooting Jada. He was only a half-decent shot, not some kind of marksman.

The guy winced in pain but didn't make himself a target. Jada might have shot him in the struggle, but he'd gotten the gun back. Now he jammed it against her skull like he was trying to drill a hole.

"Back off or she's dead!" the gunman snapped.

Drake didn't move, gun still leveled at Jada and her would-be abductor, but without a safe shot.

"Drop the damn gun, Drake," the man snarled. "You and Sullivan both."

Drake glanced at Sully and Olivia. Sully still had his back against the corner of the hotel, hidden from sight, gun still aimed at the sky. He saw the frown on Sully's face and knew it reflected his own. These guys knew their names. If they worked for Henriksen, the boss had done his homework. Of course, Olivia had

known Sully was with Jada, and she could have guessed that
Drake was the other man with her on the basis of descriptions
from the attack in New York. But Henriksen might have figured
that out himself.

"I will kill her right now!" the gunman said.

Drake started to lower his gun, then darted behind a battered,
dusty Jeep. He'd give up his gun if he had to, but he wasn't going
to stand there and wait to get shot.

"Dimitri, drive the car!" the gunman said.

The one Drake had thought Middle Eastern turned out to be
Dimitri—a Greek. He kept his weapon aimed at the Jeep and
hustled over to their BMW and slid behind the wheel. He kept
the door open, ready to shoot again.

The linebacker didn't need to be told what to do. He went to
the man Drake had shot dead and lifted the corpse under the
arms, starting to drag him around the back of the car.

"Open the boot!" he shouted to Dimitri. "The police will be
here in moments."

The Greek popped the trunk of the BMW, and it started to
rise.

Drake took several deep breaths, waiting for the moment
when the guy holding Jada would try to muscle her into the
backseat. He had seen the fear in her eyes, but he had seen the
determination as well. She would fight him if she had the chance,
and if she tried to break free again, Drake would be ready. He
would shoot the son of a bitch the second he had a target, and
he knew Sully was waiting for the same thing.

Distant sirens reached them. The police were on the way. He
tried not to think what might happen to an American with a gun
and a fake passport in an Egyptian jail.

He heard a new scuffle, and a man cried out in pain.

Go, Jada, he thought, figuring she had tried to fight back. He
swung out from behind the Jeep, aiming at the spot right beside
the BMW where Jada and the wounded thug had been a moment before. They were still there, but they weren't alone.

A darker figure had risen up behind the gunman. Hooded,
clad in flowing black, the new arrival gripped the wounded thug

by the hair and cut his throat with a long, wickedly curved blade. Jada *had* tried to twist free, had gotten her hand on the gunman's wrist and forced the gun barrel away from her skull. Now she held on to the man's wrist and watched him slump to the pavement, dead.

Others emerged from the darkness between cars, four, then six, then eight more of the hooded figures. Two of them fell upon the linebacker, killing him in near silence. Another appeared from the backseat of the BMW, flowing like liquid darkness over the seat and murdering Dimitri, who pounded the car horn—but only for a moment.

Sully had stepped out from the corner of the hotel and taken aim, but he watched in astonishment that mirrored Drake's as the shadowed figures made short work of Jada's would-be abductors. For her part, Jada staggered backward in shock.

Hooded figures put the linebacker in the trunk with the man Drake had killed. Others tossed the one Jada had wounded into the backseat of his own car. One of the assassins shoved Dimitri over and took his place behind the wheel of the BMW. Drake kept swinging the barrel of his gun back and forth, wondering if he ought to be shooting at them, though they hadn't made any attempt to attack him or his friends.

Then one of them darted at Jada so swiftly that when Drake pulled the trigger, he had no chance of hitting the man. The assassin whispered something into her ear and then retreated into the shadows between cars. The BMW's engine roared, and Drake moved aside as it shot from the parking lot, skidding into the road and vanishing up the street.

When he glanced back at the scene of the melee, Jada was alone. Sully ran toward her, and so Drake did the same thing. Of Olivia, there was no sign. She had vanished.

"Get the car," Sully snapped at him.

"But—"

"The cops!" Sully barked.

Drake ran for the car, digging out his keys. He was behind the wheel and had it started in a matter of seconds, slammed it into gear, and pulled up beside Sully and Jada, who quickly piled in.

"What about Olivia? We can't just leave her for the police," Drake said.

Beside him in the passenger seat, Jada shot him a withering glance. "Are you kidding me? She took off. You still think she didn't set us up? Let's go!"

Drake didn't have to be told twice. He hit the gas and tore out of the parking lot, raced along the street, and slowed at the corner, taking the turn just as a police car barreled toward the hotel from the other direction.

Heart hammering, he kept his speed down until they were out of the city and the desert sky had opened up above them.

"Who the hell were those guys?" Drake muttered.

"The guys who tried to take me or the guys who killed them?" Jada asked.

"Either one," Sully said.

"Jada, what did that guy whisper to you right before they did their disappearing act?" Drake asked.

She glanced at him as if deciding whether to tell. Then she exhaled. "Go home," she said.

"Wow," Drake said. "Y' know, maybe this is me going out on a limb here, but I'm going to say I think we're officially screwed."

Nobody argued with him.

10

Drake woke on Saturday morning surprised not to have been rousted by the police during the night. He was even more amazed when he turned on the television and saw nothing about the violence outside the Queen's Hotel on the news. Sully had spent the night in Jada's room, presumably sleeping in a chair—though he might have taken a pillow into the bathtub and curled up there; it wouldn't have been the first time—and when Drake phoned the room, he answered on the first ring.

"Any cops or reporters down your way?" Drake asked him.

"None. Weird, don't you think?"

Drake *did* think. "Does Tyr Henriksen have enough money to pay a restaurant full of people to keep their mouths shut?"

"Either that or pay off the Fayoum City police," Sully agreed.

"Why would he do that?" Drake asked.

"It's pretty clear he thinks we know something he doesn't want anyone knowing. If the cops question us, we might tell them."

"We wouldn't. Unless we had to," Drake replied.

"He doesn't know that."

"True."

"How you doing on your morning beauty regimen?" Sully growled. "Jada's feeling pretty vulnerable. She doesn't want to spend a minute here she doesn't have to."

"Just Jada?" Drake asked.

"You ready?" Sully replied, ignoring the question. "I've got some dates and fuul down here."

"Watch what you're calling me."

"Funny," Sully said drily.

"I just woke up. Give me twenty minutes. We should check out. Whatever happens today, tonight we find a hotel in Cairo."

"Agreed."

Drake didn't actually make it downstairs until a little more than half an hour later, but Sully and Jada must have only been a few minutes ahead of him because they were at the front desk when he walked up. Once they had checked out and settled the bill, they headed outside to the car, all of them blinking back the sunlight and glancing around for the cadre of local cops they expected to descend on them. Still, nothing happened. It was as if the events of the night before had never taken place.

"Did you ask about Olivia?" Drake said, glancing at Sully and ignoring the sharp look the question earned him from Jada.

"She's registered. We couldn't exactly ask if she came back to her room last night, and it's not likely the same clerk on duty, anyway," Sully said. "I rang her room, but no answer, and we didn't feel like knocking on the door."

Drake nodded. There had been too many surprises lately, and he wouldn't have wanted to knock on Olivia's door this morning, either. The way she'd vanished, she was either in on it or in even more trouble than they were.

"So, I take it we're not going to take spooky-ninja-assassin's advice and go home?" Drake asked.

Jada glanced at him. "No one's keeping you here, Nate."

"Hey," Drake said, holding up his hands in surrender. "We can't pretend those guys weren't intimidating. I'd feel better if I knew who they were and what the hell they were doing saving our asses."

"*If* that's what they were doing," Sully said. "Looked to me like they were killing Henriksen's guys. Was that to save Jada or just because they were Henriksen's guys?"

"If they *were* Henriksen's guys," Drake said.

"Please," Jada said, waving a dismissive hand. "Olivia may have confused you guys with her damsel-in-distress thing, but I know her. She's a part of this."

"Even if she isn't, she put the blame on Henriksen, too," Sully reminded them. "Either she was really afraid of him, which means he's behind it all, or she's in on it with him, which still means he's behind it all."

"I guess we're in agreement on Henriksen being behind it all," Drake said.

Jada punched him in the arm.

He said, "ow."

"Just drive the car, would you?" Sully said, sighing. "It's not the morning for goofing around."

Drake frowned. "People tried to kill us again last night. There were hooded assassins—and I mean really, really skilled hooded assassins. As freaked as I am, I think it's the perfect morning for goofing around."

Jada stopped short ten feet from the Volvo wagon.

Sully glanced at her. "Hey. You okay?"

She turned to Drake, stood on tiptoe, and kissed his cheek. "I thanked Sully last night. I don't think I thanked you. For saving my life, I mean."

Drake wanted to remind her that she'd done a pretty good job of helping save her own life, but he didn't want to ruin the moment.

Sully smiled. "Well, that shut him up, at least."

The clock in the Volvo had given up attempting to tell time sometime before they acquired the car, but Drake guessed it was around half past nine when they arrived in a cloud of dust at the Temple of Sobek. Though the temple had been partially excavated years ago, their interest lay beyond it, on a stretch of crenellated desert that seemed at first glance indistinguishable from any other patch of Egyptian dirt.

Only as they drove past the temple excavation and continued toward the site of the labyrinth dig did the idiosyncrasies of the land become plain. A field of tents had been erected in what looked more like a military operation than a scientific encampment. Jeeps and other vehicles suited for the desert were parked in neat rows, though not a single line delineated appropriate parking spaces. Beyond the vehicles and tents there was a great depression in the land where the desert had settled down on top of the ruins of the labyrinth. The depression hinted at the large circular design.

On the eastern edge of the excavation site, a portion of the labyrinth's walls had been dug out. Another work in progress had been covered by an awning, but Drake could make out what appeared to be the formidable stone entrance to the labyrinth. A small swarm of workers did the delicate work of slowly revealing the outer wall, but from both of the open sections of the labyrinth, buckets of earth were being carried out one by one and sifted through. Other workers carried wooden beams in through the openings, presumably to bolster the walls and ceilings that were being exposed for the first time in eons.

"It's bigger than I expected," Jada said.

"The operation or the labyrinth?" Sully asked.

"Both."

Drake studied the outline of the labyrinth again. "That may not even be all of it. There are probably lower levels, shafts and traps, other twists. These things are never as simple as they seem."

Jada glanced at the strange ripples of the desert on top of the labyrinth, indicating its basic design. "It doesn't seem simple at all."

Sully agreed. "When they were trying to dig out for the lake they were going to put in—" He pointed at the initial excavation point, the broken wall. "—probably right there, the sand started to pour down into the labyrinth. Looks like the level of the desert sank above it; otherwise we wouldn't even be seeing this much. But most of the ceilings are still intact, so the dig team isn't going to assume that the design they're seeing on top is the actual map of the maze."

"That's what I'm saying," Drake replied. "As complicated as it looks, that's only the start."

Most of the workers ignored them as they parked the car behind the row of others and got out. There were several vehicles there that obviously didn't belong: luxury vehicles among the faded old trucks and vans of the workers and the Jeeps of the foremen and archaeologists. Drake took note, but then he saw a pair of men in long blue shirts and loose cotton trousers. One had a beige and blue turban, but neither wore the traditional outer robe, the galabeya, so common among the desert dwellers.

"Excuse me," Drake said. "Can you tell us where to find Ian Welch?"

The man in the turban went on as if they were invisible and had not spoken, but the other man stopped and studied them, perhaps wondering if they worked for his employers. He chose to be careful about who he ignored, smiling and nodding and gesturing them onward toward a row of tents.

"Dr. Welch the little tent," he said.

His English was functional at best, but Drake didn't judge. How could he, when he knew barely a dozen words in Arabic?

They thanked the man and hurried on, cognizant of the sun crawling overhead, the morning burning away. They found Welch in a small tent, drinking from a canteen. The heat was brutal, and the archaeologist already had started to sweat. Drake thought the skinny archaeologist, with his mess of hair and his antic, nervous energy, might be the kind of guy who did a lot of sweating.

"I'm glad you're here," Welch said, standing to greet them. He had his glasses slipped into the crook of his shirt collar, but now he slipped them on. "I couldn't put off going into the dig much longer."

"Did you see anything strange when you left the restaurant last night?" Sully asked him. "Or anyone?"

Welch frowned. "No, why? Did something happen?"

Sully shook his head. "Never mind."

Drake studied Welch. "You're a little twitchy this morning, Ian. What's troubling you?" *Twitchier than normal*, Drake had wanted to say, but he chose his words carefully.

"Oh, just a small thing," Welch said, his voice dripping with sarcasm. "The dig's got a new sponsor as of last night. Care to guess who it might be?"

Jada blanched. "Phoenix Innovations."

Welch pointed at her. "Got it in one try."

"Henriksen," Sully growled, looking around. "Is he here?"

"I'm surprised you didn't cross paths," Welch said.

He snatched up a canvas hat and perched it on his head, then led the way out of the tent, leaving them to follow. Drake glanced at Sully, not liking this turn of events at all. Henriksen here? He had figured they would cross paths with the man eventually but had been hoping to get in and out of the dig with Welch before that happened.

"It might not be the worst thing," Jada said as she followed Drake out of the tent. "He can't kill us in front of this many witnesses."

Outside the tent, with sand blowing around them and the sun glaring, Sully had to shield his eyes to give her a surprised look.

"What?" Jada said. "I'm just looking on the bright side."

"Your bright side is pretty dark," Drake muttered. Then he smiled. "It's strangely appealing."

Jada jabbed him with her elbow as they walked after Welch. The archaeologist led them between a pair of tents and into a place where they could see the entire dig while remaining mostly hidden. A group of men and women were making their way around the outer circle of the depression, a man with a camera filming a woman who was gesturing toward the implied outline of the labyrinth and talking to the camera. The others trailed behind them, including a dark-haired woman in loose clothing and a tall, broad-shouldered blond man in a crisp white shirt and gray trousers. He looked like a politician attempting and failing to dress casually. A man constantly campaigning even if he was not running for office, Drake thought.

"Is that Henriksen?" he asked.

Jada mumbled her assent, staring at the group. She had gone pale despite the flush of the heat, and when he touched her arm to comfort her, she flinched. Her skin was cold.

"The tall woman with the dark hair is Hilary Russo. She's the director of the expedition, in charge of the whole dig," Welch said. "I take it you know the blonde."

Drake said nothing. They did indeed know the woman trailing the rest of the group. Her golden hair had been tied back in a ponytail, and she looked more suited for a safari than an archaeological dig, her clothing the female equivalent of Henriksen's Lands' End perfection.

"I guess she's a better actress than you thought, huh, kid?" Sully muttered, glancing at Drake.

"What the hell are they doing here?" Jada whispered, hugging herself now as if she were in an icebox instead of the desert.

"I told you, Henriksen's taking over funding the dig," Welch replied, hands fluttering up to tug at his hat and adjust his glasses, squirrelly as ever. "Phoenix is the sole sponsor now. He's financing this dig and the next three that Hilary undertakes—years of funding for her and her team, which includes me if you being here doesn't get me fired—but in exchange he gets control of the disposition of the relics, all media rights, and rights to museum exhibits. All of that. The documentary team is supposedly putting together some footage to prepare for a TV series he wants to make about all of this. Last night you mentioned how big a discovery this is, and you weren't wrong."

Drake paced back and forth between the tents. Jada kept staring at the group across the depression from them, but he caught Sully looking at him.

"We've gotta get down there before they do," Sully said.

Drake nodded. He turned to Welch. "What you said about your job. Are you going to bail on us, Ian? We need to know. Luka and your sister's boyfriend are dead, and we think Henriksen is the guy behind it. But it sounds to me like you're having second thoughts about helping us."

Jada turned to watch the exchange, her eyes wide with hurt. It had not occurred to her that Welch might go back on his word.

Welch hesitated, squirming, a man caught between the points of his moral compass. After a few seconds, he gave a small shrug. "Gretchen would kill me if I didn't help."

Drake thought how fortunate the man was that Henriksen's goons had been after Jada the night before and not him. His sister would kill him if he didn't help, and Henriksen might have him killed if he did. They had to warn him what kind of danger he was in—as soon as he showed them the labyrinth.

"So, how do we beat Henriksen into the labyrinth?" he asked. "They'll be going inside any minute now."

Welch smiled, nodding to himself. "Hilary wants to give them the whole tour, make a show of it. They're supposed to be filming, right? She wants to impress, which means she is going to take them in through the front."

Drake stared at him. "You're saying we go through the side door?"

Jada pointed at the larger excavation, the original part of the dig, where the wall of the labyrinth had collapsed. "Can we get in that way? Is it clear?"

"Not only is it clear, it's a hell of a lot closer to the worship chambers and the anteroom we just started digging out. One of the grad students working down there told me this morning that they've started to unearth clay jars and tablets that might be connected to whatever rituals were performed there by the Mistress of the Labyrinth."

"No one's going to stop us?" Sully asked.

Welch frowned thoughtfully, then shook his head. "For today, all three of you work for the Smithsonian."

"We're already traveling under false identities," Sully said. "You can use those names."

If Welch thought this odd, he barely frowned at the revelation. "All right. Hilary's the only one who'd know we don't have any visitors from the Smithsonian, and if we play our cards right, we won't even cross paths with her."

"I wouldn't mind crossing paths with Henriksen," Jada said.

Her hand fluttered toward the small of her back as if she were about to tap the gun she had hidden there to reassure herself of the solidity of its presence and its mortal promise. She hesitated and dropped her hand, but Drake had seen her reaching and found himself hoping they didn't run into Henriksen at all. Even if Jada managed to kill him, she would only be assuring herself a prison sentence, and the secrets her father had died over might never see the light of day.

They watched as Hilary Russo led the group from Phoenix Innovations under the awning and in through the entrance to the labyrinth of Sobek.

"Let's move out," Sully said.

They hustled out from between the tents and across a patch of desert toward the excavation of the collapsed outer wall of the labyrinth. It was a brisk walk so that they would not draw undue attention, but the men working at the dig frowned and wiped their brows as they stared at the newcomers.

There were ladders in the ditch beside the excavated wall, but Drake was surprised to find that the expedition had installed temporary stairs as well, leading down from the edge of the dig to the remaining rubble just outside the shattered wall. He wondered how many tons of sand already had been removed in the excavation. In a dig like this, archaeologists would uncover certain sections, map and photograph and study them, retrieve artifacts, and then fill in the areas they had excavated to prevent them from being damaged by the elements and by entropy trying to catch up with them. But the way Welch had described it to them, much of the labyrinth was being excavated from within instead of uncovered from above; so as long as they shored up the ceilings, they might be able to explore a great deal of the interior maze without ever having to fill it in.

They descended the stairs quickly. A pair of enormous generators growled, one on either side of the entrance. Canvas tarps had been pulled aside from the breach in the wall, and he imagined that at night they hung across the opening to keep sand from blowing back into the labyrinth tunnels. During the day, Drake presumed they needed the breeze too much to worry about the sand.

As they entered the labyrinth, he heard Jada inhale deeply, as if she could breathe in the ancient history in the air. Drake had no such romantic illusions, but even so, he could feel the age of the place. It made him feel like an intruder, but he was used to such a feeling. He had, in fact, made a career of ignoring it, though sometimes it was harder than others. The past held as many secrets as the future—more, in fact—and people would pay incredible amounts of money to unravel those mysteries and maybe own a piece of the ancient world.

Hell, he loved it himself. When he had been a boy, he had read stories of adventure, of archaeological discoveries that stunned the world. He had loved old movies full of mummies or chariot races. But unlike in those antique films, the mummies he had encountered in real life had never come to life. There had been one time, in Karpathos, Greece, when he had been sure one of them moved, but nothing before or since. Still, he found it fascinating to learn how people had lived hundreds or thousands of years earlier.

So though his breath did not hitch as they entered the labyrinth of Sobek, his pulse did quicken a bit.

The walls were a shade of orange, like clay. The line of lights that hung from pegs on the wall explained the generators growling outside. Bulbs inside plastic cages were strung along the tunnel, vanishing around the corners in either direction. A quick glance showed that they were plugged into one another like strands of Christmas lights.

"This way," Welch said, turning left.

Jada glanced at Sully as if hoping to share the excitement that seemed to have allowed her to forget her grief a moment, but he didn't notice. When she turned to Drake, he returned her smile and nodded, a confession that yes, he understood. Then they were hurrying along the tunnel, moving from pools of light to pools of shadow, and the orange walls seemed to close in around them, the dry breath of history soft on their faces.

Drake had questions he wanted to ask Welch about the construction of the labyrinth, but they were moving fast and he decided all such questions could wait. They had come here for a single purpose: to find clues to the secrets that had gotten Jada's father killed before Tyr Henriksen could do the same thing. If there was a fourth labyrinth, with or without treasure inside it, they had to get there first. More important, whatever mysteries were unraveled, they had to let the world know that Luka Hzujak had been the first to discover the truth and that he had died for it.

And if there was treasure along the way, that would be a nice bonus.

The maze turned in upon itself time and again, offering false paths and optical illusions, but the hard work of solving this part of the labyrinth had been done already. The dead ends had been roped off, the correct tunnels given away by the strings of lights, so they never slowed, even when the floor of the tunnel sloped downward or the maze took them through a door with a massive stone lintel overhead that threatened to come crashing down atop them. In many places, wooden beams had been put into place to support the ceilings and walls, hammered together hastily, and left, as if a construction crew had begun to build something and then walked out on the job.

Twice, they had to go around open shafts in the floor that went down forty feet or more into darkness.

"What's this for?" Jada asked as they circumvented the first one, a flickering lightbulb casting ghostly shadows into the hole.

"It's a trap," Welch replied.

Drake smiled but did not give voice to the obvious *Star Wars* reference. He doubted any of his companions would get it, even Sully, who he knew had seen the movies.

They passed a pair of archaeology grad students who were carrying a large plastic container in which Drake could see things wrapped in cotton batting.

"Dr. Welch," one of them—a stout Australian with bright eyes—said in surprise. "Melissa said you didn't feel well. I figured we wouldn't see you today."

He looked curiously at Drake, Sully, and Jada, but Welch trotted out his Smithsonian charade and the grad students seemed duly impressed. If they ran into anyone who was part of the upper hierarchy on the project, it might not fly so easily, but Drake hoped they wouldn't be that unlucky.

Time seemed to stretch inside the labyrinth. Drake wondered how long they had been inside, realizing they must be beneath the sand now, with thousands of tons of desert on top of them, not to mention the ceilings of the labyrinth. How far behind was Henriksen now? Still pretending to be putting together a documentary? Or would he have hurried Hilary Russo along? Drake thought the latter and began to get anxious. The only thing they had going for them was that it would take Henriksen just as long to make his way through the maze as it was taking them.

"I have no idea where we are," Jada whispered.

Sully growled. "Ain't that the point?"

"Seriously," Jada said. "I tried to keep my bearings, figure out what direction we were pointing in and whether or not we were moving nearer the center or away, but I've totally lost track."

"I didn't even try," Drake admitted.

"It would be hopeless without some kind of mapping or a GPS that could transmit through the ground," Welch said. "Daedalus was smarter than any of us. Probably smarter than all of us combined. From this point, if you tried to make it back to the entrance and the lights weren't there, there are more than a hundred combinations of turns in the maze. Unless you were very lucky, you would be lost for hours. And we've postulated that we've only been able to access an eighth of the labyrinth. From the center, you might be lost for days. You could die of starvation and thirst before getting out unless you fell down a shaft or were crushed in a trap first."

"The places you haven't been able to access," Drake said. "Did the ceiling collapse?"

"It buckled in a couple of places, allowing sand in from above. In other spots there are places where what appears to be a dead end is actually a continuation of the labyrinth, but with secret doors to hidden passages. There are portcullis blocks in the walls, but the granite framing is cracked, so the series of weights and levers that would have raised those doors are not sufficient. Essentially, they're stuck. But we'll get them open."

Drake and the others said nothing. They were all familiar enough with ancient Egyptian builders to know that the great pyramids were replete with hidden chambers and secret passages. Only recently Drake had been having a drink with an old friend in Thailand and discussing the work being done at the Great Pyramid of Giza to confirm the existence of a hidden corridor beneath the Queen's Chamber there.

"You've gotta be careful with that stuff," Sully said, reaching into his shirt pocket and pulling out a half-smoked cigar. "Those things are made to be tricky. One of them closes, you don't want to be caught on the other side."

"You can't smoke that in here," Welch said. "Poor ventilation."

Jada frowned. "Not that I want to smell the stinky thing, but actually, the air is moving a little."

"There is some sifting through cracks," Welch admitted. "But still."

"I'm not smoking it, Ian," Sully growled. "Don't get your panties in a bunch."

Welch adjusted his glasses, trying and failing to hide his irritation. Drake just smiled. Sully had his charms when he felt like using them. They were all fortunate that he had foregone the typical guayabera today. When he was clothed in his usual wardrobe, nobody would have believed for a second that he worked for the Smithsonian. *The Rat Pack museum, maybe*, Drake thought.

They heard activity up ahead, and Welch gave them a warning look. Drake was surprised when they turned the next corner and saw that the lights that were wired together had been split off so that one strand went along the tunnel to the left and one jagged to the right and then continued on ahead. They followed the right-hand path and the echoes of work in progress grew louder as the tunnel sloped downward.

If not for the noise, and the lights, and Welch leading them, Drake would have assumed they were heading for a dead end. The tunnel kept going for twenty feet or so past the opening in the wall on the right, a little zigzag that looked as if it went nowhere. The walls narrowed in the zag, and the illusion that there was no passage there at all was very effective.

When they stepped through, they found themselves in a large octagonal chamber, perhaps thirty feet across. Unlike the main tunnels of the labyrinth, which had very few hieroglyphics, the walls here were covered with paintings and raised images and symbols. Three stairs led down to the sunken floor of the chamber. A stone altar—also octagonal—stood at the center of the room. To the left was a narrow doorway capped with a line of ankhs engraved in the stone.

A camera flash came from beyond the doorway, followed by voices.

"All right, Guillermo, put that aside with the others," a woman said. "Let's start brushing the sand away so we can free that vase."

"Melissa?" Welch said.

Some shifting of equipment and clothing could be heard, and then a woman popped her head out of the side room. She had coppery ginger hair and elfin features with bright, intelligent eyes, and her face lit up with pleasure at the site of Ian Welch.

"Ian!" she said, coming out into the worship chamber. "I'm so glad you're feeling better."

"Much better," Welch lied. He looked like he might be about to become sick for real, perpetuating the fiction of their identities. "Melissa, meet Dave Farzan and Nathan Merrill from the Smithsonian."

Drake stepped forward to shake her hand. "Nate Merrill. Nice to meet you."

Sully shook her hand as well, taking the cigar stub from his mouth in an attempt at courtesy.

"And this is Jada Hzujak, Dr. Luka Hzujak's daughter. You might've heard that he passed away not long ago."

Melissa's face crinkled in sympathy. "Oh, God, no. I hadn't heard." She looked at Jada. "I'm so sorry. Your father was here not long ago. He was such a character, he kept us all laughing and fascinated at the same time."

Jada let out a shuddery breath and nodded. "Yeah. He had that effect on people."

Drake had been surprised that Welch had chosen to use Jada's real name, but now he understood why. Melissa would pay less attention to the fact that they were supposed to be from the Smithsonian if she was distracted by Jada's identity and the tragedy of her father's death. It was a crass ploy, but it worked.

A skinny, unshaven man with olive skin and dark bags under his eyes stepped out of what Welch had called the anteroom, glancing at them curiously. New introductions were made. Melissa Corrigan was an archaeologist from Colorado, lower than Welch on the ladder of command but above the grad students, including the slender Guillermo and Alan, a baby-faced black man who turned out to be the dig's photographer.

"Since Nate and Dave are visiting, I thought I'd get a consult on the whole mistress/Minotaur question," Welch told Melissa. "As you know, it was something Luka had a real passion for, and Jada was curious as well. She's sort of retracing her father's steps."

"A kind of farewell tour," Jada said, and didn't have to feign the distress the words brought her.

"Of course," Melissa said, turning back to Welch. "Do your thing, Ian. We won't get in your way."

As Melissa and her team went back to work in the anteroom, Welch showed them the worship chamber. Drake went directly to the altar. Its surface was rough and stained by blood or dye spilled thousands of years before. The base was covered with paintings, many showing crocodiles, the god Sobek, and people kneeling before a robed woman, offering her golden chalices. One painting showed the woman—the Mistress of the Labyrinth, apparently—standing by an altar quite like this one with her hands spread, as if intoning a ritual chant over an array of offerings.

"No doubt about the use of this chamber," Drake said.

"Look at this," Jada said.

She had bent over the altar for a closer look at a grouping of lines on the surface. At first glance, Drake had thought it nothing but dirt and a trick of the light, but now he realized there were designs engraved in the stone: three linked octagons, each inside a circle. Drake thought the octagonal shape was very un-usual for Egyptian builders, but he didn't dare ask about it for fear of giving their ignorance away.

"Fascinating," was all he managed.

"Three octagons," Jada said, "three labyrinths." She could get away with such things because no one had claimed she was an expert.

"That was our thinking as well," Welch agreed.

Sully had been working his way through the room, studying the angles of the joints between stones, searching for any indica-tion of a hidden chamber. This was precisely the sort of place where the Egyptians might have put one—the burial chamber of the Mistress of the Labyrinth, perhaps.

"The mistress—she was a sort of high priestess, then?" Drake asked.

He glanced at the anteroom and saw Melissa moving in there and the flash of Alan's camera, but no one seemed to think his question absurd.

"We believe so," Welch agreed. "And yet if she was a priest-ess of Sobek, what of the other two labyrinths, which had to have been dedicated to other gods? The labyrinths represent the vision of someone thinking much more broadly than a single kingdom or a single theology, but the labyrinth is clearly dedi-cated to Sobek."

"Quite a dilemma," Sully rumbled, cigar stub clenched be-tween his teeth. If these people thought he was some kind of archaeologist or museum curator, they had to be thinking he was a fairly eccentric one.

Drake leaned into the anteroom. "Mind if we take a quick look in here?"

Melissa smiled. "Of course not. Frankly, we were just waiting for the right opportunity to show Dr. Welch our most recent find. But there's no time like the present, considering the subject matter."

Welch perked up. "What is it?"

Guillermo stepped back out into the worship chamber to

make room. Alan protected his camera as if it were more fragile and valuable than any artifact they might discover, stepping out of the anteroom as well. When Welch, Drake, Sully, and Jada filed in, Melissa had a stone tablet in her hands.

"We found two of these," she began, looking to Welch for approbation. "Just this morning, in fact. This antechamber seems to have been accessible only to the Mistress of the Labyrinth. So while the paintings and tablets in the worship chamber indicate that the honey was brought to her as an offering—as does the jar we found—these tablets tell a different story."

Welch took the tablet from her and studied it, surprise dawning on his features.

"What does it say?" Jada asked.

"We'd wondered, my friends," he said, turning to them with a smile. "And now we know. The honey may have been brought to the mistress, but the offering wasn't for her. She— I'm not sure if this indicates that she served it, as with a meal, or administered it in some medical fashion to the *protector* of the labyrinth."

"That one says something like 'protector,'" Melissa said. "But the other tablet is explicit. The protector was a monster, hidden from the cult of Sobek, known only to those who dared the 'secret heart' of the labyrinth and who would never return because the monster would kill them."

"I take it the 'monster' has horns?" Sully asked.

"Like a bull," Melissa said, nodding happily. "Yes, it does."

While they continued to marvel over the tablets and translate certain bits, Drake turned to the other side of the antechamber. A single stone block had given way, but given that each one weighed about fifteen hundred pounds, putting it back in place would be a great deal of work. Sand from above had filled in that corner of the room, and he saw the brushes and other implements that Melissa and Guillermo had been using to free the tablets and other artifacts that had been discovered in this antechamber. The walls were covered with glyphs and paintings here as well, but what drew Drake's full attention was the vase caught in the packed sand.

Melissa and Guillermo had unearthed about half the vase. It was intricately painted, and he knew that without a doubt, the contents of the labyrinth would constitute one of the greatest historical finds of the modern era—perhaps the greatest. The vase was incredibly well preserved.

He picked up a brush and took a closer look. A figure had been partially revealed—that of the Mistress of the Labyrinth, he thought, since it matched the figure on the base of the altar in the worship chamber. She held a jar or chalice in front of her, proffering it to someone whose hands were visible, though the rest of the other figure was covered with sand.

Drake had a pretty good idea who that other figure must be.

He started to brush at the vase. Some of the sand was tightly packed, and though he was careful, he had to brush a bit more vigorously. He needed a little elbow grease, so he leaned his knees against the piled sand, which had remained undisturbed for thousands of years.

"Hey, dude, get away from there," the grad student Guillermo said angrily, ducking his head back into the antechamber.

Melissa turned to stare at him in annoyance. Drake smiled and held up his hands.

"No harm done. But I think I found—"

The sand gave way. He started to tumble forward and caught himself by planting his hands on either side of the vase, feeling triumphant because he hadn't damaged it. Triumphant for half a second before the vase and all the sand around it dropped as if sucked into the floor.

Drake let out a yell as he fell after it, spilling into a shaft.

Hands grabbed his legs, then his belt. As the sand sifted around him, trying to suck him down, whoever had hold of him prevented him from falling into the shaft after the vase and the granite block it had sat on and at least a few other tablets that he glimpsed before they were swallowed by the darkness below. He heard something crack and knew he had just broken a piece of history.

"Whoops!" he said.

"You stupid son of a bitch!" Melissa snapped. "What did you think you were doing?"

"Helping?"

The upper half of Drake's body still hung down inside the shaft. The hands started to pull him out. In the dim reflected light from the bulbs strung in the antechamber, he saw a painting on the wall of a figure that he could not mistake for any other.

"Guys?" he said. "You're gonna want to take a look at this."

"What did you find?" Ian Welch asked.

Drake grunted as they dragged him out, and he turned over, lying on the sandy floor, to find them all staring at him. But when he spoke, his focus was on Jada.

"The Minotaur."

11

Drake looked around for something to lower himself down into the shaft. He glanced at Sully and Jada, saw the gleam of discovery in their eyes, and knew they didn't have a moment to lose. Henriksen might be there any moment, with the authority to throw them out or even have them arrested. Whatever the dig turned up would be his to do with as he wished. There would be restrictions—the Egyptian government would see to that—but wealth had a way of bypassing rules. If the secrets Luka had sought were here, not to mention treasure, they needed to hurry.

"Welch, I need a rope or a ladder and a light," he said.

Melissa had been bent over, shining a heavy-duty flashlight into the shaft, examining the painted Minotaur on the interior wall. Now she glanced up sharply, and she and Guillermo exchanged an uncomfortable look.

"Sorry, Professor Merrill," Melissa said to Drake, shaking her head. "You're an observer. We can't allow you to—"

"Guillermo," Welch interrupted, staring at the shaft. "Run out to the breach and get one of the ladders the workers use."

Even the photographer, Alan, seemed surprised. "Dr. Welch, you're not going to let him descend the shaft?"

They were all hesitating. Welch turned toward Guillermo and gestured for him to hurry.

"Go quickly. Come on, move it!"

With a worried look toward Melissa, Guillermo dashed away. They heard his footsteps echoing along the corridor. The tension between Welch and his associate was palpable. Melissa looked as if she wanted to speak to him in private, but there was no privacy to be found in such a cramped space. Even if they went out of the worship chamber and around the first corner, whispers carried in this place like the voices of ghosts.

Alan set up his camera and started to take photos of the open shaft and the paintings in its gullet. Sully had continued to investigate the antechamber, searching for any other secrets the place might hold. Jada gave Melissa an awkward, apologetic look, and Welch only stood, vibrating with anticipation and the need for Guillermo to be swift. The way things had turned out, he would never be able to hide the fact that Jada Hzujak had been here or cover the lie about Sully and Drake being from the Smithsonian. He might be able to pretend he had been duped by them, and if it would help, Drake would be happy to back up the lie. But chances were good that unless they could uncover the truth about Luka and Cheney's murders, Ian Welch had destroyed his career today. If there were secrets below, he was damn well going to get them before Tyr Henriksen did.

"Listen," Drake said to Melissa, "we're not amateurs. Once we're in the chamber down there, you can pretend we're shadows on the wall. We won't get in the way."

Melissa gave him a look normally reserved for alcoholic circus clowns and reality TV stars with delusions of grandeur. "Really?" she asked. "You're not amateurs? Then what do you call the crap you just pulled?"

Drake winced, glancing at the shaft and thinking about the vase and other priceless artifacts he'd probably just destroyed. He saw Jada give a single nod as if to say, *She's got you there.*

"I call that discovery," Drake replied, trying for a charming smile, an effort that obviously fell short. "You had no idea the shaft was there. This could be the breakthrough you've been waiting for."

"And we could've waited another few days while we explored this chamber properly," Melissa said, her irritation only growing. She turned to Welch. "Ian, please. I know these people are your friends, but—"

"That's enough, Melissa," Welch said coldly.

"Ian—"

Welch rounded on her. "That's enough!"

It brought her up short. His voice echoed in the chamber. Alan's flash went off and they all blinked the brightness away, but the tension did not dissipate. Melissa stared at Welch, clearly wondering what had come over him. This was not the demeanor she had come to expect from any colleague, but it was clear she'd had particular affection for Welch, which was now shattered.

Then she glanced from Welch to Jada, from Jada to Sully, and then to Drake. He could actually see the moment when suspicion entered her eyes.

"What's this about?" she asked, pushing her dusty, unruly ginger hair from her eyes. "What aren't you telling me?"

Welch seemed about to crumble with regret. "Melissa—"

"Hey!" Sully interrupted.

He had sunk down onto his belly in much the same position Drake had been in when they'd pulled him out of the hole. The photographer glared at him impatiently, waiting for him to move out of the shot, but Sully wasn't budging. Shifting on the sand, unmindful of priceless antiquities that might be breaking beneath it, he pulled himself a little farther, his head dipping into the shaft.

"Does anyone else see light down there?"

"Of course there's light," Alan snapped. "It's coming from up here, reflecting off the walls of the shaft."

Sully swiveled his head to shoot the guy a look that silenced him. "I'm not an idiot," he growled. "You're the photographer. Aren't you supposed to know a thing or two about light sources and angles? Get down here and have a look at this."

The fight looming between Welch and Melissa had been short-circuited. Drake glanced once into the worship chamber, wondering what was taking Guillermo so long with the ladder and then realizing that the tunnels would be hard for him to navigate—especially with any speed—carrying a stepladder under his arm.

They all watched Alan set his camera aside and move gingerly into place beside Sully.

"This shouldn't be happening," Melissa said. "Their weight on the sand could—"

"I know," Welch said. When she glanced at him, he reached out a hand to touch her arm, his eyes pleading for understanding. "I *know*, Melissa. But there are forces at work here that you're not aware of yet."

"What forces?" she asked. "Talk to me, Ian. We're throwing protocol all to hell."

"Melissa," Alan said, looking up from the shaft. "He's right. There *is* another light source."

"How can that be?" she asked. "The only light sources possible down here are our lights and the sky, and you can be damn sure it's not sunlight or we'd have found that point of entry already."

Alan stood up, brushing off his pants. Sully stood as well but didn't bother.

"It's your light," Sully said, and he pointed into the worship chamber. "The angle's from in there."

"There must be another shaft," Jada said.

"Spread out," Sully barked, and no one argued about who was in charge.

All six of them worked their way through the worship chamber, running their hands over the walls and floor. In less than a minute, Jada called out.

"Here! I think I've found it."

Drake turned to see her kneeling in front of the altar. A sliver of a gap existed between the base of the altar and the floor. He spun and saw the lights hung from the wall behind him and nodded to himself.

"Everywhere else there's either a tighter seal or some kind of mortar," Jada said, glancing up at Welch. "But it looks like the altar is just resting here."

Melissa crouched on the other side, and they all heard her swear under her breath. "There are scrapes on the stone here." She rose quickly and glanced around, argument forgotten. "Keep looking. There's got to be a trigger."

"You think there's a shaft under the altar?" Sully growled.

Welch grinned. "Don't you?"

"I love the ancient Egyptians," Drake muttered to Jada as he joined her, the two of them running their hands all over the wall. "Sneaky bastards."

Long minutes passed during which the air in the worship chamber seemed to become thinner and dustier, and the rock and sand over their heads closed in, growing heavier, until Drake thought the whole thing might come crashing down on top of them if something didn't break the silence and the renewed tension of their search. Alan and Melissa had no idea what the hurry might be, but they felt the urgency and acted accordingly. Melissa apparently had decided that since Welch was technically her boss, she would let *his* boss worry about breaches in protocol. Drake thought it had a lot to do with her own sense of discovery. The urge to see what was beneath their feet was powerful.

"Come on," Jada whispered.

She turned and stared at the altar, causing Drake to do the same thing.

"What?" he asked.

"There's got to be some clue. Something Daedalus put in so that anyone coming from one of the other labyrinths to this one could find the trigger for whatever mechanism moves the altar."

Welch froze. He hurried to the altar and put his hand on the symbol in its center—the etching of three interlocking octagons within three circles.

"I've seen this somewhere else here. I'm sure of it." He turned to Jada. "If there's any symbol here that hints at Daedalus's presence, his design, it's this. The rest is all Egyptian, but this is clearly meant to represent his three labyrinths."

"I feel like I've seen that, too," Alan said.

"Look around," Sully rasped. "And be quick about it."

They stopped testing every stone in the room and started examining the images and symbols instead. Drake watched them, frowning, certain that if the symbol had been in this room, they would have noticed it in their search just now. He stepped outside the worship chamber and studied the door frame and lintel and saw nothing like the triple-octagon symbol. A thought occurred to him, and he reentered but passed through and into the antechamber.

It took him only seconds to locate the symbol, carved into the bottommost stone in the exposed corner of the room. Drake used the toe of his boot to put pressure on it and frowned when nothing happened. He tried again, pushing harder, hands braced on the wall. Frustrated, he dropped to his knees and began to feel around the edges, and he felt it give a little on one side.

The stone hadn't been built to slide inward. The architect had installed it to *turn*.

He pushed hard on the left side of the stone, and it shifted, turning clockwise. The stones on either side had been carved at sharp angles to allow for the freedom of movement of this keystone. Drake rotated it a quarter turn until it clicked into place again, this face of the stone carved with the same symbol.

A heavy, grinding thump resonated through the chamber. He felt it in the stones under his knees.

"That's it!" he heard Melissa say. "Who did that?"

"Nate?" Sully called.

Drake peered around into the worship chamber. "I think I found it."

"Damn right you found it," Jada said.

They were all gathering around the altar, and Drake joined them. The entire altar, base and all, had shifted two inches toward the rear wall of the chamber, away from the door. The scrapes on the floor had been from the base dragging across it, though obviously some kind of stone wheel mechanism was in place for the altar to roll on.

The gap had widened, only darkness visible within. Alan knelt down and put his hand in front of the opening, then looked up at Welch in surprise.

"There's a draft," he said, glancing at the door. "The air coming from outside—it's slipping right through here."

"What does that mean?" Jada asked.

"Means there's air circulation," Sully said. "If it's going in here, it's gotta be going out somewhere down there. Whatever this is, it's not just a room. It *goes* somewhere."

"Come on," Drake said, putting his hands on the altar and getting ready to push.

Welch and Melissa joined him, but there wasn't room for them all to push. They had to be careful. If there was a shaft underneath the altar, none of them wanted to tumble into it. But when they pushed, the altar would give only a little.

"It's stuck on something," Melissa said.

"Sully, come on," Drake said.

He joined them, and the four of them tried again. Drake pushed, low to the ground, putting all his weight into it. He felt his muscles strain with the effort.

"Come on," Sully grumbled. "It feels like it's giving a little."

"Something's blocking—" Alan began.

With a grinding snap, the altar began to shift. The four of them pushed, keeping to the sides as they uncovered the darkness below. The rumble and scrape of its movement echoed through the chamber, and then it was open.

They stood around the edges of the hole. Melissa shone her worklight downward, and Drake jerked back in surprise at the sight of the skeleton that lay on the granite stairs.

"This is incredible," Melissa said, her voice hushed. "Alan, get your camera."

Welch descended the first step, examining the skeleton and the way its arms were extended, lying on the upper stairs. The fingers of both hands were broken off, the small bones missing. Welch took out a small but powerful flashlight and studied them closer.

"Fresh breaks," he said, frowning. He sighed, then glanced up at Sully. "This is what was in the way. This poor guy had his fingers stuck. We just broke them off."

"What, he got caught like that?" Jada asked.

"More likely trapped down there," Drake said. "He died trying to dig his way out or get a grip on the altar base to try to move it aside."

Jada looked at Alan. "But you felt air moving past. Sully said it meant another way out."

"Another way for air to get out," Sully said, stroking his mustache thoughtfully as he studied the bones on the stairs. "Not for this guy, apparently."

Melissa stared at him. "Sully? I thought your name was—"

"Nickname," Sully said, brushing her off as he stepped nearer the secret stairwell. "Nate, what do you think? This guy looks bigger than the typical Egyptian to me."

Drake nodded. "I was thinking the same thing. For the standards of the time, he was huge. I've never seen a sarcophagus big enough to fit him."

Welch ran his flashlight over the bones. "Nor have I. And there's something more. His skull is—misshapen."

"Like, *The Elephant Man* misshapen?" Jada asked as they all crowded closer to the top of the hidden stairs, trying to see past the crouched Dr. Welch.

"I'm no biologist," Welch said, shifting aside to give them all a better look. "But something like that, yes."

The skull seemed inordinately large, with a jutting jawbone and several raised areas that looked rough and pitted.

"This guy was a monster," Drake said. "Look at the size of him."

The second the words were out of his mouth, he glanced at Sully.

"Wait a second," Drake went on. "Are you all thinking what I'm thinking?"

"If you're thinking this is the Minotaur, then yeah," Alan said.

"Where are the horns?" Jada asked. "He could just have been big and ugly. Besides, we don't even know it was a man. It could have been the Mistress of the Labyrinth."

"Maybe," Welch said slowly. "Maybe."

But the weirdness of the skeleton lingered, and Drake knew they were all curious enough to ponder it for a while.

"We don't have time for this," he said.

"What?" Melissa snapped, incredulous. "You don't have time for what might turn out to be evidence of the existence of a man who might have been the historical antecedent of the Minotaur legend?"

Drake shrugged. "Sorry, but no."

"He's right," Welch said. Standing, he began to pick his way down the stairs, careful not to disturb the skeleton on his way down. "We've wasted too much time already. We're being stupid."

"Wasted?" Melissa asked, and now she laughed in disbelief.

At that moment, they heard shuffling out in the tunnel, a few bumps and thuds, and then Guillermo came carefully around the corner and stood at the entrance to the worship chamber, the ladder under his arm. He looked sweaty and pale from the effort.

"Got it," he said.

Drake waved him off. "Yeah, thanks. We're all set."

Guillermo saw the open stairwell and slumped against the door frame. "Seriously?" he said to no one in particular. "Someone couldn't have come to tell me?"

"We've been a little busy," Alan said, snapping photos of the skeleton and the open stairwell.

"Holy crap," Guillermo muttered, coming into the chamber and staring at the bones.

"I know, right?" Alan agreed.

Drake had spotted a rack of industrial flashlights like the one in Melissa's hand when they had first entered. Now he snapped a couple off the rack and tossed them to Sully and Jada, then took a third for himself. Melissa and Alan stared at him, but neither made a move to stop him, perhaps because it was so clear that he had Welch's blessing.

He started down the stairs after Welch, and Sully and Jada followed, all of them treading very carefully.

"Ian, please, you have to stop," Melissa pleaded. "If you do this, I'm not going to be able to cover for you."

"Trust me," Welch called back up to her. "You're better off. Just stay up there. I'm sure Hilary will be along shortly."

Drake cast a glance over his shoulder and saw Melissa pacing, tugging at a lock of her coppery hair. She wanted so badly to be with them, to see what secrets might lie below, but she knew that if she went any farther, her job might be forfeit. She started for the stairs.

"Melissa," Guillermo said.

"Shut up!" she snapped at him.

But it stopped her. She cursed loudly, first in general and then down into the darkness at Welch. By then, Drake couldn't see her anymore and had lost interest. The labyrinth's secrets awaited.

12

At the bottom of the hidden stairs was a corridor. Their flash-lights threw ghost shadows along its length. Every twenty feet or so there seemed to be another doorway, and for a moment Drake was reminded of the optical illusion created by standing between mirrors. With one in front and one behind, the reflections seemed to go on forever in a diminishing hallway of gleaming frames. This corridor did not go on forever. It ended in a darkness that beckoned them onward, as if hungry for light.

The silence troubled Drake the most. They were underground, in a place that had been a secret even in the age in which it had been occupied. The dry, cool air seemed thick with ominous por-tent. If he had been a more superstitious man, he might have said it felt as if it had been waiting for discovery, as if—after so many years—it finally had exhaled. But superstitious or not, he wouldn't have said the words out loud. *Unless you'd had too much tequila*, he thought. *Tequila makes you say stupid things.*

He comforted himself with the knowledge that tequila could make almost anybody say stupid things.

"Spooky as hell down here," Jada whispered.

Sully chomped on a fresh cigar. When he'd smoked the stub of the other one—or lost it—Drake had no idea. But Sully didn't light up—not down here. They were surrounded by stone, but there was no telling what they might encounter. Drake figured he didn't want to drop burning ashes on ancient papyrus or the bandages of a mummy.

"How much time do you think we have?" Drake asked Welch. "If your boss gave Henriksen the full tour, I mean?"

"Twenty minutes," Welch said. "Thirty if we're lucky."

Barely time to get back up the stairs and through the labyrinth to the breach in the wall. No one addressed the renewed urgency, but they hurried a bit faster along the corridor. The slight draft Jada had noticed before persisted. It might be no bigger than a mouse could fit through, but there was an opening down here.

And "down" was the operative word. The floor slanted downward, and the four of them followed. Flashlight beams danced on the painted walls and the floor and the unadorned ceiling. Drake shone his straight ahead and saw that they were coming to an opening; a moment later, he realized it was some kind of junction.

"How far does this thing go?" Sully asked.

"It could be quite extensive," Welch replied.

"You know how these things work," Drake added. "Whatever they were hiding down here, the Egyptians loved their secret passages and halls."

"So far it's just straight ahead," Jada said. "Not much of a maze."

"Interesting, isn't it?" Welch asked. "Part of the labyrinth and yet not part of the labyrinth."

Unlike a reflection of a reflection, the corridor did not go on forever. They'd followed it for perhaps fifty yards when it opened into a small anteroom that resembled the one above, and they found themselves looking at the entrances to three separate worship chambers. Each had the triple-octagon symbol engraved in the lintel above the doorway, and each had the trio of steps leading down.

"This is different," Drake muttered. "The lady or the tiger— or the other tiger?"

"I don't think we should split up," Welch said quickly.

Jada laughed. "Yeah. Bad idea."

"No need," Sully said, flashing his light into the leftmost doorway. "They're not much bigger than the worship chamber upstairs. Altar. Same layout."

Then he stopped and glanced back at them. "Except there's a door on the other side."

Drake hurried to the central doorway and stood on the

threshold, flashing his light across the small chamber. "Here, too."

He quickly scanned the room with his torch, agreeing with Sully's assessment. The layout was identical to that of the worship chamber upstairs. He figured the dimensions would be the same. But as he let the light linger a moment on the altar, he froze, brows knitting.

"Hey, Sully? Does your room over there have the same paintings, hieroglyphics, and stuff as the chamber upstairs?"

Sully flashed his light at Drake's face. "Yeah, why?"

Drake squinted, putting up a hand to block the brightness as he turned to look at Welch and Jada. "This one has the same altar. An octagon."

"The shape of the labyrinth's design, I suspect. It's a circle, but within the circle, the perimeter of the maze is really an octagon," Welch explained.

"Yeah, great. Daedalus knew his shapes. Call Elmo. What I was saying is that this one doesn't have Egyptian writing." Drake flashed his light into the room and held it on the altar as they all moved to see inside. "It's Greek."

The look on Welch's face was almost comical. He went from surprise to childlike glee in an instant, pushing past Drake and hurrying down the few steps into the worship chamber and flashing his light around in fits and starts.

"This is remarkable," he said, pausing every few seconds to take a closer look at the writing on the wall or the paintings on the base of the altar.

As Jada, Sully, and Drake followed him into the room, Drake saw that it wasn't exactly like the chamber upstairs, after all. There were several shelves cut into the walls, each holding several large jars. Then, of course, there was also the door at the back of the room, a formidable stone block with no visible means of opening it. But Drake felt sure it was genuinely a door, just one that required some kind of trick to open.

"What does this mean?" Jada asked.

Welch nodded to her but didn't answer. Instead, he hurried

from the room and rushed into the chamber Sully had been investigating at first. Twenty seconds passed, and then he rejoined them, standing on the threshold of the central room, a fervent smile on his face.

"The room on the left is devoted to Sobek, as we would expect. But *this* one—this one is dedicated to Dionysus, the Greek god of wine and madness."

Drake focused his light on the jars on one shelf, studying the grape design there. "That doesn't make any sense."

"It makes perfect sense," Jada said, tucking a magenta strand behind her ear and lighting up with a grin. "Daedalus built the labyrinth at Knossos to impress Ariadne, but according to myth, she was the bride of Dionysus."

Sully slipped an arm around her shoulders and favored her with a proud look. "Someone's been paying attention."

" 'Bride' could mean many things," Welch said. "She could simply have been devoted to him, as a priestess, for instance."

"Like the Mistress of the Labyrinth?" Drake suggested.

Welch nodded thoughtfully. "Possibly. But you're all missing the point. The first chamber explicitly refers to Crocodilopolis, and this one to Knossos and the island of Crete."

Drake stared at him, eyebrows shooting up.

Sully chomped on his cigar and growled, "What the hell are you standing there for?"

Welch stood aside as they rushed out of the worship chamber corresponding to the labyrinth at Knossos. Jada led the way down the few steps into the third room, her flashlight beam bouncing around in front of her.

"Greek!" she said, turning to face them as they followed. "This one's in Greek, too."

But as Drake studied the octagonal altar, noticing the triple-octagon symbol in the center, he thought something looked different about the inscriptions on the base. He flashed his light at the walls and at the vases, and his suspicion increased.

"Are you sure—"

"It's Hellenic, without question," Welch said, picking up one of the jars and peering more closely at the writing. "But it isn't any variation on ancient Greek I've ever seen. Doubtless a dialect, but something rare."

He looked over at Sully. "This might be a lost language," he said excitedly.

"That's nice, Ian. Really," Sully said. "I'm sure you and your lost language will be very happy together. But the clock is ticking."

"Can you tell what god the chamber's devoted to?" Drake asked.

"Oh, that's easy enough," Welch said, moving his flashlight beam across the paintings on the walls. Drake spotted a trident. "The third labyrinth was built in worship of Poseidon. Or some aspect of Poseidon native to—wherever this language comes from."

"And?" Jada asked, frustrated. "Any idea where that might be?"

A chill went up the back of Drake's neck, and he felt a shiver. Frowning, he glanced around. Had he heard a whisper?

The four of them moved through the chamber with the flashlights, though Welch concentrated mostly on the jars. Some things required no explanation. There were images on each altar base that showed the same scene as the one upstairs of the Mistress of the Labyrinth, and there were others that depicted the Minotaur. There were labrys, the symbol for a labyrinth, carved into stone and painted on jars. He had noticed in the second chamber that there were paintings clearly showing a throne made of gold and other objects that had been painted that color and might have indicated the presence of treasure. There were similar images here. But the rest of it was unreadable to him.

A shadow moved in his peripheral vision, and he thought he heard the rustle of cloth. He glanced at the entrance to the room and thought the darkness seemed a bit darker than before.

"Did you guys hear something?" Drake asked.

"Just you," Sully said, gnawing the end of his cigar.

Jada glanced at Drake and shook her head. She hadn't heard a thing.

Welch was crouched at a lower shelf, one of the jars—or honey pots, if that was really what they were—in his hand.

"Here we go," he muttered.

Drake and the others turned to stare at him. Welch whispered to himself, translating under his breath and nodding.

He gave no warning before his legs went out from under him and he sat down hard, the jar slipping into his lap, protected from breaking by the loose cotton of his shirt.

"Thera," he said.

"Never heard of—" Sully began, but then his eyes lit up.

"Thera as in Santorini?" Drake asked.

Welch's face had gone slack. Drake thought he'd had too much revelation and epiphany for a single day and his archaeology geek brain might have blown a circuit.

"I've been there," Jada said. "It's beautiful."

Drake agreed. The whitewashed buildings and blue domes, the multicolored boats and shutters, the bells, the ocean, the wine. There was nothing about Santorini he did not love, though he'd been there only once. But he had a feeling Welch wasn't thinking about vacation spots.

"Talk to us, Ian," Drake prodded.

Welch looked up at him. "Daedalus built the third labyrinth on Thera."

"Santorini," Jada said, apparently trying to clarify that they were talking about the same place.

But Welch shook his head. "No."

"The whole thing's an active volcano," Sully said.

"Right," Jada said, snapping her fingers as she recalled. "There are a bunch of little islands that make up the rim. So you're talking Thera before it exploded or whatever?"

Welch smiled. "Oh, yeah."

Drake frowned, not sure what he was getting so excited about. In modern times, Thera was an archipelago, but really the string of islands formed a circle around the deepest spot in the Mediterranean. The islands were all that remained of the much larger Thera as it had been before the massive eruption in—he thought it was the fourteenth century B.C., but it might have been the fifteenth. He didn't remember any lava flowing on Santorini, but he knew that some of the smaller islands in the archipelago had volcanic vents and were still active.

"Minoan civilization collapsed around the same time as the destruction of Thera," Welch said.

Jada threw up her hands in frustration. "Well, that's great. So if the third labyrinth was there, we've lost any clues we might've found in a volcanic eruption thousands of years in the past."

"Maybe and maybe not," Sully said quickly, jabbing at the air with his unlit cigar to emphasize the point. He turned to Welch. "Are you saying what I think you're saying?"

Welch grinned. "I think I am."

"Would the two of you stop talking in riddles!" Drake snapped. "It hurts my head."

Sully arched an eyebrow and shook his head. "Oh, Nate, you're going to kick yourself for not getting this one. You've been to Santorini. There's only one archaeological dig going on there that's of any consequence."

"Yeah," Drake said, shrugging, the beam of his flashlight bouncing on the wall. "Akrotiri."

"Which was a Minoan settlement," Welch said. "One that many modern scholars believe once went under a different name."

Drake heard the strange rustling again but barely noticed. He stared at Welch and Sully and grinned.

"You can't be serious."

"It all fits, Nate," Sully said.

Jada punched Drake in the arm to get his attention. When he shot her an angry look, she hit him again.

"Hit *him*!" Drake said, pointing at Sully.

"Tell me!" she demanded.

Drake gestured at the other two men. "These two—they think this language was lost because all of the people who spoke it were killed in that volcanic eruption. They think the third labyrinth was in Akrotiri, on Thera."

"So?" Jada asked.

Drake smiled. "They're talking about *Atlantis*."

She hit him a third time. "I'm serious. Tell me."

"Ow!" Drake shouted. "I just did."

Jada turned to Sully. "Tell me he's kidding."

"You didn't hear the stories about the dig at Akrotiri when you went to Santorini?" Sully asked.

"I went shopping and to the beach. I flirted with guys and drank too much ouzo and rode bicycles with my friends," she said. "We didn't have the kind of fun time I seem to have with you, Uncle Vic."

"Sarcasm? Now?" Drake asked.

"Seems like it's always time for sarcasm with you," she said.

"Okay. That's mostly true," he replied. "But a lot of people think Akrotiri is what remains of Atlantis—that Atlantis was a branch of Minoan culture—the perfection of it, really. And whether that's true or not, if the third labyrinth was on Thera, the only chance we have of finding any trace of it or any records of it would be in Akrotiri."

Welch gazed at the jar, studying it closely. He spoke without looking up.

"It can't be Akrotiri. They've been excavating there since the sixties and have they found any hint of a labyrinth? I don't think so. If there's any trace of it left, it has to be somewhere else on the caldera."

The caldera—the cauldron—was how the locals referred to the part of the deep circle of water ringed by the islands of Thera.

"So we're going to Santorini," Sully said, wearing a dubious expression, "and we're going to search every crevice in each of those islands for the ruins of a labyrinth that no one—in thousands of years—has stumbled across before?"

Jada gave a small shrug, refusing to be defeated. "No one's ever known what they were looking for."

But Drake had been watching Welch and could see the man's lips moving while he studied the jar.

"You're reading," Drake said.

Welch nodded, a smile stealing across his face. "Yeah." He gestured in the direction of the other chambers. "The room dedicated to Dionysus—the writing in there is Linear B, an ancient syllabic script used primarily by the Mycenaean Greeks. Now that I've had a minute to look at this, it's really not very different. Linear B-2, let's call it."

"So?" Sully asked. "You got a point?"

"Oh, yes," Welch said happily. He lifted the jar as if it were a trophy. "Here's your link. I should've thought of this immediately, but I'm a little overwhelmed today, y' know?"

Jada smiled at him. "We know."

Welch looked grateful. "Anyway, there were texts found in the excavation of the temple at Knossos, written in Linear B, that decreed that all the gods were secondary to something called *qe-ra-si-ja*. Scholars have argued whether or not this was a god or a king or a kingdom. One school of thought translates *qe-ra-si-ja* as Therasia, a settlement on the precataclysm island of Thera."

The archaeologist looked up, inspired. "But Therasia still exists. It's small, and the side facing the caldera is all cliffs. Only a few hundred people live there."

Drake felt an old, familiar excitement building. Whatever perils they had faced, whatever tragedies had led them here, they were on the trail of a secret.

"So we're headed to Therasia," he said.

"I'm coming with you," Welch said quickly. "After Melissa's done telling Hilary what went on today, I'll be fired anyway."

"First we have to get out of here without Henriksen's goons killing us," Sully said.

Jada scoffed. "He's not going to shoot you with the expedition staff and workers around as witnesses. Rich people can get away with almost anything, pay off anyone, but it'd be pretty damn hard to cover up killing the entire crew up there."

"I hope you're right," Sully said. "Still, we need to go."

Welch held the jar he'd taken from the shelf as he stood. "All right. But I'm taking this with us. I want to have a closer look, and if we don't have time now—"

"Where's the gold?" Drake asked suddenly.

They all looked at him.

"The gold," Drake went on. "Midas or Minos or whoever

was supposed to be an alchemist, right? Daedalus paid the workers in gold. The cult of Sobek put gold crests on crocodiles."

"We found some of those already," Welch said.

"Yeah, okay," Drake replied. "But if the mistress took the offering of honey from the worshippers and fed it to the Minotaur
and the Minotaur was here to protect the gold, then where is the
gold?"

"Gone, apparently," Welch said thoughtfully.

"From here," Jada said. "But if Daedalus and his people
moved the gold from here—maybe from all three of these
chambers—the logical place for them to have moved it is to one
of the other labyrinths. Maybe they moved it around to keep it
safe. It could have been on Thera, maybe destroyed in the eruption."

Drake nodded. "Maybe. Or maybe it's in the fourth labyrinth."

"Look around you," Welch said, gesturing at the walls and
the altar. "Do you see any reference to a fourth?"

"I can't read this," Drake replied. "And no one alive is exactly fluent in ancient Atlantean."

"I told you, it's a variation on Linear B," Welch said. "I could
muddle my way through a basic translation, but so far I haven't
seen any indication of a fourth labyrinth. And the three-labyrinth
symbol is everywhere."

"So the fourth one came later," Drake said. "Companies
change their logos all the time. Daedalus didn't get a chance to
do the rebranding he needed down here before he died. The
point is, Jada's father thought there was a fourth one, and somebody killed him because he was investigating the possibility.
That's evidence right there, as far as I'm concerned."

Welch cradled the jar against his chest, looking like he was in
the mood to argue. Not too bright, Drake thought, considering
how urgent it was that they get out of there.

When Sully drew his gun, whatever Welch had been about to
say was forgotten.

"Nate. Did you say you heard something?" Sully asked, the
question almost a snarl around the cigar clamped in his teeth.

Drake reached for his gun, turning to face the entrance to the Thera worship chamber. "I did, yeah."

Both weapons were trained on the doorway. Drake narrowed his eyes and peered at the darkness out in the antechamber. Jada looked at them in confusion and then reluctantly pulled out her pistol. Welch wore a worried expression but didn't ask them about the guns, smart enough not to want to tip off whoever might be out there listening to their conversation. Drake figured if it was Henriksen or the dig director, Hilary Russo, they would have been interrupted already.

Drake padded quietly toward the door, gun at the ready. Sully used his flashlight to wave Welch back. The archaeologist shuffled backward past the altar, looking faintly ridiculous with his unruly hair and glasses.

Drake wondered if he held the vase because of its value or for comfort, the way a toddler clutches a stuffed animal.

That rustle of cloth came again. Drake frowned, all his attention on the open doorway now. He and Sully moved in, one on either side of the three stairs that led up into the darkened antechamber. They had guns in one hand and flashlights in the other, trying to figure out if there was anything for them to shoot at or if they had been spooked by nothing. They kept their flashlights aimed away from the opening, hoping that whoever lurked out there would show themselves. Jada hung back, just in front of the altar, her gun and flashlight both pointed at the floor.

Drake glanced at her, on the verge of issuing a snarky remark about how useless it would be to shoot a bullet into the floor. But when he glanced back at the doorway, he caught the shadows moving, one separating from the others, and whipped his flashlight beam up to spotlight the open doorway.

Something dashed by. Someone. No question now. They weren't alone.

"Sully," Drake said.

"Yeah."

More motion, deeper into the antechamber, shadows within shadows. Drake whipped his flashlight beam up, illuminating the man dashing across the opening so quietly that he might have been a ghost. Only he *wasn't* a ghost; they had seen him before. He was one of the killers who had stopped Jada from being abducted and killed by the hit squad Henriksen had sent to do it. Hooded and veiled, the man froze, glancing into the worship chamber at them.

They told us to go home, Drake had time to think.

The assassin narrowed his eyes and then leaped into the room, drawing a short curved blade as he raced at Sully. Drake and Sully fired at the same time. Though Drake's bullet missed, Sully's shot took the assassin in the chest, and he staggered backward, wheeling toward the steps. For a second, Drake thought he would run out of there as fast as he'd jumped in, but then the wounded, bleeding man spun and lifted his blade, about to hurl it at Drake.

Jada shot the assassin twice, once in the thigh and once in the abdomen. The blade whickered out of his hand with the speed of a boomerang, but she'd ruined his aim and the curved dagger clanged off the altar inches from her. He fell on his back, rolled, and began to drag himself out of the worship chamber.

"Don't let him get out!" Sully barked.

"*Him*? I'm worried about us getting out," Drake said.

"Where did he come from?" Jada asked.

Other rustling noises came from the anteroom, and Drake swore loudly, pressing himself against the wall beside the stairs.

"There are others!" he said. "*Of course* there are others!" It was their luck.

A scraping noise came from behind him. For a second he thought Jada was the cause, but then his mind sorted out the distance and the weight of stone on stone and realized the sound came from farther back. He glanced over his shoulder and saw that Welch's flashlight had died. In the gloom at the back of the chamber he saw shadows that did not belong, then heard the scuffle of a struggle. He swung his flashlight beam over in time to see another of the hooded assassins dragging Ian Welch through the partially open stone door at the rear of the room.

The archaeologist's hands twitched and dropped the jar, which shattered on impact.

"Welch!" Drake shouted, turning to Sully. "They're getting in through the other door!"

Jada rushed toward the stone door, beating Drake there. He wanted to tell her to back off, afraid they'd drag her in as well, but she wouldn't have listened and he didn't have time to get the words out before she was already there. She aimed her flashlight and gun together, not firing for fear of hitting Welch, and started to take a step through the gap in the door.

"Dr. Welch!" Jada called. "Ian!"

A hooded figure rushed from the darkness and grappled with her, pushing her gun away, trying to twist it from her grasp. Drake shot him in the shoulder. The attacker spun, blood spraying from the wound, and staggered back against the wall. In the shadows where Welch had vanished, others were moving. Welch was gone—maybe dead—and they had to get the hell out of the labyrinth before they joined him.

"Come on!" Drake shouted. "Jada, let's go!"

They bolted, racing around the altar on either side and then toward Sully and the three steps to the exit together. Sully had his back to the wall on the left, but when he saw them coming, he led the charge, rushing up the stairs into the antechamber.

Drake heard the first shot but didn't see it. Then he and Jada were out of the Thera worship chamber. The assassin they'd shot lay on the floor of the anteroom, bleeding but alive, but he was the least of their concerns. Two others were in the anteroom, and Drake saw motion off to his right. Several other hooded men were emerging from the darkness of the other doors.

"Look, if you want us to go home that bad, we'll go home!" he shouted, swinging his aim over to cover them.

Loud footfalls came echoing along the tunnel through which Drake and his companions had arrived. A glance showed flashlight beams bouncing off the walls. They were about to have even more company.

A woman's voice shouted in Italian and then in English.

"Who's there? Ian, what the hell is going on down here?" she called angrily.

Hilary Russo, Drake thought. But her deputy, Welch, wasn't

going to answer. He was a captive of those hooded men or had become just another part of the labyrinth's history, another thing that needed to be excavated from this place.

There were a lot of voices and a lot of footfalls, and Drake had the idea that at least a dozen people were headed their way. Maybe that was more people than the assassins were ready to kill at the moment or more people than they could risk letting live after having seen them down there in the secret corridors under the labyrinth. Drake and Sully and Jada weren't even supposed to be there. Who would believe them?

One of the hooded men Sully and Jada were aiming at lunged, and Sully shot him.

"Go!" Sully shouted, and started to run.

Trust saved Drake. He couldn't see if the way was open, couldn't tell if Sully had done any real damage to the guy he'd shot or if they had the second or two they needed to get clear, but he and Sully had been friends since Drake was a kid. They might not have always gotten along and sometimes they frustrated the hell out of each other, but Sully had been his mentor for almost twenty years. In a moment like this, they had to trust each other or they'd both have been killed years ago.

Jada rushed into the tunnel, Drake right on her heels. He flashed his light ahead of them with his left hand even as he covered the assassins coming from the Knossos and Sobek chambers with the other, arms spread wide.

He could hear Sully to his left, muttering, "Go, go, go." A swift glance showed him that the one Sully had shot had fallen but still lived, and Sully had his gun aimed at the face of the other assassin, who gazed back coolly in the semidarkness of the anteroom. The only light remaining in that junction room came from Sully's flashlight, and Drake wondered how the assassins could see so well in the dark.

It occurred to him that these were not ordinary men. He thought of the swiftness with which they killed Jada's would-be abductors in the parking lot the night before and realized that the assassins were no longer trying very hard. As he glanced back and saw Sully racing after him into the tunnel—Sully fired a bullet into the darkness as if for punctuation—he understood that they were not following. It might have been the number of people or the possibility of defeat that made them vanish back into the secret heart of the labyrinth, but whatever their reason, Drake thought they would be all right now. They would be safe, for the moment at least.

The brunette woman running toward them had to be Hilary Russo.

"Sully, gun," Drake murmured, noticing that Jada already had put hers away as she saw the people running toward them, waving flashlights in their faces.

"Who are you people?" Hilary, the dig's chief archaeologist, demanded. "Was that gunfire?"

Jada collapsed into her arms and hugged her tightly, then pushed her back and stared at her. The look on Hilary's face could only be shock.

"There are—there are people back there!" Jada said, glancing frantically from Hilary to the dark length of tunnel behind them and back.

"That's not possible! Where's Ian Welch?" Hilary demanded.

Drake and Sully surveyed the others. Past the brightness of the flashlights it was difficult to make out faces, but he was sure he'd caught a glimpse of Olivia Hzujak's hair, and the tall blond silhouette had to be Henriksen. But there was no cameraman, and most of the people seemed to be workers from the dig.

"He was with them," Guillermo said, stepping forward. "He came down here with them." He pointed. "She's supposedly Luka Hzujak's daughter."

Hilary glanced behind her, and now it was clear who she was looking at. "What about it, Mrs. Hzujak? Is this your step-daughter?"

"Olivia!" Jada cried, and rushed to her stepmother's embrace. She hugged the older woman tightly, and the beautiful mask of concern Olivia wore cracked with surprise.

That was when Drake realized he'd underestimated Jada. He had thought that she had snapped, that panic and hysteria were setting in. But the whole thing was an act. The girl was hustling them all. He wanted to kiss her. If Sully wouldn't have frowned on it, he might have. Though at this point it would have been more like kissing his sister.

"Jada, are you all right?" Olivia asked, and if she was feigning concern, her acting skills were as good as her stepdaughter's. Olivia pushed her back and stared at her face and shirt, which were dappled red from when Drake had shot her attacker. "Whose blood is that?"

"Where is Ian?" Hilary demanded. "Who was shooting?" She glared at Sully and Drake. "And who are you two? Not from the damned Smithsonian, I know that much!"

"Dr. Russo," Drake said, hoping for profound sincerity even as he tried to remember the false name he'd been using. "I'm Nathan Merrill. We're friends of Jada's, trying to help her figure out if there's any connection between her father's recent trip to Egypt and his murder."

"Murder? Oh, my God!" Hilary said, and she snapped an incredulous glance at Olivia, wondering why she hadn't been told of this before.

"You've got three worship chambers at the end of this corridor," Sully said. "There are stone doors on the other side of each. When we found the secret passage, Dr. Welch let us investigate it with him, but we weren't alone down here. There were other people here."

"That's impossible!" a voice piped up from the back.

Sheepish but worried now, ginger-haired Melissa moved forward, pushing past the towering blond statue that was Tyr Henriksen. They were clustered together now, and his face was illuminated. He stared at Drake with ice blue eyes, but he said nothing. If he wanted Jada, Sully, and Drake dead, he'd have to kill everyone else there as well and then everyone up top. He might be a vicious son of a bitch, but he still had an international corporation to run, and covering up a mass murder could have gotten messy—but he sure looked like he wanted to shed some blood.

"No one else went down," Melissa said. "I was by the entrance the whole time."

"There's gotta be another way in, then," Sully said. "Those doors in the worship chambers—people came out of them and attacked us. They've taken Dr. Welch."

Hilary Russo stared at him in obvious disbelief. "That's a lie."

"I'm sorry, but it's not," Drake said. "They dragged him through one of the doors, and—"

But she wasn't listening anymore. Hilary rushed along the corridor, picking up speed, with Guillermo and a couple of others behind her. Drake wished they could stay and help look for Ian Welch, but if the man was there to be found, his colleagues would find him. Drake, Sully, and Jada needed to get the hell out of Crocodilopolis before things got even messier for them, at which point they would not be allowed to leave. Drake didn't relish the idea of spending time in an Egyptian prison.

"We need to get Jada some air," Sully said to Olivia. "You understand."

Olivia seemed to be practically vibrating with indecision. She glanced at Henriksen, who had his hands clenched into fists. Melissa and a couple of other dig employees had stayed with them, and Drake thought it was touch and go for a moment as to whether he might start breaking people's necks with his massive hands.

"Of course," Olivia said, but her eyes were on Henriksen, keeping him in check with her pleading gaze. "I'll come up with you."

"No," Henriksen snapped, the first time they'd heard him speak in his crisp, deep voice. "I need you here."

Olivia hesitated. Drake studied her, hating that he couldn't read her. Was she really a victim in Henriksen's thrall, or was she in on the whole thing and simply trying to prevent him from doing anything stupid? Did she care about Jada at all or care that her husband had been murdered? Had she helped murder him?

"Fine," Olivia said. She gave Jada a little push. "See you outside. Don't go far."

"Yeah," Drake said, glancing at Henriksen. "We'll stick close."

Drake held Henriksen's icy stare as he backed away, cognizant of the weight of the gun he'd tucked into the back of his waistband and hoping he didn't have to use it in such close quarters.

"What did you find?" Melissa asked as they walked past her. "What's down there?"

Drake looked at her, then at Henriksen, wanting the bastard to know that they had beaten him to it and were that much closer to solving the mystery he'd killed Luka Hzujak to keep from talking about.

"Secrets," he said, smiling at Henriksen. "Stuff that's going to blow your mind. Things you never would have expected."

Henriksen lifted his chin, sneering. "Some secrets can be dangerous. Sometimes it's safer for them to remain secret. Men can become very wealthy keeping secrets."

Drake smirked. Was the guy trying to buy him? Not that he was offended by the idea of someone trying to pay him to shut up and go away. But Henriksen was the kind of arrogant bastard who thought he was king of the world. He'd had people murdered, including Jada's father, because he thought he was too special to have to follow rules or share his discoveries with the world.

Sully took Jada's hand and led her along the corridor, headed for the stairs that went up into the labyrinth. Drake hung back a moment, still locking eyes with Henriksen. Then he glanced at Melissa and smiled.

"Nothing stays a secret forever."

He didn't want to turn his back on Henriksen, but he figured if the guy was going to paint the walls with his blood, he'd have done it already. Still, it was all he could do not to run for the stairs, knowing those icy, soulless eyes were behind him, wanting him dead. *Not that I'm afraid, of course*, he thought. *I'm just also not stupid.*

Fifteen minutes later they were outside.

Four minutes after that, they were in the Volvo wagon, racing across the desert, wondering how long it would take the authorities to get out to the dig once someone radioed them.

Three hours later they were on a boat racing north on the Nile, headed for Port Said in hopes of finding a ship's captain willing to run them northwest across the Mediterranean to Santorini. There would be ferry service, but a ferry would have other stops and might take a couple of days to get them there, and they didn't have a moment to spare. They had a head start on Henriksen, but that wasn't likely to last very long. Henriksen had more money than God, and he had the luxury of traveling under his real name, not a false identity that might not hold up under real scrutiny.

They did have a few things in their favor, however. Welch had given them their destination before he'd been abducted and maybe killed—more blood spilled over this secret—and since Hilary and her team didn't know what Henriksen was looking for, they would come to their revelations more slowly. Also, Hilary and her staff would be occupied with the police, trying to figure out who had taken Welch and trying to get him back.

They would beat Henriksen to the third labyrinth, Drake decided. They had to.

As for Welch's abduction, Drake, Jada, and Sully avoided that subject as much as possible, partly because they knew the police would assume they had something to do with it. Fleeing the scene hadn't helped their case, but there had been no other choice. Now they were armed fugitives and suspected kidnappers.

Somewhere along the way, Drake figured, he had taken a wrong turn. He promised himself that if he survived this mess, he was going to find another line of work. Something quieter and safer, like fighting fires or sticking his head in a lion's mouth after hitting it with a whip. Something nice and quiet. None of the perils of racing around the world with Victor Sullivan. If they could just get to Santorini and off the island again without anyone else dying, he would consider himself lucky.

But when it came to his adventures with Sully, he couldn't fool himself for long. Their luck rarely turned out to be the good kind.

13

Santorini was unlike any other place in the world. The towns overlooking the caldera were built into the caves and folds of the cliffs left behind when the volcano at the heart of ancient Thera exploded. The blue domes of the larger buildings matched the blue of the swimming pools that dotted the cliff towns and the water of the caldera. Drake reckoned there must have been tens of thousands of stairs just in the village of Oia alone, all of them curving around the inner wall of an island that was part of the rim of a sleeping volcano. Some of the beaches had black sand— volcanic sand—and the beauty of the caldera somehow allowed the people to tell themselves that the sea would never erupt with lava and flame, killing them all.

But it might. Drake knew that, and though Santorini had a beauty and serenity greater than almost anywhere else on the planet, it was this strange peace with potentially imminent destruction that fascinated him most.

It was Sunday night, and the warmth of the day still lingered though the sun had gone down. Drake and Jada walked side by side along the alleys and stairways overlooking the caldera, surrounded by bars and restaurants and shops. Many of the shops were closed on a Sunday night in October, but some remained open, and they wandered and window-shopped, sometimes talking about their lives and sometimes in companionable silence.

They had managed a great deal in just over twenty-four hours. In Port Said they had found a marina where captains offered their boats for day trips. It was an expensive proposition and even more costly when they explained that they wanted the captain to take them to Santorini but didn't plan on making the return trip. The weathered Egyptian captain made noises about the laws they were asking him to break but was happy enough to break them when money had changed hands.

They had slept fairly comfortably on board the ship, all things considered, and arrived at Santorini in midafternoon on Sunday. It had been a stroke of genius—or luck, Drake allowed—that they had checked out of the Auberge du Lac and brought their duffels with them, guns and ammunition stuffed in among their clean and dirty clothes. They had left the Volvo abandoned in Port Said, but once they took the cable car up from the Santorini docks, getting a taxi was easy enough. Hungry as they were, they had shopped first. October nights could get chilly on the islands, so Sully and Drake each picked up sweaters, and Jada purchased a stylish leather jacket.

Or, rather, Drake purchased them all, as well as a couple of changes of clothes for each of them. He felt bad about using the fake credit card he'd gotten on the way to Montreal, but he couldn't exactly use his own, and he had to conserve the significant amount of cash he was still carrying from his adventure in Ecuador. He promised himself that when this was all over, he'd pay the store back; he'd even kept the receipt. Drake might have broken the law on a fairly regular basis—that came with the territory in his line of work—but he drew the line at ripping people off.

They'd gone into the first decent hotel they'd found in the village of Oia, pretended not to be twitchy about the exorbitant prices, and booked a suite so they could all be locked up behind the same door that night. In the summer they would never have found a vacancy so easily, but in October rooms weren't in such high demand.

Dinner had followed, and now Sully was back at the hotel, trying to figure out the best way to get them to Therasia in the morning. Even if they paid someone to take them over tonight, searching for ancient mysteries tended to be easier when the sun was shining. In the dark, Drake figured they'd just walk off a cliff and that would be the end of the whole business.

Now he and Jada were drifting into one of their comfortable

silences again. They were on the downhill side of a rise in the cliffside village, on a path among the shops and bars and eateries. There were stretches of path and then a few steps and another longer walk and a few more steps, which was as close to flat as this part of the island got. The smell of burning pipe tobacco reached them, and Jada inhaled and smiled.

"You like that smell?" Drake asked.

She shrugged. "When I was little, my dad smoked a pipe."

"His doctor made him give it up?"

"No. When I got to high school, I told him it was pretentious and embarrassed me," she said, a melancholy smile on her face. "He gave it up for me. This thing that gave him pleasure and some kind of peace of mind, and I—"

She couldn't finish the sentence, her voice quavering. Her eyes filled with tears, but Jada seemed resolutely against shedding them. A moment later she brushed at her eyes, but her cheeks were dry.

"What happened to your parents?" she asked. "Uncle Vic would never tell me."

"You were asking about me?" Drake said, teasing her.

"I was curious," she admitted. "But don't flatter yourself."

Drake smiled, but after a moment he looked down at the homes and hotels and shops on the cliff beneath them and at the surf smashing the rocks on the rim of the caldera farther below.

"Okay. Sorry," she said. "I didn't know it was a taboo subject."

"It isn't really," Drake replied, turning to look at her. "Just something I don't enjoy talking about. You know what a ronin is?"

"Something Japanese, right?"

"A masterless samurai," he said. "One who has left his master's house and cut off all connections to his past, gone into the world, and made his own path. I know it sounds ridiculously geeky and self-important—"

"Actually, it sounds like something that takes a lot of courage. Having no one."

"Sully was around when I needed someone there," Drake

said, voice low. He wasn't used to opening up, to letting the
court jester that seemed to rule his tongue half the time go silent.

"He's always been like that," Jada agreed. "He plays it like
he's a rogue, like he doesn't care. He vanishes for months at a
time, makes out like he's only out for himself, pretends that the
money is his top priority—and maybe most of the time it is. But
my dad used to say that with his back against the wall, when it
counts, there wasn't anybody he'd rather have in his corner than
Victor Sullivan."

"Yeah," Drake agreed, and they walked on a couple of minutes longer before he spoke again. "Listen, I wish none of this
had ever happened, but if it had to happen, I'm glad I'm here
with you both. You've got me in your corner, too."

"I know," she said. "And it's appreciated."

They fell silent again, but this time the quiet between them
had a breathless quality, as if each of them feared the next words
that might be spoken. A burst of song, Greek voices raised in
alcohol-fueled camaraderie, caught on the breeze and swept by
them. It came from the nearest bar and was followed by a round
of laughter. A man jogged by, intent on the effort of his athletic
self-discipline. Two stylishly dressed young women came up the
walkway, exuding sexy confidence. But for those few seconds,
Drake and Jada couldn't take their eyes off each other.

Blinking, taking a quick breath, Jada forced a nervous smile.
"It's beautiful here. Romantic. Gives you all kinds of crazy
thoughts."

Drake felt grateful. If she'd kissed him, he might have kissed
her back, and that wasn't the way any of this was meant to go.
For just a moment, the dynamic between them had been on the
verge of drastic changes. He smiled, waiting a few seconds before speaking, wanting to be certain the moment truly had
passed them by.

"I haven't had a lot of luck in that department," Drake said.

"Yeah. Me, either. Maybe I should come back here afterward,
meet some handsome fisherman, and open a dress shop."

Drake laughed. "You've seen too many movies."

When Jada punched him in the arm, back to her usual abuse,

he knew that the moment was officially over. They were allies. In a strange way, they were almost siblings. And nothing else. Drake knew that that was for the best, that anything else would be far too complicated, but he knew he would always be curious about the road not traveled. It wouldn't be the first time he'd felt that way in his life, and he knew it wouldn't be the last.

"Look," she said, shifting her weight from one foot to the other, pushing magenta bangs away from her eyes as she huddled into the leather jacket as if the night was colder than it felt. "There's something we've been avoiding talking about, and I don't think we can go any further without at least addressing it."

Aw, no, Drake thought. *We had the perfect moment, the silent acknowledgment. Talking about it is only going to lead to crippling awkwardness and me babbling like a fool.*

"The hooded guys," Jada went on.

Drake arched an eyebrow, his mind shifting gears. "Yeah. Of course. Them."

"I mean, yeah, we talked about them in the sense of 'those guys are creepy, who the hell are they and why are they trying to kill us and why did they try to warn us to go home before they tried to kill us . . .' And I'm babbling."

"Yes." Drake leaned against the railing over the cliff. "Yes, you are."

Jada smiled. He thought she might punch him again, but apparently she was too tired from all the other times she had punched him.

"We haven't really talked about what I think is the big question."

"Which is?"

"Those doors in the labyrinth of Sobek," Jada said. "I don't know about you, but I've kind of been avoiding it because I'm trying not to think about Welch being taken. His sister's boyfriend was murdered because he tried to help my father solve this puzzle, and now Ian's missing, maybe dead, because he did the same for us. It's weighing on me. I can't help feeling responsible."

Drake nodded grimly. "It goes away, that feeling. Not as

quick as you'd like, but it does. The thing to remember is that we didn't force him to help us. He knew there was danger, and he wanted to help anyway. That won't make you feel less guilty, but it's a good thing to remind yourself that you can't control other people. Not the ones who want to help you and not the ones who want to kill you."

"They dragged him through the door at the back of that worship chamber. And the rest of the hooded guys had to have come through the sealed doors in the other rooms. Even if we assume there's a simple way to open those—triggers, something to make them swing easily, that we just hadn't found yet—how did they get down there?"

"They could've gone down the night before and been waiting for us," Drake said. "They told us to go home, but they figured either we were going to find those rooms or Henriksen would."

"Uh-uh, no," Jada said, shaking her head. "The skeleton, the Minotaur or whatever—his fingers broke off when we slid the altar back. If anyone else had gone down that way before us, that would've happened *then*, not now."

Drake pondered that, running a finger inside the collar of his new sweater. The tag was bugging him, distracting him, but there was no arguing with Jada's point. Not that he had actually believed the hooded killers had slipped past the dig workers or security and gone down through the upper-level worship chamber. Sure, he'd seen the way they seemed able to melt silently in and out of shadows like some kind of crazy ninja assassins, but if they wanted to, he would have bet they could have killed every person working on the dig team.

So why hadn't they? They had rules, he thought. They weren't going to kill people who didn't break them.

Had they been giving Drake, Sully, and Jada the benefit of the doubt? The hooded men had told them to go home; had they been waiting for the three of them to cross some invisible line? To trespass?

"We already talked about there being another way in," he reminded her. "We felt the air moving. By now, Hilary Russo and her people—and probably the antiquities minister or whoever—have already found the other entry point."

"Agreed," Jada said. When she nodded, her hair veiled her face again. "But the labyrinth was buried for, like, thousands of years. If the archaeologists unearthing the site didn't know there was another way in, how did *they*?"

"Now you're just creeping me out," Drake said.

"I'm creeping myself out!" Jada said. " 'Cause the next question is, if they knew the bat cave entrance to that labyrinth, do they know about this one?"

Drake caught another whiff of the pipe smoke he'd smelled before. Mixed in with that odor were delicious aromas of frying onions and spices. From another bar, a ways back along the walk, loud music had begun to play, the kind of thumping dance noise that roared in the sort of nightclub he had always avoided. But earlier they had passed a young bearded guy playing a bouzouki, and Drake had allowed himself a moment to wish they were here on some less troubling errand and without the specter of Luka's death looming over them.

"I don't think I want the answer to that," he admitted. "But I figure we'll find out when we find the labyrinth on Therasia."

"Can't wait," Jada muttered.

They turned together, in silent agreement that they were moving on from both the topic and the location. Something caught Drake's attention, a shifting of the night shadows on top of the darkened jewelry store to their left. He glanced up and froze, staring.

Jada walked on several steps before she realized he wasn't with her.

"Nate?" she asked, turning to see what had snagged his attention.

Drake started walking again, taking her elbow and hurrying along the path. He glanced over his shoulder, looking at the jewelry store's roof and then checking others on both sides of the path. They went down five steps, and he picked up his pace further.

"What the hell's wrong with—" she started. "Wait, did you see one of them? The hooded guys?"

"I'm not sure," Drake said.

And he wasn't. It had been a momentary glimpse, little more than a shadow detaching itself from another shadow and retreating out of sight. But something had been moving up there, and even if Henriksen had caught up with them this quickly, the men he'd hired thus far weren't clever or stealthy enough to lurk in shadows.

"You think they're trailing us right now?" Jada asked.

"Maybe."

"Why just watch? They don't know what to make of us? Or they're biding their time?"

Drake wanted to comfort her, but he'd had a lifetime of telling people what they needed to hear instead of what they wanted to hear. And Jada wasn't exactly a damsel in distress.

"These guys are like shadows. They don't like being seen," Drake said. "They took a risk back in Egypt with so many people seeing them. My guess is they didn't like it. They're doing what any decent hunter would do, waiting for the right moment. They'll want us alone, away from a crowd. Better still if they can take us one by one."

Jada's face went slack. "Oh, no. Uncle Vic."

Drake felt his heart sink. He couldn't be sure of what he'd seen, but if they were being shadowed—if these ninja assholes really did want to take them out—and they'd left Sully alone—

He took Jada's hand, and together they ran.

They raced along the walkway, past the bars and darkened shops, watching rooftops and shadows for any further threat. But Drake's thoughts had shifted away from self-preservation. The fear that made his heart race, thrumming in his skull, had nothing to do with his own safety. He hadn't seen the corpse of Luka Hzujak, but he knew how the dead man had ended up—in a trunk with his arms and legs cut off and his decapitated head resting on his chest, abandoned on a train platform. He had to force himself not to picture Sully's face staring up from inside that trunk, a bloodstain spreading out beneath it on a vintage guayabera, the copper stink of blood mixing with the earthy odor of old cigars.

Jada let go of his hand, and he wished she had held on. But they needed to run faster, and that didn't leave time for them to soothe each other's fears.

Drake darted along a narrow path that led down, cut into the cliff face. The island fell away to the right. There were homes and hotels and even a few more restaurants below, slashed into the rock, but none of them were likely to save them if they fell. Small trees and bushes grew around the path, along with fall flowers, a minor miracle considering the severely arid climate of the island. Drake scratched his arm on something as he whipped by, but those were the sorts of things that grew on Santorini—the prickly, dangerous ones.

A chorus of laughter rippled into the air ahead. They descended narrow steps carved from stone and came to another long slash of a terrace, a walkway filled with middle-aged Germans on holiday. Several of them swore as Drake and Jada elbowed through them. One man tried to grab Jada's arm, but she popped her open hand against his chest, shoving him away. Drake smelled licorice and knew that one of them had spilled ouzo on his clothes. These were the details he absorbed as he ran, the minutiae he tried to use to drive back the dark thoughts.

"He'll be all right," Jada whispered as she ran beside him. "He has all the guns."

The guns had occurred to Drake the moment he saw the dark figure on the rooftop. He and Jada had not wanted to risk carrying illegal weapons in public unless they were sure they would need them. *Stupid*, he thought now. *Careless*. They weren't on holiday. The very idea of a moonlit stroll had been ridiculous. The three of them should have holed up in their suite until morning, waiting for daybreak, when they could search for the labyrinth.

The hotel lay ahead. They reached a narrow set of stairs winding up the cliff face and ran up the seventeen steps to the top, and the doorway loomed on their left. Straight ahead was the pool, still bright blue under the lights, heated just enough that a few brave souls stood quietly flirting with one another in the water and admiring the view of the caldera far below, glistening in the moonlight.

Drake scanned the entrance, checked the darkness beyond the lights of the pool. Nothing. He hauled the door open and hurried inside, Jada darting along in his wake. They hurried through the lobby, trying to move fast without attracting too much attention. Drake ignored the elevator. They were only two stories up. He vaulted the first three steps, gaining speed as he ascended, holding on to the railing. By the time he reached the third floor corridor—the walls curved to follow the line of the cave in which the hotel had been built—he had a lead of half a flight of stairs on Jada, but he didn't wait for her.

He sprinted, slowing as he neared his room so he could retrieve the key card from his wallet. As he slid the key into the slot, he held his breath. Jada came rocketing toward him and skidded to a halt on the carpet as the light turned green and he shoved the door open, his hands aching for a gun.

They entered, and Jada pushed the door quietly shut behind them.

Drake led the way into the suite. He glanced into the bathroom, where the faucet dripped and there was evidence that Sully had shaved. The suite's bar was open, a bottle of wine open on the small table in the common room. Jada ducked into her room, poked around a moment, then emerged, shaking her head. No sign of Sully. But she held the gun that had been in her duffel, so that, at least, had been left alone.

Jada frowned, glancing around in alarm. It took Drake only a moment to realize what was troubling her—the breeze. He shivered a little at the cool night air that eddied around them and turned to stare at the door to the last place Sully might be, the other bedroom. The door hung open wide, but only a dim light glowed within. Drake and Jada moved to either side of the door and took a breath. Jada motioned for him to wait, showing him the gun, indicating she wanted to go first.

Drake slipped into the bedroom, forcing her to follow. But as she came up beside him, they both stared at the French doors, holding their breath. The doors were open, the curtains rustling with the breeze. They could see through to the balcony and the Mediterranean night beyond, but the only trace of Sully was the cigar smoke that lingered in the room.

A sick feeling swept over Drake. He closed his eyes and pressed his palms against his temples, trying not to scream in fury and anguish, trying not to think about heads and torsos in railway trunks.

Jada found their duffels, and the sound of her rustling through Sully's made Drake open his eyes. She pulled out the gun Sully had been carrying, and Drake stared at it. Whoever had come for him had been stealthy enough that he hadn't had enough warning even to go for his gun.

She handed the gun to Drake and then sat down on the bed. Her face looked drawn and pale, her eyes hollow.

"Uncle Vic," she whispered, hanging her head, the gun dangling from both hands, down between her knees.

Just as she said it, Drake frowned. The cigar smoke hadn't dissipated. If anything, the odor had grown stronger.

"Wait a—" he started to say.

"Who's there?" asked a voice from the balcony.

"Sully?" Drake called.

"Out on the terrace, making friends," Sully replied.

Drake and Jada both exhaled, chuckling softly at their panic and the grief that had come and gone in half a minute. She rolled her eyes at him, mocking them both, but Drake knew he had not been wrong in chiding himself. They had gotten careless. Paranoia had to be their ruling emotion if they wanted to stay alive.

Jada hurried to the door, putting her gun in the rear of her waistband. Drake didn't even do that, holding on to Sully's gun but keeping it out of sight as he followed her to the balcony. He stood half inside and half out. The noises of Santorini were dim and distant enough not to intrude on the breathtaking vista of the caldera and the rest of the islands that ringed it.

Sully stood at the balcony to the left, leaning with his back to them. On the next balcony, separated from theirs by a gap of barely a foot, a thirtysomething black woman with flawless skin and copper-penny eyes smiled as Jada and Drake emerged.

"These must be your mates," the woman said in a bright British accent. She held Sully's cigar in one hand and a wineglass in the other. "Nice to meet you both."

"Jada and Nate, meet Gwen," Sully said, barely looking at them, clearly enchanted. As he half turned to make the introduction, Drake saw the wineglass in his hand. "Gwen, say hello to Jada and Nate."

Gwen raised her nearly drained wineglass in a salute. "Cheers."

"Hi," Jada said.

"Hello," Drake added.

They had come onto the balcony—Drake only halfway, still hiding the gun—carrying an air of urgency that Gwen must have seen. Her eyes narrowed, and she gave a small, reluctant smile.

"Looks like you have business to attend to," Gwen said. She puffed on the cigar, coughing a little before handing it back to Sully. "There, I've tried it. And it sort of tastes sweet and like crap at the same time. I hope you're happy."

Sully smiled at her. "Very."

Gwen glanced at Jada and Drake. Sully did as well, though he had an irritated smile on his face, as if wondering why they weren't going away. It was obvious he had been doing some serious flirting with the woman, and it seemed like he might have been making some progress. Now she handed him back the second wineglass.

"I'll only be a few minutes," Sully promised her. "It's a sin to leave a bottle of wine this good half full."

"Sorry. It's getting late, and I have to meet some friends," Gwen said. "Maybe tomorrow night?"

Sully smiled. "I'll be here."

"It's a date."

Gwen turned to go back inside, and Sully shot Drake and Jada an unforgiving look. They retreated to the suite together, and Sully closed the French doors before turning toward them.

"This better be good," he grumbled.

"You won't be here tomorrow night," Drake said. "Well, probably not."

"Thanks, genius," Sully muttered, one eyebrow raised. "As if I didn't know that."

"But you just told her—"

"Hey, a guy can hope. It's about all I *can* do if you two are going to barge in on me any time I've made a new friend."

Drake lifted the gun, drawing Sully's attention to it. "We barged in because we thought the spooky ninjas were about to cut your throat and chuck you over the cliff. Then we got here, and hello, no sign of Sully. The doors are open, and we're thinking 'intruder.'"

"It was so hard to imagine I might be smoking a cigar and relaxing with my thoughts?"

"We didn't see you," Jada said, obviously irritated with his truculence. "Not until we smelled your stinky cigar."

Sully actually looked wounded. He brandished the smoldering cigar. "This is a Cuban. They're harder to smuggle into the States than guns, drugs, or antiquities."

"Oh, well, in that case, good job, Uncle Vic," Jada said, her voice dripping with sarcasm.

"We were worried about you, dumbass," Drake said. "Or did you miss that part?"

Sully gave him a devious smile. "No, I got that. I just like to rile you guys up. You deserve it after interrupting what could've been a beautiful— Wait. Why were you so worried? Did something happen?"

Drake opened his mouth, then closed it again. He glanced at Jada.

"We're not sure."

"What do you mean, 'not sure.' Either something happened or it didn't."

"It might've," Jada said. "We might've seen one of the hooded men from the labyrinth up in the village, on a roof."

"I guess it's pointless to ask if you noticed anything weird or saw anyone skulking around," Drake said. "Your attention being otherwise occupied by the lovely Gwen."

Sully grinned. "Smokin' hot, right?"

Drake gave a nod of appreciation. "No argument."

"Okay," Sully said, turning to Jada. "So you maybe saw something and you maybe didn't. We'll stay vigilant—"

Jada shot him a dubious look.

"We'll work on our vigilance. Get better with that," Sully corrected. "But since none of us has had their throat cut tonight, can we talk about something that's actually important?"

"Like?" Drake asked.

Sully stabbed his cigar out in an empty hotel water glass, then made a beeline for Drake's duffel. He dug through it and pulled out the maps and journal Luka had squirreled away for Jada to discover in Egypt. He set the maps aside and started flipping through the pages again.

"Before I went out for a smoke, I had a little wine and took a closer look at the journal."

"We've been through the whole thing," Jada said.

Sully found his page, stroked the paper with a finger, holding it open, and nodded to her. "I know. But sometimes things like this don't make sense until you've gotten new information. When you look back through it, it's like you've got new glasses on, and you can see things you didn't see before."

"How much wine did you *have*?" Drake teased.

"Two glasses," Sully said. "I opened a beer, but it tastes like crap."

"Focus?" Jada prodded, hands on her hips. Drake would have thought it difficult to look stern with magenta bangs, but somehow she managed.

"Right." Sully nodded. "So I found a book about Akrotiri in the little library in the hotel—it's out in the living room—and I was reading about the excavation there. If there ever was an Atlantis, I understand why so many people believe this was it. Atlantis was supposed to be advanced, right? Well, Akrotiri was so far ahead of the rest of the world for its time, it's amazing. They only unearthed one tiny tip of the town. More of it is there, and some is underwater. But what they found—we're talking multistory buildings, neighborhoods, looms to weave textiles that they exported. They had hot and cold running water. Think about that. Four thousand years ago, before anyone else, hot and cold running water. Then the volcano erupted, and it was bye-bye Akrotiri."

"This is all fascinating," Drake said, "but—"

"Yeah, yeah," Sully said, frowning. "I'm getting to it. The volcano wasn't the only thing. They had a lot of earthquakes on Thera in those days, leading up to the big blow. But the earthquakes didn't stop then. They're not as frequent, but they still happen. There was a major one here in 1956—did a lot of damage to the modern village of Akrotiri, which is near the excavation but not right next door. The modern village had been built around a medieval fortress that stood at the top of a hill, but the earthquake in '56 did a ton of damage, destroyed a lot of houses, and turned the fortress into unsafe ruins. They rebuilt the houses at the bottom of the hill, but the fortress has essentially been abandoned and off-limits for more than half a century."

Sully smiled. "All interesting, right. But a hell of a lot more interesting when you consider this."

He opened the journal to the page he'd marked with his finger. There were labyrinth designs and notes scribbled all over the two-page spread, so it took a moment before Drake noticed the sideways scrawl in the margins of the left-hand page.

"Quake of '56," Luka had written. "Under Goulas?"

"What the hell is 'Goulas'?" Drake asked.

"I'm guessing the Greek name for this fortress you're talking about," Jada said.

Sully grinned. "Smart kid." He beamed, almost as proud of her as he seemed of himself.

"Wow, look at that," Drake said. "I didn't think Victor Sullivan had ever done homework in his life."

Sully flopped onto the bed, set the journal on his chest, and put his hands behind his head—the picture of relaxation.

"I guess you *can* teach an old dog new tricks," he said.

"So we're not going to Therasia tomorrow, I take it?" Jada

asked. "Ian seemed so sure that the reference to Therasia on that jar meant that's where the labyrinth must be. And you've gotta admit, there was logic to that."

Drake went to the French doors and looked out at the moon-lit water of the caldera. "There still is. But it's been awhile. What's called Therasia now is not the same as what was called Therasia then. We can't know until we look, but if you think about Knossos and Crocodilopolis, the labyrinths there were not in the city or next to the temple; they were a short distance away. That fits with the location of the fortress."

"Which would mean the labyrinth was underground," Sully said. "Built right into the hill. That would've taken a hell of a long time."

Drake ruminated on that a minute, then glanced at Jada.

"Your father thought it was under Goulas."

Jada came up beside him, and together they stared out at the water for a moment. Then she smiled and turned to Sully.

"That's good enough for me."

14

The sun had started its leisurely crawl across the sky shortly after Drake hauled himself out of bed. Now the clock on the dashboard of their taxi ticked toward nine a.m. as the Greek cabbie steered around the potholes on the road to Akrotiri village.

The first sight of the village made Drake wonder if they somehow had ended up in the wrong place, but the taxi driver explained that the tourists who made the trip out to see the ruins didn't bother to stop in the village and that that was just how the villagers liked it. The place reminded Drake of little American towns that had dried up and blown away when highways were built that took most of the traffic off the byways of earlier days.

Other than the single blue dome at the center, the rest of the village that sprawled around the base of the hill looked like a scattering of child's blocks, painted white and left to fade in the sun. Rising in the middle of that ordinariness was the hill Sully had read about, and atop it the Goulas—the tower—and the fortress around it.

As the taxi wound its way through the narrow streets of the village, people paused to watch them pass, eyes narrowed with curiosity, some of their expressions not at all welcoming. People worked here, going about their lives with no interest in the more commercial concerns of the rest of the island. Driving through Akrotiri village, Drake felt as if they were slipping back in time.

The driver took them up the hill as far as he could manage, past the single blue-domed building, and then in toward the crumbled wall of the fortress, but there he had to leave them off. Drake paid him double his asking price and promised twice as much if he would retrieve them at five o'clock. He took the cab company's phone number along with the driver's promise and then watched the man drive off, raising a cloud of dust with his departure. He spotted several other, smaller clouds in the distance—vehicles on the road, either to the village or, more likely, to the dig site.

"You think he'll come back?" Jada asked, standing beside him and watching the shrinking dust devil that indicated the retreating cab.

"We can hope."

They had eight hours before the taxi driver returned—if he returned. Drake figured that gave them plenty of time to explore the ruins. If the labyrinth was there and there was a way in, they would find it. And if they came up empty-handed, he could always call and try to get the taxi driver to return sooner, though he worried that they could end up with a lot of walking ahead of them.

Drake unzipped his pack and took inventory, making sure he hadn't forgotten anything vital: water, fruit, and cheese from the hotel, rope, flashlight, gun. They all carried the same essential supplies, but Drake hoped they wouldn't be down there long enough to require the use of anything but the flashlights.

"Nice place," Sully muttered, looking up at the fortress. "We should convert it into a bed-and-breakfast."

"I feel like I'm in some Greek version of *Dracula*," Jada said, gazing up at the fortress. "We've got the remains of a castle and the little village of people who stare at you as you go by. All we're missing is a Greek Dracula."

"That'd be just our luck," Sully sighed, and started walking.

"Good thing there's no such thing as vampires," Jada replied, setting off after him.

Drake said nothing. He slipped his backpack on and started walking.

"Wait, there *aren't*, right?" he heard Jada ask.

"Not that we've ever run across," Sully admitted. "And we've seen some wild stuff. Sometimes stories are just stories. Vampires are absurd, anyway. They're always better dressed than everyone else, right? But they're up all night killing people and drinking blood, and half the time they live in graves and crypts or whatever. Yeah, these are not creatures well versed in the laundry arts. Stupid. Who believes that crap?"

Drake smiled. Laundry. He could always trust Sully to find the practical angle.

Jada and Sully caught up with him. Sully patted his pockets in search of a cigar but apparently had left his last one behind in the hotel. He'd managed to remember his gun but not a cigar. Drake almost suggested it might be his subconscious trying to make a statement about smoking but decided not to antagonize his friend. *Don't poke the bear*, Sully had often said when Drake was younger. As rules went, it was a smart one.

They began by making a complete circuit of the fortress, following the perimeter and examining the places where the walls had crumbled. The medieval stone structure had begun to collapse like a sand castle in some places, eroded by entropy, but in others the walls remained standing strong. They found only a handful of places where crevices had formed in the exterior of the ruin, and none of them yielded evidence of anything beneath the structure.

In the most dangerous places, haphazard attempts had been made to block off entry. There were signs and in one place a piece of railing that looked new enough to be a recent effort, but if so the village or the island had run out of money before it could be completed. A twelve-foot stretch of metal railing with nothing on either side of it would do little to keep inquisitive visitors away. It slowed Drake and his friends not at all.

At the rear of the fortress they encountered a partially collapsed doorway. Wooden supports had been put in place to prevent more of the stone above the door from falling, and makeshift wooden doors had been put in place to block the entrance. Once upon a time, the wood might have been strong and new, but the arid weather and sea air had dried and weakened it. A chain looped through the door handles, but it took Drake three kicks to smash the doors open, one of the handles tearing right out of the wood.

And they were in.

"Now let's see what we can find before the police show up," Jada suggested.

Sully pushed the doors closed, then dragged a couple of heavy blocks of broken masonry over to keep them from swinging inward.

"Do they even have cops here?" he asked.

"Maybe not in the village, but on the island?" Jada said. "Yeah."

"This is as remote as you can find on Santorini," Drake said. "I'm guessing there aren't a ton of cell phones. And no matter what weird looks we got on the way up here, they must see the occasional tourist checking this place out. They're more likely to think we're idiots than thieves or vandals or something."

"So we're relying on them thinking we're just American fools?" Sully asked.

Drake shrugged. "Pretty much."

"It's probably a safe bet," Sully agreed after thinking about it for a second. "But if we're out here long enough, *someone* will get the police to check on us or come looking themselves."

"Then stop talking and get to work," Jada said, smiling.

Sully snapped off a salute. "Yes, ma'am."

For more than an hour, they explored the courtyard and the rooms of the fortress. Some were completely shattered and full of debris, and Drake tried not to wonder what was beneath the rubble. If what they sought had been closed off by the earthquake, it would take a lot more than bare hands to uncover it.

Other rooms were well preserved but empty, dust on the floor a reminder of the unsteadiness of the whole structure. The wind off the Mediterranean gusted powerfully from time to time. When it whistled over the hill and through the cracks in the walls, it seemed to make the very foundations shiver.

The second and third hours found them peering beneath fallen stairs and investigating darkened alcoves. Throughout the fortress there were cracks in the walls, and in some places the floor had given way. They treaded carefully there, warily creeping through rooms Drake wouldn't ever have dared to enter by choice. They all carried their guns, and Sully and Jada each had one of the industrial flashlights they'd stashed in their duffels before boarding the ship from Egypt. Sully's kept flickering, the battery threatening to die, but so far it worked well enough.

Many of the breaks in the walls and floor opened into jagged nooks, and they examined those holes carefully, searching for any indication that there might be more open space below. In one of the less damaged corners of the fortress, Drake found a doorway with stairs leading downward.

"Jada, I need a light," he called.

She and Sully abandoned their searches to join him, shining their flashlight beams down into the dark of the old stone stairwell. One part of the left-hand wall had fallen in, but Drake started down, careful not to get ahead of the pool of illumination. They managed to pick their way over the debris on the stairs and found a bit of hallway at the bottom. Only a bit, however, as the corridor to the left had been entirely blocked by a rockfall from above. The ceiling had given way there, and whatever lay in that direction was closed to them.

The right-hand side held much more promise.

If the door had been made of metal, they'd never have gotten through. The earthquake had shifted and buckled the frame enough that the lintel pressed down on the door from above. The whole frame seemed off kilter, slanted to the left, and the door was tightly jammed within the new angles of the frame, squeezed from the top and sides. But the pressure had been enough to split the wood down the middle. The boards were thick planks, but they had splintered and now the two sides of the door were held together only by thin iron bands on the top and bottom.

"I'm a little worried the whole thing's going to come down on top of us if we try to break through," Jada said.

Drake and Sully studied the doorway. Sully ran his fingers along the top of the broken door, where the ceiling pressed down onto it.

"I can't promise you it won't," he said.

Drake scoffed. "Come on. You think this piece of wood is holding up the thousands of tons of rock above us?"

"No," Sully said, frowning as he looked at the door. "But if it's what kept the doorway from collapsing—"

He shrugged—"Ah, screw it"—and put all his weight behind a kick that made the wood shriek and dust sift down from above. Sully kicked the door twice more in rapid succession and then winced, backing away. He massaged his knee.

"You all right, old man?" Drake asked, smiling.

"Why don't you give it a shot, wise guy?" Sully growled.

"I would've been happy to if you'd let me know before you started unleashing all your righteous kung-fu fury on the mean old door."

Sully sighed heavily and stood, preparing to kick the door again. Jada covered her mouth, trying not to let him see her laugh.

"All right, grumpy," Drake said. "Let me give it a shot before we end up having to carry your geriatric butt out of here."

"My geriatric butt is still young enough to knock you unconscious," Sully warned. Then he stretched his leg, still trying to work the kinks out of his knee. "But yeah. Have at it."

Drake smiled, knowing it was a cocky grin but unable to help himself. He stared at the door, determined, and shot a hard kick at the split in the wood. It shrieked, the crack widening, but the thin iron straps were not going to give so easily. The impact on the door had shot up his leg hard enough to rattle his teeth, but he wasn't going to let Sully know that. Drake kicked again, and it might have been that the stone lintel shifted a little, or it might have been the door frame. It was hard to tell.

He glanced at Jada, wondering if she was right to be concerned. If they hadn't run out of fortress to search, he would have suggested that they keep looking, but this room was their dead end. If they found nothing beyond the door, they would have to start over. Drake would go over the various chambers and sublevels of the fortress even more carefully, and Jada would go with Sully into the village to start asking around about the earthquake and what might have been on the hill before the fortress was built.

"This is turning out to be a waste of a day," he said.

Jada had her hair back in a ponytail, and when she frowned and crossed her arms, she looked like someone's recalcitrant teenage daughter.

"Are you giving up?" she asked.

"Nah," Drake said, deciding this was not the moment to suggest they call the taxi back and head somewhere for a drink. He slid the gun from the back of his waistband and handed it to her. "Hang on to that for a second, will you?"

As she took it, he drew a deep breath, glanced at the door, then ran at it. Even as he launched himself off the ground, he knew what a stupid idea it was. Trying to be Action Man always ended in bruised ribs and a bruised ego. His regret lasted a millisecond, and then his feet struck the crack in the door and it burst inward in a shriek of metal and wood.

Drake tried to put a hand down to break his fall but still rapped his knee hard when he struck the ground. He grimaced, sucking air between his teeth, and got up slowly, massaging the same knee Sully had been nursing a minute before.

"You're no Bruce Lee," Sully muttered.

"I got the damn door open," Drake countered, dusting off his trousers.

"Do you two ever not bicker like children?" Jada asked.

Drake and Sully exchanged a look, and then both of them grinned.

"Not really," Sully said.

"It's always his fault," Drake said. "I'm innocent."

Sully rolled his eyes. "How is it I've let you tag along with me so many times over the years?" he asked, stepping through the wreckage of the door, shining his flashlight around a room that had been closed up for more than half a century.

"You? I'm the one who lets you tag along. But that's going to change, trust me. Grumpy old man with stinky cigars."

"Enough with the cigars," Sully called back to them, his voice echoing off the walls of what seemed like a fairly large room.

"I agree," Jada whispered to Drake. "Enough with the cigars."

"I heard that," Sully said.

"Good," she shot back.

Jada handed the gun back to Drake, who returned it to his waistband as they followed Sully through the shattered door. As they passed over the threshold, Drake looked up at the buckled frame. He said nothing to Jada, but he didn't like the look of it. The split door had been acting as a massive support beam, just as she had feared. Grit sifted down from cracks in the stone above the ruptured wooden frame. But it was only a single room and the last one open to them. If they left without examining it, they would always wonder.

"Suddenly I'm thirsty," Sully said, waving his flashlight around.

As Jada swept her light across the ceiling and then aimed it forward, Drake understood the joke. They were in a medieval wine cellar. Unlike the rest of the fortress, this room had been carved right out of a section of ancient stone, part of the hilltop. The curved ceiling was built of stone blocks, and arched alcoves lined the walls. Old casks were stacked in several of the alcoves, but over time the wood had dried so badly that the seals had opened and the wine had long since drained away and evaporated, leaving only stains and a dull but distinctive odor.

"Nice. How come I don't have one of these?" Drake asked.

No one answered. Jada and Sully had both begun searching the room. He figured they were checking the alcoves for secret passages, since there was no obvious sign of cracks or breaks in the cavern floor. The fortress had been built eons after the labyrinth would have been abandoned, but if this was the location of Daedalus's third maze, it was entirely possible that whoever had built the fortress would have known about the labyrinth and constructed some kind of hidden access. And given that the wine cellar had been carved out—or plugged into an existing split in the rock—it made sense that if there were any kind of access, it would be through here. But with a single circuit of the room, half in darkness since he didn't have a flashlight, Drake could tell that the builder of the fortress had given this room only one purpose, and that was storing wine.

"Guys, this isn't the place," he said.

"Maybe not," Sully allowed.

But Jada kept looking, trying to haul a cask out of the way so she could shine her light behind it.

"Jada," Drake began.

"Hang on," she said.

He shoved his hands into his pockets. If she wanted him to wait, he would wait. She had more riding on solving this puzzle than he did. Drake glanced at Sully, who had started to examine the ceiling with his flashlight. There were cracks there that Drake hadn't noticed upon entering, and he didn't like the look of them at all.

"We should get out of here," he said.

Sully kept searching. In the far corner of the wine cellar, a long, jagged crack—several inches across at its widest—had opened in the ceiling. Drake followed the beam, walking over for a closer look. He didn't like it at all.

"Do you hear that?" Sully asked.

They all paused to listen. Jada had given up her search behind the cask and now stood at rapt attention. At first, Drake couldn't make out any particular sound. In the cellar of the abandoned fortress, all noise seemed so far away, and he expected the keening of the wind or some muffled cry or perhaps footfalls in the hallway. Then he realized that the sound Sully had heard existed on a different level, a low groaning that seemed to come almost from inside his own skull.

No. It's not in your head. It's coming up through you. And it was. The groaning, grinding noise traveled up his legs from the floor, his bones vibrating almost imperceptibly.

He stared at his feet, anxiety rising, but then he noticed something that distracted him from his alarm. The wine casks in the alcove right behind him had long since given up their contents, and a small river of wine must have flowed across the floor, leaving a dark bloody stain on the stone when it dried up. Drake followed the zigzag course of the trickling wine stain with his gaze and realized it ended against the back wall.

"Sully, give me your flashlight," he said.

"Nate, we've gotta go," Sully said.

"Just for a second."

Sully complied, and Drake used the beam of the flashlight to follow the dry river of wine to the wall. The floor had been slightly canted at the time the casks gave way. But there was no large stain near the wall to indicate the wine had pooled there, which made no sense at all.

Drake dropped to his knees, following the wine with the light, and then he saw where the wine had gone. Along the seam where wall met floor, though the wine cellar was mostly carved out of the rock, a split had occurred at the juncture of floor and wall. The spilled wine had not puddled there because it had poured into that crack and down into the hill below.

"Look at this," Drake said.

"Nate," Jada said worriedly, studying the cracks Sully had found in the ceiling.

"Just for a second," Drake insisted. "The wine went somewhere. I know it could just be a fissure, that it doesn't necessarily mean Luka was right about the labyrinth being here, but—"

"Of course he was right," Jada said. "I mean, fathers think they're right about everything, but when it came to his research, mine didn't like to guess. He would hypothesize, sure, but if we found that reference in the journal, it's safe to assume there were other clues and bits of evidence he gathered that we don't know about. Maybe there's even stuff in the journal but we just don't know how to interpret it."

Sully went rigid. A second later, Drake felt the tremor that had frightened him.

"Know what?" Drake said. "If there's a way down there, it isn't from this room. I vote we—"

The crack was so loud that it shut him up. The whole room began to rumble, and that was enough for Drake.

"Go!" he shouted, shoving Jada ahead of him.

Drake led the way with Sully's flashlight. Jada twisted as she ran, shining the flashlight above them, and Drake couldn't keep himself from glancing up to see the long cracks racing across the ceiling, opening wide spaces between the rows of stones that had been laid there centuries ago.

The noise grew so loud that it drowned out his thoughts, and just as he was about to shout for Sully to run faster, the roof of the wine cellar started to cave in. A piece of stone hit his shoulder, and again he shoved Jada, but harder this time. She careened into Sully, and the two of them fell through the open door, sprawling on the floor in the corridor, near the bottom of the stairs.

Drake swore as he saw the wooden door frame buckling further as the weight of the ruin above them shifted and the frame began to give way.

He dived through the opening just as the frame splintered and a huge slab of rock crashed down, barely missing his legs. The three of them scrambled backward, rising unsteadily, the corridor pitching around them. The slab seemed for a moment as if it would block the wine cellar from view, but then it tilted away from them, and they watched in astonishment as it fell into a hole where the floor of the wine cellar had been.

An entire section of the fortress above collapsed into the room and crashed through the floor, smashing it open in two places, rubble sliding down to half fill the gaping openness of the broad corridor beneath them.

Rubble shifted, and they coughed, covering their mouths and noses until the dust had begun to settle.

"You've got to be kidding me," Sully murmured, shining his flashlight across the holes in the shattered floor.

"We almost died," Jada said, unsteady on her feet.

"Yeah," Drake said. "On the other hand—"

Jada shone her light into the rubble and the ancient corridor below them. "Yeah. The labyrinth of Thera."

"It better be," Sully said. "Or we've done all this damage for nothing."

"All we did was open a door," Drake reasoned.

"Says Captain Dropkick," Sully rasped.

"Guys, can we just find out if this is the labyrinth, please?" Jada asked.

Sully put an arm around her. "Come on, kid. You know we entertain you. It's like going on a Mediterranean adventure with a couple of vaudeville stars."

"Or the bickering brothers I never had," Jada mused.

Drake crouched at the edge of the pit that had opened where the wine cellar had been moments before. Dust still lingered, a low cloud misting above the rubble. The huge piece of masonry that had been above the door made a sort of ramp down into the more treacherous wreckage, but the fortress had ceased its trembling. The rubble shifted a little, bits of rock sliding down to find a new resting place.

"Jada, can I ask you a question?" he said.

"Of course."

Drake turned from the rubble and arched a mischievous brow. "Are you old enough to even know what vaudeville is?"

"Hey. Don't knock vaudeville," Sully protested.

"I'm not. I'm saying you're old."

Sully sat down beside him and slid his legs over the shattered edge of the floor. "I'm not old. I'm seasoned. And for your information, I wasn't alive in the vaudeville era. I've just seen a lot of old movies."

Drake smiled but said nothing more. He couldn't really tease Sully about old movies because he loved them, too.

"Are we really doing this?" Jada asked.

For a second, Drake thought she was still talking about their bickering. Then he saw that she'd come up to stand behind him and Sully and was staring down into the pit. So much of the roof had come down that in places they could see the blue Aegean sky. But Drake was much less interested in what had been opened above than he was in what had been revealed below.

Sully pushed off the edge of the floor.

"Damn it, Uncle Vic, be careful!" Jada said.

Drake figured all three of them were holding their breath, but the huge slab of stone did not shift as Sully slid down it. When he reached the rubble, he waited as Drake slid down after him. The stone was warm under Drake's steadying hands. At the bottom, he glanced up at Jada.

"This is really stupid," she said as she sat down on the shattered edge of stone that had once been the wine cellar's threshold.

Drake and Sully grinned at each other.

"We've never let that stop us before," Drake said.

Jada slid the length of the slab, and Drake caught her at the bottom. The three of them exchanged weighted glances, none of them wanting to admit just how dangerous their next step would be. Under their feet was hundreds of tons of stone both from the part of the fortress that had given way and from the buckled floor of the wine cellar. But the opening at the far end of the debris called to them. There were secrets there, and that was what they'd come for. None of them would have turned back now.

They picked their way carefully across the rubble. Several times, the stone shifted under Drake's feet, and he nearly toppled over before Sully or Jada grabbed him. He did the same for them, and soon they were sliding down a slope of debris, loose stone cascading around and beneath them.

Drake pitched forward and jumped the last few feet down into the ancient corridor below. As Jada and Sully followed suit, he glanced up into the ruin that once had been the wine cellar, peered through the openings above into the blue sky, and wondered how difficult it was going to be to climb back up the rock pile with it all giving way beneath them. He thought it might be like Sisyphus trying to roll his stone uphill. He figured they had four or five hours before the taxi driver returned. He hoped that would be enough time to figure a way out of the ruins.

"All set?" Sully asked.

Jada took a deep breath, tested her flashlight, and shone it down the throat of the dark corridor ahead. "Set."

Drake would have been happier if he'd had a flashlight, too.

But the ones Sully and Jada were carrying provided plenty of illumination. He had a lighter with him in case he needed to make a torch in an emergency.

"Follow the yellow brick road," Drake said softly, his words slipping down the corridor and coming back in a whispery echo.

The stones rustled behind them, settling further. It occurred to him that as unstable as it was, the rest of the fortress might collapse while they were underground, trapping them. He tried to push the thought away, but it lingered in the back of his head, haunting him.

The corridor led them north about a hundred paces, sloping downward the whole way, and then turned west, where it ended abruptly in a steep set of stairs. Small cups had been carved into the stone at intervals. Drake rubbed the inside of the bowl and then licked his finger. His nose wrinkled with distaste.

"Lamp oil," he said. "Nothing left, but these were lights."

As they descended the stairs, Jada and Sully used their beams to illuminate the walls and ceiling, searching for any art or ornament and finding nothing. They had found some kind of subterranean complex built into the hill beneath the Akrotiri fortress but no indication they were in a labyrinth.

That did not come until they were deeper.

There were flowers over the door. Not actual flowers but an engraving in the stone depicting a small array of large-petaled blossoms. Sully kept his light on the engraving, and they all studied the flowers for several long seconds.

"What are they?" Drake asked.

Sully grunted. "I look like a florist?"

They both looked at Jada.

"What?" she said, shrugging. "Because I'm a girl I'm supposed to know botany? I have no idea what they're supposed to be, aside from flowers."

Drake tried to play off their presumption, ready to make some excuse, but Jada gave him a look that warned him not to try and then went through the arched doorway.

"What?" Sully said. "Girls like flowers."

Drake shook his head. "You're such a Neanderthal."

"And you're what, Mr. Sensitive?"

"Come on!" Jada snapped at them.

Their bickering was really starting to get to her, which amused Drake no end. It was also, he hoped, distracting her from her grief and from the danger they were in and from the burden of guilt they all felt for Ian Welch's abduction and possible murder. They were all on edge, aware that they had to at least accept the possibility that the hooded men who had been waiting for them in the labyrinth of Sobek might be lurking down here already.

"She loves us," Drake whispered to Sully.

Sully nodded sagely. "How could she not?"

The corridor jagged to the left, then to the right, and in a dozen steps they came to a junction with three possible avenues ahead.

"Looks like we're in the right place," Drake said.

Jada stared at the three doorways, shaking her head. "This isn't going to work. We need rope—something better than bread crumbs to leave a trail. Otherwise we could be down here forever. We could get so lost, we might die before we found our way out."

Drake shook his head. "I don't think so."

"How do you figure?" Sully asked.

Drake lifted his shirt and tugged a cloth packet from his waistband. He unwrapped the cloth napkin he had taken from a room service tray left in the hotel corridor to reveal Luka Hzujak's journal and maps, folded tightly and all tied together with shoelaces he'd purchased in the small store in the lobby.

"I didn't think we should leave this in the room for sneaky ninja guys or Henriksen's thugs to find if they searched it. Also, y' know, maps."

Sully frowned. "What the hell good will those do us? None of them are for this place. No one's been here in forever."

"He's right," Jada said. "My father was working with Maynard Cheney, studying labyrinths in general, including the design of what had already been uncovered at Crocodilopolis. His sketches in the journal refer to the maps in some places. It might not tell us every turn to take, but it could be the Rosetta Stone as far as figuring out the logic of this place."

Sully shone his light on the journal while Drake flipped pages. Jada unfolded a map and then a second, finding what she wanted.

"Here," she said, pointing to a junction in the labyrinth map that mirrored the one they were standing in. "It's not the middle door. That's going to double back into one of the other two. We'd be going in a circle."

"If you're right," Sully told her.

Drake flipped another page, then went back three. "She's right," he said. "Luka has half a dozen variations on this, and only one of them has the middle door being the right one."

"How do we know this isn't one of those instances?" Sully asked.

"I don't have all the answers," Drake replied. "And neither did Luka. If it's gotta be trial and error, then that's what it'll be."

Sully nodded. "Okay." He went over to the corner of the right-hand door, where the stone seemed worn by time, and kicked at the rough edge of the frame, knocking several chunks of rock to the floor.

"Just in case," he said, holding up the biggest shard of stone. "Which way?"

"Let's try this one first," Jada said, shining her light into the left side tunnel.

Holding the journal open in his hands, Drake followed her. Sully seemed thoughtful but said nothing as he took up the rear. Drake studied the doorway, then looked along the corridor, which seemed to turn left again just ahead. Behind him, Sully paused to scratch something into the wall just inside the doorway.

"Your initials?" Drake asked.

"Hey, at least I didn't write 'Sully was here.'"

"But you were tempted."

Sully shrugged. "Of course."

Drake started to turn, but something caught his eye. He

reached out for Sully's arm and pulled him over, making him shine the flashlight beam at the wall just above the door. Something else had been inscribed there, and it wasn't Sully's initials.

"Jada!" Drake called.

She hurried back to join them, merging her light with Sully's. In the bright splash of illumination, they could all see the small diamond shape engraved into the stone above the door.

"Do you think that means we chose right?" Jada asked.

Sully stepped back out into the junction, but Drake had a glimmer of memory. In the light from Jada's flash, he scanned pages of Luka's journal again, and a smile crept across his face. He tapped the same page he'd looked at before, showing several variations on the three-choice junction. In each instance, Luka had drawn a small diamond shape on two of the possible avenues but not the third.

"Look at the map," Drake said quickly.

Jada set it on the floor and unfolded it. They huddled over it, studying it in the light.

"The middle path isn't marked," Sully called from the junction.

"He's drawn them here, too," Jada said, tapping a fingernail on the map, where her father had inscribed tiny diamond shapes in many places.

Drake got up and went out to the junction with Sully. He snatched the flashlight away and went into the middle tunnel, searching the wall above the door. Then he went into the third tunnel.

"Yes!" he shouted in triumph.

Sully and Jada stood in the junction watching him.

"So the diamond marks the path?" Sully asked.

"No," Drake said, gesturing to the stone above the doorway. "It's here, too. Only on the inside. No way to see it from out there."

"But if it's on two of them, how do you—" Sully began, and then he grinned, nodding. "Oh, I like that. The right way is the one that isn't marked."

"Exactly," Drake said, glancing excitedly at Jada. "Your

father had it figured out. But we never would've realized it if we'd only run into forks in the labyrinth. If it was one or the other, the diamonds wouldn't have helped. But this has three choices, and if two are marked, that's gotta mean that the absence of a diamond is what shows the right path. Which means we were wrong. It's the middle door."

The three of them stared at one another, smiling in triumph.

They hurried through the middle door and had gone about twenty feet when Sully halted abruptly.

"Wait, wait," he said, running back to the entrance and scrawling his initials just inside the door. "Just in case we're idiots."

15

Though the difference was gradual and subtle, there could be no mistaking the fact that their travels through the labyrinth were taking them deeper. Drake had the impression they were also moving farther away from the fortress. In Egypt, they had explored only a small section of a sprawling maze that might have been the size of a town. The temple at Knossos had thousands of rooms, and he suspected that they were inside a structure just as vast as that one. There were small chambers off the tunnels and corridors; some apparently were for storage, whereas others appeared to have been used for rituals. Several had frescoes on the walls that were neither Egyptian nor Greek in style but a merging of both. Those rooms surprised them, as did the presence of the flower motif they had encountered at the entrance, which was repeated in many of the small rooms.

In the tunnels, however, there were no decorations, no frescoes, nothing that might be used as a landmark for those lost in the maze. Only those side chambers might have given an intruder clues, but although their contents might be different, their design was consistent from one to the next.

They had come three times to what seemed a dead end only to discover hidden doorways, and twice they had descended secret stairways into lower levels of the labyrinth. Sometimes it felt as if they were traveling far from their origin point, and at others it seemed to Drake they were going in ever diminishing circles.

The diamonds or lack thereof had not failed them yet. Not once had they had to retrace their steps. Yet Drake had wondered if the trail without diamonds was leading them to the center of the labyrinth or to some trap for fools who thought they were clever and ended up instead broken after a fall through a shaft in the floor.

There had been dozens of shafts. After Drake had come around a corner and had to hurl himself across one, nearly tumbling into it, they were taking corners more carefully now. The air that came up from the shafts was warm enough that each of them had built up a sheen of sweat. The deeper they descended, the more the temperature increased.

"I guess this is what comes from digging into the skin of a volcanic island," Jada had said the first time she touched a wall and pulled her hand away, surprised at the heat.

But it didn't slow her down. If anything, it spurred her on so that half the time she was in the lead, though they didn't let her get too far ahead. There was no telling when some hidden trap might be sprung.

They worked their way through a series of narrow openings, nearly missed a turn made invisible by the placement and coloration of stone, and had to backtrack when they discovered they had entered a tunnel marked with a diamond. When they had righted themselves, they found a tunnel so low that they were forced to crouch to pass through.

Once they had reached a place where they could stand again, they found themselves at a fork where both tunnels sloped downward at steep angles, the first time they had encountered such a significant drop without stairs.

"How deep are we?" Jada asked as she looked for the markings inside each of the doorways, shining her flashlight into the darkened passages.

"Good question," Sully replied, studying the walls inside the left passage. "Look at this."

Drake crouched to get a closer look at the engraving. Near the floor, just inside the door, was an octagon inside a circle like the ones they had found in Crocodilopolis. Just one, which made sense given that only in the worship chambers had they encountered that triple-octagon design that seemed to represent the three labyrinths designed by Daedalus. But this one was different in another way. Etched inside the octagon was the same flower design they had seen all through this labyrinth.

"What the hell is that flower?" Drake asked, but it was a rhetorical question. None of them knew the answer.

"No diamond here," Sully said, shining his light on the stone above the door.

"Jada, come on," Drake said. "It's this one."

He poked his head out and saw her standing just inside the entrance to the right-hand passage of the fork. She wore a puzzled expression.

"Hey," he said. "What's up?"

Jada looked at him. "I hear water."

Drake went to join her, Sully hurrying to catch up. He gestured for Jada to take the lead, and she did, making her way cautiously down the sloping tunnel, using her flashlight to study the floor in front of them before taking a step. The incline grew steeper until only the roughness of the surface gave them enough traction to avoid sliding down into the dark.

The noise of the surf grew louder as they descended, and Drake wondered if they possibly could have gone so far from the hill. Granted, Akrotiri village was a stone's throw from the cliffs overlooking the ocean, but how far had they gone underground? The question seemed moot as the sound of the crashing water increased.

"Anyone notice the temperature difference down here?" Sully asked.

"I made the mistake of touching the wall," Jada replied.

Drake tested it, placing his palm against the stone. Though it was not hot enough to burn him, the temperature had risen. When the floor began to level out, they found themselves in a small chamber whose floor was shot through with circular vents. Unlike the shafts they had seen on the upper levels of the labyrinth, these seemed natural. Steam rose from the openings.

"Kill the lights," Drake said.

Jada cast an odd glance his way, but when Sully shut his flashlight off, she complied as well. He heard her small gasp. Though dim, each of the vents gave off a reddish glow.

"We really are on top of a volcano," Jada said softly.

"Did you think it was an urban legend?" Drake asked.

She clicked her flashlight back on. "No. It's just so hard to imagine how anyone can live here, knowing that it might all be obliterated at any time."

"People will give up a lot for paradise," Sully rumbled.

Drake glanced at him. "That may be just about the smartest thing you've ever said. Seriously."

"Inside this grizzled exterior is a great philosopher," Sully advised him.

"I'll try to remember that," Drake replied.

They continued through the small chamber and into a series of short zags and switchbacks, the water growing louder. Only a minute or so later, their flashlight beams were swallowed by vast gray nothing. Sully grabbed Drake's arm as Jada came to a startled halt. They swept the lights back and found the precipice half a dozen feet ahead. Part of the labyrinth had collapsed, opening up a cavern thirty feet above them and at least sixty feet wide. Stone blocks and what looked like the remnants of walls painted with frescoes were amid the rubble strewn far below, picked out by the flashlight beams as Sully and Jada investigated.

They were in a sea cave, but no light came from outside. Perhaps at low tide there might have been an opening, but the entrance to the cave was submerged. The water crashed on the rocks not in waves but in a churning ebb and flow that reminded Drake of breathing, in and out, filling and emptying. If this had been the path to the center of the labyrinth and the worship chambers, they would have been out of luck.

"The earthquake must have shaken this wing of the labyrinth apart," Jada said.

"*Some* earthquake," Sully said. "I'm sure there've been a hell of a lot of them since the island blew up in the first place."

For several seconds, they just stared at the sea cave and the salt water washing over the rubble far below the precipice. Drake thought he could make out some of the details on the shattered frescoes down there. There were images of flowers yet again, but another caught his eye: a veiled woman kneeling before a horned figure, offering a chalice. He would not have been able to make out the image if not for the fact that he'd seen one quite like it in the labyrinth of Sobek. Then the water washed over it, falling against the debris, and he reminded himself that whatever they were supposed to find, it would await them at the heart of the labyrinth.

"Come on," he said. "We're wasting time. Don't want to miss our taxi."

Sully took point as they retraced their steps. After the small cave with its steaming volcanic vents, the three of them had to make their way up the steep tunnel. Bent into the effort, sometimes using their hands to steady themselves on the severe incline, they climbed back toward the fork in the maze.

"Damn, I need to cut back on the Oreos," Drake muttered as he hiked after Sully. The heat of the labyrinth had begun to affect him more, and he wished they had brought more water.

They ascended for several seconds in silence before Jada chuckled.

"Wow," she said. "Uncle Vic doesn't even have the energy to be snarky."

"I'm taking the high road," Sully rasped tiredly.

Drake chose not to comment. Either they both were taking the high road or they both were too busy clambering up through the steep tunnel to bicker. As they reached the fork, where the labyrinth leveled out again, Sully sighed in relief. But as Drake looked up, seeing Sully illuminated by the golden glow of the flashlight, which threw strange shadows all around the labyrinth corridor ahead, he saw a figure dart from the right and strike Sully across the head.

Sully cried out in pain and went to his knees, clutching his skull where he'd been struck.

Tyr Henriksen stood over him, brandishing a blue-black pistol with cruel confidence. He stepped back so that Sully couldn't lash out at him but kept his gun aimed at Sully's head.

"I know you're armed," Henriksen said. "But I've got kind of a head start, and bullets travel fast."

Drake took the warning, keeping his hands where Henriksen

could see them as he emerged from the steep tunnel. He could vaguely hear the sound of water behind him, but that sea cave seemed distant and beautiful now, like some forgotten grotto.

"Leave him alone, you son of a bitch," Jada said, pushing past Drake and hurrying toward Sully. She knelt by him protectively, and Henriksen did nothing to stop her, though he kept the gun on them both.

Others began to emerge into the split corridor. From the other sloping tunnel in the fork came two gunmen, one short but powerfully built and the other the kind of dead-eyed, buzz-cut mercenary whose very aura suggested a military career gone wrong. Three others appeared from the tunnel Drake, Jada, and Sully had used to get this far. By their complexion and the curiosity in their eyes, Drake decided they must be local talent: homegrown Greek thugs. One had long since gone gray, and his skin was taut and weathered so that it looked almost like tree bark. The other two looked enough like him to be his sons. They were also armed. Counting Henriksen, that made six guns against three, but Henriksen and his goons had theirs drawn already, which made the odds moot.

"You followed us," Drake said.

"Of course," Henriksen said, giving a small shrug, blue eyes shining in the illumination from the flashlights. Several of the thugs carried them, and the corridor was lit up brightly now.

"You had a chance to talk to Welch before our mysterious hooded men snatched him away," he went on. "And we knew you had Luka's notes. The Russo woman was helpful at the Temple of Sobek, but she had to bring in others to interpret the writing there, and we couldn't wait for her and track you at the same time. It was a gamble, but we put all of our faith in you."

His smile made Drake's hands ball into fists.

"I'm glad we could help," Sully said, voice dripping with sarcasm. "You want to point that thing somewhere else?"

Henriksen glanced down at his gun as if he'd forgotten it was there. "This? Not just yet." He gestured with the barrel. "What I'd like is for the three of you to take out your own weapons and set them on the floor, then back away slowly. We wouldn't want anyone to get shot."

Drake frowned. Something in the man's tone surprised him. It almost sounded as if Henriksen meant it. Quickly glancing around, Drake noticed the easy stance of the other men. They might be thugs and even—particularly in the case of the one with the buzz cut and the stumpy musclehead—killers, but they didn't look ready to kill. Not at this moment. Certainly, if Drake went for his gun, that would change, but these guys seemed way too relaxed for men who had tracked down prey.

For the first time, he wondered if they had somehow gotten it all wrong.

"Guns," Henriksen repeated, because none of them had moved.

As Jada reached delicately for hers, Drake stopped her, a hand on her arm. Every one of the gunmen shifted to aim at him.

"I don't think so," he said, studying Henriksen's face. "If you're going to kill us all the same, you might as well get it over with."

Henriksen arched an eyebrow. "You're an enigmatic man, Mr. Drake. Most people don't volunteer to be shot."

"I've been shot before. I'm still alive. Not that I really like the idea. The food on this island is amazing, and I had my heart set on the lamb special tonight."

With a grim smile, Henriksen nodded. "That does sound enticing. And truth be told, I have difficulty with the idea of murder. You've all been so useful in helping me reach my goals. I wonder, perhaps, if you could be trusted to continue that usefulness under a more formal arrangement."

"I'd rather die," Jada said, and this time when she reached for her gun, it was not to surrender.

Drake grappled with her for a second, stripping the pistol from her hand.

"Whoa, whoa," Sully said, standing up to fill the space between Jada and the gunmen, putting himself between his goddaughter and death. Then he glanced at Drake. "What's your play here, Nate?"

"I'm working on it," Drake replied.

"Are you kidding me?" Jada shouted. "There's nothing to work on. This son of a bitch murdered my father."

Henriksen looked affronted. "I did no such thing."

"Then you paid to have it done," Sully said.

The gunmen shuffled aside to make room as another figure emerged from the darkness of the left-hand fork. Olivia looked lovely as ever, her hair golden in the electric light. She gazed at Jada with something resembling true sadness.

"He's telling the truth," Olivia said.

"Where the hell were you hiding?" Sully asked.

"It's a little crowded in here," she said, and then dropped her gaze. "I don't like any of this. Guns and tight places. This isn't a life I ever dreamed for myself."

"You've been in on this from the start," Jada said. "Admit it! You show up at our restaurant in Egypt playing damsel in distress. The grieving widow—"

"I *am* grieving!" Olivia shouted, tears springing to her eyes. She wiped at them. "I loved your father. He had his suspicions about this research, and he withdrew from the project. He might've ruined everything, and I know how it looks. But I can promise you, Tyr had nothing to do with his death and neither did I. Who does that? The way he was—mutilated . . ."

Her voice trailed off. Her shoulders shook as she tried to contain her grief, and Henriksen put a comforting arm around her.

"You told us you thought Henriksen had killed him," Sully said.

"I would not do such a thing," Henriksen said. "And if I had, why would I have done such a grisly job of it and then left him out in public in a way that would cause such an uproar?"

Drake hated to say it, but someone had to. "It's a fair point."

Jada looked at him as if he'd betrayed her.

But Sully nodded. "Nate's right. I'm not convinced Henriksen would've let his secret project fall apart, but when you're trying to keep a lid on things, you don't draw that kind of attention. Whoever murdered Luka, they were trying to send a message."

"I think we know the message," Drake said. "We got it in the parking lot outside the restaurant back in Egypt."

Jada looked at him, eyes alight with reluctant understanding. " 'Go home.' "

"In New York, we caught a glimpse of the man who killed Maynard Cheney. The guy who cut the video feed before doing the deed. Did he look like any of these goons to you?" Drake asked.

The goons in question stiffened, some of them intelligent enough to be insulted, but Henriksen gestured for them not to react, watching Jada. Drake studied him, knowing that nobody would have the patience to stand and listen to this if he intended to commit triple homicide.

Jada pointed a shaking finger at her stepmother. "You told us you were afraid of Henriksen! That you thought he'd killed Dad!"

Olivia seemed ashamed, glancing away.

"My suggestion," Henriksen confessed. "We wanted to know what you know. We wanted Luka's journal."

Drake stared at him. He doubted the man had chased them down with murder in mind, but he had a hard time buying the level of innocence Henriksen was attempting to cloak himself in.

"So now what?" he said. "We're here. You're here. Maybe the answers you're looking for are here. Maybe you can figure out the location of the fourth labyrinth—if Daedalus even designed one—and find the treasure you're after."

Henriksen frowned. "Treasure?" Then he blinked, smiling, and his eyes lit up. "It would be nice."

Drake shook his head. Something was *off*. He just couldn't put his finger on it.

"Say you find it," Sully put in. "What happens then? You try to hurt Jada and I will kill you."

"I don't doubt it," Henriksen said. "And you have my word. We have no intention of killing any of you."

Sully glanced at Drake and Jada. "Strangely, I don't feel comforted."

Neither did Drake. There were pieces that didn't fit. The

hooded men might have murdered Luka and Cheney. They might even have set Luka's apartment on fire. But the van full of guys with guns who tried to kill all three of them at the site of that fire in New York? That wasn't the spooky ninja dudes' style—not at all.

Drake glanced at Jada, then at Sully, and he had a feeling they were putting it together as well. Maybe not specifics, but he figured they had their suspicions. None of them was in a frame of mind to join forces with a guy who had sent a hit squad after them, not to mention the thugs who'd tried to abduct Jada in Egypt. All along they had wanted the journal and whatever information Drake and Sully had helped Jada gather. Whether Henriksen had ordered Luka murdered and hacked apart didn't really matter in the end.

"I'm glad to hear you say that," Drake told Henriksen. He smiled at Olivia, making sure to put as much of a chill in his expression as possible. "Thing is, we're not interested in partnering up. We're doing this for Luka. And whatever we find at the end of the rainbow, it's not going to end up in your pocket."

For a long moment, Drake thought Henriksen would change his mind about killing them. The man stiffened, his smile frozen into a mask that barely hid his fury. But then Olivia touched his arm, stroking his bicep before gripping his wrist. The thugs all sensed their boss's tension, and the promise of violence seemed to wake something in their eyes.

"Tyr," she said.

Henriksen exhaled. Relaxed. The thugs seemed disappointed.

"If this ends in bloodshed, it won't be because I didn't attempt another way," he said to Jada. Then he focused on Drake and Sully. "You've been doing such a good job of making your way through the labyrinth so far," he said, nodding once at Sully. "Thank you, Mr. Sullivan, for so clearly marking the way with your initials. We might've gotten lost if not for you."

"Bite me," Sully growled.

Any trace of amusement in Henriksen's face faded away. "As I said, you've done well thus far. I'm inclined to let you continue."

With the barrel of his gun he gestured them toward the left-hand fork, where the floor sloped steeply away, just as it had on the right. The gunmen moved out of the way to let them by. Olivia studied Jada as if hoping for some kind of acknowledgment, but Jada wouldn't even look at her.

"Lead on," Henriksen said.

Grimly, Drake and Sully exchanged a look, both well aware that moving forward was their only choice and only hope. Sully shone his flashlight down into the sharply sloped tunnel, and they began to descend.

A gunshot split the air like the crack of a bullwhip. Drake turned in a crouch and drew his gun, pushing in front of Jada and Sully. Shouts came from the split in the corridor behind them. Flashlight beams crisscrossed, blinding him for a moment, throwing shadows that separated a moment later to reveal a scuffle that sent echoes bouncing off the walls.

He saw Henriksen struggling with a black-clad hooded figure. The big blond man slammed the hooded killer against the wall and tore a long curved blade from his hands. A flashlight beam illuminated Henriksen's back, and Drake saw the blood spreading from a knife wound there. Now the big man returned the favor, driving the blade into the hooded man's gut.

"I wondered when those sons of bitches would show up," Sully rumbled. He gripped his pistol and moved to pass Drake, headed toward the fighting.

"No, don't," Jada said, grabbing his arm. "This is our chance."

"Chance for what?" Sully said. "To see who wins the right to kill us?"

More gunshots rang out. Men shouted in pain and grunted with the effort of their struggle. One of the Greeks lay on the floor of the corridor, throat cut, bleeding out onto the stone. Drake tried to make out how many of the hooded men were there and wondered if Henriksen had any other thugs waiting outside. Had the hooded men followed them as well, or had they already known the labyrinth was here?

"No!" Olivia screamed.

For a second, they could hear only her voice. Then she appeared ahead, framed in the mouth of the tunnel, running toward them down the steep slope with a flashlight in her hand. The light blinded Drake for a second, but when he blinked and his vision returned, he saw one of the hooded men rushing after her.

Drake raised his gun, aiming right for the tip of Olivia's nose. "Down!"

She saw the gun, glimpsed his determination, and dropped to the ground just as he fired. The bullet took the hooded man in the chest, stopping him cold. He fell across her legs, both of them skidding down the steep tunnel floor, and Olivia screamed again as she extricated herself from the dead man's burdensome weight.

"Who the hell are these guys?" Sully growled, shaking free of Jada.

He climbed the sharp incline and knelt to tear the hood away from the corpse, shining his light on the face he had revealed. The dead man's eyes were already glazed and empty, staring forever into the void. His features were distinctively Asian, his eyes dark and almond-shaped. Whoever he was, he wasn't Greek and he wasn't Egyptian. Chinese or Tibetan, Drake thought.

"Thank you," Olivia said, grabbing hold of Sully and rising shakily.

The fighting went on back in the corridor before the fork. Another gunshot boomed and the scuffling and cursing and grunting continued, but with the flashlight beams darting around, it was impossible to make out much detail. Shapes and shadows fought, and the copper stink of blood filled the air, along with the acrid odor of cordite from the guns.

Olivia grabbed Jada by the arms, unmindful of the gun in the younger woman's hand.

"Do something," she said, her pristine beauty tarnished by desperation. "If they kill Tyr and his men, we're next!"

Jada shoved her with such force that Olivia slammed into the wall, skull thunking against stone.

"There's no 'we,' Olivia," Jada snapped. "You and me— there's no we."

Drake didn't take the time to tell Jada that Olivia had a point, and he suspected she wouldn't have listened if he had. But there was no doubt that they were in trouble. If Henriksen survived, he might stab them in the back at some point, but if the choice was that or death for him and his friends in the next ninety seconds or so, he'd take a knife in the back somewhere down the line.

"Sully," Drake said.

"Yeah."

They started past the dead man, bent low to keep from toppling backward, and climbed back toward the split in the corridor. Drake caught a glimpse of the man he'd thought of as Buzzcut staggering past the doorway ahead, the hilt of a blade jutting from his back. One of the hooded men followed, intent on finishing the job he'd begun.

"Hey!" Sully shouted.

The killer turned.

"This is for Luka," Sully said, and shot the hooded man three times.

"Overkill, maybe?" Drake suggested. "We don't know how many bullets we're going to need."

They reached the door, sliding their backs along the walls opposite each other, guns raised. Drake studied Sully's face, wondering how many times the two of them had been stuck like this, trapped somewhere they might be imprisoned just for entering, with merciless killers between them and the exit. But he didn't bother to count. Once was once too often.

"On three," Drake said. "One. Two—"

Olivia screamed again, even more frantic than before.

Drake and Sully turned to see Olivia scrambling up the sheer stone, climbing over the dead man, eyes wide with terror. Jada had her back to them, her flashlight aimed farther down the severe drop-off of the tunnel. More hooded men were coming up from deeper within the labyrinth, scrabbling up the stone slope like spiders.

"Damn it!" Sully shouted.

Jada shot one of them, tried to turn and flee up the steep

incline, but slipped and fell onto her side on the stone floor of the corridor. The hooded men swept toward her. In the glow of Sully's flashlight, Drake made out four of them, not counting the one Jada had just shot. They had swarmed over their wounded comrade as if he weren't there.

"I thought they followed us in, like Henriksen," Drake said.

"They flanked us," Sully muttered.

Drake had wondered before if the hooded men knew about this labyrinth, if they were as knowledgeable about its secrets and hidden chambers as they had been about the one in Egypt, and now he had his answer.

Olivia kept screaming, and Drake wished she would shut up. He took aim and was about to pull the trigger, but then Sully blocked his shot. Drake shouted at him to get out of the way, but with Jada in danger, Sully wasn't going to be able to be reasoned with. Drake realized he didn't want to risk trying to shoot the killers unless he was right up close.

With a roar that managed to be warning and battle cry and profanity all in one, Sully hurtled down the sheer slope with his gun and flashlight both held out in front of him. One of the hooded men reached Jada, grabbed her leg, and brandished the curved blade they all seemed to carry. Sully shot him in the head, but Drake knew the shot was pure luck. At that angle and speed, careening out of control, Sully's next move was no longer his choice to make.

"Sully, no!" Drake shouted.

The words echoed off the walls as Sully lost his footing, moving too fast, yet managed to lunge at the three remaining killers, passing right over Jada. He crashed into them, knocking two of them backward, and they all fell sprawling and rolling down the tunnel into the darkness, Sully's flashlight shattering and winking out.

The scuffling from that darkness chilled Drake's blood.

"Son of a—" he began.

Jada cried out for her godfather. Drake slid and skidded down the tunnel toward her, stepping over the man he'd shot and calling out for Sully, hearing only the whisper of movement below.

Jada stood, recovering her flashlight and shining it down into the dark, and they both saw the figures twisted around one another. The three hooded men struggled with Sully, one of them clamping a hand over his mouth. His eyes were wide and gleaming in the beam from Jada's light, and Drake wanted to look away, sure that any second a curved blade would slice Sully's throat.

"Down here!" Olivia shouted behind them. "There are more of them down here!"

"Drake!" a low voice called.

He didn't turn. The voice belonged to Henriksen, and he put together what it meant. The man was wounded but alive, and if he and Olivia and others—given the footfalls Drake could hear—were starting down the sloped fork, it meant they had won back there at the split in the corridor.

"Let him go!" Drake roared at the hooded men.

They did not, but neither did they cut Sully's throat. Instead, they dragged him deeper into the tunnel, scrambling back into the darkness.

"Crap!" Drake barked. It was just like Welch. They had lost the fight and were retreating, but they were taking Sully with them.

Drake spun as Henriksen came down the slope toward him. The wounded man had lost his gun but still held a flashlight.

"Give me that," Drake demanded.

"He's as good as dead," Henriksen snapped.

"No," Jada said. "They took him! They didn't kill him!"

Drake snatched the light from Henriksen. "I'm going after him."

He started down into the forgotten heart of the labyrinth, and when he sensed Jada behind him, heard her footsteps, and saw her flashlight beam merging with his to illuminate the darkness below, he didn't argue. With her father dead, Sully was the closest thing either one of them had to a father. They would save him together or not at all.

16

Drake stood in total darkness, his forehead pressed against hot stone, trying to contain the urge to scream. He could hear the rustle and click of Jada going through her pack nearby, putting a fresh set of batteries into her flashlight. She spoke in a low voice, but he barely heard the words. Was she trying to comfort him or herself? He couldn't be sure. Probably both.

How much time had passed since the hooded men had dragged Sully away? An hour and a half? Two?

At first it had felt as if Drake and Jada were giving chase, and he had believed they could catch up with the murderous bastards. He had reminded himself that if they'd wanted Sully dead, they could have killed him right there in the tunnel, and they hadn't done it. But still the image of Sully struggling with the hooded men as they hauled him into the shadows haunted Drake. Would it be the last time he would see his friend and mentor alive? After a time, he forced himself not to think about it, focusing entirely on the pursuit.

But soon the chase gave way to something more closely resembling a search. They had followed the twists of the labyrinth, ignoring blind alleys thanks to the diamond markings that indicated the proper path. They stopped from time to time to listen for the sounds of scuffling or any hint that the killers were up ahead. Sully would call out, Drake had told himself. But the only scuffling they heard was the sound of their own shoes on the stone floor, and the loudest sound was the pounding of Drake's heart inside his chest.

After fifteen minutes, Drake had begun to fear that they had been wrong in assuming the hooded men would have taken the marked route toward the center of the maze, and they had backtracked to search the side tunnels and blind alleys. With no trace of the killers and no shout from Sully, they'd had no choice. Some of the tunnels led to dead ends, though in a couple of places Drake thought there might be some mechanism that would lead them to a secret chamber. Other avenues ended in a collapsed section of the maze, and twice they came to places where the labyrinth had given way and the underground caverns had opened up enough that the sea had made its way into the subterranean world. Turgid water ebbed back and forth.

Those sunken rooms were full of water, but Drake saw a glimpse of the split at the top of a cave entrance in one, and he thought the tide must be going out.

There had been more shafts as well, and Drake had rounded a corner too fast and plunged into one, barely catching himself on the edge. He had managed to haul himself up, bathed in the heat and glow coming from the volcanic vents down below, but the flashlight he had taken from Henriksen had been lost— sacrificed to the volcano.

Eventually they had given up on dead ends. They had begun searching not for a secret passage where the killers might have taken Sully but for the center of the labyrinth. Drake thought they might try sacrificing him to Poseidon or whoever else this temple had been dedicated to, and if that were to happen, it would be in the worship chamber.

And now they had found it.

"Damn it," Jada muttered.

Drake heard a soft thunk and realized she had dropped one of the batteries. He froze, thinking they were going to be trapped down there in the dark and wondering how they would ever find their way out, and then the light snapped on, so bright that he had to shield his eyes.

"Sorry," she said, moving the beam from his face.

"I thought you'd dropped a battery."

"I did. One of the dead ones."

Drake only nodded. Neither of them smiled. They had lost the heart for the banter that had kept them going for the past few days and allowed her to focus on something besides her father's murder. Now neither of them could think of anything but Sully meeting the same fate, a head and torso in a steamer trunk left on a train platform somewhere.

Jada looked tired and pale. They still had water and food in their packs, but Drake wasn't hungry. It was all he could do to stop himself from shaking with fury, though he knew the rage only masked his fear for Sully and the sadness he felt in his bones. More than once before he had been convinced Sully had died, only to discover otherwise, and they had been in dozens of tight scrapes. He liked to tell himself this was because Sully was a tough son of a bitch, but he knew there had been just as much luck involved as toughness or determination.

They had to get him back.

"Come on," he said. "We're not going to find them just waiting around."

Jada shone the light around the worship chamber. The flash had flickered out while they were descending the three steps down into the room, and she had stumbled and fallen to her knees. It was only sheer luck that she hadn't broken the flashlight. They were going to have to be more careful; their only flashlight might be more important to their survival than the water bottles they carried.

As the light swept across the walls and the octagonal altar and found the antechamber where the Mistress of the Labyrinth would have prepared for the rituals that took place there, Drake knew there could be no doubt that Daedalus had designed this chamber as well as its Egyptian counterpart, but there were no hieroglyphics here. Jada's light illuminated frescoes painted on the altar depicting the Mistress of the Labyrinth receiving honey from kneeling worshippers, along with images of Minotaurs, but the writing on the walls was the same ancient dialect that had been on the jar Ian Welch had found in the Atlantean chamber in Egypt. Some variation on Greek. If Welch had been there, he could have read it.

"It's exactly like the one in Egypt," Jada said.

"Let's hope so," Drake replied, striding directly into the anteroom. The details of this chamber didn't interest him. All he cared about were the true worship chambers below, the ones dedicated to each of the gods of the three labyrinths: Dionysus, Sobek, and Poseidon. If this labyrinth truly had the same design, there would be stone doors in those chambers that led into secret recesses, and he would find a way to get them open somehow.

In the glow of Jada's light, he went straight to the corner where he expected to find the false stone block that would trigger the altar to slide back. Yet the stones along the bottom of the wall did not move when he tried to push them, and when Jada came closer with the light, they saw no symbol engraved there. The chill that had clutched at Drake's heart for the last two hours turned to ice. Had they reached their last dead end?

"Look around?" he said.

But Jada didn't need his urging. She had begun to search the anteroom for the octagon with a circle symbol that had indicated the trigger in the labyrinth of Sobek. There were symbols everywhere that he could only imagine must be some Atlantean arcanum. Shelves held painted jars, just as in Egypt, and a side shelf had a shaft built into it, hot air wafting up from below.

"Here!" Jada said.

He turned to see her pushing a spot on the wall between two shelves, and they both heard the grinding of stone as hidden weights and balances shifted. Wiping sweat from his brow, he rushed from the anteroom and saw that the altar had moved several inches. The mechanism that locked it in place had released, and Drake ran to it and threw his weight against it. It slid back easily so that even as Jada joined him, the huge stone octagon rolled away to reveal the stairs beneath. No skeleton awaited them this time, and Drake started down.

He'd reached only the third step when he heard Jada gasp.

"Nate, look at this."

"Jada, come on," he urged, looking up to see her shining the flashlight on the top of the altar.

Her eyes were wide with surprise. Reluctantly, he went back to the top of the steps and stood beside her. The moment he saw the symbol engraved on the top of the altar, he understood her reaction. In the Temple of Sobek, they had found a pattern of three octagons within circles, all interlinked.

Here there were four.

Drake looked up at Jada. A sheen of sweat made her face almost luminescent in the glow from the flashlight. It brought home to him how truly hot it had become inside the labyrinth and reminded him of the danger they were in. Volcanic vents, collapsed corridors, caverns where the sea had flooded in, and killers who would not hesitate to cut their throats or drag them off through secret passages to some unknown fate.

But they had found what they had been looking for all along.

"There really is a fourth labyrinth," Drake said.

Jada's lower lip quivered a moment, and he could only imagine the emotions flooding through her.

"I *knew* there had to be," she said. "My father knew."

At the mention of her father, Drake felt the ice in him melt in the renewed heat of his anger and his fear for Sully.

"Come on," he said, leading her to the stairs.

They descended together, Jada guiding their steps with her flashlight. At the bottom, they hustled along the corridor. Drake kept an eye out for open doorways but was certain that the only ones that mattered would be the ones that led into what he now knew would be four worship chambers at the end of the hall.

Their footfalls echoed off the walls. Drake felt his hands clenching into fists. A thousand images of Sully strobed through his mind, memories of the man laughing at one of his own jokes, smoking his cigars, or looking up in triumph from some discovery, face covered in grime but eyes alight with childlike excitement. Sully had been like a kid on Christmas morning every time they found something the rest of the world had told them would never be found or didn't exist at all. He often behaved as though the money was all he cared for, but Drake knew him better than anyone alive. Sully appreciated all kinds of treasure.

Where are you, old man? Drake thought.

But the only way to answer that question was to figure out who the hooded men were. Who were they working for? They had murdered Luka and Maynard Cheney and many others since to keep the location of the fourth labyrinth secret. That seemed clear. Drake had believed Henriksen's denials—about those killings, at least. But the hooded men had taken Welch and now Sully. In both instances, the abductions had occurred only when the killers had realized they were about to be defeated. They had retreated to fight another day, apparently, and taken prisoners.

Though it did not slow him, he had the terrible feeling that the chambers ahead of them were empty and that even if they were able to find a way to open those recessed doors at the back of the chambers, the passages beyond also would echo with the stillness of the ages.

They heard the shush of water even before they reached the turn in the corridor. Dread curled tightly in Drake's gut.

"Nate—" Jada began.

"No!" he said, sprinting the last twenty feet, almost outpacing the flashlight beam.

He rounded the corner, slowing before he would have entered the darkness ahead. He could feel the vastness, the emptiness of the cavern ahead and heard the ripple and wash of water, and then Jada appeared behind him and the scene illuminated by her flashlight surprised him. To the right, the labyrinth had collapsed. All that remained of whatever worship chambers had been there had fallen into a massive rift that had opened in the rock. Only the upper arch of a doorway was still visible to indicate that anything had ever been there.

But to the left, two worship chambers remained.

Drake ran to the nearest door and darted inside, taking care on the three steps to the chamber floor.

"Jada, the light!" he called, though she was right behind him.

She flashed the beam around the room, dispersing ancient shadows, and Drake realized he had been holding his breath. Now he swore. The writing on the walls was in Greek, the engravings of grapes immediately signifying Dionysus to him. He glanced at the massive slab of a door at the back of the chamber, tempted to test it, but instead he spun toward Jada.

"Let's check the other one."

The symbol on the altar upstairs had included four octagons inside four circles. That had to mean four labyrinths and one chamber down here dedicated to the primary gods of each. Two of those chambers had caved in and been eroded by seawater for more than half a century. The clues they needed might be lost forever.

Outside the last worship chamber, Drake hesitated a moment. As Jada entered, descending the three entry stairs, the shadows closed around him. He put a hand on the hot stone wall and watched her. For a moment, he thought he heard a rustle of whispers back in the corridor, but it might have been the undulating sea washing against the ruins down in the collapsed cavern.

Then he saw Jada turn toward him, a look of wonder on her face, and the only thoughts in his mind were of Sully. They had found it.

He ran down the three steps and joined Jada. Side by side they examined the walls of the worship chamber. The style of the painting on the walls was entirely different from anything they'd seen thus far, and he recognized the Far East influence instantly. The Minotaurs were there, but the most frequently repeated image was that of the flower that they had seen upon entering the labyrinth this morning. All around the images, on columns in the chamber, and on the octagonal altar at the center of the room were ancient Chinese characters.

"The fourth labyrinth—" Jada began.

"Is in China," Drake finished.

They looked at each other and swore, sharing a chorus of profanity.

Drake followed Jada's light as it traveled across the walls, and what he saw disturbed him profoundly. There were images of men being hung from wooden braces and skinned alive, being burned, and having long spikes hammered into their bodies. They were horrifying, all the more so for the paintings of the same flowers and other plants and tree branches decorating the hideous imagery.

"I don't think I want to know what god they worshipped in the fourth labyrinth," Jada whispered.

"Swing the light over here," he said, going to the door at the back of the chamber.

For long minutes they searched for a trigger, but to no avail. The walls were hotter here than anywhere else they had been in this subterranean maze, and he wondered what kinds of vents might wait on the other side. His shirt, damp with sweat, stuck to his back and shoulders.

When Jada paused to take a drink of water from her pack, she looked as if she felt guilty, and when she passed the bottle to Drake, he felt the same way. But it was no use. Even if they found a way to trigger the door open, they weren't going to find Sully.

A scuffing noise at the entrance to the chamber made them both spin, Drake reaching for his gun. Flashlight beams blinded them momentarily.

"Don't shoot, Mr. Drake," a deep, accented voice said.

Henriksen.

As the bright lights moved away from his face, Drake kept his gun aimed at the figure in the doorway while his eyes adjusted. Henriksen's blood-soaked shirt had been torn open and the knife wound on his shoulder bound to stop the bleeding. The man looked pale, but his eyes were alert and glittering with a zealot's joy. He descended the three steps into the room, smiling as he gazed around, totally unmindful of the gun in Drake's hand.

Henriksen's short, powerfully built sidekick followed him into the room, followed by the gray-haired Greek and then Olivia, who still managed to look beautiful despite her unruly hair and the sheen of sweat on her. Her features had a hard, flinty edge and her eyes had gone cold, but the moment she spotted Jada, she softened and seemed to wake from the haze of heat and fear that had entranced them all.

The old Greek's surviving son stayed just outside the door, guarding the entrance with a gun in his hand and grief for his dead brother burning in his eyes. He wanted more of the hooded men to come. Drake had seen that look in the eyes of anguished men before. His loss hurt so much that he wanted to kill until it didn't hurt anymore or die and end it completely. It was probably for the best that he remained in the hall. With that kind of rage, he could not be counted on to remember who his enemies were.

"China," Henriksen said, shaking his head. "I never would have guessed it."

"They let you live?" Jada asked, staring at Olivia. Her meaning was clear; she wished the hooded men had done a more thorough job.

Olivia flinched, and the innocence with which she had approached Jada all along fractured, letting a flicker of dark intelligence and hatred show through. Then the mask was in place again, but Drake had seen the cold, calculating face of the real Olivia for a moment, and now he was even more on guard. He still had his gun out, and the old Greek and the short sidekick were both also armed, their weapons aimed casually at the ground. The promise of bullets made the hot air in the chamber go still.

"We fought them off," Olivia said softly. "Nico lost a son. Tyr lost one of his best men."

Drake figured she must be referring to Buzzcut, and Nico was the old Greek.

"We lost someone, too," Drake said.

That made Henriksen look up, his blue eyes somehow even paler in the glow of the flashlights. "Sullivan may still be alive. If they were going to kill him, why not just do it? Why bother abducting him? He only slowed them down."

Drake had had the same thought, but he didn't want to agree with anything Henriksen said. He nodded slowly, narrowing his eyes.

"So what now?" Drake asked. "These guys have a history of coming back in greater numbers. We drove them off this time, but they obviously would rather see us all dead than let us make it to the fourth labyrinth."

Tyr Henriksen smiled, revealing sharp little teeth. Despite his handsome features, in that moment he looked more like a shark than a man.

"I'm a businessman, Mr. Drake, and I've been successful at it. That means I'm used to there being people out there in the world who would like to see me dead."

Drake hesitated. His heartbeat pulsed in his temples, and his breath came in short, angry inhalations. The gun in his hand seemed to thrum with an urgency all its own, pleading to do its brutal work. Henriksen hadn't killed Luka or Cheney and he hadn't taken Sully or Welch, but someone had burned Luka's apartment and sent gunmen after Jada in New York. The hooded men didn't seem overly fond of guns, and it was clear Henriksen didn't have a problem with killing when necessary. But where did all that leave them?

Henriksen watched him closely now, his instant fascination with the Chinese worship chamber set aside for a moment. The so-called businessman must have been able to see the indecision— the temptation toward violence—in Drake's eyes, because he took a step forward, closing the space between them.

He waved at his men, and they holstered their weapons. "Mr. Drake," he said. "You can put the gun away now. The danger has passed."

"Has it?" Jada asked, never taking her eyes off her stepmother.

Olivia ignored her, taking out a camera and beginning to photograph the writing and the paintings that decorated the worship chamber. Nico used his flashlight to help dispel the shadows so that she could get the clearest shots. There were shelves of jars there as well, and the short man began to lift them one at a time for her to photograph.

Henriksen looked meaningfully at Drake. "These men, whoever they are, clearly do not want to squander their lives. In a conflict where they don't see the possibility of achieving their goals, they withdraw and await another opportunity. They are gone, Mr. Drake. They have given up on the idea of preventing us from learning what we can about the fourth labyrinth from this chamber. If they had more men with them, we would all be dead. Instead, they have taken your friend Sullivan. Why they took him and didn't kill him, I don't know, but for the moment let's assume he's alive. You have two choices.

"You and Jada can continue to be obstinate and hostile, working to find the fourth labyrinth on your own—as finding the killers who strive to protect its secrets is your only hope of locating Sullivan—or you can accept that we are all seeking the same answers. If our motivations differ, isn't that a debate that can be postponed to another day?"

Drake glanced at Jada and then took a sideways shuffling step so that he was beside her. From the outset they had been convinced that Tyr Henriksen was their enemy, and even now they couldn't be sure he was not. When Luka Hzujak had discovered Henriksen's plans for the fourth labyrinth, he had quit working with Phoenix Innovations and tried to beat Henriksen to the punch. Henriksen wanted the treasure of the labyrinth for his purposes, and to make sure he could claim it, he intended to keep secret the historical revelations involved in his discovery. Jada would never let that happen, and Henriksen had to know that.

But the selfish, entitled bastard was right. It was an argument that could wait. The only thing that really mattered at the moment was finding Sully.

Drake lowered his gun. After a moment, he slipped it back into his waistband and nodded toward Henriksen.

"We'll settle our differences later."

Henriksen smiled. "I look forward to it. But for now—" He turned toward Jada's stepmother. "Olivia, what can you tell us?"

Olivia paused in her photography. "Not a lot yet. The writing is ancient Chinese, but we'll need to transmit these pictures to Yablonski for translation. No idea what the flower motif is meant to represent, but it's all through here, an addition to the same repetitive imagery we've seen in the other chambers."

Drake frowned and glanced at Jada. If she seemed surprised that her stepmother was the expert on Henriksen's team, she didn't show it.

"Any idea what god this chamber is dedicated to?" Drake asked. "The paintings over by the door look like something out of Dante's *Inferno*."

Olivia stared at him. Drake thought about the way she had come into the restaurant in Egypt the other night, pretending to be the damsel in distress from some film noir. Olivia might not be as evil as Jada had made her out to be—she hadn't murdered her own husband, at least—but that didn't mean she wasn't a manipulative bitch and a hell of an actress.

Now though, Olivia seemed to deflate a little, and most of the remaining tension in the chamber dissipated. They were all there together, hundreds of feet underground, sweating from the heat of volcanic vents, and they shared a goal. If they were going to work together, now was the time.

"I'm not as familiar with ancient Chinese mythology as I'd like to be, and as I said, I can't read this. So I'm not sure of the name of the god."

"But?" Jada asked.

Olivia took another photograph, then grabbed Nico's wrist to aim his flashlight at the hideous paintings Drake had seen before of men and women being flayed and tortured. They were arrayed in a curling, descending pattern, the torment growing gradually more horrific and explicit toward the bottom of the wall.

"In Chinese mythology dating back to the twelfth century B.C., after death, tainted souls were taken to a subterranean hell called Diyu, where they were punished until they had atoned for their sins. According to the legend of Diyu, they existed in a cycle of torment, enduring gruesome torture until they died, only to have their bodies restored so the punishment could start again."

"I didn't even know the Chinese believed in hell," Jada said.

Olivia shook her head. "It's not the Christian hell. Diyu was said to exist underground and be composed of many levels, each with its own ruler. But above them all was a kind of king." She snapped another picture. "I wish I could remember his name, because I'm guessing he's the god this chamber is meant to worship."

Henriksen had been studying the paintings on the walls more closely while she talked, but now he turned.

"Don't worry about that. Yablonski will figure out what all of this means," he said. "Let's just get it all photographed and take our leave. The police have been well paid to stay away, but I would rather not be discovered in the presence of men who have been murdered."

Drake saw Nico flinch at that, but the old Greek kept his grief to himself.

"We'll bring our own people out, of course," Henriksen continued. "And see to it that they're properly buried."

Jada sneered at him. "How noble of you."

Olivia snapped one last photograph of a jar the short man held, then gestured for him to return it to the shelf. She turned to regard the rest of them.

"There's something else," she said.

Drake didn't like the smugness of her tone. "Just spill already."

Olivia traced her finger over one of the most repulsive paintings of the Chinese hell.

"I told you that Diyu was believed to be underground," she said, a thin smile forming on her lips as she glanced at Henriksen. "According to the myths, it was also a *maze*."

"You're not saying you think this place actually existed?" Drake asked, the idea of such tortures in the real world making him sick.

"Some real-life version?" Olivia replied. "I think we have to conclude that it did. Look at all of the evidence around you. What does it say, Mr. Drake?"

Jada pushed her hair from her face and wiped sweat from her eyes. "It tells us that Diyu *was* the fourth labyrinth."

"Exactly," Olivia replied.

"Hell?" Drake said, turning to Henriksen. "We're saying *hell* is the fourth labyrinth?"

"Hell or something like it," Henriksen replied. "And when Crocodilopolis was abandoned and the volcano destroyed Thera, where do you think Daedalus and his followers brought all of their accumulated wealth? What better place to hide it than an underground maze where the people believed they were already dead? It's insane, but what other conclusion can we draw?"

Speechless, Drake had no reply. He turned it over and over in his head, examining it from every angle, and he couldn't deny that it felt like there were at least shards of truth to the theory, as crazy as it sounded. The frescoes on the wall said as much.

"How did my father know?" Jada asked, her gaze locked on her stepmother.

Olivia managed to look sad at the mention of her late husband, but Drake knew that might well be just part of the mask she wore.

"In researching the historical origins of the myths connected to the labyrinths, he developed the theory that King Minos of Crete and Midas were the same man—"

"We got that much," Drake interrupted. "But the archaeologist at the labyrinth of Sobek thinks it wasn't Midas who was the alchemist. It was Daedalus."

Olivia narrowed her gaze, smirking. "Aren't you clever."

Jada scoffed. "No such thing as alchemy."

Henriksen leaned against the wall, wincing at the pain from his wound. "Then where did all that gold come from?"

"Not from magic," Jada said. "Or even some pseudo-science. You can't make gold."

"Maybe not," Olivia replied. "Probably not. Your father believed that Daedalus must have been some kind of charlatan, but he kept an open mind because he had no other explanation. And the more he researched Daedalus and alchemy, the more he began to see other connections that defied explanation. There were stories of the ancient alchemist Ostanes—"

"The Persian," Drake said. "Sure, there were similarities in his background. Same with St. Germain and half a dozen others. They were all alchemists. Half of what they did was about creating the illusion that they had abilities they didn't have to give them that mysterious, mystical aura. They all claimed to be immortal. Fulcanelli even claimed he *was* St. Germain."

"What if he was?" Olivia asked.

"Seriously?" Drake scoffed. "You are an entire jar of nuts."

Henriksen started to speak up, but he hadn't gotten half a word out when there came a boom and rumble from far above them and the whole chamber began to shake. A jagged crack raced across the ceiling. Dust and debris rained down, and a jar fell to shatter on the floor.

Olivia screamed and pressed herself against the wall as Drake grabbed Jada and ran toward the doorway. Nico's son looked around in fear and surprise but did nothing to stop them as they joined him in the corridor. They froze there, unsure what to do. The rumbling continued, a grinding roar from far off but loud enough that the muffled noise reached them despite how far they had come into the subterranean maze.

Olivia staggered toward Henriksen, and he put a protective arm around her.

"Is it the volcano?" Olivia shouted, looking at Nico.

The old Greek did not move. He seemed resigned to whatever fate held in store for him. His eyes were narrowed as he tried to make sense of the noise from above.

Then the rumbling subsided and the last bits of grit rained down from the ceiling. Whatever had happened, it was over as abruptly as it had begun.

"If it was the volcano, we'd be dead already," the short, stocky thug muttered. "It's the fortress."

Henriksen flashed him a dark look. "Corelli?"

The stocky man—Corelli—looked at him, dark certainty in his eyes. "Explosives, Mr. Henriksen. The assholes brought the whole place down on top of us. We're not going anywhere."

"Oh, my God," Olivia whispered. Her gaze turned haunted. "I can't die down here." She looked around at the walls as if they were about to start closing in.

Drake frowned, shaking his head. No way. He couldn't even let himself wrap his mind around it. The hooded men had used explosives to destroy the rest of the fortress ruins, trapping them down here? They used daggers. They were killers from another era, all about stealth and secrecy. Explosives?

But there was no other answer. It wasn't as if Henriksen would have trapped himself down here voluntarily.

"What do we do?" Nico's son said, his Greek accent think and frantic. He stared not at Drake or Henriksen but at his father. "What are we going to do?"

"There are other ways out," Jada said, turning to Henriksen. "Those hooded men—they got out with my godfather, and they didn't go back the way we came in."

Henriksen trembled, gaze shifting around the room. Drake thought others, watching him, might have thought he shook in fear, but he understood that the man was filled with anger at having been trapped like this—at having his will thwarted. At length, Henriksen aimed his flashlight at the huge stone slab of the door to the secret passage at the rear of the chamber.

"We figure out how to open that door."

"And what if we can't figure it out in time?" Olivia demanded.

"There's another way," Drake said. As they all turned to him, he pointed at Olivia. "Please tell me that camera is waterproof."

17

Drake raced out of the Chinese worship chamber ahead of them. A crack had appeared in the wall of the corridor outside and chunks of stone had broken off the support pillars in the hall, but he knew that would be nothing compared with the damage they would encounter if they attempted to retrace their steps. They had only one chance of getting out of the labyrinth quickly—perhaps at all.

There had been four worship chambers in Daedalus's original design for this junction in the secret heart of this labyrinth. Two of them had been destroyed, collapsing into the cavern formed by the earthquake of 1954. Now even more of the stone floor had calved off into the large cavern. The others followed Drake with their flashlights as he led them to the sheer ledge. Below, the sea churned in and out like a watery bellows.

"You can't be serious," Corelli said. "And you thought Olivia was nuts?"

Henriksen shot him a dark look. "Shut your mouth, idiot. We could all die down here."

"Yeah. I'd like to avoid that," Drake said.

Jada stood on the verge of the chasm. Drake took her arm and pulled her back a foot or two. Part of that ledge had given way already. After the explosion, cracks might have formed to make it even more unstable.

She did not try to pull her arm away but glanced up at him.

"How far do you think we'd have to swim underwater?"

Nico and his son were back in the entrance to the Chinese worship chamber, whispering quietly to each other. Corelli shook his head, scratching the back of his skull in doubt. But

Henriksen's eyes were lit with anticipation. Drake had to hand it to him; the man was motivated.

"There's no way to tell," Drake said.

"I don't know how long I can hold my breath," Olivia said, walking up to the edge and looking down into the roiling water.

"Look, the tide is low," Drake said. "It could still be going out; I don't know. But we're not going to get a better shot than this for another twenty-four hours."

Jada, Olivia, and Corelli all looked dubious. But Drake noticed the Greeks watching him and thought he saw interest and encouragement in their gazes. They were locals, and they looked as though they thought he might not be entirely crazy, after all.

"The camera," Drake said, looking at Olivia. "I asked you before, is it waterproof?"

Olivia nodded. "Supposedly."

"And there's a waterproof pouch in my pack," Henriksen said, gesturing to the backpack Corelli carried. With his wound, Henriksen apparently had given up the burden. "We can double up protection."

"And if the camera's ruined?" Olivia complained. "What then?"

"Then we come back," Henriksen said sharply. "Or I do, with or without you."

"We could try through those stone doors," Corelli argued. "There's gotta be a way to trigger them open."

"If there were any easy way, we'd have found it in the Temple of Sobek," Henriksen argued. He looked at Drake and nodded. "We go."

Drake shook his head. "No. I go." He made his way to the edge and sat down, taking off his boots and then stripping his khakis off. He balled up the trousers and stowed them in his pack, hesitated, and then decided to put the boots back on. The climb down would be jagged, and even underwater he'd hesitate to be barefoot. Despite their weight, he decided he was better with the boots than without them, although he knew he looked ridiculous in his boxer briefs and boots.

He swung his legs over the edge of the broken floor, then turned back to Henriksen. "You're filthy rich, right?"

Henriksen nodded gravely. "Yes. Yes, I am."

Of course, Drake thought. *The guy wants treasure. The rich want to get richer.*

"You're a man who wants the best of everything. Who spares no expense?"

"That's right."

Drake smiled. "Good for you. Give me your flashlight. If you're that particular, I'm guessing it's waterproof."

Henriksen walked over and handed his flashlight to Drake. His boot shifted and a piece of the cliff broke off, but he scrambled backward in time.

Drake turned to Jada. "I'm going to see if there's a way through. It may not be far to the outside, or if it is, there may be air pockets along the way, even open caverns. I figure no more than half an hour. If I'm not back, you'll have to move to plan B."

"What's plan B?" Corelli asked.

"Anything but dying," Drake replied.

He checked that his pack was tightly zipped and then turned around and slipped over the edge of the shattered floor. There were handholds, but halfway down a chunk of stone broke off under his fingers, and he slid the last ten feet, turning as he fell. He turned his ankle on the debris below as he landed in the churning water at the edge of the cavern, and he bit his lip to keep from crying out.

"Are you all right?" Jada yelled, her voice throwing haunted house echoes all across the cavern.

Drake tested his ankle and found it only a little sore. He shone his flashlight upward to find the entire group, including the Greeks, staring down at him.

"I'm good," he said with a wave. "I'll be back."

He told himself that they wouldn't hurt Jada, that if they had any intention of doing so, they would have done it already. And then he dived into the water, surfacing a moment later. The flashlight beam illuminated a patch of the water, unaffected by being submerged, and he felt a sliver of relief. He shifted over to the left side of the cavern, where he could scrabble along the wall and his boots would not drag him down.

Drake kept his head above water all the way to the other side of the cavern. He kept his breathing steady, calming his heart, and then he ran out of room. The tide had lowered the water level in the cavern, but it wasn't low enough that he wouldn't have to swim underwater to find an exit.

He took a deep breath and went under, stepping away from the wall and letting his boots drag him down. With the flashlight out in front of him, he kicked forward, swimming as best he could despite the light in his hand and the weight of his clothes and boots. He blinked his eyes against the sting of the salt water, and only then did he realize how hot the water was. It came from the sea, pushing in and dragging back out again, but the volcanic vents underwater heated it while it churned in these caves.

As long as he didn't boil or drown, he figured he'd be fine.

Kicking off the walls and bottom of the crevasse he had entered, Drake waved the flashlight left and right. Cave fish, unused to the light, darted away from the beam. He saw silver eels rippling in the ebb and flow of the current that tugged him along. For once, fortune was with him. The tide was still going out. He only hoped it did not turn before he went back to get the others.

What are you thinking? Just hope you make it back to them.

He could almost hear Sully's gruff voice in his head, telling him to focus. His anger returned full force, and he had to tamp it down to stay calm and hold his breath.

Ahead, the dark water seemed to lighten, and he let himself hope. Clicking off the flashlight for a moment, he confirmed the glow, but as he swam toward it, he saw the gloomy luminescence came not from daylight but from cracks in the floor of the cave. As he swam over the pair of volcanic vents, he could feel the heat from below, and again he wondered how the people of Santorini could knowingly make their lives on the rim of an active volcano.

His lungs began to burn. Clicking the light back on, he kept swimming even as he began to realize that he would have no choice but to turn around. Searching upward with his free hand, he hoped to find an air pocket where he could get a sip of oxygen, but there was no space between water and stone.

Drake cursed the weight of his boots, wishing he had risked taking them off. They had slowed him, and now they felt heavier than ever. He wondered if they would be the death of him, if he would be able to make it back even if he turned around now. Though his thoughts had turned sluggish, he tried to figure out how far he had come, how far the cavern with the ruined worship chambers might be from the outside, but he knew it was foolish even to wonder. Any guess would be nothing more than that.

The pressure built in his head, and he felt his chest constricting with the need for air, and suddenly he understood that he'd come too far, that turning back was no longer an option. Forward was his only chance.

Even as the thought struck him, he saw light ahead yet again. It might have been more vents, but this time, when he clicked off his flashlight, he realized the glow luring him forward came not from below but above. Desperate for air, he swam another ten feet, then fifteen, and finally twenty-five, and then he could stand it no longer.

Chest burning, mind screaming, he kicked for the surface and emerged with a wheezing gasp into a much narrower cavern, perhaps as little as eight or nine feet in width. The afternoon sunlight that streamed in came from a crevice another twenty yards ahead, but beyond it, he could see a sliver of deep blue sky.

A grin split his face.

And then he realized he had to swim back and let Jada and the others know and then lead them through the underwater passage. His lungs hurt just from thinking about it. But they would be out, and that meant the real search could start. He would find Sully, and together they would expose the secrets of the hooded men to the world so that the murderous bastards couldn't get their hands on anyone else. He thought about the paintings in the Chinese worship chamber, the hellish images of torment in Diyu, and he felt more determined than ever.

Drake clung to the wall, catching his breath for the swim back.

This time he would take off his boots.

He couldn't help but wonder if, when they finally got back up to Akrotiri village, the taxi driver would be waiting.

18

Turbulence jostled Drake from an unsettling dream. He had been standing in the rain at Sully's funeral, the only person without a black umbrella. Among the sea of faces he could see through the veil of dream and rain were many of the less savory characters he and Sully had encountered over the years. Thieves and cutthroats, smugglers and corrupt politicians—all of them had gathered to pay their respects. Jada stood by the grave, her magenta bangs now dyed a bloody crimson, and the priest who stood at the head of the gathering, one hand on the coffin, was Luka Hzujak.

The priest had looked at him, dry beneath his huge black umbrella.

"When you lie down with snakes, you've gotta learn to hiss," the priestly Luka had said, his voice like a whisper in Drake's ear. "But that doesn't mean you have to slither."

He had laughed then, and the entire gathering of mourners had laughed with him, their voices the shush of rain pattering on umbrellas. Drake, soaked to the skin, had not found it funny. Sully had used that line about snakes with him ten years earlier, the morning they had paid a ship's captain in Valparaiso to carry them and their cargo home to the States. The man had had a huge cache of drugs on board, also headed for the USA, and Drake had needed to be persuaded not to throw them overboard. Sully had reminded him that if they didn't want the captain to interfere in their business, they couldn't interfere with his.

When he woke from the dream, he found Tyr Henriksen watching him.

Drake sat up, groggily reaching for his gun.

Henriksen nodded. "It's all right, Mr. Drake. Your weapon is still there and still loaded."

Drake's hand closed on the butt of the gun, but he didn't take it out of his waistband. The guttural drone of the engine made him blink, and only as he glanced around did he remember that they were on an airplane chartered by Henriksen for the journey from Greece to China. Out the oval window beyond Henriksen the sky was dark. He wasn't sure how long they had been flying or how long he'd been sleeping, but it was still night.

The plane Henriksen had chartered was of a sort he rarely had been inside: a private jet with seating for twelve in the center and a cabin for business in the rear, complete with a narrow conference table. Henriksen, Olivia, and Corelli had been in the back when Drake had fallen asleep, and it disconcerted him to wake with the man studying him as if he were some kind of exotic pet.

"You slept soundly," Henriksen said. "You snore."

"Back off, pal. You're freaking me out."

Feeling something sticky on his chin, Drake wiped his mouth and realized he had been so deeply asleep that he had been drooling a little. Henriksen had had the good grace not to mention it.

"I guess I was more tired than I thought," Drake said.

Henriksen leaned back in his seat. "We all were. I dozed for several hours myself. Jada is still sleeping."

Drake craned his neck to look back along the aisle and saw her stretched out in her wide, fully reclined seat, a blanket over her. She looked peaceful, and Drake felt happy for her. Peace had been hard for Jada to come by of late. Only sleep offered any respite from her grief and the fears and tensions of recent days. Olivia and Corelli were nowhere to be seen, which he assumed meant they were still in the rear cabin. Whether they had gotten any sleep, he didn't know. Not that he had a lot of concern for their well-being.

"How much longer?" Drake asked, sitting up straight.

He had fallen asleep so quickly that he hadn't even taken the trouble to recline his seat completely, and now his back ached from slouching in the chair for so long.

"We have several hours yet," Henriksen replied.

When he shifted in the seat, he winced, and Drake realized that the knife wound was bothering him badly. Corelli had stitched him up, and it seemed their first aid kit had included some serious painkillers, but if Henriksen had taken anything, Drake hadn't seen him do it.

After escaping from the labyrinth beneath the Goulas in Akrotiri village, they all had spent a little time recovering and letting their clothes drip-dry on the rocks at the bottom of the cliff not far from the village. Getting topside had been a time-consuming process. Drake had hoped the taxi that had dropped him and Jada off in the morning would be there waiting, but night had fallen by the time they returned to the village, and he and Jada had reluctantly accepted a ride back to their hotel from Henriksen. They had ridden in relative silence, all the suspicion and ill will poisoning the air in the limousine.

Drake and Jada had returned to the suite, entering with guns drawn, just in case the hooded men were waiting. Not that Drake had believed they would be. All they seemed to want was for everyone to stop searching for the fourth labyrinth, and now that they realized Henriksen and Jada were both on the verge of locating it, Drake figured they would retreat and just wait. He wondered how many killers would be waiting for them when they got to China.

They had showered and put on clean clothes, then packed up what little they had. Without a word, Jada had put all of Sully's things in his duffel, including the sweater he'd bought when they had shopped the night before. Neither one of them was willing even to consider the possibility that he wouldn't have need of the contents of that duffel again.

A door clicked open at the rear of the passenger cabin. Drake turned and saw Corelli poke his head through.

"Mr. Henriksen," the short man said. "Olivia has something you're going to want to hear."

Drake frowned, turning to Henriksen, who popped up from his seat with the exuberance of a child.

"Well?" he said, turning to Drake. "Are you coming?"

"What is it?" Drake asked, still not completely awake. The echoes of his dream had lingered like cobwebs in his mind.

"I'm going to guess it's a translation of all the ancient Chinese back in that chamber," Henriksen said. "Or don't you want to know if my people have figured out the location of the fourth labyrinth?"

Drake stretched and started to rise. "I'm coming."

Henriksen went on without him, hurrying excitedly to the back of the plane and slipping through the door to the rear cabin. As Drake watched him go, a voice from his dream came back to him.

You've gotta learn to hiss, but that doesn't mean you have to slither.

He crouched to shake Jada awake. When he saw that she had been drooling as well, he smiled and used the edge of his shirt cuff to wipe her mouth.

"Wake up, sleeping beauty."

She blinked and then sat up quickly, pulling away from him in a tangle of blanket, eyes wide. For a second she seemed almost not to recognize him, and then she relaxed, remembering where she was and how she had gotten there.

"Bad dreams?" he asked.

"No. Good ones," she replied, but she didn't elaborate. Jada glanced around. "And now I wake up to the nightmare."

Drake nodded, giving her a moment to come more fully awake. Then he hooked his thumb toward the rear of the plane.

"Henriksen just went into the back. I guess Olivia's got something new."

At the mention of her stepmother's name, Jada's eyes darkened. She didn't bother using the control to put her seat upright, just shoved the blanket aside and joined Drake in the aisle. She ran her fingers through her sleep-mussed hair and nodded to him, then led the way to the door to the rear cabin.

Jada didn't knock, just opened the door and stepped through.

Olivia and Corelli were seated at the narrow conference table and glanced up from the laptop open in front of them when Jada and Drake entered the cabin. Henriksen had expected them and did not bother to turn away; he stood over the nearer end of the table, studying one of the maps Luka had left with his journal for Jada to find. Drake knew the sight must have given Jada pause—her father had hidden his research to keep it out of Henriksen's hands, and now she had handed the journal and maps over to the man who'd been his rival. It had been the right choice at the time, the only choice—they had more dangerous enemies to be wary of—but Drake could tell the decision didn't sit right with Jada at all.

Drake had no doubt they would come to regret it. The only question was when that moment would arrive and whether they would be ready for it.

"What've you got?" Jada asked, staring at her stepmother. Henriksen might be Olivia's boss, but when the two women were in the same room, the bitterness and tension existed for the two of them alone.

Olivia smiled thinly. Either she had wearied of her stepdaughter's hatred and suspicion or she had decided it was time to stop pretending she gave a crap what Jada thought. Whatever happened now, it was all business. They shared certain goals—all of them—and for the moment that was enough to keep them cooperating.

"Quite a lot, actually," Olivia said. "Why don't you have a seat."

Drake waited for a cue from Jada, wondering if she might refuse to sit. But she hesitated for only a moment before sliding into one of the remaining chairs around the table. Drake sat next to her, glancing for a moment at the large screen at the rear of the cabin, which flickered with blank light. The monitor was on but displayed nothing at the moment.

"Are we gonna have a slide show?" he asked. "Fair warning, I tend to fall asleep. Unless it's the one on fire safety. I like the sirens. And the Dalmatian."

Henriksen shot him a disapproving glance, and Corelli scoffed like a man about to start a fight in a bar. The women ignored them all. Jada stared impatiently at Olivia, who tapped a couple of keys on the laptop. The plane's engine whined loudly enough that they had to raise their voices slightly to be heard, and the pungent smell of urine and industrial cleanser came from the bathroom. Drake figured no amount of money could build an airplane without those two elements, but wealthy people liked to pretend they didn't notice them. The thought crystallized a feeling he'd had in the back of his mind all day: Henriksen was a brat, just a spoiled rich kid grown up into a spoiled rich man. He wanted the secrets and treasures of the fourth labyrinth because he liked to own things that nobody else could have.

"Phoenix Innovations employs a man named Emil Yablonski," Olivia said. "Yablonski is the most brilliant man I've ever met, but he's almost incapable of functioning socially. He's a historian and archaeologist, but he hadn't done fieldwork in more than twenty years. He doesn't mind e-mail or even the phone, but he doesn't like talking to people in person. He'd rather you be in the next room than in his office."

Henriksen waved a hand to indicate she should move along. He slipped into a chair, though still studying the map unfolded in front of him.

"They don't care about Yablonski," Henriksen said. "The guy works for me, and I don't care, either." He shot a look at Jada. "Part of my company is a think tank. Yablonski has his own division. Now we move on."

Olivia smiled at her employer, but there were sharp edges to her expression and it was clear she didn't like being spoken to so brusquely. Drake couldn't muster much sympathy.

"Yablonski is practically paralyzed with geek joy over the information he's getting from these translations," Olivia said. "His exact words were, 'This changes everything.' Frankly, I think that's a rash overstatement. The ancient Chinese writing on the walls and on the ceremonial jars clarifies certain things, confirms others, and gives us some vital clues as to our next step.

"We start with Daedalus. With the writings from the three chambers in the labyrinth of Sobek for comparison, Yablonski has confirmed that Daedalus designed the first three—Knossos, Crocodilopolis, and Thera—though if you want to refer to the Thera structure as the labyrinth of Atlantis, it would make Yablonski very happy."

"He really thinks Atlantis was there?" Drake asked.

Olivia shot him a withering look, cold and beautiful. "Atlantis is a myth, Mr. Drake. The labyrinth of Poseidon on Thera is the seed from which the roots of that myth grew."

"Are you saying Daedalus didn't design the fourth labyrinth?" Jada asked.

Olivia arched an eyebrow. "Someone was listening. Let me back up, though. The temple at Knossos was built around 1700 B.C., the same era in which the Egyptians built Crocodile City. But what's become clear here is that these cities were already under way or already built by the time the labyrinths were constructed. We're putting our best guess at around 1550 B.C. Knossos came first. Daedalus tried to impress Minos—or Midas—in order to win his approval so that he could marry Ariadne. But one entire wall of the Chinese worship chamber on Thera is given over to telling the story, and it's clear that Daedalus only met Ariadne when he went to the king with his plans to build the labyrinth."

Henriksen grunted. "The labyrinth came first."

Olivia nodded. "It did."

"So what was Daedalus? The traveling inventor?" Drake asked. "He just wandered around the ancient world saying, 'Hey, want me to build you something cool?'"

"He was an alchemist, of course," Olivia said, her smile genuine for once.

"That's crap," Jada snorted.

Corelli hit a key on the laptop, and an image appeared on the monitor screen on the rear wall of the cabin, showing several paintings and a lot of ancient Chinese characters.

"The people who wrote this disagree," Corelli said.

Drake stared at him. "Relax, junior. The grown-ups are talking."

Corelli froze, his features practically turning to stone. For a moment, Drake thought he might lunge across the table or pull a weapon, but then Olivia put a firm hand on his arm and he relaxed, forcing a smile.

"Go on, then. Why don't you tell me what it says?" Corelli said.

Drake shrugged. "It's all chicken scratches to me," he said, looking back at Olivia. "But I know a little bit about alchemists. You can't make gold."

"It doesn't matter," Henriksen said. He pointed to the screen. "They believed it could be done, and they believed Daedalus could do it."

Olivia leaned back in her chair. "Exactly."

"So Daedalus was a snake-oil salesman," Jada said. "He didn't fulfill a need; he invented it."

Drake glanced down at Luka Hzujak's journal, which had been in the center of the table since they'd entered. He picked it up and flipped to the first maze sketches he found, and then he looked up at Jada, ignoring the others.

"Your father had figured that part out, I think."

"Why do you say that?" Olivia asked.

Drake ignored her, opened the book, and leaned over to show Jada a page where Luka had titled one maze drawing "The Labyrinth of Anygod."

Jada's eyes were bright as she lifted her gaze. "He knew." She looked at Olivia and Corelli and then turned to Henriksen. "Daedalus went to the kings and high priests with the labyrinth design and claimed he could make them all as much gold as they could ever want. And he promised them that the labyrinth would be the perfect treasury, a place for them to store their own gold where it could never be stolen."

"And then he stole it," Drake said, grinning. "The lovable bastard."

"You can't know that," Olivia sniffed.

"Sure we can," Drake said. "It makes sense. Dionysus, Poseidon—Sobek? The crocodile god? Daedalus would dedicate his labyrinth to whichever god was best loved where he wanted to build. Real estate developers do basically the same thing every damn day."

Olivia and Henriksen studied each other a moment, and then Henriksen nodded. Once again, Drake felt sure they were hiding something. Not all of this stuff about Daedalus, because he sensed their excitement about the revelations that Yablonski's translations had turned up. But they had a piece of the puzzle they weren't sharing.

"It could be," Olivia said.

"What else did your supergeek turn up?" Drake asked.

Corelli hit another key. More of the flowers that had been a part of the design throughout the labyrinth under the fortress and the Minotaur.

"There are about a dozen flowers this could be," Corelli said. "The research team thinks it's most likely something called false hellebore or white hellebore. They're poisonous."

Drake had been wondering why he'd take an interest until Corelli mentioned poison, and then he saw the thug's eyes light up. The information had stuck with him because he had a fascination with ways to hurt and kill people. Drake had met his kind before and didn't like the unpredictable quality they brought to the table.

Olivia typed a couple of things. Images flashed by, ending with the large painting of the Chinese hell—Diyu—that they'd found in the chamber.

"Obviously the labyrinth on Thera was begun later than the other three," Olivia said. "It may be that Daedalus was moving his hoard from one to the next, abandoning the kingdoms he had duped. By the time the construction of the worship chambers on Thera had begun, he had obviously found a new sucker and a location where he could break ground on a fourth labyrinth. It would've been under construction while the labyrinth on Thera was still being completed.

"By the time of the eruption on Thera—which destroyed the Minoan offshoot colony there—"

"Atlantis," Drake put in just to irritate her.

"—the fourth labyrinth was being built in a place called Yia-jiang in southern China," Olivia continued. "Yiajiang was a tiny settlement that grew and later became known as Yecheng."

"It doesn't really ring a bell," Drake said.

Olivia turned to Henriksen. "Today we know it as the city of Nanjing."

"That's nuts," Drake said. "I've been to Nanjing. The original city wasn't built until—what, fifth century B.C. That's a thousand years after Thera exploded."

Olivia nodded. "That was my first reaction, too. But Yablon-ski confirms there were tribal settlements in the area all through that period. And would you care to guess what myth is consistent with every one of those settlements?"

Drake sat back in his chair, letting it sink in. He glanced at the hideous painting on the screen.

"Diyu."

"You're not as dumb as you look," Corelli muttered.

Henriksen had his phone out. He punched a couple of keys, and a moment later he was barking orders. It took Drake a minute to realize that he must have a whole new batch of hired thugs either already in China or on their way and had just instructed them to rendezvous in Nanjing. A second later, Henriksen hit an intercom switch and the pilot answered. Henriksen gave him their new destination and then signed off, turning his attention back to the conversation.

"The gold was on Thera during the eruption," Jada said, eyes narrowed as she worked it out. "Had to be. The labyrinth there was unstable but only partially destroyed. Once they'd finished the fourth labyrinth, they would've moved Daedalus's hoard there. But what about Daedalus?"

Olivia clicked past several other images and stopped on one of the ceremonial jars, which showed the Mistress of the Labyrinth, a Minotaur, and what Drake realized was a funeral pyre.

"They burned him?" Drake asked.

"He died," Olivia said. "His nephew, Talos, finished the design for the fourth labyrinth and altered it considerably. Beneath the painting of Diyu in the chamber, it is written that Talos wanted an army of slaves to build the labyrinth for him, and that would require overseers and protectors."

"The Minotaur was supposed to be the protector," Drake said.

"Of the labyrinth, yes," Olivia replied. "But the Minotaur would've been like a guard dog. They'd have selected the biggest, most frightening warrior they could find."

"So, not Corelli, then," Drake said.

Corelli made a rude gesture but said nothing.

"Talos wanted what Yablonski translated as 'Protectors of the Hidden Word,'" Olivia finished.

Henriksen looked at her. "Tell me about Diyu. What did the research team find?"

Olivia glanced at her laptop screen. "According to the myth— as opposed to the writings we found—the labyrinth was ruled by Yan Luo, sort of a god himself. Yablonski's translations confirm that the Chinese worship chamber was dedicated to Yan Luo, the king of hell. On Thera, Daedalus had started to expand more with the idea of underground, multilevel labyrinths, and that matches up with the myth of Diyu, which was a maze of levels and chambers where souls were supposed to be brought and punished for their earthly sins. Once they had redeemed themselves, they could be given the Drink of Forgetfulness and return to the world, or so they were promised."

Drake felt something unlocking in his mind, tumblers clicking into place. Jada must have sensed a change in him, because she gave him an odd look.

"Nate? What is it?" she asked.

Corelli, Olivia, and Henriksen were all looking at him. The airplane's engine seemed louder than ever. Sudden turbulence shook them hard enough that his teeth clacked together, and it felt like the plane veered to the right. Drake chalked it up to the pilot correcting their course for Nanjing.

"Daedalus's nephew wanted slaves. The people believed in hell. What if that's the reason they chose this location and the reason they changed the design? What if they *built* hell and then abducted people, maybe drugged them and pulled them down there and made them think they were in Diyu? Who knows, maybe there really was some kind of Drink of Forgetfulness. When they grew too old to be useful, they'd drug them again and return them to the surface."

Drake glanced around, the plane taking a bounce that jarred his knees against the underside of the table. He grimaced, then threw up his hands.

"Am I crazy?"

Henriksen frowned and cast a dark look toward the front of the plane, apparently irritated at the pilot. But then he turned back to Drake.

"That may not be as far-fetched as it sounds," he said.

Jada rolled her eyes. "Everything about this is far-fetched. But all the pieces fit together too neatly not to be true."

"Nanjing has a long history of stories about people vanishing. Three Jin princes and their courts went missing in the third century. During the Ming Dynasty, when Nanjing was the capital of China, hundreds of thousands of workers were brought in to rebuild the city, and there were stories that a demon lived under the old city gates and would eat the workers if it caught them out at night. Many of them supposedly vanished."

"The Minotaur?" Jada asked. "Or whoever the Mistress of the Labyrinth made up to look like a Minotaur?"

"Could be," Drake said.

"These guys in the hoods," Corelli said. "If they're still down there, how many do we think there are?"

Drake could see he was thinking in terms of combat. How many guns would they need to get past the hooded killers of the labyrinth, the Protectors of the Hidden Word?

"Are there still slaves?" Olivia wondered aloud.

Drake thought of Sully and Ian Welch, and he knew the answer. It enraged him to think what Sully might be going through—he didn't want to think about the images of torture in Diyu—but it reassured him as well. If all of their conjecture held together, it meant that Sully was still alive.

Henriksen looked contemplative. "There's a famous story about an army detachment—three hundred men—who disappeared while returning to Nanjing in 1939. They were expected, but they never arrived."

"Maybe they did," Drake said. "But they hit a detour."

Olivia cried out as the plane shook violently. The laptop slid from the table. Corelli made a grab for it, but the aircraft pitched to starboard and he toppled after the computer to the floor. The large screen winked out as the laptop landed with a crack, Corelli sprawling on top of it.

Jada slid into Drake, who held on to the table to keep from falling from his chair. Henriksen stood, but the pitch of the plane threw him into the wall. He made his way to the door and flung it open. Drake could see into the vacant passenger cabin, and his stomach lurched as he got a better view of just how badly they were listing.

"What the hell is going on?" Drake asked, following Henriksen into the passenger cabin. They leaned on seats and braced themselves on the overhead compartments as they struggled toward the cockpit. The tall man had a small spot of blood seeping through his shirt where his knife wound had been bandaged.

"I don't know," Henriksen replied, eyes dark with resignation. "But this isn't turbulence."

They reached the front of the cabin. Henriksen began pounding on the door to the cockpit, shouting for the pilot or the co-pilot to let him in. Drake shifted his stance and felt something sticky under his boot. When he glanced down, he swore under his breath and tapped Henriksen, pointing out the narrow pool of blood trickling out from underneath the door.

"Back up!" Drake shouted, drawing his gun.

Henriksen moved aside, eyes wide, and covered his ears against the boom a gunshot would make in such a closed space. Drake tried not to think about the possibility of a ricochet and what would happen to the plane at this altitude if a bullet ripped through the aircraft's skin.

Then he pulled the trigger three times, blowing apart the cockpit's lock.

Drake kicked the door in, Henriksen right behind him.

The pilot lay dead on the floor, his slashed throat gaping like a bloody, mocking grin. The copilot held a disturbingly familiar curved blade, the same sort used by the Protectors of the Hidden Word. The guy looked Greek; he sure as hell wasn't Chinese. For a second, Drake wondered if everything they had been assuming was wrong, if they really knew nothing at all about the threat they were facing and the people trying to keep them from finding the fourth labyrinth. Then he noticed the glazed look in the copilot's eyes, his lost and distant gaze, and he knew the man was not in his right mind.

"Drop the knife or I *will* shoot you," Drake said.

The copilot didn't even acknowledge them. Instead, at the mention of the knife, he glanced down at the gleaming blood-streaked blade, eyes wide with recognition. His face slack and expressionless, he slashed his own throat.

"No, damn it!" Drake shouted, reaching for the copilot with his free hand.

The man crumpled to the ground, twitching, blood pulsing from his wound. The cut was deep and long, blood vessels severed. There would be no saving him.

Henriksen stared slack-jawed at the two dead men even as the hull of the plane screamed around them, air currents twisting the craft, dipping it even harder to starboard. Any second, the plane would begin to dive.

Drake tucked away his gun and dived for the pilot's seat. He grabbed the stick and held on, trying to keep the plane from shaking apart around them.

"Please tell me you know how to fly an airplane," Henriksen said.

Drake didn't spare him a glance as he replied. "Does 'sort of' count?"

19

Tyr Henriksen seemed capable of wielding his wealth like a scalpel or like a club, depending on the circumstances. Either way, the man clearly was used to smoothing the path of his life with money. But no matter how rich he was, he could do nothing to hurry the Nanjing police. When a handful of Americans and a filthy rich Norwegian made an emergency landing at the local airport with two dead men on board, the cops were going to have questions.

Any other day, the boredom drilling into Drake's brain would have had him on the verge of screaming. But considering that a couple of hours earlier he had landed a jet, talked in to the runway by air traffic controllers whose entire English vocabulary seemed to have been learned from old Tom Cruise movies, all he really wanted was a beer. Not that he blamed the air traffic controllers for not speaking his language—he was in *their* country, after all. But the first time one of them called him "Maverick," he had pretty much assumed he was going to die.

Not dying, in contrast, had made his day.

They'd left Santorini just after eight p.m.—two in the morning, Nanjing time—and the flight had taken just under twelve hours even with the unfortunate murder/suicide interruption. Now looking out the windows of the airport security office, Drake could see the shadows growing long as the daylight turned late afternoon gold. The clock read just after five p.m.

Jada had curled up on a sofa and fallen asleep—adrenaline hangover, he figured. Corelli sat on an uncomfortable-looking plastic and metal chair across from Drake, hands in his lap. He looked like a waxwork dummy of a 1940s movie gangster,

Jimmy Cagney's bulkier brother. Or a robot someone had shifted into the idle position.

Through a glass partition, Drake could see Henriksen and Olivia standing in sullen silence as Nanjing police, airport security, and a dark-suited representative of the Chinese government argued with representatives from the Norwegian and American embassies. The copilot had been a paid assassin or a terrorist, the diplomats were insisting, bent on the murder of a prominent and wealthy businessman. Henriksen and his people were lucky to be alive; they shouldn't be treated as victims.

That was essentially how the argument was going from the snippets of it Drake had heard through the glass and through the door when security agents went in and out. The real conflict going on in that room had to do with the guns that had been found on the plane. While Drake had been trying not to crash the aircraft, Corelli had gathered all the weapons from their bags, wiped them down, and hidden them inside a food service cabinet. Now Henriksen and Olivia were insisting that they knew nothing about the cache of guns and that they must have belonged to the copilot assassin. The Chinese authorities were having difficulty believing that one killer would need half a dozen guns, but the representatives from the U.S. and Norwegian embassies were putting the pressure on. Drake had a feeling that it wouldn't be long before they were allowed to leave, though not without the government putting some kind of surveillance on them. It was going to be an interesting night.

Drake stood and walked toward the exit. Corelli frowned, shattering the notion that he might be a robot, and watched his progress. A pane of glass was set into the metal door, and through it Drake could see a pair of guards in the corridor outside. The security director and the police investigators had been polite enough, though their manners came with a frosty demeanor. Polite or not, though, there could be no mistaking this for anything other than a detention area. As far as Drake could tell, nobody had said they were in custody, but until they were released, they might as well be behind bars.

His thoughts turned constantly to Sully. While they were locked up here, spinning lies and deception, where was he? Drake had put all his faith into the belief that the Protectors of the Hidden Word had taken Sully with them back to the fourth labyrinth, and all signs pointed to the labyrinth being here. But until they found the labyrinth, he wouldn't know for sure if Sully was still among the living. What bothered him most was that they were prisoners not only of the authorities but of their own ignorance. They were in Nanjing, but in reality they were no closer to the labyrinth. Until they knew exactly where it was, the facts they *did* know were useless.

So, while Jada slept and Corelli zoned out, Drake had been racking his brain for what he knew about Nanjing, trying to bring logic to bear on the problem. They had no Internet access. Corelli couldn't even contact Yablonski back at Phoenix Innovations to see if the brilliant recluse had come up with anything else that might be helpful. For the moment, Drake was alone with the puzzle.

While the security team was hustling them in from the tarmac, they had passed down a corridor with advertisements on the walls. One of them had shown a subway train and had a map of various underground transportation lines. Drake couldn't read Chinese, but the words "Nanjing Metro" were in English, and the poster had gotten him thinking. If the city had been built on top of the fourth labyrinth, there had to have been thousands of opportunities over the years for builders to break through into the ancient maze. There were basements, subway lines, underground malls, and, most recently, subterranean bomb and earthquake shelters.

He suspected that if they did the research, they would find all sorts of stories about workers vanishing while engaged in excavation for those projects. If the Protectors of the Hidden Word had been active for two thousand years before the foundations of the first real city had been built in Nanjing, they would have been careful all along to keep excavators away. The labyrinth might be deep underground, but Drake doubted it would have been deeper than the subway.

They needed a map of the Nanjing Metro. They had to find a piece of the city with no tunnels underground, a space wide enough for a labyrinth the size of the one on Thera. He had been thinking about the legend of the demon that supposedly had lived under the city gates during the construction phase of the Ming Dynasty. Once upon a time, Nanjing had had thirteen gates, but now only one remained. Drake knew it had another name, but it was known simply as the China Gate, a major tourist attraction. He'd only ever seen pictures, but he had to wonder.

He turned to find Corelli still watching him. Jada began to stir and opened her eyes. For a moment she smiled at Drake, but then it was as if a veil of hurt had been drawn over her eyes, and he knew that she had remembered where they were and why and all the events of the last week. He thought of that blissful moment she'd had in the haze between sleeping and waking, and he envied her.

The door to the inner office swung open, and the three of them looked around to see a security guard emerge. Drake exhaled with disappointment, but the guard didn't let the door close behind him. Instead, the man held it open for Henriksen and Olivia, who wore matching facial expressions, a mixture of arrogance and irritation at the inconvenience they had been forced to endure. The two diplomats followed, along with a Nanjing police officer. Through the glass partition, Drake could see the dark-suited government agent speaking with the director of airport security. They did not look happy, which confirmed Drake's suspicion that they were being allowed to leave.

"Come on," he said to Jada. "We're going."

A limousine awaited them outside. Porters carried their bags out and put them into the trunk, and Corelli slammed it shut. Drake and Jada climbed in after Olivia while Henriksen had a quick conversation with the Norwegian and U.S. embassy men. Corelli went and stood by him, taking up a position as his employer's bodyguard. None of them had guns anymore—they couldn't exactly have asked for them back after denying ownership of the weapons—but Corelli looked like he knew how to hurt people without bullets. Drake assumed the conversation had to do with Henriksen's gratitude for the diplomats' intervention and the manner in which his thanks would be expressed. *In cash, probably*, Drake thought.

Henriksen opened the passenger door and looked in at the driver.

"Get out."

"Mr. Henriksen," the blond man said, his accent much thicker than Henriksen's, "the embassy sent me. I'm to take you anywhere you like."

Henriksen glanced back at the diplomats on the sidewalk, then looked at the driver again.

"You'll be paid. But I have my own driver."

As he spoke, Corelli opened the driver's door and gestured for the man to get out. The driver hesitated, then shrugged and climbed out, leaving the car running. He said something in Norwegian, calling to the embassy man over the top of the limo. The diplomat nodded tersely, and the driver threw up his hands and moved out of the way, letting Corelli slip behind the wheel.

The driver still stood mystified beside the limo as Corelli slammed the door. Henriksen joined Olivia, Jada, and Drake in the back and shut his door, and moments later they were gliding out into the traffic leaving the airport. Jada and Drake exchanged a glance.

"Have you ever driven in Nanjing before?" Jada asked.

"Never been to China," Corelli replied. He nodded toward the dashboard. "We got a GPS. How hard can it be?"

"Hand me that," Henriksen said.

Corelli passed the GPS back through the open window between the driver's seat and the rear of the limo. Henriksen tapped the touch screen, quickly switching languages, and then keyed in an address before handing it back.

"Thanks, boss," Corelli said.

"Where are we going?" Jada asked.

Olivia stretched her legs, the leather seat creaking beneath her. Drake couldn't help noticing how shapely those legs were, straining against the fabric of her pants, and he wondered if she did such things on purpose to draw attention or if it was just a reflex after decades of wanting to be the center of attention.

"We're going to the hotel," she said.

Drake frowned, shaking from his musings about her. "I don't think so. These ninja bastards have Sully. I'm not lounging around in some hotel suite while they're doing who knows what to him."

"Ninjas are Japanese," Corelli supplied from behind the wheel, glancing in the rearview mirror as the GPS gave him instructions in a soft feminine voice.

"Shut up," Drake snapped. "You think I don't know—oh, forget it." He stared at Henriksen. "Listen, I've been trying to work out where the labyrinth might be. We need to take a hard look at the China Gate. And we need a subway map."

He explained his reasoning, and Henriksen listened calmly. Jada nodded in support, but Olivia only stared through the limousine's tinted glass window at the lights of Nanjing coming to colorful life as night fell around them. The cityscape included a strange mix of gleaming modern office towers and pagoda-like buildings. They passed cars and buses and bicycles, the city teeming with people, but Drake shut it all out. They weren't here to sightsee.

"I've been to the China Gate," Henriksen said when Drake had finished.

"You've been to Nanjing before?" Jada asked, eyes narrowed in suspicion.

Henriksen gave her an amused look. "I do business around the world. I've been almost everywhere at one point or another. But the last time I was here, nearly fifteen years ago, I was touring the country with my ex-wife. Mr. Drake's logic is sound. The China Gate was built during the Ming Dynasty, but its builders included portions of the original city gate, which dates back to the Tang Dynasty in the eighth century. I specifically remember that it was once called the Jubao Gate, which translates as the 'Gathering Treasure' Gate."

Drake felt a chill. "You think that's a reference to the gold Daedalus's nephew moved from Thera?"

"It's possible," Henriksen said.

"Wouldn't someone have found it by now?" Olivia asked, her eyes alight with interest now. Eager, she leaned forward in her seat. "It sounds like this gate must get a constant stream of tourists. Even if you assume the labyrinth's protectors would abduct or kill anyone who found an entrance, they would have to come and go themselves. It doesn't seem likely there'd be a way into the labyrinth from somewhere so public."

"Maybe it isn't there at all," Jada said. "How many people could vanish in that one spot without the authorities taking a much closer look?"

Drake nodded and stared out the window as the limo crossed a bridge over the Qinhuai River, the calm water replete with yellow-canopied riverboats. Jada's argument made sense, and his momentary excitement had been extinguished.

"Regardless, we can't simply go there and start searching," Henriksen said. "Whatever we do, we require the cover of night, and if we find the labyrinth, its hooded killers are sure to be waiting for us, which means we need reinforcements. I have a security team on the way. They'll be here by midnight. And of course the government and the police will be watching us. I need time to put the appropriate bribes in place to make sure they look the other way when the moment comes."

Drake swore, hands clenched into fists as he thought of Sully.

Jada touched his arm. "He's a tough old guy. He'll be all right until we can get to him."

"We go to the hotel," Henriksen said, pulling out his phone. "Meanwhile, we get Yablonski looking at the Nanjing Metro map and see what else is as old as the China Gate."

"He's already compiling a database of disappearances," Olivia said. "If we see a concentration of people going missing in one particular spot over the centuries, that'll help, too."

Drake couldn't argue with any of them, and that made his frustration all the worse. Several long minutes passed as Henriksen phoned Yablonski, and then the interior of the limo fell into a silence broken only by the white noise of the engine and the hum of the tires on pavement. He stared out the window toward the east, where the city gave way to a forested mountain. When he glanced over at Jada, she looked as if she wanted to crawl out of her skin. She and her stepmother were on the same seat but sitting as far apart from each other as the space inside the limo would allow.

How did it come to this? Drake wondered. *Relying on the people we were out to stop from the beginning?* Henriksen and Olivia might not have killed Jada's father, but Luka had wanted nothing more than to stop Henriksen from getting to the fourth labyrinth before him.

So what would you have done if you got here on your own? he thought. *What would be the next step?*

Drake turned to Henriksen and held out his hand. "Give me your phone."

The big man narrowed his icy blue eyes. "What?"

Jada studied them both, a what-the-hell-are-you-doing look in her eyes.

"Phone?" Drake said.

Henriksen shrugged and handed him the smart phone. Olivia seemed nervous, as if she was worried Drake had something tricky up his sleeve. The limo slowed a bit as Corelli glanced in the rearview again, apparently thinking the same thing. Drake thought about reminding them that *he* wasn't a ninja, either, and it wasn't like he was going to be able to use the phone as a deadly weapon. He decided to let it go. If wondering what he had in mind kept them nervous, that was probably for the best.

Internet access was limited in China, so that was no good, but a quick call to London information services got him the phone number for the archaeology department of Oxford University, and moments later he sat listening to the phone ringing half the world away.

"Margaret Xin, please," he said when a male voice answered.

Henriksen's eyes widened in alarm, and he reached for the

phone. Drake slapped his hand away, though he was impressed that the man had recognized Margaret Xin's name.

"Relax, blondie," Drake said. "We're in this together for now."

He hated saying the words, wanted to spit to clear the taste of them out of his mouth. As far as he was concerned, they were in it together as long as their fate was twined together and not a moment longer. He figured Henriksen felt the same way.

A quiet female voice came on the line. "Hello?"

"Maggie, it's Nathan Drake."

"Nate? This is a surprise. Are you in London?"

"No, Maggie, listen—Sully's in trouble," Drake said. "I know you two ended kind of messy, but I need your help."

He heard a deep intake of breath, and when she spoke again, there was a tremor in her voice.

"This isn't cheating-at-cards sort of trouble, is it?"

"Would I be calling you if it was?"

"I guess not," Maggie said softly. "You're right, Nate. It ended messy between Victor and me. In fact, messy probably doesn't begin to cover it. I wish he was a different sort of man, but I can't blame him for that. How can I help?"

Drake let out a breath, relieved. He gave a slight nod to Jada.

"Nanjing," he said. "Something old. Maybe underground. Catacombs, maybe, or a fortress or palace."

"You're in China?" Maggie said. "What are you doing in—"

"Now's not the time. When it's all over, I'll call you and tell you everything. Right now I just need to know what you can tell me."

Maggie hesitated, thinking. "Well, you're not going to find real catacombs there. The rest—I mean, fortresses, palaces—there are all sorts of things. But underground, the only thing that comes immediately to mind is the palace of Zhu Yuanzhang, who you might know as the Hongwu Emperor. He was the first emperor of the Ming Dynasty. The palace is supposed to be under the Ming Xiaoling Mausoleum, inside the Treasure Mound."

Drake froze, his heart thrumming in his chest along with the limousine's engine. "Treasure Mound," he repeated, wanting to be sure he'd heard her right.

"Well, there isn't any actual treasure there," Maggie explained. "It's a reference to the emperor's tomb and whatever might have been buried with him."

"Why do you say it's supposed to be there? Don't you know?" Drake asked.

"Nobody does for sure. The mausoleum is a complex of twenty buildings that took decades to complete. The Treasure Mound is a hill in the midst of the complex, which is east of the city. Archaeologists have used geomagnetic surveying equipment to confirm the presence of tunnels under the mound. Turned out the whole mound was covered with large bricks from the Six Dynasties, dated to the fifth century, which suggests there was another structure there at some point.

"In any case, the team analyzing the Treasure Mound found tunnels that go right to its heart. Part of the mausoleum complex is a structure called the Soul Tower, the base of which goes fairly deep into the mound. They were able to map the tunnel, and it leads to the base of the Soul Tower and some kind of opening, but couldn't go any further."

Drake frowned. "What do you mean they couldn't go any further? Was there a cave-in?"

"I'm not clear on some of the details," Maggie said. "I found the research fascinating, but I haven't written about it or taught it in class, so I can only tell you what I remember, which is that some kind of room was found but no real entrance. Still, the archaeologists working at the mound were convinced they'd found the actual burial site of Zhu Yuanzhang."

Drake gazed out at the glittering lights of Nanjing. "I don't get it. Why didn't they excavate?" he asked.

"It's against the law."

"What?"

"The only one of the Thirteen Imperial Tombs of the Ming Dynasty that's been excavated is the tomb of Emperor Wanli in

Beijing, and that was back in the 1950s. After that, the government forbade the excavation of any of the other 'underground palaces.' "

Drake was silent as he felt puzzle pieces clicking into place in his mind. He glanced at Jada and Olivia, then at Henriksen.

"Nate, are you still there?" Maggie asked.

"I'm here. But I should go now."

"Is that helpful at all?"

An image flashed through Drake's mind of the hooded men dragging Sully down into the darkness of the labyrinth of Thera.

"I sure as hell hope so," he said.

"So do I," Maggie replied. "When you catch up to Victor—"

"Yeah?"

"Give him my love."

Drake could feel years of regret in those four words, but he could offer her no comfort other than to promise that he would pass the message on. In a way, it was a promise to himself as well, a vow that he would see Sully again and be able to tell him that Margaret Xin sent her love.

He reiterated his assurance that he would tell her the whole story when he could and then ended the call and handed the phone back to Henriksen.

"What was all of that?" Henriksen asked.

"What's this 'Treasure Mound'?" Olivia added.

Drake leaned back in his seat, feeling the soft leather crinkle beneath him. "What would you say if I told you the tomb of the first Ming emperor is under a hill not far from here but archaeologists have never been inside it because the Chinese government has forbidden them to excavate it?"

Henriksen and Olivia stared at him. In the front seat, Corelli swore.

Jada smiled. "I'd say somebody in the government is either well paid to keep a secret or too afraid not to."

"I don't know," Olivia said. "It doesn't prove anything."

"Maybe not, but it's a start," Drake said. "And you can bet there's no subway underneath it."

20

Henriksen seemed reluctant to go along with Drake and Jada's insistence that his men not kill the guards at the Ming Xiaoling Mausoleum. Corelli, in contrast, seemed actively disappointed.

Seven hours had passed since Drake's phone conversation with Margaret Xin, and Henriksen had used the intervening time wisely. Two separate mercenary groups had arrived to report for duty, a total of sixteen men and women willing to take orders without questioning things such as morality and legality. They were introduced to Drake and Jada as employees of private security firms on loan to Phoenix Innovations, but that was just a fancy way of saying they were ex-military personnel willing to put their training to use in the service of whoever could afford to pay.

Henriksen's latest thugs came complete with an arsenal of weapons that would have made the Nanjing police officers who'd questioned them at the airport go into cardiac arrest. When Drake had asked for guns for himself and Jada, Henriksen had started to speak up, on the verge of telling Perkins, the ranking officer, not to give them weapons. Then he apparently had remembered that they were all still pretending to be on the same side and gave Perkins the nod.

It had underscored the question that had been on Drake's mind for a while. Henriksen knew they weren't looking for the same result from this mission. Yes, Drake's first priority was Sully's safety, but he and Sully had promised Jada that they would follow through on Luka's last wish and make sure the world learned the secrets of the fourth labyrinth. If Henriksen planned to loot Daedalus's hoard, how did he expect to hide that theft from the public?

The obvious answer was that he didn't. That meant, of course, that he also didn't intend to let the secrets of the labyrinth get out. To prevent that, he'd have to kill Drake, Jada, and Sully, and what better place to do it than down in the labyrinth, where they probably would never be found?

But if Henriksen hadn't killed Luka and Cheney, was he a killer? Did he really intend to come to some compromise with them? Drake knew only one way to find out. It gave him a small sliver of hope when Henriksen ordered his people not to kill the mausoleum guards. They were bound and gagged and several were knocked unconscious, but in the morning they'd still be alive, and that boded well.

They were almost certainly in the right place. In addition to their suspicions after what Margaret Xin had told Drake, Yablonski had come through with another small fact that solidified their belief: the three hundred soldiers who had vanished near Nanjing in the 1940s had been camped on Dulongfu, a hill at the foot of the Zijin Shan Mountains.

The site of the Ming Xiaoling Mausoleum.

Now in the moonlight, they raced north through the grounds of the mausoleum toward the Soul Tower and the Treasure Mound beyond. On a curving path, they passed carved stone figures of animals both real and mythical and then figures of humans. Crossing several small bridges, they reached a red stone gate and then hurried across an open plateau where the bases of temple pillars were all that remained of one of the original buildings. Another bridge and then a tunnel, and at last they approached the Soul Tower, an enormous stone structure that abutted the Treasure Mound.

Yablonski's research team had dug up articles and reports from the archaeology team that had confirmed the location of the tomb, so they didn't have to scour the mound for the location of the tunnel. Henriksen had a map that pinpointed it exactly, and Corelli and Perkins led them all directly to it. The hired guns were stealthy; Drake had to give them that. They moved in relative silence even carrying weapons and packs, and the wind was the only sound up there on the hill. With the trees all around the perimeter of the mausoleum complex, even the late night noises of the city could not reach them. It felt to him as if the night were holding its breath.

A chain-link gate had been installed to block the tunnel entrance. Perkins gestured to a grim-faced brunette woman, who hurried forward, slid off her pack, and pulled out a set of folding bolt cutters. In thirty seconds, she had the chain cut, and Perkins caught it so that it wouldn't clank when it hit the ground. The gates screeched a little as they were dragged open, and then they were pouring two by two into the tunnel.

Absent the wind, they were swallowed by the ancient stillness of the place. Footfalls, no matter how stealthy, seemed to scrape the walls all around them, echoing off the floor. Drake glanced at Jada and saw the anticipation on her face. His heart raced, and he knew that hers must be hammering. It was still possible that they might be wrong, that the labyrinth would not be found beneath the emperor's tomb, but he felt the rightness of it and a certain menace in the air. It might have been the menace that truly convinced him they had reached their goal.

Flashlights searched the darkness at the end of the tunnel, where it ran into the base of the Soul Tower, underground. Four of the mercenaries guarded their flank, lights and guns aimed back toward the entrance.

"Mr. Drake," Henriksen said, gesturing for him to come forward.

Drake and Jada joined Henriksen and Olivia at the horn-shaped opening in the base of the Soul Tower, then slipped through and into a small oval chamber. The walls were constructed of stone blocks, unmarred by paintings or engravings, and the chamber was small enough that with the four of them inside it felt claustrophobic.

Flashlight in one hand, Drake started testing every block with the other hand. He pressed edges and crevices, and Henriksen followed suit. Jada and Olivia joined in. Olivia tried setting her shoulder against a wall, perhaps thinking the whole thing might move. They found no trace of the genius that had gone into using counterweights and perfect balance to create hidden doors and secret passages in the other labyrinths. Unless they were missing something, it was just a room.

"Damn it," Olivia muttered. "I was so sure."

"We all were," Henriksen said.

Jada shook her head. "No. We've got to be missing something. Otherwise what purpose does this chamber serve? It's no ritual space. They built a tunnel to get to it. It's absurd to think there isn't something we're missing."

"The geomagnetic survey showed crevices in the mound and in this tunnel," Henriksen said. "Maybe there's an entrance near one of those. Whether the labyrinth is here or not, there's no question the emperor's tomb is, so we've got to find a way in."

Drake shined his flashlight along the base of the wall, all around the chamber, frowning deeply. He examined the floor, which had been made of the same stone blocks as the walls. Some of the stones seemed to go beneath the walls, as though they continued on the other side, which made sense if the entrance was in one of the walls.

He got on his hands and knees and ran his fingers along the crease between floor and wall on the north side of the small room. The wall definitely sat on top of the stone blocks that made up the floor. Flashing his light around, he realized that the same was true on the eastern and southern walls.

"You've got something," Jada said. "What is it?"

Drake stood and rushed from the tiny chamber, nearly colliding with Corelli, who had been standing just outside, watching the proceedings.

"Watch yourself, moron," Corelli growled.

"Back up," Drake snapped at him. He waved his light at Perkins and the goon squad. "All of you, give me room."

They obliged, and he stood just outside the room, using the flashlight to study the horn-shaped entry and the walls around it. The stones just above the point of the horn were a variety of shapes, as if they were remnants of quarried rock put into place solely because they would fit together. But six inches above the point was a stone that had a roughly octagonal shape. It wasn't perfect, but studying it now, he felt sure the shape could not be an accident. At first none of them had noticed because they had been searching for an engraving, as they'd found in the other labyrinths.

Drake looked into the chamber again, stared at the floor, and gestured toward Jada.

"Come out of there," he said. "All of you."

Jada and Henriksen did as he asked, and he stood aside to let them pass. Olivia frowned. She didn't seem to like the idea of Drake telling her what to do. After a moment, though, she followed her boss out of the chamber. For the moment, they were all still sharing the same goal.

He turned to Perkins and Corelli.

"Give me a boost?"

Corelli sneered. "I'll give you a boost, all right."

But Perkins turned to the largest of his squad. "Massarsky. Help the man out."

The massive thick-necked mercenary slung off the strap of his semiauto and handed it to Garza, a Latina with cold eyes who had her hair tied back in a tight knot. She took it, but Drake noticed that her own weapon remained steady, aimed not quite at him but not away, either.

"Up you go," Massarsky said.

Drake handed Jada his flashlight—he hadn't yet drawn his gun tonight—and steadied himself on the edges of the horn-shaped entrance as he stepped up onto Massarsky's back. Several flashlight beams converged on the octagonal stone he had identified. When he pressed his fingers against the stone, it did not move, but when he put one hand over the other and put his weight behind it, the octagon slid backward an inch and then two.

He thought of Sully and allowed himself to hope as he heard the grinding of stone and the heavy thunk of weights shifting in the walls. He dropped down from Massarsky's back and peered into the chamber beneath the Soul Tower, but nothing was happening.

Then Jada tapped his arm, and he turned to see a square block sliding out of the wall to the left of the entrance. Dust fell to the ground. Flashlight beams swung over to illuminate the ten-inch square.

"There's another one," Corelli said.

Drake turned and watched the second stone, exactly opposite the first, sliding from the wall. With a loud double thud, the noises in the walls ceased. Henriksen pushed past Massarsky and examined the square on the left. Garza handed Massarsky his gun, but her gaze was on the other square. Jada had her flashlight on it, and now Drake joined her, running his fingers around the edges.

"There's open space behind this one," Henriksen said.

"Here, too," Drake said. His fingertips touched what felt like a smooth stone cylinder, like a post or the axle of a wheel.

A *wheel*, he thought, gripping the square and trying to turn it. When he twisted to the right, he felt it give.

"Turn it!" Drake told Henriksen. He glanced over his shoulder and saw the big Norwegian doing just that.

Simultaneously, they rotated the squares until they wouldn't turn any further. Drake felt something in the wall give way, and this time the grinding and thumping inside the walls was much louder, and he heard Jada cry his name at the same time he realized much of the noise was coming from the small room under the Soul Tower. The mercenaries were well trained—not one of them moved, ready for whatever happened next—but Corelli, Olivia, and Jada crowded in front of the horn-shaped doorway, and Drake had to crane his neck to get a glimpse inside.

The stone blocks that made up the floor of the small chamber were sinking in horizontal rows, each dropping a foot farther than the last, and Drake quickly realized they had released the mechanism they had been searching for. The floor had transformed into a set of stairs leading down into darkness.

"Massarsky," Perkins said, "you and Zheng take point."

The two mercenaries slipped through the horn-shaped entry, flashlights clipped to their guns, and started down the stone steps, weapons ready to fire. Drake had entered ancient temples and ruins before, and normally he'd have thought their caution unwarranted. But they were expecting an attack here. The Protectors of the Hidden Word would be waiting, but they didn't know what kind of number to expect. It was possible that most of the hooded killers had died in their skirmishes in Egypt and on Santorini.

Still, better safe than dead.

Henriksen, Olivia, and Corelli followed the first half dozen mercenaries, ignoring Drake and Jada. Now that they had found the way into the emperor's tomb, their former animosity was forgotten. Their full focus was on the yawning darkness below, and Drake understood why. As much as he wanted to find Sully, he had no problem letting some of the goon squad precede him. If the spooky ninja dudes were waiting, he was more than happy to let the hired guns take the first few hits.

They descended the stairs and found themselves in a long, sloping corridor. The rest of the mercenaries fell in behind Drake and Jada, though two of them hung back, staying to guard their exit. That made fourteen in Perkins's squad and nineteen all together, counting Drake and Jada, Henriksen and Olivia, and Corelli. Nobody spoke as they moved along the corridor, listening for any sign of a potential attack coming from ahead and watching for hidden doorways.

The tunnel spiraled downward, taking them deeper, and then straightened out again and ran on for perhaps fifty yards before it ended in a vaulted chamber that caused them all to come to a halt. Two passages led away and farther downward from the chamber, and mercenaries were investigating both paths. But the rest of the group had focused elsewhere, and as flashlight beams illuminated the walls and ceiling, Drake stared in amazement.

"This isn't man-made," Henriksen said. "It's a natural cave."

Moss grew in thick patches on the walls. Stains on the solid rock showed the patterns where water had dripped down from above, and Drake shone his flashlight upward. He pressed himself against the wall alongside Olivia, who was doing the same thing.

"Do you see it?" she asked.

"A crevice," he said.

Long, thick roots jutted from stone and earth and hung down, partially blocking the view, but Drake could see the glint of his light off jagged stone. Far above, where his beam could not reach, was a thin sliver of moonlight.

"Another one over here," Garza called from the other side of the cave.

Corelli swore softly. "Olivia. Better have a look at this."

Drake frowned and glanced at Henriksen, who had turned to look at Corelli. The bodyguard had his light trained on a blanket of moss, but there were hints of white among the green and brown.

"They're flower buds," Olivia said, a tinge of wonder in her voice.

"Not just buds," Jada said, from a jagged alcove where the moss grew particularly thick. She shined her flashlight at a spot perhaps ten feet off the cave floor, where a trio of white flowers grew, dangling and half wilted.

"Those look familiar to you?" Drake asked.

Jada nodded. "Sure do."

Henriksen came over to inspect them. "These aren't white hellebore at all. They look similar—could be related—but the petals have a different shape."

"And white hellebore can't grow in moss with this little light," Olivia added, coming up behind him.

Drake pushed against the wall and looked up, spotting another crevice. The moss was wet from the rain that ran down into the cave when it stormed. He pushed back and thrust his fingers into the moss, finding thick vines beneath it. He tugged them out to show the others.

"There you go," Corelli said, as if to himself.

Perkins called for Henriksen, but Drake kept his eyes on the flowers. *Cave hellebore*, he thought, wondering if they had discovered a new species of flora.

"—no sign of diamond carvings or any other differentiating marks," Perkins was saying.

Drake stiffened and turned. He stared at the two men and then at the two doors, and he realized something they obviously had figured out already. Two doors—two possible choices—this was the start of the fourth labyrinth.

"Jada," he said. "Where's the emperor's tomb?"

Jada nodded slowly, but it was Olivia who answered.

"Maybe it was never here. Your professor friend in Oxford said they'd established it was here because they knew *something* was here. It made sense to assume it was the burial site—the underground palace."

Corelli had gone over to the right-hand passage and begun to explore it, searching for markings the mercenary team already had established weren't there. Drake liked the man less and less as the minutes ticked by. For a flunky, he seemed fairly presumptuous, almost as if he forgot from time to time that he was just an employee.

Henriksen glanced at Drake. "I have a theory."

Drake nodded. "Let's hear it."

"It never made any sense to me that Daedalus would've marked the correct path through the Thera labyrinth."

"He didn't," Jada said. "He marked the *wrong* path."

"Granted," Henriksen replied, blue eyes turned gray in the reflected illumination of so many flashlights. "But how long did it take us to figure that out? A man who would design such a puzzle would never offer so simple a solution. But what if those markings were added later, when it no longer mattered if intruders could find their way?"

"After the Thera eruption?" Drake asked. "Why bother?"

"No, it makes sense," Jada said, and he could see it pained her to admit that Henriksen had a point. "If we're going on the theory that there even was a golden hoard and that Talos—or someone—supervised the removal of Daedalus's treasure from Thera, wouldn't it go faster and much more smoothly if those moving the gold couldn't get lost?"

Drake thought about it, then nodded reluctantly. "I guess. If they were really abandoning it."

"Half of it had already collapsed," Henriksen reminded him. "They wanted to move the gold to the fourth labyrinth, as Daedalus had done at least twice before."

"It's all about the gold with you, isn't it?" Drake asked.

Henriksen smiled. "There are other treasures, but as far as motivations go, gold has its appeal."

Drake knew he was supposed to hate the man, so he turned away before he let himself smile. Henriksen had a point. He had been motivated by gold plenty of times in his own life. This time, he had other interests: saving Sully's life and getting vengeance for Jada's father. The thought made the smile die on his lips.

"How do we choose a path?" Olivia asked. "I don't think splitting up is a good idea."

"Why not?" Jada asked. "There are plenty of us."

Corelli snorted derisively. "Maybe because we're not the only ones down here."

Nobody acknowledged the comment. The mercenaries were already wary—they were paid to be—and Drake didn't need reminding. He went over to the doorways into the two passages and studied them with his light. Runnels had been carved in the cave floor over time by rainwater from heavy storms searching for somewhere to drain. But in both of the doorways he saw that gutters had been cut into either side of the sloping passages. More of the runnels seemed to go to the left-hand passage, but that seemed like it must be a natural phenomenon. Still, the different levels of wear had him searching his mind. The water erosion triggered a thought.

Drake slipped off his pack and pulled out a sports bottle full of water. He uncapped it, went to the entrance of the left passage, and knelt to pour a few ounces across the threshold there. Jada had followed, giving him the benefit of her flashlight.

"What the hell are you doing?" Corelli asked.

"Thinking," Drake replied. "Try it sometime."

He went to the right-hand passage and repeated the process, nodding as he saw the water running into tiny cracks and pooling into depressions as it trickled down the slope into the tunnel.

"This way," he said, standing and going back to stow the water and slip his pack back on.

"What was that?" Henriksen asked. "Are you Tonto now?"

"If they had so much gold then they had to mark the path for workers to carry it all out of the labyrinth on Thera, there was a hell of a lot of traffic going in and out of here at one point," Drake explained. He pointed to the right-hand passage. "There's a hell of a lot more wear on that side and hardly any erosion on the left. Not a lot of foot traffic that direction."

Henriksen considered that but looked unsure.

Drake shrugged. "Do what you want. Sully's here somewhere. Jada and I are going to find him."

He glanced at her to make sure he had the right to speak for her, but she already was following. She had put her hair up in a ponytail, magenta on black, and without it veiling her features, her face had a soft vulnerability that was deceiving. But when she met his gaze, he saw the familiar determination in her eyes and knew there was no turning back for either of them.

As if there ever could have been, he thought.

"The man makes sense," Perkins said.

Henriksen glanced over at the mercenaries, who had spread out, some of them still investigating the cave while others were on alert for any sign of approach.

"The logic is solid, Mr. Henriksen," Perkins continued. "I can't say we're going to be able to determine which path is correct at each turn in the labyrinth, but right now, I advise we take the tunnel on the right."

Henriksen glanced at Olivia, but her face was an unreadable mask.

"Right it is," he said. "But everyone be on guard. The protectors know these corridors intimately. And I have no doubt they have doors we'll never see. Perkins, make sure someone is covering the rear."

"Yes, sir," Perkins said, gesturing for two of his people to guard their flank.

But that was the problem in a labyrinth full of hidden chambers and secret passages. It was impossible to know where an attack would be coming from. Anything could be hiding in the shadows.

21

They set off down the sloping tunnel in twos, as before, and the twists of the labyrinth quickly revealed themselves. Several times they were able to find the right path by measuring the wear on the floor, but in other places they were forced to explore wrong turns for long minutes before realizing they had chosen poorly.

This labyrinth differed significantly from the others in that it was a combination of man-made tunnels and natural caves. In another of the caves they passed through they found moss growing and fissures that led up to the surface, and Drake wondered how far underground they had traveled. There were vines as well, but only small blossoms of cave hellebore, nothing in full bloom.

A curving stone staircase had been carved into the side of a large cavern that dropped away precipitously on the right. Drake kept a hand on Jada's shoulder as they went down the stairs, feeling the presence of the mercenaries behind him. He had been careful to make sure that Corelli preceded them down, not trusting the man to follow. At the bottom of the steps, they found the first writing on the walls and familiar paintings of cave hellebore, as well as the symbol of the four interlaced octagons that stood for the four labyrinths.

At the sight of that symbol, Henriksen could not hide his elation. Olivia did not smile, but Drake thought she looked flushed and heard her exhale as if she were trying to steady her breathing. Corelli's face gleamed with anticipation. Drake worried that they were allowing themselves to be distracted and were letting their guard down. But as long as Perkins and his goon squad were with them, he figured someone was making sure they weren't going to get dragged into the shadows and have their throats cut.

He nudged Jada. "You all right?"

"Is that a joke?" she asked, one eyebrow arched.

"I'm not in a joking mood."

"That's a first," she said.

After a few more steps, Jada bumped lightly against him. "I'm just wondering how it all got turned around."

She didn't have to explain what she meant. Right about then, he figured she must be wondering what her father would have said if he could have seen her exploring the fourth labyrinth with his traitorous wife and his rival.

"It's not over yet," he said. "What matters is how it all turns out."

Jada nodded, but her knitted brow showed she was still troubled. "That's not all that matters."

He knew she was right, but it would give her no comfort for him to agree with her, so he said nothing. At the bottom of the steps, a tunnel opened to the left, and they entered a complex series of alleys, forks, corners, and dead ends that vexed them for nearly half an hour until Jada forced them all to stop and just listen. It wasn't what they heard that showed them the right path, however, but what they felt. Air moved through the labyrinth—this strange combination of natural caverns and man-made maze—and by following the drafts they found a side passage off what they'd thought was a dead end and were on their way again.

When they reached a sloping tunnel that seemed more crevice than passage, the path downward nothing but jagged edges of stone that would barely function as steps, there was some doubt that they had chosen the right path, but they forged ahead nevertheless. They had to descend as if climbing down a ladder, seeking footholds among the sharp striations of stone. Drake clutched his flashlight in one hand and used the other to steady himself, knowing a fall would mean torn flesh and broken bones. He scraped his left knee and right forearm and nearly shattered his flashlight when he momentarily lost his footing.

"Where the hell are they?" Henriksen asked aloud as they clambered down through the treacherous terrain.

No one asked who "they" were. Henriksen wasn't the only one who had expected to fall under attack by now, but Drake didn't let himself surrender to the temptation to think that the Protectors of the Hidden Word had abandoned their duty. Unlike the others, which had the dry stillness of age, this labyrinth felt alive to him. *Aware.* They were there, he felt sure.

In the narrow confines of that tunnel, clambering on the sharp, jutting stones, he felt almost alone in spite of the string of people ahead of and behind him. Drake had rarely suffered from claustrophobia—being trapped beneath tons of earth in the cave-in of an Aztec tomb seven years earlier had been a rare exception—but his heart began to hammer in his chest, an edge of panic gnawing at him. His body ached for open sky and fresh air the way it did when he went diving and stayed under the water too long, and he didn't like being jammed into a place so vulnerable to attack with no way to defend himself.

When he heard the commotion ahead and below—the thump of boots and clatter of slides being racked back on assault weapons—his need to get out of that sharp-toothed tunnel only grew. He could hear the soldiers muttering, and when he glanced down, he realized he was almost there. Olivia had been right in front of him, and he saw her carefully extricating herself from the jagged rocks and stepping into an open chamber. Corelli and Henriksen and the mercenaries on point were already out of the tunnel.

"What is it?" Jada asked from behind him.

Below, he heard Olivia suck in a harsh breath, and he glanced down again, watching as she swung her flashlight around.

"Diyu," she said, almost to herself.

"It's hell," Drake replied.

But it wasn't until he reached the bottom safely and emerged into the chamber—a natural cave with jagged walls and a peaked ceiling like some kind of primeval chapel—that the reality of it struck him. There were stone altars with the carved faces of Chinese demons, and along one pitted wall, massive iron hooks had been driven into the rock face. The wall and floor were stained a horrid copper brown, caked with centuries of spilled blood and viscera. The place *breathed* with the anguish of tortured souls. If it was not quite an abattoir, it was the nearest to such a place Drake had ever entered.

"Oh, my God," Jada said as she came in behind him.

Drake flinched at the sound of her voice. The other mercenaries came behind her, some of them voicing their own surprise but most too hardened to the worst cruelties of humanity to react. Drake hoped he never became so callous.

"Look at this," Corelli said, pointing to a sacrificial altar.

Sluices had been carved around the edges of the table to carry blood away. It ran like a gutter down the side of the altar and across the floor, into a spill-off cut into the far wall, next to the cave's exit.

Horrified as he was, Drake felt ice fill his veins as he remembered the map on the wall in the Chinese worship chamber on Thera.

"This is just one room," he said. "There are others—maybe a lot of others."

"Nate, look at this," Jada said.

He turned to find her shining her flashlight on a wall painted with horrible images of demons and torture. There were hulking men with horns and brutish faces—Minotaurs—and a woman with a veil over her face who had to be Diyu's version of the Mistress of the Labyrinth. Despite the Chinese characters painted on the wall and the difference in visual style, the most significant difference Drake noticed between these images and those they'd seen before had to do with the huge chalice or vase in the mistress's hands. Seven slaves knelt in a semicircle before her as if awaiting an anointment. They were all reaching for the chalice, and she seemed to be extending it, as though willing to hand it over.

Henriksen and Olivia came up behind them. He glanced back at them and saw Olivia nod once, as if she'd just confirmed an earlier suspicion, and then she turned away, uninterested. Henriksen lasted only a moment longer before he, too, had moved on.

The mural hadn't surprised them at all.

"Is that supposed to be Daedalus's honey?" Drake asked.

"That was my thought," Jada said.

Massarsky sidled up next to them. "Come on. We're moving out."

Drake spun to see that he was right; Perkins had ordered his people forward. Henriksen and Corelli were vanishing through the exit from the torture chamber already, and Olivia followed. Like the soldiers, she had her gun drawn and now held it at her side. He wondered if seeing this bit of Diyu had unnerved her. She didn't seem easily shaken.

"Thanks," Jada said.

Massarsky nodded, but he wasn't paying any attention to them. He and Garza and a few others were covering the flank, which meant they couldn't proceed until Jada and Drake got moving. Drake reached for his own weapon—a ten-millimeter Glock that carried fifteen rounds—and unsnapped the guard on the holster. He hesitated only a moment and then drew the gun.

"What are you doing?" Jada whispered.

"Making sure I'm ready when the moment comes."

"You're certain there's going to be a 'moment'?"

Drake nodded. "There always is."

He and Jada hurried after Olivia, ducking through the low exit. The others had gotten a distance ahead, and only the scuff of their boots and the bouncing beams of their flashlights gave away their location in the long tunnel. Drake picked up the pace. He heard Massarsky and the others behind them, equipment jostling as they, too, made better time.

The tunnel ended at a narrow ravine perhaps a dozen feet across at its narrowest and four times that at the widest. Its walls rose precipitously. High above, a glimmer of moonlight showed through, and when they shone their flashlights upward, they could just make out the shapes of thick roots that had burrowed their way through the stone. The walls a hundred feet above them were caked with moss and vines and dotted with the white blossoms Drake thought of as cave hellebore.

Narrow ledges had been carved into the walls above and

below, walkways that zigzagged up toward those blossoms and down toward the dark depths of the ravine. The flashlights picked out jagged rocks far below.

"There was a bridge here," Corelli said.

Flashlight beams illuminated the remnants of wooden supports that once had held up a footbridge that must have spanned the gap.

"Are you kidding me?" Olivia said. "We have to walk all the way down and then up the other side. On *that*?"

She pointed out the rocky ledge with her flashlight. The walkway couldn't have been more than three feet wide.

"How do we do that?" she continued.

"Carefully?" Jada suggested.

Her stepmother cast her the darkest glance Drake had ever seen pass between the two women.

Drake glanced across the ravine, where a wide, diagonal split in the wall showed what he assumed was the door into the rest of the labyrinth. There were probably other torture chambers in the warren of tunnels that he presumed they would find on various levels as they climbed down into the ravine and up again, but the fact that a bridge once had existed suggested that their path lay ahead.

"We could jump," he said.

Henriksen scoffed. "It's too far."

Drake wasn't sure about that. The ledge on the other side looked wider, and it was a good six feet lower. If it weren't for the fact that a fall onto the rocks below almost certainly would kill them, he would have been willing to gamble that with the right footing and trajectory, he could have made it.

"So we walk," Drake said.

Olivia gave a pensive sigh and then raised her gun and took aim at Drake's chest.

"Well, *we* do," she said.

As Jada reached for her holstered weapon, Drake started to bring his Glock up to shoot her. All over the ledge there was movement, guns coming up, flashlight beams dancing around. Corelli let out a cry that sounded like a celebration.

Tyr Henriksen stepped between Olivia and Drake.

"Olivia, what do you think you're doing?"

It seemed to Drake that she had removed her mask at last. The smile that lifted the corners of her mouth was cruel and lovely and tinged with madness.

"Finally disabusing you of the notion that you're in charge here," she said, raising the pistol and aiming it at Henriksen's face.

Drake blinked in surprise even as Jada let out a small gasp. Neither of them had seen this coming. Apparently, Henriksen hadn't, either. He stiffened, lifted his chin, and glared at her, then tilted his head toward his bodyguard.

"Corelli," he said. "Try not to kill her."

With a laugh, Corelli shuffled over beside Olivia, but his gun was trained on Drake and Jada. "Nothing to worry about on that score, *boss*."

Even as Henriksen absorbed this shock, the mercenaries took aim as if they were a firing squad, but all the guns were pointed at Henriksen, Drake, and Jada.

"You incredible bitch," Jada said. "You killed my dad, after all, didn't you?"

Olivia gazed at her with regret. "I know you'd like to believe that, but I actually really liked Luka. Sweet man. In the end, he was too innocent for me. I wanted him to be a part of this, but when he went off on his little crusade—well, somebody was going to kill him. It just didn't end up being me. The protectors got to him first."

"You knew they existed?" Drake asked.

"Not until Luka turned up dead. Then when I heard about Dr. Cheney, well, it was obvious someone didn't want us to find this place."

"Us," Drake echoed.

Corelli smiled. "Us."

Drake narrowed his eyes, feeling his hand tighten on the grip of his gun. "You came after us in New York. In the van. You set Luka's apartment on fire."

"I coordinated," Corelli said, correcting him. He glanced at

Perkins. "You can hire anyone to do anything if you know who to call."

Drake turned to Perkins. "If those were your guys, they were pretty sloppy."

"Not my people," Perkins said. "This is my first time working for Mrs. Hzujak."

Henriksen winced at the words, this confirmation that Perkins was taking orders from Olivia instead of from him.

"I'm the one who hired you, damn it!" Henriksen snapped at the mercenary commander. "How the hell is she paying you?"

"What you offered them is nothing compared to a cut of what's waiting for us in the treasure chamber," Olivia said, her eyes alight with greed and zealotry.

"It's a calculated risk," Perkins admitted. "We consider it an investment."

Massarsky shifted uncomfortably. When Drake glanced at him, the huge ex-soldier shrugged.

"Sorry, man."

"Yeah." Drake laughed drily. "No hard feelings."

"Enough," Olivia said, tilting her head toward Jada. "Get the girl's pack."

When Corelli came forward, keeping his weapon trained on Drake, Jada started to shuffle away from him, dangerously close to the edge of the ravine.

"Give it to him," Drake said. "She wants your father's journal and the maps. They're useless to us down here. Luka never made it this far. If he guessed the fourth labyrinth was in China, he didn't write it down. There's nothing in there that can help us."

Olivia laughed. "Nothing can help you."

"God, when did you become so cold-blooded?" Henriksen asked.

"Says the man who'd stab his own brother in the back to get what he wants," Olivia said.

"Never literally," Henriksen said. "I've never killed anyone."

"Too bad you missed your chance," Olivia said.

Perkins cleared his throat. "Can we just get on with this? It's a long climb down and up again, and we've gotta do it again coming back."

Olivia shot him an irritated look, then gestured to Corelli.

Corelli lifted his gun and pressed the barrel against Drake's temple. "Drop the gun, dumbass. You're slightly outnumbered."

He snickered. That, more than anything, was what flipped the switch inside Drake.

"Dropping it," he said. "Just don't talk anymore. Your breath is terrible."

Corelli shoved the gun against his temple. Drake held his gun away from him and bent down slowly, lowering it to the ground.

"This guy," Corelli said, glancing over at Olivia. "Can I kill him now or what?"

The second his gaze shifted away, Drake knocked his arm back, throwing off his aim, and kicked him in the chest. Corelli staggered backward, arms pinwheeling, right over the edge of the ravine. He screamed on the way down and pulled the trigger twice, but the bullets vanished in the darkness above them.

"Son of a bitch!" Olivia shrieked, striding toward him, leaving Garza and another mercenary to cover Henriksen.

Perkins and Massarsky were on Drake instantly, guns pointed at his head, but Drake wasn't stupid. He didn't try picking up his weapon, just laced his fingers at the back of his neck.

"Come on, guys," he said. "Tell me you weren't tempted to do that yourself. I mean, I know you're going to shoot us, but that clown had to go first."

"Nate?" Jada said quietly.

His bravado failed when he heard the crack in her voice. But he didn't regret what he'd done. Corelli had been about to kill him, which meant he'd bought them a couple of extra minutes of life. And now Olivia had no sidekick, no one to share her plan, no one else who knew where to find what they were looking for. Perkins had just become her best friend, but he cared only about the gold. Olivia was alone, and she deserved that.

"What are you waiting for?" Olivia snapped, glancing at Perkins even as she kept her weapon aimed at Henriksen.

"What's wrong, Olivia?" Henriksen said. "Afraid to get blood on your own hands?"

Drake had been fighting his instinct to like the guy. But since they were both about to be shot, he figured that put them on the same side, and he couldn't help but admire the big Norwegian's fearlessness.

"Just waiting for your order," Perkins said.

Fourteen mercenaries and one coldhearted witch, all with guns aimed at them. Drake felt a terrible sadness grip his heart as he thought about Sully and realized that whenever they caught up with him, they were going to kill him, too.

He stood, ignoring the mercenaries who shouted at him not to move, and reached out to take Jada's hand. Hell, they were family. She squeezed, and he glanced at her.

"Now I know how Butch and Sundance felt," she whispered, but her smile was strained and her eyes were damp with unshed tears.

"Do it," Olivia said. "Kill—"

Massarsky shouted and backed away from the ravine, swinging his assault rifle around to aim at the edge.

"What the hell?" Garza yelled, and pulled the trigger.

All eyes turned toward the ravine as hooded men clutching metal claws dragged themselves onto the ledge, moving inhumanly fast. Garza's bullets punched through one of them, sending blood spraying out into the gap, the body tumbling down onto the rocks below. Gunfire echoed off the walls of the ravine, mercenaries shouted, but the Protectors of the Hidden Word were silent as they attacked, killing and dying in equal measure.

One of them lunged at Drake, his blade whistling through the shadows in a wide arc, aimed for his throat.

22

The gunshot made Drake flinch even as he tried to dodge the killer's knife. But the hooded man fell short, his lunge losing momentum, and he crashed to the rocky ledge at Drake's feet and twitched once, then went still.

Jada stood behind him, gun in hand, looking like she might throw up. Her weapon was still holstered; she had managed to pick up his Glock. Amid the chaos of gunfire and voices, bloodshed and brutality, he darted forward and snatched the gun away from her. A hooded woman—one of the first females he'd seen among them—raced up, metal climbing claws like brass knuckles on her hands, ready to slash him to ribbons. Drake held his breath when he took aim and shot her in the chest.

They had no time for hesitation, but it would haunt him. Even in self-defense, killing haunted him. *Almost always*, he thought. Corelli might have been an exception.

With a glance around, he spotted Olivia up against the wall of the ravine, gun held out in front of her, firing at the hooded killers still swarming up from over the ledge. But Perkins and Garza were nearby, and they had firepower to spare. The semiautomatic weapons' fire ripped at the air, the echoes punishingly loud.

Drake grabbed Jada's hand and dragged her back into the tunnel that led back up to the torture chamber. For a moment, they were out of sight of both sets of killers. Drake turned to her, put a hand under her chin, and forced her to look up at him. Her gaze was far away, and he worried that she was in shock.

"Jada, listen to me."

"I shot that man."

"If you hadn't, he'd have gutted me," Drake said. "You saved my life. But we're both on borrowed time here. Whoever wins out there, they're going to kill us, so we've gotta run for it."

She blinked as if coming awake. "If we try to go back, they'll catch us. We'll never make it to the surface."

Drake shook his head. "No, no. I don't want to go back."

Jada glanced at the end of the tunnel and saw one of the hooded men straddling a mercenary on the ledge, slashing at the ex-soldier's throat with a curved blade. Arterial blood sprayed in an arc.

"We can't walk down the cliff paths. We'll never get past them, and even if we did—"

"There isn't time," Drake said, his heart like a tiger trying to smash free of its cage. He thought his chest might burst, it was hammering so hard. "There's only one way we're surviving the next hundred seconds or so."

One of the hooded men slipped into the tunnel, spotted them, and cocked back a hand in which he clutched a throwing knife. Drake shot him twice. Twelve shots left in the Glock's magazine before he'd have to reload. The killer and his blade hit the rock floor at the same time. The man dragged himself to his knees, blood raining from his chest, and reached for the knife.

It was Jada who put the third bullet in him.

She had her own gun out now, the two of them staring at that opening, waiting for more of the killers to come for them. But through the opening, they could see the flashlight beams slashing the darkness, and enough of that light bounced off the walls that they could make out the dim outline of the tunnel across the ravine.

Jada stiffened and then spun toward him. "You can't be serious. If we fall short, we're dead."

Drake holstered his gun. "We don't jump for it, we die anyway." He shoved his flashlight into his backpack, working fast, zipped it, and slipped it back on. "Sully's waiting for us, kid."

Jada swore, snapping her gun back into its holster. She kept swearing over and over again, the profanity like a mantra as she jammed her flashlight into her backpack and then turned to look at him defiantly.

"It's gonna be—" he began.

Jada punched him in the arm. "Just shut up and run."

Drake felt a strange, mad surrender then. Not to death but to fate. An old song floated into his mind, one Sully played from time to time: *Freedom's just another word for nothing left to lose.* He'd never understood just how true that was until this moment. Free, exhilarated by his terror and hope, he took Jada's hand, and they ran to the tunnel's end and onto the ledge. Their hands unclasped just as they reached the edge, and then they launched themselves full speed across the twelve-foot gap.

For an eyeblink, Drake felt weightless, with the jagged rocks below and the slivers of moonlight high above. Then gravity took hold, and they began to fall. He windmilled his arms to keep balanced in the air, and then he slammed into the far wall, cracking his head against it. He slid to the ledge, then spun around and saw Jada land on her belly, legs hanging out over the yawning darkness below. Her fingers scrabbled for purchase and found none, and he knew she was going over, knew she would die broken and bloody.

He caught her wrist, throwing himself backward so he wouldn't be pulled along with her. He slammed the heel of his boot against the remains of a support that once had held up this end of the missing bridge. The rocky ledge scraped his back and legs as he dragged her up on top of him, and for a moment they lay there, hearts racing together. Then a stray bullet struck the wall above them, sending tiny shards of rock flying, and they were in motion. Drake rolled Jada off him, and the two got to their knees and turned to look at the scene playing out across the ravine.

Half a dozen hooded men were still scaling the wall below the opposite ledge. Many lay dead, crumpled in bloody heaps around the mercenaries and protectors who were still trying desperately to murder one another. Olivia remained pinned against the wall, with Perkins putting himself between her and the hooded men. At least five of the mercenaries were down, wounded or dead—he figured probably the latter. The Protectors of the Hidden Word didn't seem like the wounding kind.

Henriksen let out a primitive, furious roar and grabbed hold of the hooded man who'd been trying to cut him open. The big Norwegian, a blond silhouette captured in the illumination from someone else's flashlight, slammed the hooded man against the wall twice, then a third time. The echo of cracking bone mixed with the sounds of death and battle, and then Henriksen hurled the man into the ravine.

Then he spun and stared right at Drake.

"He's looking at—" Jada started.

"Us," Drake agreed, standing up and waving. "Jump! It's your only shot!"

"What are you doing?" Jada demanded.

But even as she spoke, Henriksen stooped and snatched the gun from a dead mercenary, slung it across his back, and retreated a couple of steps before sprinting for the edge.

Olivia screamed and pushed past Perkins, taking aim and firing while Henriksen was airborne.

The Norwegian crashed into the wall and almost fell backward into the ravine before Drake steadied him. Only then did Drake realize that Olivia had missed. Across the gap, she shrieked in anger and started shooting at the three of them. There were still hooded men trying to get to her, to cut her throat, but she was more concerned with trying to make sure they died first.

Perkins knocked her back against the wall, saving her from a blade that whistled through the air and would have caught her in the chest. But the action cost him, and as he turned to take aim, two of the hooded men descended on him, their blades rising and falling, blood spattering the lens of his flashlight so that its beam was darkened with spots of shadow that had been his life, now extinguished.

Still, the odds had changed. Assault rifles tended to have that effect. The last few hooded men came over the ledge and were shot before they could make it a handful of feet. The mercenaries were going to win this, but either way, Drake knew that he, Jada, and Henriksen needed to be gone.

"We can't stay here," he said.

Henriksen risked one last hate-filled glance at Olivia, and then all three of them rushed for the tunnel entrance near the supports of the long-ruined bridge.

"Go get them!" Olivia screamed at someone. "Get over there and kill them!"

As Drake ducked through the tunnel entrance, he thought it was Massarsky's voice he heard behind him.

"You're out of your mind, lady. No one's jumping that. You'd have to be crazy or out of choices, and we're neither. They can't get out without going past us."

There was more, but as Drake, Jada, and Henriksen hurried into the twisted knot of tunnels on the other side of the ravine, the voices were muffled and they could hear only gunshots.

Henriksen had no flashlight, but Drake and Jada lit the way ahead. They made wordless progress, coming to junctions and doors, narrow passages and dead ends, as they had before, but they had become veritable experts in navigating through labyrinths by now, and when they chose the wrong direction, it was never for very long.

Soon they had left the echoes of gunshots and murder behind, but Drake knew the danger would catch up to them eventually and hadn't a clue what they would do when it did.

In another piece of hell—these torture rooms like the chambers of this diabolical labyrinth's heart—they stopped to catch their breath. Drake and Jada leaned against the edges of the entry passage while Henriksen walked around the hideous cavern, plunging unwisely into the shadows.

"Throw some light over here?" he asked.

Jada ignored him, so Drake raised his flashlight. Henriksen had his back to them, staring at an enormous mechanism composed of a huge stone wheel with hooks jutting from the rock. The wheel had been stained dark with ancient blood, yet Drake thought he detected the scent of copper in the air. He wondered if pain could have a ghost, if the stink of human suffering could haunt a place when even the most tenacious souls had long since departed.

He wanted out of the fourth labyrinth. Out of Diyu. He didn't care about gold or treasure. From the moment Sully had been dragged off, this job had been about getting his best friend back alive, but the sense of adventure and the promise of gold had maintained a certain secondary allure in the back of his head. No more.

"Hey," Jada whispered.

Drake looked over at her. In the glow of their flashlights, he saw that magenta strands had come loose from her ponytail. To someone who hadn't been at her side these last days, she might have looked fragile, but to Drake, she seemed as strong as if she'd been forged in fire.

"Thanks," she said.

He didn't feel deserving of her gratitude. What had he done for her thus far except be by her side while people died around her, while she took a life for the first time, while her godfather had been stolen from her and her stepmother betrayed her? He couldn't bring her father back to life.

The best he could do was finish the job they'd started.

"Any time," he said, grinning. "I wouldn't want to go on a suicide mission with anyone else."

Jada pushed off from the wall and went to punch him.

"Enough!" Drake said, holding up his hands in surrender.

Jada smiled. "Tough guy." Then she walked toward Henriksen. "All right, Tyr. Time to tell us what the hell that was all about back there."

Henriksen turned, still in the pool of Drake's flashlight. He hung his head, shadows gathering under his eyes, and it made him look a century older.

"I never thought she would go so far," he said. Lifting his head, he turned his sorrowful gaze upon Jada. "Tonight I have blood on my hands for the first time."

"Join the club," she said. She tried to sound cavalier, but Drake heard the pain in her voice. "But you're not exactly an innocent. Your whole career has been about doing whatever it took to get what you wanted. If you never killed someone or had anybody killed, I'm willing to bet people have died because of you before."

The words scuffed the walls, but they were nothing compared to the screams that once had reverberated here.

"She's got you there," Drake said.

Henriksen glanced at him and managed to look almost ashamed. "You are not what I expected, Mr. Drake." He nodded toward Jada. "Either of you. You are survivors, and you have my admiration."

"Yeah, well, considering we thought you were pretty much the devil when this all started, I guess you're not what we expected, either," Drake said. "But we don't have time for group therapy, Tyr. I'm going to bet there are still some spooky ninja guys—"

"And girls," Jada put in.

"Yeah, I noticed that," Drake said. "My point is, no matter how many Protectors of the Hidden Word were killed by Perkins's goon squad, I doubt they're all dead. If I was calling the shots, I'd have held some of my people back. They've got Sully and Ian Welch somewhere, and maybe others. Never mind the gold. There could be one or two right around the next turn. So we're not going another step until you tell us what it is you've been holding back."

Henriksen frowned. Jada aimed her flashlight at his eyes, and he squinted, turning away.

"Come on," she said. "No more secrets. If the three of us are going to make it through till morning, we need to work together."

Several seconds ticked by in the silence of the torture chamber. Its gruesomeness struck Drake anew, and he became more impatient than ever to be gone from there, to find the heart of the labyrinth and make an end to things.

"Tyr—"

"Knossos," Henriksen said.

Drake shrugged. "What about it?"

"The labyrinth there is in ruins," Henriksen went on, his gaze shifting from Drake to Jada. "But I've had theories about Minos for years, and I've had teams going through the ruins, doing small excavations, all through museums and universities but with my people running it. One of those excavations turned up the wreckage of a chamber."

"A worship chamber," Jada said, her voice low.

Henriksen nodded. "I brought your father in after my people had translated fragments of several tablets and the writing on a shattered sacramental jar we had recovered. I had been keeping track of progress at Crocodilopolis for a while, but once your father confirmed my suspicions that Daedalus had designed both the labyrinth at Knossos and the one in Crocodile City, it became my priority. I'd hoped to find a complete worship chamber there, and of course we found even more than that."

"But there are things you knew already," Drake said, studying his face. "Things you learned from the fragments from Knossos."

"Bits and pieces. Suppositions," Henriksen said. "The first Mistress of the Labyrinth was Ariadne herself. Her beauty and gentleness kept the Minotaur calm—"

"There's no such thing—" Jada began.

"But there was!" Henriksen snapped. "You don't understand."

He took Drake's flashlight and shone it upon the wall, where a gruesome painting in the ancient Chinese style represented the Mistress of the Labyrinth tipping a cup of honey into the mouth of a slave whose back was streaked with scars from the lash. Others awaited the same communion. One of them, off to the right, was hunched over, having already received the cup. Horns jutted from his head, and his features were contorted, almost savage.

"You've gotta be kidding me," Drake rasped, staring. "The honey? What, it turned them into monsters?"

"Not with horns," Henriksen said, waving his disbelief away. "Those were an affectation, something to frighten the others, I think, and to perpetuate the legend that Daedalus had so carefully built. The skeleton we examined in the labyrinth of Sobek—the one you found on the stairs under the altar—had the horns of an actual bull. They were probably tied to his head with some kind of leather strap.

"There are conditions that could explain many of the Minotaur's legendary features. The chemical composition of the honey might have triggered hypertrichosis, causing the growth of thick, shaggy hair all over their bodies, their faces included. I also suspect they attained their monstrous size through slave labor and the honey's activation of the pituitary gland's growth hormones. It's even possible that one or two grew cutaneous horns, prompting the legend to begin with and leading Daedalus and his inner circle to use fake horns to perpetuate the monstrous image of the Minotaur in order to keep people too terrified to attempt to explore the labyrinth. But the key element is strength and aggression. Savagery. Perhaps an edge of lunacy."

Jada's flashlight beam wavered. "What are 'cutaneous horns'? Is that even something real?"

"They're not actual horn. In rare cases, people have seemed to grow horns on their heads or faces or hands, but it's a buildup of keratotic material, like hair or fingernails. Sometimes there's cancer involved . . ." Henriksen waved the topic away. "This is not important."

"Agreed," Drake said. "And it's pretty gross. How the hell do they do it? What's in the honey?"

Henriksen smiled slightly, as if he couldn't help it. "The white blossoms you've seen? Much of what we learned from the fragments discovered at Knossos concerned them. White hellebore."

Drake turned his flashlight back on the wall painting of the slaves being given honey in a ritual presided over by the Mistress of the Labyrinth. Images of those flowers were mixed amid ancient Chinese characters and portrayals of hellish torture.

"But those flowers aren't white hellebore," Jada said. "We've established that."

Henriksen arched an eyebrow. "Tell me what you know about *Helleborus*."

She shrugged. "Only what your research team turned up. The

ancients thought there were two species, white and black, both poisonous."

"In the legends, black hellebore was a cure for madness," Drake said.

"But the flower they thought was white hellebore back then—" Jada began.

"It's still called white hellebore—" Drake put in.

"—isn't white hellebore at all. It's a different species. Like Nate said, they still call it that, but it's something else."

Henriksen nodded. "But what if, in ancient times, true white hellebore did exist? What if the flower they call by that name today, knowing it isn't the same species, is not the same flower the ancients called white hellebore? What if true white hellebore has been all but extinct for more than two thousand years— except inside this labyrinth, where it had continued to be culti- vated all down through the ages?"

Drake stared at him. "You're telling me this whole thing has been about flowers?"

"More than you can imagine," Henriksen said.

"Why?" Jada asked. "You want to create an army of Mino- taurs or something?"

Henriksen's expression hardened; whatever camaraderie they had built through their mutual survival was shattered.

"I don't," he said. "But I'm sure there are more than a few governments that would love that."

"Oh, my—" Jada started.

"I don't think it's that simple, though," Henriksen said, forg- ing onward. "Look at that painting. There are six or seven slaves being fed that honey, but not all of them are Minotaurs. What we've translated suggests that creating the Minotaurs was a happy accident, a by-product of the intended purpose of the white hellebore and the honey made from it. Daedalus—and later Talos—wanted slaves, and the primary effect of the dis- tilled essence of the white hellebore was to make those who in- gested it suggestible. Controllable. In theory it's not unlike the manner in which Haitian 'witch doctors' were once supposed to have used tetrodotoxin from puffer fish and other species to induce a trance state, but without the motor and mental impairment associated with those toxins. In small doses, Daedalus's honey left his subjects none the wiser, and in larger doses it either turned them into mindless drones or triggered the physiological and psychological changes that created Minotaurs. At Knossos, the honey had another name. In English, it translates as—"

"The hidden word," Drake interrupted. "The word they all had to obey."

Henriksen nodded. "Precisely."

"You're saying the hooded men aren't protecting Daedalus's treasure," Jada said. "They're protecting the white hellebore."

"This is where Olivia and I disagree," Henriksen replied, his voice echoing off the torture chamber's walls. "I believe that all references to treasure in the ancient records are really references to the flower. Mr. Drake, if you're the expert you claim to be, you must know that historically, white hellebore has also been reputed to be one of the key ingredients used—"

"In alchemy," Drake finished for him. He shook his head, waves of disbelief washing over him. He just had to make sure he didn't drown in them.

"I don't think alchemists turned base metals to gold any more than I think you can pull a rabbit out of a hat," Henriksen said. "I think all the great alchemists did was get their hands on some white hellebore and use it to influence the minds of those around them to control their perceptions and make them believe they had seen something they had not seen."

"There's no treasure," Drake said. "No gold?"

"Oh, I'm sure there must be something, or there was once upon a time," Henriksen said. "Do I think that Daedalus paid his workers with gold from inside the labyrinths? No. At Knossos, I suspect he paid them in stones or nuts before he realized that it would be much easier to simply take over their minds entirely and enslave them, which is what he likely did while building the labyrinth of Sobek.

"Olivia disagrees. She believes that Daedalus must have accumulated vast wealth, and perhaps she's right. But we won't know until we reach the center of the labyrinth. If she cared only for the white hellebore, she'd have turned around the moment we found it as we entered Diyu. But she wants that gold."

Drake scowled. "While all you want is to sell mind control to whichever government is the highest bidder."

Henriksen shrugged. "Someone's going to profit from this. I'd rather it were me."

Jada took a step backward. "This is what my father wanted to stop," she said, staring at him.

"I have no doubt," Henriksen agreed. "But I'm not some James Bond villain, Jada. It's not as if I'm going to try to take over the world. I'm only a businessman."

"Do you have any idea what this could be used for?" Jada demanded. "Think of the espionage applications. Dosing world leaders so you could control their decisions. Never mind the military uses. You know that soldiers would be experimented on. And what about dictatorships that want more pliable people?"

"As I said," Henriksen replied, "someone's going to do it."

"Unless we destroy the white hellebore," Jada said. "Burn it all."

Henriksen clenched his fists. "I'm afraid I can't allow that."

"Whoa!" Drake said, dropping his hand to the gun on his belt. "Let's all take a breath, okay?" He shone his flashlight at Jada and saw the emotions wracking her features. "Henriksen might not be a world conqueror, but right now, we have no idea what Olivia has in mind."

"Oh, make no mistake," Henriksen said. "If whoever she hires for the science can synthesize the chemicals, there's nothing Olivia would like more than to have presidents and despots as her puppets."

Drake glanced back and forth between them. "Our goals haven't changed. I'm here for Sully."

"I'm here for my father," Jada corrected him. "I love my Uncle Vic, but I'm here to stop Henriksen—*or* my stepmother—from getting what they want."

"Just hang on!" Drake snapped. "Do not fight this fight right now. We have two choices, all three of us. We go forward or we go back. If Sully's really still alive, I'm not leaving here without him, and I'm guessing both of you need to know what's at the heart of this place, yes?"

"I'm not going back," Jada said.

Henriksen's eyes blazed with his own intent.

"Then let's get going," Drake said. "One fight at a time."

They had lost time with revelations and argument, and as they renewed their exploration of Diyu, Drake felt constantly aware of the darkness they'd left behind. Every shadow and crevice breathed with menace because they had no idea how many hooded men might remain, but the longer they went without being attacked, the more his main concern became Olivia and the surviving mercenaries. It had sounded like Massarsky had taken charge when Perkins had been killed. He'd seemed okay for a guy who used his military training as a soldier for hire, and maybe a killer for hire if the price was right. But Drake had a feeling they wouldn't be having a beer together anytime soon.

They moved swiftly, making fewer wrong turns, working half on instinct now. Jada froze Henriksen out as if he weren't there at all, and that sat just fine with Drake. If the two of them weren't talking, it meant he didn't have to worry about breaking up a fight. Having to walk through three additional torture chambers—they were more plentiful down in the twisted bowels of the maze—only put more of a damper on any idle conversation. No one was feeling chatty except for Drake, and even he stopped trying to fill the silence after a while.

When they discovered the living quarters of the Protectors of the Hidden Word, they drew their guns and didn't holster them again. Yet amid the stone chambers—filled with wooden frame walls and floor platforms, as well as blankets and makeshift beds from a variety of eras—they met no resistance. Drake tried counting rooms and beds but decided the quicker they left the place, the better.

"Nate, do you hear it?" Jada whispered, her breathing low

and even, her gaze shifting about with a new degree of skittishness.

Drake nodded. They could hear the sound of running water, but not from pipes. He led the way with his flashlight, and at the rear of the warren of rooms that made up the living quarters, he found a small door that led into a natural fissure. The smell hit him even before he entered, and he knew he'd found what passed for a bathroom. Twenty feet below, a narrow river sliced through rock, rushing along an underground course it must have followed for centuries, even millennia.

"That's disgusting," Jada said.

"But necessary," Henriksen said. "Somewhere they'll have a kitchen. They must hunt for their food and gather greens in secret. They might even go into the city to find—"

"We don't care about their culture," Drake said, giving him a hard look.

Henriksen nodded. Interested as he was, he understood this wasn't why they had come. It wasn't an anthropology study.

Drake threaded back through the rooms, ducking through doorways until he had led them back to the tunnel they'd diverted from to investigate the quarters. The river had him thinking, wondering if the ravine they'd jumped also once had had water at the bottom. He had a feeling they had almost reached their destination, so he was surprised when the contortions of the labyrinth began to take them upward.

The sound began as a dull roar.

"What *is* that?" Drake asked.

They backtracked along a dead end turn and then started along a zigzag tunnel that had started as a natural cave and been smoothed and widened by human efforts. The sound diminished and then built again, growing ever louder, until the hissing roar filled the tunnel around them.

When Drake's flashlight beam picked up the gleam of moisture on the tunnel wall ahead, he knew what they had found.

The cavern was longer and wider than either of the others they'd encountered thus far. The river came rushing in from the right and over a ledge, creating a forty-foot wall of crashing

water that filled the vast cavern with a damp chill and a deafen-
ing white noise. Their tunnel ended on a plateau at the top of the
waterfall.

"It's beautiful," Jada said in surprise, raising her voice to be
heard.

Their flashlight beams strobed the walls, picking out faded
characters and symbols painted in some places and engraved in
others. Far above, slits of moonlight provided no real illumination but a glimpse of eyelet crevices that would allow the tiniest
bit of sunlight in on a clear day. Long strips of moss ran down
the far wall and covered the rocks on either side of the waterfall,
both there on the plateau and in the lower half of the cavern
below them, and vines of white hellebore, long since adapted to
this bizarre subterranean hell, were plentiful amid the moss.

Though the flashlights were powerful, they could make out
few details below. But Drake saw at least one tunnel leading
away from the area around the bottom of the waterfall, and he
suspected that what looked like deeper patches of darkness beyond all but the dimmest glow of their lights might be other such
tunnels.

"This is it," he said. "Down there somewhere."

Jada scanned her flashlight beam across the other side of the
rushing river, then ran it along the plateau toward the edge of
the waterfall. Drake saw the stairs the same moment she discovered them, carved into the wall beside the waterfall, descending
into the lower cavern. They gleamed with spray, and he knew
they would have to watch their step.

The violence began so quickly, Drake barely knew what was
happening. Henriksen grabbed his shoulder and spun him
around, reaching for his wrist. Drake held his gun in one hand
and the flashlight in the other, and for several heartbeats he
thought that Henriksen was attacking, making his move now to
eliminate them to save the white hellebore. He cracked the man
across the skull with the barrel of the Glock, and Henriksen
staggered back, dropping to one knee, blood welling on his forehead.

But he was waving his gun the other direction along the plateau, toward the dark cave mouth from which the river spouted.

"There!" Henriksen shouted. "Turn the bloody light over there!"

Drake swung the flashlight beam. Out of the corner of his eye he saw Jada just beginning to turn.

Then he saw them, five shadows rushing along the river's edge into the pool of light. *Only five*, Drake thought, which had to mean that their numbers were thinning badly. Their odds of surviving to see the sky again were improving.

One of the figures broke away, picking up speed. Henriksen raised his gun, steadied his aim, and fired. The killer crumpled, but forward momentum brought him rolling along the rock shelf toward them, and in the circle of Jada's flashlight beam, he tumbled to a halt and lay dead, gazing up at them with hollow, lifeless eyes.

Ian Welch.

Sick dread clutching at his heart, Drake directed his light at the others. Henriksen was taking aim again.

"Don't shoot!" Drake shouted.

His flashlight found four faces, but only one of them was not half hidden beneath a black hood. Drake swore.

"Sully, stop!"

But Drake could see in his eyes that Sully did not know him. The Sully who had been his best friend for nearly twenty years did not live behind those eyes anymore. Sully did not know him.

For half a second, Drake wondered if he could shoot him just to wound, but he wasn't that good a marksman and they'd never be able to carry him out of the labyrinth if he couldn't walk on his own.

It was half a second too long.

"Sully, it's me!" Drake yelled.

Then Sully barreled into him with enough force to knock the flashlight from his hand and the air from his chest. Drake staggered backward, only just managing to hold on to his gun as Sully put both hands around his throat and squeezed.

Struggling, trying to retreat, Drake felt his boot slip off the plateau's rocky edge. Jada screamed his name, and then he and Sully were falling. They plunged into the cold, roaring river, Sully still with his hands wrapped around Drake's throat. Drake's mind was screaming for oxygen, his chest tight and burning after Sully had knocked the air out of him, and he wondered if Sully or the river would do him in.

Then they were spilling over the waterfall, falling, punished and dragged downward, and he realized it would be the fall that killed him.

23

Drake thrashed in the water, tearing loose from Sully's grip. The river rushed around him, but for long drowning seconds he could not discern up from down, life from death. Then his left foot hit something hard and unyielding, and he knew that it must be below. Fighting to keep himself from flipping over again in the powerful current, he thrust his legs down, struck bottom, and propelled himself upward. His chest convulsed with the need for air, and when at last he broke the surface, he gave himself over to a helpless primal gasping, his mind devoid of reason, desiring only to breathe.

A hand snagged his shirt, and then Sully latched on to him, arms and legs wrapped around him from behind, trying to force him down. Drake shot an elbow into his gut, felt the sharp exhalation behind him, then reached around and put Sully in a headlock. Choking and dragging him at the same time, he pushed for the rocky riverbank. He'd dropped his flashlight up on the plateau, and though he didn't remember letting go of his gun, he had lost it when they'd plunged over the waterfall. All he had to fight with were his hands and his wits, and he hoped they wouldn't fail him.

Only the dimmest light existed down there in the lower cavern. It might as well have been pitch-dark save for the gleam of moonlight and reflected illumination from wavering flashlight beams above. That wet blackness gave form to rocks and walls and its absence indicated the presence of tunnel mouths, but otherwise Drake was in darkness.

He felt the river bottom underfoot and knew he must be near the bank. The roar of the waterfall on his right made it hard to hear much else, yet another churning noise came from his left, and he glanced that way to see the glistening blackness of a vertical rock face—the far end of the cavern. The river flowed into a tunnel at the base of the rock.

Panic raced through him. His throat raw from nearly drowning, his profanity-laced mutterings came out a meager rasp, but in his mind he was shouting. If they were dragged into that river tunnel, the darkness would be complete, and there was no way to know when or if they would enter another cavern where they might climb out. The underground river might go on for miles, joining the Qin Huai or Yangtze somewhere beyond the city of Nanjing. By then, they probably would be dead.

Drake tried to hoist Sully from the water, staggering toward shore, fighting the current. Sully had seemed disoriented, but now he thrashed against Drake's choke hold, elbowed his ribs, and clawed at his hands. He twisted and bucked, and Drake lost his footing. Then he fell into the torrent again, washing toward the back of the cavern to vanish into the subterranean river's hidden path forever.

"No!" Drake screamed, getting his footing, grabbing Sully around the torso as if tackling him.

He drove Sully toward the shore, dragging them both waist deep through the water even as Sully tried to break his grip. In the shallows, where the river turned almost gentle, Drake gave Sully a shove and sent him careening onto the rocky bank. Lungs burning and heart thundering, Drake stood with his hands on his knees. His muscles were exhausted from fighting the river, and though the air tasted sweet, each sip made his ragged throat ache even worse.

In the dark, he saw the black silhouette of his best friend rise and turn toward him. The only feature he could make out was Sully's eyes, which glistened in the dark, as wet and black as the rocks by the river.

"Sully, please," Drake rasped. "It's me. It's Nate. I know you're still in there. Don't make me fight you."

Silent as the hooded men, Sully lunged at him. Drake dodged left, grabbed his outstretched arm, and used it for leverage, slamming his knee up into Sully's gut. He heard the explosion of breath as he knocked all the air out of Sully's lungs. But Sully held on, wheezing and groaning, as Drake kneed him a second time.

Sully bit his arm, teeth sinking into flesh, and Drake cried out in pain that merged with the waterfall in a roaring chorus. With his free hand he punched Sully in the temple five times in quick succession until Sully's jaw let go. Drake reeled away from him, careful not to fall into the deep current again. He felt hot blood coursing down his arm, smelled its coppery stink, and knew he had to finish this before Sully killed him.

Drake waded toward him, feinted twice, and then landed a blow to Sully's gut and followed up with three quick strikes to the face. In the dark, he could make out only the shape of his old friend, but he didn't need to see the details, didn't want to see the lack of recognition in those blank eyes, especially now.

With one final blow, he sent Sully crashing to the rocky bank again, but as his friend began to rise, Drake got him into a choke hold again. This time Drake had solid ground beneath him and held on tightly as Sully's struggles grew weaker. In what seemed only moments, his friend began to sag in his grasp, and Drake released him. Sully crumpled to the ground, where Drake felt for his pulse and found it still beating. He wrapped his arms around his friend and let out a shuddering breath.

Sully's alive, he thought, frozen with shock and relief. For the first time, he admitted to himself that he had been half convinced that the hooded men had killed him. He had no idea how he would get them out of the labyrinth or what it would take to shake Sully out of the honey's effects, but he knew he had to take it one step at a time.

Something dark floated by on the swift current, jutting from the water. Drake cursed himself and set Sully down, standing and turning to look up at the plateau. A pair of flashlights moved down the water-sprayed stairs, slowly descending toward him.

"Nate!" a voice cried, carrying to him over the crushing thunder of the waterfall.

"Here!" he shouted back, wading a few feet into the shallows. "I've got Sully!"

The two beams of light continued down the stairs carved beside the waterfall, and slowly he began to make out the shapes behind them. Jada and Henriksen had managed to defeat the three attackers who had come at them on the plateau with Sully and Ian Welch. One of them had just floated by in the river, dead or dying, and Drake figured the other two were probably dead as well, as was Welch.

"How deep is it?" Henriksen called. "Can we cross?"

Drake thought about that. At its deepest, would Jada's feet reach the bottom?

"I don't know. The current's pretty strong!"

When Jada and Henriksen reached the bottom of the steps, standing on the rocky shelf on the opposite bank of the river, they began to scan the lower cavern with their flashlights, and Drake got a much better idea of his surroundings. The blossoms he still thought of as cave hellebore grew all over the walls on vines and in the moss. Where nothing grew, the cavern walls were carved with octagons, flowers etched inside of them, and ancient Chinese symbols had been painted and repainted over centuries.

"Nate, look!" Jada called, flashing her light on something at the end of the cavern, where the river flowed into the rock face.

It took a second for him to realize that the stony edges that glinted in the light were steps. He frowned, then started along the rock shelf on the riverbank, pacing their progress on the other side. As they searched with their flashlights, Drake saw the steps on his side as well and ran toward them. He passed high, rounded tunnel mouths but could see nothing but deeper darkness inside as he hurried by, and in seconds he had reached the bottom of those steps.

"There's a bridge!" he called to them, amazed at the way the solid rock above where the river left the cavern had been cut away to form a crossing above the water.

Jada and Henriksen picked up their pace. Drake hesitated. He'd left Sully on the bank and still could make out the silhouette of the man lying in the dark. He went up the half dozen steps to the bridge but halted there. As Jada and Henriksen hurried toward their side of the bridge, Drake studied the tunnel mouths on the other side. Jada barely spared them a glance, but Henriksen slowed and shone his light inside as he went past, searching for the worship chamber they all expected to find.

As Henriksen continued, it seems for a moment that the illumination from his flashlight remained behind in the last of the tunnels. Drake blinked, staring at the phenomenon, and then realized the light inside the mouth of that tunnel was moving, jittering and swinging and growing brighter.

Company, he thought. He was about to shout to the others when staccato gunfire came from the tunnel, muffled but echoing out into the vast waterfall cavern. Drake flinched before he realized that whoever was coming wasn't shooting at him, Jada, or Henriksen.

Jada turned, pausing on the steps on the other side of the bridge.

"Run!" Drake shouted, racing toward her over the rushing river.

Henriksen did the running for her, linking arms with her and sweeping her along as he bolted toward Drake. They both still had their flashlights and guns out, and it made for an awkward flight, lights bobbing and legs almost becoming tangled.

More gunshots rang out, and then the first of the mercenaries came hurtling out of the tunnel mouth, twisting around to cover the others with both light and weapon. They poured from the labyrinth and into the cavern; Drake counted five, including Olivia, Massarsky, and Garza, and when he saw the hooded men dart from the tunnel, hurling knives and what looked like small, sharpened metal rings, he knew the rest of their team must be dead.

"Go, go!" Jada yelled.

Drake already was turning back the way he'd come. The way Jada and Henriksen's lights were bouncing, it was hard to make out the top of the stairs, and he had to go slowly. Henriksen had let Jada go, but now she nearly collided with Drake as they ran down the half dozen slippery steps to the rock shelf of the riverbank.

"I thought you were dead!" she said.

"So did I!"

"Don't do it again!"

Drake had no snappy comeback. His focus was on the tunnel mouths on this side of the river.

"Jada!" he said, pointing. "Check those; see if any of them lead out of here. Olivia and her goons found another path to get into this cavern; there might be more than one way out."

"I'm not going until I find the worship chamber!" Henriksen snapped.

Gunshots, and they all looked over to see a hooded woman with long black hair streaming beneath her hood drive a long blade through one of the mercenaries, momentum carrying them both into the river. But Olivia and the others were already at the base of the bridge. Drake knew she had spotted them—flashlights were dancing all over the cavern—but she had only three more thugs between her and certain death, and she was running like hell.

"You can do whatever the hell you want!" Drake snapped at Henriksen. "After you help me get Sully to cover!"

Henriksen blinked, but only once, and then they were running along the bank toward where Sully lay sprawled, still unconscious. They grabbed him under the arms as they heard Jada shouting their names and began to drag him toward her. She stood in the mouth of the tunnel closest to the waterfall, and they ran to join her, Sully's boots trailing across the ground between them.

Back on the bridge, Massarsky, Garza, and a square-jawed black guy Drake thought was named Suarez were making a stand. They stood on the stone walkway above the river and shot the two hooded men who were out in the open on the riverbank. One or two more—perhaps *only* one or two more; it was impossible to tell—remained in the tunnel they had just vacated, but Massarsky and his people pinned them down. They couldn't come out without being killed. Olivia stood behind Garza, gun in hand. Her blond hair was a tangled, dirty mess, and her face was etched with grim determination.

Olivia turned and looked right at Drake as he and Henriksen dragged Sully into the open tunnel. He could read the profanity on her lips. Then they were inside the tunnel and out of her sight, and she out of his.

Only when Drake turned to look for Jada did he see that the tunnel rounded a slight curve and then ended just ahead.

With three steps down into a worship chamber.

The octagonal altar sat in the center of the room. Drake felt himself go cold, a numb amazement spreading through him. They had found it. After all this, they were here.

He and Henriksen dragged Sully down the three steps, and then Henriksen let go. Drake had to catch Sully to keep him from crashing to the stone floor of the worship chamber as Henriksen raced around the room, shining his flashlight on the Chinese characters and the symbols and paintings all over the walls.

Jada already had rushed into the anteroom, the ritual preparation space that had been built next to the worship chamber, its design identical to that of the other labyrinths Daedalus had created. In every other way, Diyu was different from the first three labyrinths, but here at its heart, its origins echoed loudly.

Several more gunshots rang out, and then he heard Olivia shouting. He feared they were not going to be alone in the chamber much longer.

"The trigger!" he called to Jada. "Find the—"

"Already on it!" she replied, searching the corners of the anteroom with her flashlight. In the reflected illumination, he saw her eyes light up, and then she bent, pushing and then kicking at a stone block in the wall of the anteroom.

With a loud clunk of stone, the altar shifted a couple of inches. Jada had found the trigger.

Henriksen and Drake stood staring at the altar for a few seconds. On the ground, Sully began to groan and then move as he slowly came around. Drake had no idea which Sully would be waking up, the one he knew or the one the white hellebore poison had made.

He glanced at Jada. Regardless of her intentions toward the flower that had caused so many so much grief and suffering, he could see that she needed to know just as much as he did what they would find in the chamber below.

"Push!" Drake said, glancing at Henriksen.

In the short tunnel behind them, they could hear the footfalls and voices of Olivia and her trio of mercenary survivors. On the floor, Sully groaned louder, and in the most pissed-off, most graveled voice Drake had ever heard, he started muttering colorful curses about the Protectors of the Hidden Word and payback.

Henriksen threw himself against the octagonal altar, and Drake did the same thing; the whole thing slid back with a rumble of stone on stone.

The first thing Drake noticed about the darkness yawning below was the nauseating stink that wafted up at them. Then he saw two yellow eyes gleaming against the black and heard the bestial snarl that grew into a roar as the Minotaur thundered up the steps, slavering and reaching for Henriksen's throat.

Drake had no gun. He threw the hardest punch he had in him, aiming for the vulnerable muscle cluster under the Minotaur's arm. He felt his knuckles crunch on impact, and pain shot up his arm as he swore and reeled back. As the Minotaur closed one hand around Henriksen's throat, it twisted and snarled at Drake. Jada shone her flashlight into its eyes, and it flinched, startled.

Henriksen shot it twice in the chest, and the human monstrosity rocked with the bullets, relaxing its grip enough for Henriksen to shake free. The Minotaur looked down at the holes in its chest, blood weeping and then spilling from the wounds, and Drake had a better look at its face and head. There could be no doubt that this was a man, deformed and hideous to behold but no less human for it. A light coat of hair covered even his cheeks, and ridges of what looked like bone were visible through the hair, but the horns on top of his head were those of an animal, clamped inside a frame of tarnished gold and held there with leather straps. The beast had no clothes, and the matted hair that covered its body had begun to thin in places. It looked almost sickly.

But the bullets had not stopped it.

A clatter of footsteps came from behind Drake, and he heard Garza swearing.

"Son of a bitch!" Suarez yelled.

Massarsky grabbed Olivia and shoved her behind him even as Garza lifted her weapon, taking aim.

"Get clear of that thing!" Garza shouted.

Drake didn't have to be told twice. The single glance the Minotaur had given him had chilled his bones, so now he grabbed Jada and backpedaled with her into the wall. Henriksen backed up as well, and Drake wondered why he hadn't kept shooting. He had his weapon leveled at the Minotaur, but it was almost as if now that its attention was elsewhere, he had no interest in destroying it.

Sully had risen unsteadily, and now he wavered on his feet, half blocking Garza's aim.

"Get down!" Garza shouted.

"Just shoot!" Olivia screamed at her. "Kill him, too! You're going to kill them all anyway; just shoot through the bastard!"

The Minotaur roared, batting at the flashlight beams that blinded it for a moment, but the way it twisted, gaze narrowing, Drake thought it had zeroed in on Olivia's shrill voice, as if it recognized that she was giving the orders. And why not? Once upon a time, it had been just a man.

It barreled toward Olivia despite the others in the way. Sully dived from its path, dropping wearily to his knees as the Minotaur continued past. Garza pulled the trigger, bullets chipping the walls, the echo of the semiautomatic fire assaulting their ears. Three bullets stitched the Minotaur's hip and arm and shoulder, and it screamed in pain, but it was inhumanly fast and changed direction in an instant.

Garza's weapon clicked on empty, dry-firing, the clip out of bullets. She might have had another, but her time had run out. Her eyes went wide as the Minotaur reached for her, grabbing her head and giving it a savage twist. The dry snap of breaking bone was like a whip crack in the worship chamber.

"Come on, kid," Sully said, grabbing Drake's shoulder, half for support and half to get him moving.

Drake turned and saw that Henriksen already had started down through the secret passage beneath the altar. He slapped Sully's back and pointed, then called to Jada, and the three of them were following fast. Gunfire ripped the air behind them, and Drake heard the sound of bullets punching through flesh. This time when the Minotaur roared, it came out as a scream, but then they left the sounds of violence behind, descending into the heart of the fourth labyrinth at long last.

In the shadows, with only Henriksen and Jada's flashlights to guide them, they found the corridor leading from the bottom of the steps. The heavy, musky stink of the Minotaur seemed to coat the walls and floor, so strong that Drake scowled in disgust.

Sully stumbled a bit, and Drake looked at him, still wary of the way the protectors had toyed with his mind and still feeling the bruising on his neck from Sully trying to strangle him. He was alive, and the relief of that still felt like victory, but Drake didn't want to celebrate just yet.

Then Sully tripped and would have fallen if Drake hadn't caught him. He ducked under Sully's arm, helping him stay balanced as they moved down the corridor. Under his breath, Sully grunted something that might have been words.

"What was that?" Drake asked.

"You deaf?" Sully rasped. "I said it smells like your laundry down here."

Drake blinked in surprise, and then a smile spread across his face. "Glad to have you back, old man."

Jada caught up to them, then, and they had to stop in the corridor as she threw her arms around Sully. Drake backed away to give them a moment, and for several long seconds they just held each other, Jada's shoulders trembling with emotion as she buried her face in the crook of Sully's neck.

"I'm so glad you're not dead," she murmured into the collar of his shirt.

"You and me both, darlin'," Sully replied.

"Look at this," Henriksen said.

Drake glanced up and saw Henriksen shining his flashlight through an open side passage. When Drake looked inside, he saw a warren of tunnels as well as an opening that seemed to lead into a kind of living space decorated with crude wall paintings that looked as if they'd been made in blood. The stink of filth and death was powerful, and Drake knew it must be where the Minotaur slept.

"Let's go," Sully said. "Let's finish this."

In moments they had reached the end of the corridor. It couldn't have been more than sixty feet in length, so short that the beams of the surviving mercenaries' flashlights still provided some illumination back on the stairs. At the end of the corridor was a heavy wooden door with iron bands holding the thick planks together. They had encountered nothing like this in the other labyrinths, but Drake noticed the age of the wood and realized the door had been added within the past century or so, as if in this one place the hooded men had acknowledged the passage of time. It didn't jibe with the Minotaur's savagery, this tiny concession to civilization.

And there was light under the door.

"What the hell—?" Drake began.

Henriksen handed Sully his flashlight and tried the latch. The door opened, swinging inward, and Henriksen gave it a shove with his gun. Empty-handed, Drake felt more vulnerable than ever, but as the door swung wide, he forgot about protecting himself—forgot almost everything.

Consistent with Daedalus's design, there were three steps down, but this room dwarfed any of the other worship chambers they had seen. Fires burned in braziers set at intervals that went deep into the cave. A pair of iron chandeliers hung from chains hooked to the ceiling, fat white candles burning brightly. But even all that light could illuminate only a portion of the shadowed cave, which seemed to be some bizarre combination of vault and sepulcher.

The treasure of Daedalus lined the walls and filled the dark recesses at the back of the cave. Stone jars and vases overflowed with gold coins struck in ancient Greece and Egypt, with gem-encrusted headpieces and golden necklaces and gleaming scepters. A solid gold crocodile three feet in length must have come

from the Temple of Sobek. And in the middle of it all, on a pedestal, stood a golden statue of a Minotaur, its horns massive
shards of ruby.

In a single glance, Drake drank in the forgotten majesty of the
place and the enormity of the secret truths it confirmed. But a
moment was all he allowed himself, for the menace in that cave
was far more dominant than its promise.

In the middle of the floor were three stone tombs, massive
things like sarcophagi but with a Chinese influence on the design
and the engravings. Beyond the three tombs, a small cluster of
people waited, watching the intruders with eyes full of fear and
loathing. There were three hooded men—one guardian for each
tomb, perhaps. A woman stood in their midst, tall and veiled,
the firelight throwing shadows across what little of her face was
visible. Her eyes seemed to flicker yellow like the Minotaur's.
Behind her was an altar above which were shelves arrayed with
vases and chalices. Upon the altar were drying white flowers,
fragments of bone, and a variety of small stone cups. One cup
had spilled a coppery powder across the pale stone.

The Mistress of the Labyrinth. It could be no one else.

Yet Drake's gaze was drawn past her, to the right of the three
tombs, where a withered monster lay ailing on a wooden pallet,
swaddled in thick woolen blankets. Its eyes were opalescent,
blind and seeking, and its ugly, wrinkled, misshapen head was
covered with scabs and the stains of age. Once it had been a
Minotaur, but now it was only a pitiful, mindless old man on the
verge of death.

"We should never have come here," Jada whispered.

Drake understood. The scene wrenched at his heart so powerfully that for a moment he allowed himself to forget more than
two thousand years of slavery, torture, and murder. And then
the mistress of the fourth—and last—labyrinth pointed one
trembling finger at them and barked an order with a sneer of
such cruelty and disdain that he could feel the venom in her.

The hooded men attacked, leaping on top of the three tombs
and launching themselves through the air. Henriksen fired, but
the black-clothed protector was too fast, twisting and lunging.

The two careened to the ground and fell, struggling, onto the floor. Henriksen's gun skidded away across the stone.

Jada shot the one nearest her. The bullet struck his shoulder and spun him around, but Drake missed whatever happened next. The third killer came at him, darting and moving, swaying like a serpent, a curved blade flashing in his grip. Drake waited for him to attack, then swung Henriksen's flashlight, which shattered the hooded man's wrist. The dagger clattered to the floor, but the killer kept coming, striking Drake in the throat with his good hand. Drake spun, trying to avoid the strike, and the hooded man missed his larynx by inches, punching the side of his neck instead.

Sully tackled the killer, lifting him off the ground and slamming him into one of the tombs so hard that the hooded man cried out in pain and fell to the ground, wheezing and grabbing for the small of his back, dragging his legs behind him uselessly.

Automatic gunfire stitched the firelit vault, bullets chinking into gold and shattering vases.

Everyone froze except for Henriksen, who delivered a final blow that knocked his opponent senseless. The hooded man groaned, barely conscious, and Henriksen glanced up, his enemy's blade in his hand.

Drake and Sully stood together. Jada hovered near the corpse of the hooded man she apparently had shot a second time. But they all stared at the entrance to the vault, where Suarez and Olivia were descending the last step, his arm around her. Blood soaked his left side and pain etched his face, but his grip on his gun was strong enough and his eyes seemed clear.

Olivia gazed at the gold with open lust, her grin fervent with glee. The Minotaur had clawed the right side of her face, slicing deep furrows in her cheek, and she hardly seemed to have noticed. In her left hand, she still clutched a pistol.

She started to speak but couldn't get the words out without bursting into a fit of laughter. Blood trickled down her chin and neck, staining her shirt and jacket.

"Look at this!" Olivia said. "Damn it, Tyr, *look* at all of this!"

"I'm looking," Henriksen said warily.

"We were both right!" Olivia said, extricating herself from Suarez, who managed to stay standing on his own. "Go on, soldier. Finish them. All of them."

Suarez's gun barrel didn't even twitch. "I don't think so. No way am I getting out of this pit without help, and you can't exactly carry me."

Olivia turned to sneer at him.

As she did, a shriek came from behind Drake, and he turned, ready for a fight. *The mistress*, he thought. She and her dying charge had seemed helpless, and for a moment they'd forgotten her. Even as he turned, he saw the tall veiled woman grab Henriksen from behind, one hand clamped over his face as she drew the wickedly curved blade across his throat. Dying, he tore at her veil, revealing a grotesque countenance without the bestial features of the Minotaur but ruined by a lifetime's slow poisoning by white hellebore.

Suarez opened fire, blowing her back among the tombs in a heap of tangled limbs and a growing pool of blood. The final hooded man began to rise groggily from the beating Henriksen had given him, and Olivia took aim and tried to kill him, but she had run out of ammunition. With a short burst from his weapon, Suarez finished the job.

Drake reached for Jada, as much to take comfort as to give it. He put an arm around her, and Sully joined them. Only Jada still had a gun, but whatever happened next was going to be up to Suarez. Drake felt sick looking at Henriksen and the Mistress of the Labyrinth and the bodies of what he could only assume were the last of the Protectors of the Labyrinth.

He glanced over at the ancient dying Minotaur on its worn pallet. It shivered, staring blindly into nothing, as if its mind was so far gone that it barely knew they were there in the vault with it. Perhaps that was true. If so, Drake thought it was for the best.

"There's nothing here I want," he said.

Sully looked sick. It was clear he and Jada shared that sentiment.

But Olivia still wore the same lunatic grin. She left Suarez standing at the bottom of the steps and rushed to the wall on her left, digging her hands into the stone jars of coins and letting them run through her hands. Drake tried not to calculate the worth of so much gold pressed into such ancient coins. Each was practically priceless.

"Stop," Sully said. "There isn't—"

Suarez took a step toward him, gesturing with the gun. "For the moment we're all friends here, 'cause I want to live. If you folks don't want to be richer than sin, that's your business. Me, I have no objection to treasure."

Drake could have told him that the flowers they had passed upon first entering the labyrinth and seen many times since were worth more than all the treasure in the vault combined. But he doubted Suarez would believe him and didn't much want to share the information, anyway. For her part, Olivia knew all about the white hellebore, and Henriksen had suggested she would not hesitate to do as he'd planned and sell it to the highest bidder, but it was clear that gold was her first priority.

Olivia took out a heavy Egyptian necklace of beaten gold and put it around her throat, smiling like a little girl playing dress-up in Mommy's closet. She stepped on top of the golden crocodile and glanced around, shaking her head as if it were too much for her to take in, and then her gaze locked onto the gold statue of the Minotaur with its ruby horns. She jumped down and ran to the pedestal where it stood.

As she reached for the statue, Drake felt a surge of shame. He glanced over at the dying Minotaur, an old man ravaged by poisons and physiological side effects his entire life, and saw the monster lower its head and turn away. Perhaps it was not entirely blind, but what, Drake wondered, did it not want to see?

Drake turned and stared at Olivia, firelight and shadows playing across her slim body, and as her fingers touched the gold and ruby statue, somehow he knew. He broke away from Jada and Sully and ran toward her even as she hefted the statue from its pedestal, admiring its shine.

A wide octagonal stone began to rise out of the top of the

pedestal. The statue had been a counterweight, and now it had been removed. Loud grinding noises filled the walls, the thunking and crashing of stone blocks shook the room, and Drake turned and ran.

"Get out of here!" he shouted at Sully and Jada.

Suarez looked at him, and the man's eyes went wide. He didn't know what had just happened, but he saw their panic and turned and started to limp toward the three stairs.

"Where the hell are you—?" Olivia screamed after them.

A huge block of stone in the wall of the cave pushed inward, falling onto the coin jars. They shattered, spilling coins all over the floor, just as a torrent of water rushed in through the hole the block had left behind. The rumbling and grinding went on. Another block slid from the wall, then a third and a fourth, and water crashed in, filling the vault with all the power of the river. So much water flooded in so quickly that in moments it began to rise around them.

Jada reached the stairs first, helping Suarez out of the rising water, which already had reached the second step. Drake and Sully were right behind them, but Sully turned to look back into the vault.

"What about her?" he said.

Drake turned to see Olivia in the middle of the maelstrom formed by the half dozen raging torrents coming through the walls. Treasures were flooded, knocked over, swirling and sinking, and Olivia screamed not in panic for herself but in anguish over the loss of the gold. She clutched the Minotaur statue to her chest as if it were her child, trying to keep it above the swiftly rising water.

"Come on, damn it!" Drake shouted, wading back toward her.

"Nate!" Sully called.

"Just go," Drake snapped, waving him on. "I'm right behind you!"

The water had risen with stunning speed, washing around his waist now and still churning into the vault.

"Olivia! Drop the statue and swim!"

She glared at him with such hate that it stopped him cold. Olivia struggled to hold the heavy statue and forge her way through the maelstrom inside the vault. Drake swore and pushed toward her again, the river still flooding higher.

Something underwater must have tripped her, because she went down with a splash, submerging instantly. Drake thought she would drop the statue then, but there was no sign of flailing arms until suddenly she surfaced twenty feet to his right.

But Olivia was not alone. The dying Minotaur held her from behind, its gauzy white eyes shining in the light from the chandeliers above. The floodwater had knocked over the braziers and put them out, but the candles still burned. At first Drake thought the Minotaur had found the strength to attempt to survive and was trying to drag Olivia toward him and toward the door, but then he saw the way one of its clawed hands was tangled in her hair and the other gripped her throat, and the two of them sank under the water together.

Drake hesitated, furious with Olivia and with himself. Then, over the roar of the water, he heard Sully shouting to him from outside the vault and knew he had to go. He turned and slogged back toward the door, the floodwater swallowing him.

By the time he reached the steps, the water was up to his shoulders. As he climbed the submerged steps, he saw a flashlight up in the corridor and realized Sully had waited for him.

"Go!" he called, struggling out of the water and up the last step.

Sully hit him with the flashlight beam—Suarez must have had it in his pack—and shouted at him to hurry.

"Turn around!" Drake snapped as he ran toward Sully.

Then the water reached the top of the steps and began to pour into the corridor, and Sully's eyes widened as he understood. They had a hundred feet or more of corridor to cover, and the water would keep churning, keep rising, until it matched the level of the river—at least ten feet above them.

The water washed around their legs, flooding along the tunnel. Sully stumbled once and Drake caught him, but they kept going. Up ahead they saw Jada helping Suarez up the stairs of the secret passage into the worship chamber. Suarez slipped and fell and didn't rise again until Drake got there to help Jada with him, the water already above their knees.

They had to drag Suarez the last couple of steps and through the opening of the hidden entrance, where the altar remained rolled back from the stairs. Panting, bent over, with a single flashlight and only Suarez's gun, they staggered out of the worship chamber, past the corpses of Massarsky, Garza, and the younger Minotaur, even as the water rushed up the stairs after them.

Three more steps took them out of the worship chamber, and then they were in the short tunnel that brought them to the rocky shelf of the riverbank, where the waterfall roared and the white hellebore grew as it always had.

Suarez died there only moments after they had set him down gently, too much blood lost from the wound in his side. Drake sank to his knees beside the man, sick to the bone of death and greed.

"Thanks for not killing us," Drake whispered before he reached out and closed the dead man's eyes.

He glanced at Sully and Jada, who were leaning against each other, exhausted and drained. Then he sat back on his haunches and glanced around the vast cavern, waiting long seconds to see if any of the Protectors of the Hidden Word would spring from one of the tunnels and try to kill them. No one appeared.

Far up in the ceiling of the cavern, he thought he could make out tiny slits of morning light.

"What do we do now?" Jada asked.

"What your father would have wanted," Sully replied.

Drake nodded, rising wearily to his feet. He stared around at the blossoms on the walls among the moss and vines.

"Exactly," he said. "We rip it all down, and then we burn it. We make sure white hellebore—the real thing—stays a myth."

"We could set a charge, blow the tunnel under the Treasure Mound," Sully suggested.

Drake shrugged. "Why bother? Once we close it up, the entrance is hidden, and the government forbids anyone from excavating."

"Perkins left two of his people on guard. What do we say to them when we get out of here?" Jada asked.

Sully laughed. "Tell 'em they got lucky."

Drake clapped him on the back, and the two of them smiled at Jada.

"Better yet," Drake said, "tell 'em they're fired."

24

Five days later, Luka Hzujak finally got his funeral. The autumn sun cast a golden hue across the quiet beauty of the cemetery. Woodlawn was one of the most famous burial grounds in New York City, an oasis of peace and quiet in the Bronx. Jada said she had chosen it for that reason, and Drake could understand.

In late October, there were as many red and gold leaves on the ground as there were on the trees, and with every breeze they skittered across the broad lawns, catching on tombstones and statues of angels. Aside from the distant rumble of car engines that seemed the eternal background music of New York City, the only sounds were the wind in the leaves and the voice of the minister.

Drake stood on Jada's left, Sully on her right. She had wept as any grieving daughter would, but she held her chin high. Her father had loved nothing better than unraveling the secrets of history. Even if he hadn't been attempting to beat Henriksen to the discovery of the true history of Daedalus and his labyrinths, once Luka knew about them, he would have been unable to resist the temptation to learn more. But his intentions had been pure.

Drake knew that he and Sully usually could not claim such innocent ambitions. They walked a fine line, often on the razor edge of both criminality and greed. Olivia had been willing to hurt anyone—kill anyone—to fulfill her desire for gold, and the idea of turning people into puppets for her personal amusement had inspired her. It was easy for Drake to think of her and to know that he and Sully were different. Like Luka, they loved history and the thrill of uncovering its secrets, but half the excitement came from the fact that those secrets were so often *treasures*. They wanted the rewards that came along with the risks they took along the way, and that was certainly part of their motivation.

How different did that make them from Henriksen? That was the question that had been haunting Drake ever since they had emerged from Diyu, beaten and exhausted. He and Jada had watched over Sully for a day and a half in a Beijing hotel suite, where they had checked in under false identities and prayed they wouldn't be arrested. Though he hadn't been given enough doses to alter his mind permanently, the poison he'd been fed needed to work itself out of his system.

During that time, Drake had thought a lot about Tyr Henriksen. In the end, he'd decided that although the gulf between his philosophy and Henriksen's might not be as wide as he would like, it was wide enough for him to be able to sleep at night. Henriksen loved history and discovery, and he coveted the treasures of the past. But though he might not have been as deeply tainted as Olivia, he was still a black hat. He hadn't been willing to kill or ask others to kill for him, but he hadn't cared at all how many might die because of his actions. He had intended to sell the white hellebore to the highest bidder, and Drake, Sully, and Jada had burned it, no matter that it could have given them unimaginable wealth if they had done as Henriksen or Olivia would have.

Drake would never be able to say that what he and Sully did wasn't at least partly about the treasure—about the money. But in his heart he knew that it had never been only about the money and it never would be. That distinction would have to be enough.

The minister finished his blessings and then gestured to Jada. She knew what he expected and started forward. Her father's casket rested on a riser beside the open grave, which had been covered by a green tarp. Enormous floral arrangements created a kind of path for mourners to pass by the coffin, and Jada led the way. A gust of wind tousled her hair, blowing magenta strands across her face, but she did not bother to tuck them back as she drew a flower from the first arrangement, walked to her father's casket, and threw the flower on top. She paused, kissed the fingers of her right hand, and then pressed those fingers to the smooth metal. She drew in a long, shuddering breath and then let it out. If she said goodbye to him, it was in her heart rather than aloud.

Drake and Sully tugged flowers from the arrangement and tossed them onto the casket before escorting her away as the line of mourners formed behind them to take part in the same ritual farewell.

Jada had cousins and a couple of aunts at the funeral, but Sully was her godfather, and she had wanted him with her through the service. Now she stopped and waited for her other relatives, but she turned to Drake and took his hands.

"Thank you."

Drake nodded. "Nothing to thank me for. He was a good man."

Jada turned to Sully, her eyes welling up again. Her lower lip trembled.

"I don't think I could've handled this—" she began, but then words failed her. She glanced at the ground, watching the leaves that danced across the lawn at her feet.

Sully put a hand on her shoulder, leaning forward to kiss her head. "It's okay. We're not going anywhere. Go talk to your family and we'll wait."

Shaking, she looked up at him. Her eyes were red and glistening but filled with a ferocious love.

"You're my family," Jada said. She glanced at Drake. "Both of you."

She threw her arms around Sully and hugged him so hard that he grunted in surprise, his eyes widening comically. Then he relaxed into her embrace and just held her for a minute, until she exhaled and stepped away from him.

"You'll be here?" she asked. "I know you have a life to get back to."

Sully pointed toward one of Jada's aunts, who already had left her flower on the casket and was hovering, not wanting to interrupt.

"Go. We're here for days still."

Jada smiled, wiped at her tears, and then went to talk to her aunt. Others gathered around her, and for a while Drake and Sully were forgotten.

Sully straightened his tie, uncomfortable in the suit he'd bought for the funeral.

"Thanks," he said.

"What for?"

"For coming when I asked and for staying alive."

Drake shrugged. "You'd do the same for me."

Sully gave a pensive nod and turned to watch Jada talking to other mourners who wanted to give her their condolences.

"Are you worried about her?" Drake asked.

"A little. But she'll be all right. She's smarter than either one of us."

Something in his tone gave Drake pause. He cocked his head and studied Sully a little more closely.

"What's on your mind?" he asked.

Sully gave him a sidelong glance, thoughtfully smoothing his mustache. "I got a phone call from Massimo last night. Did you know he has a cousin who's a cardinal in Rome?"

Drake frowned. "No. Did you?"

"No. Point is, his cousin the cardinal isn't a cardinal any-more. Sixty-seven years old and he's quit the priesthood, left the Vatican. Disillusioned, apparently. But he didn't leave empty-handed."

"Spit it out, Sully," Drake said. "Massimo's cousin the former cardinal took something with him when he left. So what was it?"

Sully smiled thinly, almost a smirk. "You know the story about the Italian archaeologist—this is about ten years ago—who found a report in the Vatican archives about this mission-ary, Andres Lopez—"

"I know the story," Drake interrupted. "What was it, end of the sixteenth century? Lopez supposedly found Paititi in the Amazon basin in Peru, but he and the Vatican kept it a secret for four hundred years. We've heard a million stories like that. There's no evidence, and I need a break from lost cities and an-cient treasure."

Sully arched an eyebrow. "You do, huh?"

Drake nodded. "I do."

"What if I told you Massimo's cousin worked in the Vatican archives before he decided he didn't want to be a cardinal anymore? What if I told you that not only was the Italian archaeologist right, that Andres Lopez *did* find Paititi, but that Massimo's cousin has the secret map Lopez made that shows exactly how to get there? What would you say to that?"

Drake looked over at the minister and then at the casket covered with flowers that were spilling all over the ground. He glanced at the trees and the autumn colors and the buildings in the distance, New York unfolding all around them. Sully was right, of course. Jada would be okay. She would go home to the embrace of her friends, she had family to check on her, and she had made it clear that the perilous adventure she'd shared with them was a one-time thing.

He was going to miss her.

With a quiet, rueful laugh, Drake shook his head. "You know you're going to get us both killed one of these days?"

"Someone's going to find Paititi, Nate," Sully replied. "I'd rather it be us."

"Well, then," Drake said, turning up his collar as the October breeze turned chilly. "I guess I'd say we're going to Peru."

About the Author

CHRISTOPHER GOLDEN is the award-winning, bestselling author of such novels as *Of Saints and Shadows, The Myth Hunters, The Boys Are Back in Town,* and *Strangewood.* He also has written books for teens and young adults, including *When Rose Wakes, Soulless, Poison Ink,* and *The Secret Journeys of Jack London,* coauthored with Tim Lebbon. The online animated series he wrote with Amber Benson, *Ghosts of Albion,* received a special citation at the Prix Europa and boasted 100,000 unique hits per week in its original run.

A lifelong fan of the "team-up," Golden frequently collaborates with other writers on books, comics, and scripts. He cowrote the lavishly illustrated novel *Baltimore, or, The Steadfast Tin Soldier and the Vampire*—and the subsequent comic book series—with Mike Mignola. With Tim Lebbon, he has cowritten four novels in the Hidden Cities series. With Thomas E. Sniegoski, he is the coauthor of the book series *OutCast* and *The Menagerie,* as well as comic book miniseries such as *Talent,* currently in development as a feature film.

As an editor, he has worked on short story anthologies that include *The New Dead, The Monster's Corner,* and *British Invasion* and has also written and cowritten comic books, video games, screenplays, and a network television pilot. He also is known for his many media tie-in works, including novels, comics, and video games, in the worlds of *Buffy the Vampire Slayer, Hellboy, Angel,* and *X-Men,* among others.

Golden was born and raised in Massachusetts, where he still lives with his family. His original novels have been published in more than fourteen languages in countries around the world. Please visit him at www.christophergolden.com.